"[Furst's] depictions of wartime Europe have the richness and complexity of the fiction of John le Carré and Somerset Maugham. . . . With the authority of solid research and a true fascination for his material, Mr. Furst makes idealism, heroism, and sacrifice believable and real."

—David Walton, *The Dallas Morning News*

"Furst's scrupulous attention to spycraft and period detail . . . evokes the mood of conquered cities like Warsaw, Paris, and Barcelona. . . . Language this lovely vaults the categories we lazily constrain literature with."

—Maureen Corrigan, *Fresh Air*

"Some books you read. Others you live. They seep into your dreams and haunt your waking hours until eventually they seem the stuff of memory and experience. Such are the novels of Alan Furst, who uses the shadowy world of espionage to illuminate history and politics with a gripping immediacy."

—Nancy Pate, *The Orlando Sentinel*

"Imagine discovering an unscreened espionage thriller from the late 1930s, a classic black-and-white movie that captures the murky allegiances and moral ambiguities of Europe on the brink of war. . . . Nothing can be like watching *Casablanca* for the first time, but Furst comes closer than anyone has in years."

—Walter Shapiro, *Time*

"Furst has somehow discovered the perfect venue for uniting the European literary tragedy with the Anglo-American spy thriller. Nobody does it better."

—*Kirkus Reviews*

PHOTO: JERRY BAUER

ALAN FURST is widely recognized as the master of the historical spy novel. He is the author of *Night Soldiers, Dark Star, The Polish Officer, The World at Night, Red Gold,* and *Kingdom of Shadows.* Born in New York, he has lived for long periods in France, especially in Paris. He now lives on Long Island, New York.

Also by Alan Furst

THE WORLD AT NIGHT

A NOVEL

ALAN
FURST

THE
WORLD
AT NIGHT

RANDOM HOUSE TRADE PAPERBACKS NEW YORK

Copyright © 1996 by Alan Furst
Reader's guide copyright © 2001, 2002 by Random House, Inc.

All rights reserved under International and Pan-American Copyright Conventions.
Published in the United States by Random House Trade Paperbacks, a division
of Random House, Inc., New York, and simultaneously in Canada by
Random House of Canada Limited, Toronto.

RANDOM HOUSE TRADE PAPERBACKS and colophon are trademarks
of Random House, Inc.

This work was originally published in hardcover by Random House, Inc., in 1996.

Library of Congress Cataloging-in-Publication Data

Furst, Alan.
The world at night : a novel / Alan Furst.
    p.   cm.
ISBN 0-375-75858-5
1. Motion picture producers and directors—Fiction.   2. World War,
1939–1945—France—Fiction.   3. Paris (France)—Fiction.   [1. France—
History—German occupation, 1940–1945—Fiction.]   I. Title.
PS3556.U76 W67 2002
813'.54—dc21   2001048533

Random House website address: www.atrandom.com
Printed in the United States of America
987654

Avec remerciements à Ann Godoff, pour son
support et ses encouragements

The boat left the Quai de la Joliette in Marseilles harbour about midnight. It was new moon and the stars were bright and their light hard. The coast with its long garlands of gas lamps faded slowly away. The lighthouses emerging from the black water, with their green and red eyes, were the last outposts of France, sleeping under the stars in her enormous, dishonored nakedness, humiliated, wretched and beloved.

—Arthur Koestler, 1940

THE 16TH ARRONDISSE-MENT

L 10 May, 1940.

ong before dawn, Wehrmacht commando units came out of the forest on the Belgian border, overran the frontier posts, and killed the customs officers. Glider troops set the forts ablaze, black smoke rolling over the canals and the spring fields. On some roads the bridges were down, but German combat engineers brought up pontoon spans, and by first light the tanks and armored cars were moving again. Heading southwest, to force the river Meuse, to conquer France.

In Paris, the film producer Jean Casson was asleep. His assistant, Gabriella Vico, tried to wake him up by touching his cheek. They'd shared a bottle of champagne, made love all night, then fallen dead asleep just before dawn. "Are you awake?" she whispered.

"No," he said.

"The radio." She put a hand on his arm in a way that meant there was something wrong.

What? The radio broken? Would she wake him up for that? It had been left on all night, now it buzzed, overheated. He could just barely hear the voice of the announcer. No, not an announcer. Perhaps an engineer—somebody who happened to be at the station when news came in was reading it as best he could:

"The attack . . . from the Ardennes forest . . ."

A long silence.

"Into the Netherlands. And Belgium. By columns that reached back a hundred miles into Germany."

More silence. Casson could hear the teletype clattering away in the studio. He leaned close to the radio. The man reading the news tried to clear his throat discreetly. A paper rattled.

"Ah . . . the Foreign Ministry states the following . . ."

The teleprinter stopped. A moment of dead air. Then it started up again.

"It is the position of the government that this aggression is an intolerable violation of Belgian neutrality."

Gabriella and Casson stared at each other. They were hardly more than strangers. This was an office romance, something that had simmered and simmered, *and then, one night.* But the coming of war turned out to be, somehow, intimate, like Christmas, and that was a surprise to both of them. Casson could see how pale she was. Would she cry? He really didn't know very much about her. Young, and slim, and Italian—well, Milanese. Long hair, long legs. What was she—twenty-six? Twenty-seven? He'd always thought that she fitted into her life like a cat, never off balance. Now she'd been caught out—here it was *war,* and she was smelly and sticky, still half-drunk, with breath like a dragon.

"Okay?" He used *le slang Américain.*

She nodded that she was.

He put a hand on her cheek. "You're like ice," he said.

"I'm scared."

He went looking for a cigarette, probing an empty packet of Gitanes on the night table. "I have some," she said, glad for something to do. She rolled off the bed and went into the living room. *Merde,* Casson said to himself. War was the last thing he needed. Hitler had taken Austria, Czechoslovakia, then Poland. France had declared war, but it meant nothing. Germany and France couldn't fight again, they'd just done that—ten million dead, not much else accomplished. It was simply not, everybody agreed, *logique*.

Gabriella returned, lit a cigarette and handed it to him. "May I take a bath?" she asked.

"Of course. There are towels—"

"I know."

Casson found his watch on the night table. 5:22. Water splashed into the bathtub. The tenant on the floor below was a baroness—she didn't like noise. Well, too bad. She already hated him anyhow.

He got out of bed, walked to the glass door that opened on the little balcony. He pushed the drape aside; you could see the Eiffel Tower across the river. The rue Chardin was quiet—the 16th Arrondissement was always quiet, and Passy, its heart and soul, quieter still. One or two lights on, people didn't know yet. So beautiful, his street. Trees in clouds of white blossom, dawn shadow playing on the stone buildings, a lovely gloom. He'd shot a scene from *No Way Out* here. The hero knows the cops are onto him, but he leaves his hideout anyhow, to see his rich girlfriend one last time.

The telephone rang; two brief whirring jingles. Paused a few seconds. Rang again. *Jesus, the baroness.* Gingerly, Casson picked up the receiver.

"Yes?"

"Have you heard?"

It was his wife. They had been separated for years, living their own lives in their own apartments. But they remained married, and shared a set of old friends.

"Yes," he said.

"I'm not disturbing you, am I?"

"No, Marie-Claire. I was up."

"Well, what shall we do?"

Fight, he thought. Support the troops, hold rallies, you had to—

"About tonight, I mean."

Now he understood. They were giving a dinner party at her apartment. "Well, I don't see how, I mean, it's war."

"Bruno says we must go on. We must not give in to Hitler."

Bruno was Marie-Claire's boyfriend. He owned an agency that sold

British motorcars, had his hair cut twice a week, and spent a fortune on silk dressing gowns.

"He's not wrong," Casson said.

"And the cake has been ordered." The twentieth wedding anniversary of the Langlades—a cake from Ponthieu.

"All right. Let's go ahead. Really, what else is there to do?"

"Are you going to the office?"

"Of course."

"Can you telephone later on?"

"I will."

He hung up. The door to the bathroom was half-open, the water had stopped. Casson paused at the threshold.

"You can come in," Gabriella said.

Her skin was flushed from the heat of the bath, wet strands of hair curled at the back of her neck, her breasts and shoulders were shiny with soapsuds. "They are going to arrest me," she said, as though it were hard for her to believe.

"Why would they do that?"

She shrugged. "I am Italian. An Italian citizen."

Enemy alien. It was absurd, he wanted to laugh, but then he didn't. Mussolini was Hitler's ally, a treaty had been signed in 1939. The Pact of Steel, no less. But it was only ridiculous until police came to the door. Gabriella looked up at him, biting her lip. "Now look," he said. "It's too early for tears. This is *Paris*—there's always somebody you can talk to, always special arrangements. Nothing's final here."

Gabriella nodded gratefully, she wanted to believe he was right.

Casson caught a glimpse of himself in the steamy mirror. Dark—like a suntan that never really went away—naked, lean, with a line of hair up the center and shoulders a little heavier than his suits suggested. Not so bad—for forty-two. Still, if he were going to be authoritative, he'd better get dressed.

He stood in front of his closet, gazed pensively at a row of suits. In the distance, a two-note siren, high/low. Police or ambulance, and coming nearer. Casson went to the balcony and looked out. An ambulance, rolling to a stop just up the block. Two women ran into the street, one clutching a robe against her chest, the other in the black dress of a concierge. Frantically, they urged the men from the ambulance into the building.

Casson went back to the closet. On the radio, the premier of France, Paul Reynaud, was reading a statement: "The French army has drawn its sword; France is gathering herself."

A little after ten, Casson left for the office. In the streets of Passy, the war had not yet been acknowledged—life went on as always; *très snob,* the women in gloves, the men's chins held at a certain angle. Casson wore a dark suit, sober and strong, and a red-and-blue tie with a white shirt—the colors of France. But the blue was teal, the red faded, and the shirt a color the clerk had called "linen". He stopped at a newspaper kiosk for *Le Temps,* but it was not to be. A huge crowd was clamoring for papers, he would have to wait.

The day was fine, cool and sunny, and he liked to walk to his office, just off the Champs-Elysées on the rue Marbeuf. Like it or not, his usual cabdriver was not at his customary spot on the place Iéna so it was walk or take the Métro, and this was no morning to be underground. Somewhere along the way, he would stop for a coffee.

He was, to all appearances, a typical Parisian male on his way to the office. Dark hair, dark eyes—France a Latin country after all—some concealed softness in the face, but then, before you could think about that, a small scar beneath one eye, the proud battle trophy of soccer played with working-class kids when he was young, in fact the most violent moment he'd ever experienced.

In real life, anyhow. *Last Train to Athens* had a murder in an alley in the Balkans, pretty nasty by the time they'd got it cut. Emil Cravec! What a ferocious mug on him—where the hell was he, anyhow? *No Way Out* was tame by comparison, except for the ending. Michel Faynberg had directed for him, and Michel had never really left the Sorbonne. He'd had the hero clubbed to death at the base of a statue of Blind Justice—what a load of horseshit! *No Way to Make Money* the exhibitor Benouchian called it. Yet, in all fairness, that hadn't really turned out to be true. The students went.

He liked *Night Run* best of all, he loved that movie. It was better than *The Devil's Bridge,* which had got him the little house in Deauville. He'd almost directed *Night Run,* stood with old Marchand all day long, watched rushes with him every night. Marchand was a legend in the industry, and the great thing about stature, Casson had discovered, was that egoism was no longer the issue—now and then, anyhow. Even a producer, despised moneyman, might have an idea that was worth something. Marchand had been in his seventies by then, was never going to get the acclaim he deserved. White hair, white beard, eyes like a falcon. *"Tiens,* Casson," he'd said. "You really want it right."

It was, too. The smoke that billowed from the locomotive, the little cello figure, the village scenes they shot around Auxerre—every frame was right. A small story: beginning, middle, end. And Marchand had found him Citrine. She'd had other names then, what she'd come north with, from Marseilles. But that was eleven years ago, 1929, and she'd been eighteen. Or so she said.

Casson strode along, through the open-air market on the place Rochambeau. The fish stall had a neat pile of fresh-caught *rouget* on chipped ice. Gray and red, with the eye still clear. A goat was tied to the back of a wagon and a young girl was milking it into a customer's pail. The market café had tables and chairs out on the sidewalk, the smell of coffee drawing Casson to the zinc bar. He stood between a secretary and a man with red hands and a white apron. Unwrapped the sugar cube and set it on the spoon and watched the walls crystalize and tumble slowly down as the coffee rose up through it. He brought the cup to his lips: hot, black, strong, burnt. Casson allowed himself a very private little sigh of gratitude. To be alive was enough.

Ah, a band.

Casson stopped to watch. A unit of mounted Gardes Republicains in hussars' uniforms, chin straps tight beneath the lower lip. On command they rode into formation, three lines of ten, horses' hooves clopping on the cobbled street. Then played, with cornets and drums, a spirited march. In the crowd, a veteran of the 1914 war, the tiny band of the Croix de Guerre in his lapel, stood at rigid attention, white hair blowing in the breeze from the river, left sleeve pinned to the shoulder of his jacket.

Now the band played the "Marseillaise," and Casson held his hand over his heart. War with Germany, he thought, it doesn't stop. They'd lost in 1870, won—barely—in 1918, and now they had to do it again. A nightmare: an enemy attacks, you beat him, still he attacks. You surrender, still he attacks. Casson's stomach twisted, he wanted to cry, or to fight, it was the same feeling.

28, rue Marbeuf.

Turn-of-the-century building, slate gray, its entry flanked by a wholesale butcher shop and a men's haberdashery. Marbeuf was an ancient street, crowded and commercial, and it was perfect for Casson. While the big production studios were out at Joinville and Billancourt, the offices of the film industry were sprinkled through the neighborhood in just such buildings. Not *on* the Champs-Elysées, but not far from it either. Honking trucks and taxis, men carrying bloody beef haunches on their shoulders, fashion models in pillbox hats.

To get to Casson's office you went to the second courtyard and took the east entry. Then climbed a marble staircase or rode a groaning cage elevator an inch at a time to the fourth floor. At the end of a long hall of black-and-white tile: a sugar importer, a press agent, and a pebbled glass door that said Productions Casson.

He was also PJC, CasFilm, and assorted others his diabolical lawyers thought up on occasions when they felt the need to send him a bill. Nonetheless, the world believed, at least some of the time. Witness: when he opened the door, eight heads turned on swivels. It brought to mind the favorite saying of an old friend: "One is what one has the nerve to pretend to be."

As he went from appointment to appointment that morning, he began to get an idea of what the war might mean to him personally. For one thing, everybody wanted to be paid. Now. Not that he blamed them, but by 11:30 he had to duck out to Crédit Lyonnais to restock the checking account from reserves.

When he returned, the scenic designer Harry Fleischer sat across the desk and bit his nails while Gabriella prepared a check: 20,000 francs he was owed, and 20,000 more he was borrowing. "I can't believe this is happening," he said gloomily. "My wife is home, selling the furniture."

"I wish I knew what to say."

Fleischer made a gesture with his hand that meant *just because I am this person.* He was heavy, face all jowls and cheeks, with a hook nose, and gray hair spreading back in waves from a receding hairline. "I ran from Berlin in 1933, but I thought: so, I have to live in Paris, the whole world should be tortured like this."

"Where are you going?"

"Hollywood." Fleischer shook his head in disbelief at what life did. "Of course I could say '*Hollywood*!' I know plenty of people who'd see it that way. But I'm fifty-six years old, and what I'll be is one more refugee. Arthur Brenner has been trying to get me to come to MGM for years. Well, now he'll get. I don't want to leave, we made a life here. But if these *momsers* do here what they did in Poland . . ."

There was a big, dirty window behind Casson's chair, open a few inches. Outside was the sound of life in the Paris streets. Casson and Fleischer looked at each other—that couldn't end, could it?

"What about you?" Fleischer said.

"I don't know. Like last time—the thing will settle into a deadlock, the Americans will show up." He shrugged.

Gabriella knocked twice, then brought in Fleischer's check. Casson signed it. "I appreciate the loan," Fleischer said, "It's just to get settled in California. What is it in dollars, four thousand?"

"About that." Casson blew on the ink. "I don't want you to think about it. I'm not in a hurry. The best would be: we give Adolf a boot in the ass, you come back here, and we'll call this the first payment on a new project."

Casson handed the check to Fleischer, who looked at it, then put it in the inside pocket of his jacket. He stood and extended a hand. "Jean-Claude," he said. That was Casson's affectionate nickname, in fact his first and middle names.

"Send a postcard."

Fleischer was suddenly close to tears—didn't trust himself to speak. He nodded, tight-lipped, and left the office.

"Good luck, Harry," Casson said.

Gabriella stuck her head around the doorway. "James Templeton is calling from London."

Casson grabbed the phone with one hand while the other dug through a pile of dossiers on his desk, eventually coming up with one tied in red ribbon. *Mysterious Island* was printed across the cover. The movie wouldn't be called that—somebody else had the rights to the

Jules Verne novel—but that was the idea. *When their yacht sinks in a tropical storm, three men and two women find themselves* . . . In one corner of the folder, Casson had written *Jean Gabin?*

"Hello?" Casson said.

"Casson, good morning, James Templeton." Templeton was a merchant banker. He pronounced Casson's name English-style; accent on the first syllable, the final *"n"* loud and clear.

"How's the weather in London?"

"Pouring rain."

"Sorry. Here the weather is good, at least."

"Yes, and damn it all to hell anyhow."

"That's what we think."

"Look, Casson, I want to be straight with you."

"All right."

"The committee met this morning, in emergency session. Sir Charles is, well, you've met him. Hard as nails and fears no man. But we're going to wait a bit on *Mysterious Island.* It's not that we don't like the idea. Especially if Jean Gabin comes on board, we feel it may be exactly right for us. But now is not the moment."

"I understand perfectly, and, I am afraid you are right. We are at a time when it doesn't hurt to, uh, not continue."

"We were hoping you'd see it that way."

"Without confidence, one cannot move ahead, Monsieur Templeton."

"Do you hear anything, on the situation?"

"Not really. The radio. Reynaud is strong, and we know the Belgians will fight like hell once they organize themselves."

"Well, over here Chamberlain has resigned, and Churchill has taken over."

"It's for the best?"

"Certainly in this office, that's the feeling."

Casson sighed. "Well, thumbs-up."

"That's the spirit."

"*Mysterious Island* will wait."

"This doesn't leave you—I mean . . ."

"No, no! Not at all. Don't think it."

"Good, then. I'll tell Sir Charles. In a year we'll all be at the screening, drinking champagne."

"The best!"

"Our treat!"

"Just you try it!"

"Good-bye, Casson. We'll send along a letter."

"Yes. Good-bye."

Merde. Double *merde*.

Gabriella knocked and opened the door. "Your wife on the line," she said.

He always had a mental picture of Marie-Claire when he talked to her on the phone. She had tiny eyes and a hard little mouth, which made her seem spiteful and mean. Not a fair portrait, in fact, because there were moments when she wasn't that way at all.

Of course—*Parisienne* to the depths of her soul—she made herself beautiful. She smelled delicious, and touched you accidentally. Had you in bed before you knew it, had life her way after that. Knowing Marie-Claire as he did, Casson had always assumed that Bruno, a pompous ass at the dinner table, was a maestro in the bedroom.

"The Pichards cannot come," Marie-Claire said. "Yet Bruno insists we have this dinner. Françoise called and said that Philippe's younger brother, an officer, had been wounded, near the town of Namur. A sergeant had actually telephoned, from somewhere in Belgium. It must have been, I don't know, dreadful. Poor Françoise was in tears, not brave at all. I thought well, that's that. Cancel the cake, call the domestic agency. But Bruno *insisted* we go on."

Casson made a certain Gallic sound—it meant refined horror at a world gone wrong. Again.

Marie-Claire continued, "So, I rationalize. You know me, Jean-Claude. There's an elephant in the hall closet, I think, oh some circus performer's been here and forgotten his elephant. Now Yvette Langlade calls, Françoise has just called her—to explain why she and Philippe won't be there. And Yvette says we *are* going to cancel, aren't we? And I say no, life must go on, and she's horrified, I can tell, but of course she won't come out and say it."

Casson stared out the window. He really didn't know what to do. Marie-Claire had a problem with her lover and her circle of friends—it didn't have much to do with him. "The important thing is to get through today," he said, then paused for a moment. The telephone line hissed gently. "Whatever you decide to do, Marie-Claire, I will go along with that."

"All right." She took a breath, then sighed. "Will you call me in an hour, Jean-Claude? Please?"

He said yes, they hung up, he held his head in his hands.

He thought about canceling his lunch—with the agent Perlemère—and asked Gabriella to telephone, cautiously, *to see if Monsieur Perlemère is able to keep his lunch appointment.*

Oh yes. A little thing like war did not deter Perlemère. So the good soldier Casson marched off to Alexandre to eat warm potato-and-beef salad and hear about Perlemère's stable of lame horses—aging ingenues, actors who drank too much, the Rin-Tin-Tin look-alike, Paco, who had already bitten two directors, and an endless list beyond that. A volume business.

Perlemère ordered two dozen Belons, the strongest of the oysters, now at the very end of their season. He rubbed his hands and attacked with relish, making a *thrup* sound as he inhaled each oyster, closing his eyes with pleasure, then drinking the juice from the shell, a second *thrup*, followed by a brief grunt that meant arguments about the meaning of life were irrelevant once you could afford to eat oysters.

Perlemère was fat, with a small but prominent black mustache—a sort of Jewish Oliver Hardy. *Perlemère, Perlmutter, mother-of-pearl,* Casson thought. Curious names the Jews had. "I saw Harry Fleischer this morning," he said. "Off to MGM."

"Mm. Time to run, eh?"

"Maybe for the best."

Perlemère shrugged. "The Germans hit first. Now we'll settle with them once and for all."

Casson nodded polite agreement.

"What'd you do last time?" Perlemère demolished an oyster.

"I graduated lycée in 1916, headed for the Normale." The Ecole Normale Supérieure the most exclusive college in the Sorbonne, was France's Harvard, Yale, and Princeton all rolled into one. "My eighteenth birthday, I went down to the recruiters. They asked me a few questions, then sent me off to install cameras on Spads flying recon-

naissance over German lines. I changed film, developed it—really the
war started me in this business."

"*Normalien,* eh?" He meant Casson was well-connected; a member,
by university affiliation, of the aristocracy.

Casson shrugged. "I guess it meant something, once upon a time."

"School of life, over here." *Thrup.* "But I haven't done too badly."

Casson laughed—as though such a thing could be in question!

"I expect this war business will go on for a while," Perlemère said.
"Your German's stubborn, I'll admit that. He doesn't know when he's
beaten. But we'll give them a whipping, just watch."

Casson took a bite of the potato-and-beef salad, which would have
been delicious if he'd had an appetite, and a sip of the *Graves,* which
he didn't care for. "You represent Citrine, Jacques?"

"Not any more. Besides, what do you want with her?"

"Nothing special in mind. I just remembered she used to be with
you."

"Suzy Balcon, Jean-Claude. Remember where you heard that."

"Oh?"

"I'll send a photo over. She's tall and sophisticated—but she puts
your mind in the gutter. Mm. Never mind Citrine."

Two businessmen maneuvered down the packed aisle and managed
to squeeze themselves around the tiny table next to Casson. "Two hundred German tanks on fire," one of them said. "Just imagine that."

Back at the office, Gabriella: "Your wife called, Monsieur Casson. She
said to tell you that the dinner has been canceled, and would you please
telephone her when you have a moment. She's at the beauty parlor until
three-thirty, home any time after that."

"Gabriella, do you think you could find me *Le Temps?*" For Casson, a day without a newspaper was agony.

"I can go to the *tabac.*"

"I would really appreciate it."

"I'll go, then. Oh, Maître Versol asks that you call him."

"No."

"Yes, monsieur. I am afraid so."

Back in his office, Casson retrieved the swollen dossier from the bottom drawer where he'd hidden it from himself. In 1938, someone at

Pathé had woken up one morning with a vision: the world could simply not go on without another remake of *Samson and Delilah*. And Jean Casson had to produce. Costume epics were not at all his specialty, but Pathé was huge and powerful and deaf—the only word they could hear was *yes*.

He got a script. Something close to it, anyhow. Signed a Samson who, from medium range in twilight, looked strong, and a reasonable Delilah—overpriced but adequately sultry. Pathé then canceled the project, paid him based on the escape clauses, and went on to new visions. Casson tied up the project, or thought he did.

One small problem: his production manager had ordered four hundred beards. These were for the extras, and were composed of human hair, prepared by the estimable theatrical makeup house LeBeau et cie. Cost: 5,000 francs. Somewhere just about here the problems began. The beards were, or were not, delivered to a warehouse Productions Casson rented in Levallois. Subsequently, they were returned to LeBeau. Or perhaps they weren't. LeBeau certainly didn't have the beards—or thought he didn't. Casson didn't have them either—as far as he knew. It was all *très difficile*.

Casson made the telephone call, writhing in silent discomfort. LeBeau couldn't actually sue him—the money was too little, the loss of business too great. And Casson couldn't tell LeBeau to take his beards and the rest of it—films could not be made without a theatrical makeup supplier. Still, this was an affair of honor, so Casson had to endure Maître Versol's endless drivel as a weekly punishment. The lawyer didn't attack or threaten him; the world—a murky, obscure entity—was the villain here, see how it took men of exquisite integrity and set them wandering in a forest of lost beards. Where were they? Who had them? What was to be done? *Très difficile.*

When he got off the phone, Gabriella came in with a copy of *Le Temps*. It had a certain puffy quality to it—obviously it had been read, and more than once—but a look in Gabriella's eye told him to be thankful he had a newspaper and not to raise questions about its history.

There wasn't all that much to read: Germany had attacked Belgium and the Netherlands and Luxembourg, the French army had advanced to engage the Wehrmacht on Belgian territory, a stunning assortment of world leaders were infuriated, and:

The characteristics of the French soldier are well-known, and he can be followed across the ages, from the heroic fighters of the feudal armies to the companies of the *Ancien Régime,* and on to the contemporary era. Are they not the characteristics of the French people? Love of glory, bravery, vivacity?

5:20 P.M.
Headed for the one appointment he'd looked forward to all after-noon—drinks at a sidewalk table at Fouquet—Casson left the office ten minutes before he really had to, and told Gabriella he wouldn't be back.

Marie-Claire had called at four; the dinner was now definitely on for tonight. They had, in a series of telephone calls, talked it out—Yvette Langlade, Françoise, Bruno, and the others—and reached agreement: in her hour of crisis, France must remain France. Here Marie-Claire echoed that season's popular song, Chevalier's *"Paris Reste Paris."* It was, Casson suspected, the best you could do with a day when your country went to war. Children would be born, bakers would bake bread, lovers would make love, dinner parties would be given, and, in that way, France would go on being France.

And would he, she would be so grateful, stop at Crémerie Boursault on the way home from the office and buy the cheese? "A good *vacherin,* Jean-Claude. Take a moment to choose—ripe, runny in the middle, French not Swiss. Please don't let her sell you one that isn't perfect."

"And we're how many?"

"Ten, as planned. Of course Françoise and Philippe will not be there, but she telephoned, very firm and composed, and said it was imperative we go ahead. We must. So I called Bibi Lachette and explained and she agreed to come."

"All right, then, I'll see you at eight-thirty."

For the best, he thought. He walked down Marbeuf and turned onto the Champs-Elysées. At twilight the city throbbed with life, crowds moving along the avenue, the smells of garlic and frying oil and cologne and Gauloises and the chestnut blossom on the spring breeze all blended together. The cafés glowed with golden light, people at the outdoor tables gazing hypnotized at the passing parade. To Casson, every face—beautiful, ruined, venal, innocent—had to be watched until it disappeared from sight. It was his life, the best part of his life; the night, the street, the crowd. There would always be wars, but the people around him had a strength, an indomitable spirit. *They cannot be conquered,* he thought. His heart swelled. He'd made love all his life—his father had taken him to a brothel at the age of twelve—but this, a Paris evening, the fading light, was his love affair with the world.

He reached in his pocket, made sure he had money. Fouquet wasn't cheap—but, an aperitif or two, not so bad. Then the *vacherin,* but that was all. Marie-Claire's apartment was a ten-minute walk from the rue Chardin, he wouldn't need a taxi.

Money was always the issue. His little house in Deauville was rented. Not that he told the world that, but it was. He did *fairly* well with his gangsters and doomed lovers—they paid his bills—but never *very* well. That was, he told himself, just up ahead, around the next bend in life. For the moment, it was enough to pay the bills. Almost all of them, anyhow, and only a month or two after they were due.

But in Paris that was typical, life had to be lived at a certain pitch. His father used to say, "The real artists in Paris are the spenders of money." He'd laugh and go on, "And their palette is—the shops!" Here he would pause and nod his head wisely, in tune with the philosopher-knave side of his nature. But then, suddenly, the real ending: "And their canvas is life!"

Casson could see the performance in detail—it had been staged often enough—and smiled to himself as he walked down the crowded avenue. Casson wondered why, on the night his country went to war, he was thinking about his father. The father he remembered was old and corrupt, a rogue and a liar, but he'd loved him anyhow.

Casson needed only a moment to search the crowded tables—what he was looking for was easy to find. Amid the elegant patrons of Fouquet, the women with every inch of fabric resting exactly where they wished, the men with each hair exactly where they'd put it that morning, sat a ferocious, Bolshevik spider. Skinny, glaring, with unruly black hair and beard, a worker's blue suit, an open-collar shirt, and bent wire-frame Trotsky eyeglasses. But this one was no artsy intellectual Trotskyite—you could see that. This one was a Stalinist to his bloody toenails and, momentarily, would produce a sharpened scythe and proceed to dismember half the patronage of Fouquet's, while the waiters ran about hysterically, trying to present their bills to a dying clientele.

Ah, Fischfang, Casson thought. *You are my revenge.*

Louis Fischfang was Casson's writer. Every producer had one. Casson told the agents and screenwriters that he spread the work around, and he did—different people were right for different projects. But in the end, when the chips were down, when somebody had to somehow make it all come out right for the people who handed over their hard-earned francs for a seat in a movie theatre, then it was Fischfang and no other.

Though he quivered with political rage, spat and swore like a proletarian, marched and signed and chanted and agitated, none of it mattered, because that fucking Fischfang could write a movie script that would make a banker weep. God-given talent, is what it was. Just the line, just the gesture, just the shot. There could be no Jean Cassons—no Alexander Kordas, no Louis Mayers, no Jean Renoirs or René Clairs—without the Louis Fischfangs of this world.

Fischfang looked up as Casson approached the table. Offered his usual greeting: a few grim nods and a twisted smile. *Yes, here he was,* the devil's first mate on the ship of corruption. Here was money, nice suits, *ties,* and the haughty 16th Arrondissement, all in one *bon bourgeois* package called Casson.

"Did you order?" Casson asked as he sat down.

"Kir." White wine with blackcurrent liqueur.

"Good idea."

"Royale." Not white wine, champagne.

"Even better."

The waiter arrived with Fischfang's drink and Casson ordered the same. "It's a strange day to work," he said, "but I really don't know what else to do."

"I can't believe it's come to this," Fischfang said angrily. "They"—in Fischfangese this always meant *the government* and *the rich and the powerful*—"they grew Hitler. Watered him and weeded him and pitch-forked manure all around him. They gave him what he wanted in Czechoslovakia and Poland—now he wants the rest, now he wants what *they* have. Hah!"

"So now they'll stop him," Casson said.

Fischfang gave him a look. There was something knowing and serious about it—*you're naive*—and it made him uncomfortable. They sat for a time in silence, watched the crowd flowing endlessly down the avenue. Then Casson's drink came. *"Santé,"* he said. Fischfang acknowledged the toast with a tilt of the tulip-shaped glass and they drank. Fischfang's grandfather had crawled out of a shtetl in Lithuania and walked to Paris in the 1850s, Casson's roots went back into Burgundy, but as they drank their Kir they were simply Parisians.

"Well," Casson said acidly, "if the world's going to burn down we should probably make a movie."

Fischfang hunted through a scuffed leather briefcase at his feet and brought out a sheet of yellow paper crammed with notes and ink splatters. *"Fort Sahara,"* he said. He took a packet of cheap cigarettes; short, stubby things, from his breast pocket. As the match flared, he screwed up his face, shielding the cigarette with cupped hands as he lit it. "Lisbon," he said, shaking out the match. "The slums. Down by the docks. Women hanging out washing on a line stretched across the narrow street. They're dark, heavy, sweating. All in black. The men are coming home, in twos and threes, carrying their oars and their nets. Kids playing soccer in the street—tin can instead of a ball. Now it's nighttime. Men and women going to the—*cantina*? Wine's being poured from a straw-covered jug. There's a band, people dancing. Here's a young man, Santo. He's tough, handsome, sideburns, rolled-up sleeves . . ."

"Michel Ferré."

"Yes? That's up to you. For some reason I kept seeing Beneviglia—he speaks French with an Italian accent."

"Hunh. Not bad. But remember, this is a quota film—life will go smoother if everybody's French."

To protect the film industry, the government had decreed that a certain portion of a foreign company's French earnings be spent on French films—which meant that major studios, in this case Paramount, had frozen francs that had to be used on what had come to be called "quota films."

"Even so, Michel Ferré is perhaps a little old," Fischfang said. "Santo is, oh, twenty-five."

"All right."

"So he's taking his girl dancing. There's a thwarted suitor, a knife fight in the alley. Suitor dies. We hear whistles blowing, the police are on the way. Cut to the train station—Marseilles. All these tough-guy types, Santo looks like an innocent among them, with his cheap little suitcase. But he survives. Among the thieves and the pimps and the deserters, he somehow makes a place for himself. Maybe he works for a carnival."

"Good."

"I see him backlit by those strings of little lights, watching the young couples in love—it should be him and his girl, holding hands. But his friend at the carnival is no good. He plans a robbery—asks Santo to keep a revolver for him. So, he's implicated. They hold up a bank. We see it. The manager runs outside waving his arms, they shoot him—"

"Why not hold up the carnival? The owner's a cheat with a little mustache . . ."

Fischfang nodded and crossed out a line in his notes. "So they're not gangsters."

"No. Men on the run from life. The carnival owner knows that, he thinks he can hold back their wages because they can't go to the police."

"So, once again, Santo has to run. We see him staring through the train window, watching the world of everyday life go by. Then he's someplace, oh, like Béziers. Down to his last sou, he enlists in the Foreign Legion."

"Then Morocco." Casson caught the waiter's eye and raised two fingers.

"Well, the desert anyhow. Last outpost at Sidi-ben-something-or-other. The white buildings, the sun beating down, the tough sergeant with the heart of gold."

"Camels."

"Camels."

A woman in a white cape swept past them, waving at someone, silver bracelets jangling on her wrist. Fischfang said, "Can we do anything about the title, Jean-Claude?"

"It's from Irving Bressler, at Paramount. It says 'Foreign Legion,' it says 'desert.' By the way, who are they fighting?"

Fischfang shrugged. "Bandits. Or renegades. Not the good Moroccans."

"Where's the girl, Louis?"

"Well, if the fisherman's daughter goes to Marseilles to be with Santo, she sure as hell can't go to the desert. Which leaves the slave girl, captured by bandits many years ago . . ."

"Kidnapped heiress. She's been rescued and is staying at the fort . . ."

"Native girl. 'I'm glad you liked my dancing, monsieur. Actually, I'm only half-Moroccan, my father was a French officer . . .' "

"Merde."

"This is always hard, Jean-Claude."

They were silent for a moment, thinking through the possibilities. "Actually," Casson said, "we're lucky it's not worse. Somebody in the meeting mumbled something about the hero *singing,* but we all pretended not to hear."

The waiter arrived with the Kirs. *"Fort Sahara,"* Casson said, and raised his glass in a toast. The sky was darker now, it was almost night. Somewhere down the boulevard a street musician was playing a violin. The crowd at Fouquet's was several drinks along, the conversation was animated and loud, there were bursts of laughter, a muffled shriek, a gasp of disbelief. The waiters were sweating as they ran between the tables and the bar.

"Ending?" Casson said.

Fischfang sighed. "Well, the big battle. Santo the hero. He lives, he dies . . ."

"Maybe with French financing, he dies. For Paramount, he lives."

"And he gets the girl."

"Of course."

"She's the colonel's wife . . ."

"Daughter."

"Cat."

"Chicken."

❖❖❖

8:30 P.M.

Casson took the long way on his walk from the rue Chardin to Marie-Claire's apartment on the rue de l'Assomption. A blackout was in effect, and the velvety darkness of the Passy streets was strange but not unpleasant—as though the neighborhood had gone back a hundred years in time. In some apartments there were candles, but that was typical French confusion at work: a blackout didn't mean you had to cover the light in your windows, it meant you couldn't turn on the electricity. If you did, it would somehow—one never quite understood these things—help the Germans.

The walk to Marie-Claire's took less than fifteen minutes, but Casson saw two moving vans working that night. On the rue des Vignes, three men struggled with a huge painting, something eighteenth century, in a gilded frame. On the next street it was a Vuitton steamer trunk.

Rue de l'Assomption stood high above the Bois de Boulogne, and the views were dramatic. Lovely old trees. Meadows and riding paths. Marie-Claire's horsey friends had their polo club in the Bois, Bruno served in some vaguely official capacity at Le Racing Club de France, there was a season box at the Auteuil racetrack, and a private room could be rented for late supper parties at Pré Catalan, the fin-de-siècle restaurant hidden at the center of the park.

Casson paused at the entry to the building. This had been his apartment when he'd married, but it belonged to Marie-Claire now. Well, that was the way of the world. The history of ownership of apartments in the 16th Arrondissement, Casson thought, would probably make a more exciting epic of France than the *Chanson de Roland*.

The concierge of the building had always loved him:

"Ah, Monsieur *Casson*. It's good to see a friendly face. What a day, eh? What a horror. Oh the vile Boche, why *can't* they leave us alone? I'm getting too old for war, monsieur, even to read it in the papers. Let alone the poor souls who have to go and fight, may God protect them. What's that you have there? A *vacherin!* For the dinner tonight? How Madame *trusts* you, monsieur, if I sent my poor—ah, here's the old elevator; hasn't killed us yet but there's still time. A good evening to you, monsieur, we all would love to see more of you, we all would."

The elevator opened into the foyer of Marie-Claire's apartment. He had a blurred impression—men in suits, women in bright silk, the aromas of dinner. Marie-Claire hurried to the door and embraced him, *grosses bisoux,* kisses left and right, left and right, then stepped back so he could see her. Emerald earrings, lime-colored evening gown, hair a richer blonde than usual, tiny eyes scheming away, clouds of perfume rolling over him like fog at the seaside. "Jean-Claude," she said. "I am glad you're here." Something to say to a guest, but Casson could hear that she meant it.

And if any doubt lingered, she took him gently by the arm and drew him into the kitchen, where the maid and the woman hired for the evening were fussing with the pots. "Let's have a look," she said. Lifted the lid from a stewpot, shoved tiny potatos and onions aside with an iron ladle and let some of the thick brown sauce flow into it. She blew on it a few times, took a taste, then offered it to Casson. Who made a kind of bear noise, a rumble of pleasure from deep within.

"Ach, you peasant," she said.

"Navarin of lamb," Casson said.

Marie-Claire jiggled the top off the *vacherin*'s wooden box, placed her thumb precisely in the imprint made by the woman in the *crémerie,* and pressed down. For his effort, Casson was rewarded with a look that said *well, at least something went right in the world today.*

"Jean-Claude!" It was Bruno, of course, who'd snuck up behind him and brayed in his ear. Casson turned to see the strands of silver hair at the temples, the lemon silk ascot, the Swiss watch, the black onyx ring, the *you-old-fox!* smile, and a glass full of *le scotch whiskey.*

Suddenly, the sly smile evaporated. The new look was stern: the hard glare of the warrior. *"Vive la France,"* Bruno said.

They toasted the Langlades with champagne. Twenty years of marriage, of that-which-makes-the-world-go-round. Twenty years of skirmishes and cease-fires, children raised, gifts the wrong size, birthdays and family dinners survived, and all of it somehow paid for without going to jail.

Another glass, really.

With the exception of Bruno, they had all known each other forever, were all from old 16th-Arrondissement families. Marie-Claire's grandfather had carried on a famous, virtually lifelong lawsuit against Yvette Langlade's great-aunt. In their common history all the sins had been sinned, all the alliances broken and eventually mended. Now they were simply old friends. To Casson's left was Marie-Claire's younger sister, Véronique, always his partner at these affairs. She was a buyer of costume jewelry for the Galéries Lafayette, had married and separated very young, was known to be a serious practicing Catholic, and kept her private life resolutely sealed from view. She saw the plays and read the books, she loved to laugh, was always a charming dinner companion, and Casson was grateful for her presence. To his right was Bibi Lachette—the Lachettes had been summer friends of the Cassons in Deauville—the last-minute stand-in for Françoise and Philippe Pichard. Her last-minute escort was a cousin (nephew?), in Paris on business from Lyons (Mâcon?), who held a minor position in the postal administration, or perhaps he had to do with bridges. Bibi had been a great beauty in her twenties, a dark and mysterious heartbreaker, like a Spanish dancer. The cousin, however, turned out to be pale and reticent, apparently cultivated on a rather remote branch of the family tree.

With the warm leeks in vinaigrette came a powerful Latour Pomerol—Bruno on the attack. Casson would have preferred something simple with the navarin, which was one of those Parisian dishes that really did have a farmhouse ancestry. But he made the proper appreciative noise when Bruno showed the label around, and for his politeness was rewarded with a covert grin from Bibi, who knew Casson didn't do that sort of thing.

They tried not to let the Germans join them at dinner. They talked about the fine spring, some nonsense to do with a balloon race in Switzerland that had gone wrong in amusing ways. But it was not easy. Somebody had a story about Reynaud's mistress, one of those *what does he see in her* women, ungainly and homely and absurdly powerful. That led back to the government, and that led back to the Germans. "Perhaps it's just a social problem," Bernard Langlade said gloomily. "We never invited them to dinner. Now they're going to insist."

"They insisted in 1914, and they were sorry they did." That was Véronique.

"I don't think they've ever been sorry," said Arnaud, a lawyer for shipping companies. "They bleed and they die and they sign a paper. Then they start all over again."

"I have three MGs on the Antwerp docks," Bruno said. "Paid for. Then today, no answer on the telephone."

This stopped the conversation dead while everybody tried to figure out just exactly how much money had been lost. When the silence had gone on too long, Casson said, "I have a friend in Antwerp, Bruno. He owns movie theatres, and seems to know everybody. With your permission, I'll just give him a call tomorrow morning."

It helped. Madame Arnaud began a story, Bernard Langlade asked Véronique if he could pour her some more wine. Bibi Lachette leaned toward him and said confidentially, "You know, Jean-Claude, everybody loves you."

Casson laughed it off, but the way Bibi moved her breast against his arm clearly suggested that *somebody* loved him.

"Well," Marie-Claire said, "one can only hope it doesn't go on too long. The British are here, thank heaven, and the Belgians are giving the Germans a very bad time of it, according to the radio this evening."

Murmurs of agreement around the table, but they knew their history all too well. Paris was occupied in 1814, after the loss at Waterloo. The Germans had built themselves an encampment in the Tuileries, and when they left it had taken two years to clean up after them. Then they'd occupied a second time, in 1870, after that idiot Napoleon III lost an entire army at Sedan. In 1914 it had been a close thing—you could drive to the battlefields of the Marne from Paris in less than an hour.

"What are the Americans saying?" asked Madame Arnaud. But nobody seemed to know, and Marie-Claire shooed the conversation over into sunnier climes.

They laughed and smoked and drank enough so that, by midnight, they really didn't care what the Germans did. Bibi rested two fingers on Casson's thigh when he filled her glass. The *vacherin* was spooned out onto glass plates—a smelly, runny, delicious success. Made by a natural fermentation process from cow's milk, it killed a few gourmets every year and greatly delighted everyone else. Some sort of a lesson there, Casson thought. At midnight, time for cake and coffee, the maid appeared in consternation and Marie-Claire hurried off to the kitchen.

"Well," she sighed when she reappeared, "life apparently *will* go on its own particular way."

A grand production from Ponthieu; feathery light, moist white cake, apricot-and-hazlenut filling, curlicues of pastry cream on top, and the message in blue icing: "Happy Birthday Little Gérard."

A moment of shock, then Yvette Langlade started to laugh. Bernard was next, and the couple embraced as everyone else joined in. Madame Arnaud laughed so hard she actually had tears running down her cheeks. "I can't help thinking of poor 'Little Gérard,' " she gasped.

"Having his twentieth wedding anniversary!"

"And so young!"

"Can you imagine the parents?"

"Dreadful!"

"Truly—to call a child that on his very own birthday cake!"

"He'll never recover—scarred for life."

"My God it's perfect," Yvette Langlade panted. "The day of our twentieth anniversary; Germany invades the country and Ponthieu sends the wrong cake."

Everything was arranged during the taxi ballet in front of the building at 2:30 in the morning. Bibi Lachette's cousin was put in a cab and sent off to an obscure hotel near the Sorbonne. Then Casson took Bibi and Véronique home—Véronique first because she lived down in the 5th Arrondissement. Casson walked her to the door and they said good night. Back in the cab, it was kissing in the backseat and, at Bibi's direction, off to the rue Chardin. "Mmm," she said.

"It's been a long time," Casson said.

Bibi broke away in order to laugh. "Oh you are terrible, Jean-Claude."

"What were we, twelve?"

"Yes."

Tenderly, he pressed his lips against hers, dry and soft. "God, how I came."

"You rubbed it."

"You helped."

"Mmm. Tell me, are you still a voyeur?"

"Oh yes. Did you mind?"

"*Me?* Jean-Claude, I strutted and danced and did the fucking can-can, how can you ask that?"

"I don't know. I worried later."

"That I'd tell?"

"Tell the details, yes."

"I never told. I lay in the dark in the room with my sister and listened to her breathe. And when she was asleep, I put my hand down there and relived every moment of it."

The cab turned the corner into the rue Chardin, the driver said "Monsieur?"

"On the right. The fourth house, just after the tree."

Casson paid, the cab disappeared into the darkness. Casson and Bibi kissed once more, then, wound around each other like vines, they climbed the stairs together.

Suddenly, he was awake.

"Oh God, Bibi, forgive me. That damn Bruno and his damn Pomerol—"

"It was only a minute," she said. "One snore."

She lay on her side at the other end of the bed, her head propped on her hand, her feet by his ear—her toenails were painted red. Once in the apartment, they'd kissed and undressed, kissed and undressed, until they found themselves naked on the bed. Then she'd gone to use the bathroom and that was the last he remembered.

"What are you doing down there?"

She shrugged. Ran a lazy finger up and down his shinbone. "I don't know. I got up this morning, alone in my big bed, and I thought . . ." Casually, she swung a knee across him, then sat up, straddling his chest, her bottom shining white in the dark bedroom, the rest of her perfectly tanned. She looked over her shoulder at him and bobbed up and down. "Don't mind a fat girl sitting on you?"

"You're not." He stroked her skin. "Where did you find the sun?"

"Havana." She clasped her hands behind her head and arched her back. "I always have my bathing suit on, no matter where I go."

He raised his head, kissed her bottom; one side, the other side, the middle.

"You are a bad boy, Jean-Claude. It's what everyone says." She wriggled backward until she got comfortable, then bent over him, her head moving slowly up and down. He sighed. She touched him, her hands delicate and warm. *At this rate,* he thought, *nothing's going to last very long.*

Worse yet, their childhood afternoons came tumbling back through his memory; skinny little dirty-minded Bibi, been at the picture books her parents hid on the top shelf. What an idiot he'd been, to believe the boys in the street: *girls don't like it but if you touch them in a certain place they go crazy—but it's hard to find so probably you have to tie them up.*

But then, what an earthquake in his tiny brain. She *wants* you to feel like this, she *likes* it when your thing sticks up in the air and quivers. Well. Life could never be the same after that. "Thursday we all go to the Lachettes," his mother would say in Deauville. His father would groan, the Lachettes bored him. It was a big house, on the outskirts of the seaside town, away from the noisy crowds. A Norman house with a view of the sea from an attic window. With a laundry room that reeked of boiled linen. With a wine cellar ruled by a big spider. With a music room where a huge couch stood a foot from the wall and one could play behind it. *"Pom, pom, pom,* I have shot Geronimeau."

"Ah, Monsieur le Colonel, I am dying. Tell my people—Jean-Claude!"

From the front hall: "Play nicely, *les enfants.* We are all going to the café for an hour."

"Au revoir, Maman."

"Au revoir, Madame Lachette."

There were maids in the house, the floors creaked as they went about. Otherwise, a summer afternoon, cicadas whirred in the garden, the distant sea heard only if you held your breath.

"You mustn't put your finger there."

"Why not?"

"I don't think you're supposed to."

"Oh."

A maid approached, the Indian scout put his ear to the waxed parquet. *"Pom, pom!"*

"I die. Aarrghh."

Aarrghh.

Bibi's head moving up and down, a slow rhythm in the darkness. She was coaxing him—knew he was resisting, was about to prove that she could not be resisted. Only attack, he realized, could save him now. He circled her waist with his arms, worked himself a little further beneath her, put his mouth between her thighs. *Women have taught me kindness, and this.* She made a sound, he could feel it and hear it at once, like the motor in a cat. *Now we'll see,* he thought, triumphant. *Now we'll just see who does what to who.* Her hips began to move, rising, a moment's pause, then down, and harder every time. At the other end of the bed, concentration wavered—he could feel it—then began to wane.

But she was proud, a fighter. Yes, he'd set her in motion, riding up and down on the swell of the wave, but he would not escape, no matter what happened to her. It was happening; she too remembered the afternoons at the house in Deauville, remembered the things that happened, remembered some things that could have happened but didn't. She tensed, twisted, almost broke free, then shuddered, and shuddered again. *Now,* the conqueror thought, let's roll you over, with your red toenails and your white ass and—

No. That wouldn't happen.

The world floated away. She crawled back to meet him by the pillows, they kissed a few times as they fell asleep, warm on a spring night, a little drunk still, intending to do it again, this time in an even better way, then darkness.

A loud knock on the door, the voice of the concierge: "Monsieur Casson, *s'il vous plaît.*"

Half asleep, he pulled on his pants and an undershirt. It was just barely dawn, the first gray light touching the curtain. He unbolted the door and opened it. "Yes?"

Poor Madame Fitou, who worshiped propriety in every corner of the world. Clutching a robe at her throat, hair in a net, her old face baggy and creased with sleep. The man by her side wore a postal uniform. "A telegram, monsieur," she said.

The man handed it over.

Who was it for? The address made no sense. CASSON, Corporal Jean C. 3rd Regiment, 45th Division, XI Corps. Ordered to report to his unit at the regimental armory, Chateau de Vincennes, by 0600 hours, 11 May, 1940.

"You must sign, monsieur," said the man from the post office.

A
COUNTRY
AT WAR

*T*he column came into the village of St.-Remy, where the D 34 wandered through plowed fields of black earth that ran to the horizon, to the fierce blue sky. The mayor waited in front of the boulangerie, his sash of office worn from waist to shoulder over an ancient suit. A serious man with a comic face—walrus mustache, pouchy eyes—he waved a little tricolor flag at the column as it passed. It took two hours, but the mayor never stopped. All along the village street, from the Norman church to the Mairie with geraniums in planter boxes, the people stood and cheered—*"Vive la France!"* The war veterans and the old ladies in black and the kids in shorts and the sweet girls.

A unit of the *Section Cinématographique,* attached to the Forty-fifth Division headquarters company, headed north in the column of tanks, gasoline trucks, and staff cars. The unit, assigned to take war footage for newsreels, included the producer Jean Casson—now Corporal Casson, in a khaki uniform—a camera operator named Meneval, like Casson recalled to service, and a commander, a career officer called Captain Degrave. They were supposed to have a director, Pierre Pinot, but he had reported to the divisional office at Vincennes, then disappeared; averse to war, the Wehrmacht, or the producer—Casson suspected it was the latter. The unit had a boxy Peugeot 401 painted army green, and an open truck, loaded with 55-gallon drums of gasoline, 35-millimeter film stock in cans, and two Contin-Souza cameras, protected from the weather by a canvas top stretched over the truck's wooden framework.

The village of St.-Remy disappeared around a bend, the road ran for a time by the river Ourcq. It was a slow, gentle river, the water held the reflections of clouds and the willows and poplars that lined the banks. To make way for the column a car had been driven off the road and parked under the trees. It was a large, black touring car, polished to a perfect luster. A chauffeur stood by the open door and watched the tanks rumbling past. Casson could just make out a face in the window by the backseat; pink, with white hair, perhaps rather on in years. The column was long, and probably the touring car had been there for some time, its silver grille pointed south, away from the war.

Casson had hoped, in the taxi on the way to the fortress at Vincennes, that it was all a magnificent farce—the work of the French bureaucracy at the height of its powers. But it wasn't that way at all and in his heart he knew it. At the divisional headquarters, a long line of forty-year-old men. The major in charge had been stern, but not unkind. He'd produced Casson's army dossier, tied in khaki ribbon, his name lettered in capitals across the cover. "You will leave for the front in the morning, Corporal," he'd said, "but you may contact whoever you like and let them know that you've been returned to active duty."

From a pay phone on the wall of the barracks he'd called Gabriella and told her what had happened. She asked what she could do. Call Marie-Claire, he said, keep the office open as long as possible, explain to the bank. Yes, she said, she understood. There was nothing but composure in her voice, yet Casson somehow knew there were tears on her face. He wondered, for a moment, if she were in love with him. Well, he hoped not. There was nothing to be done about it in any event, the life he'd made was gone. Too bad, but that was the way of the world. Over, and done. Part of him thought *well, good.*

"Perhaps," she'd said, "there are certain telephone numbers you should have, monsieur. Or I could call, on your behalf."

Gabriella, he thought. I never appreciated you until it was too late. "No," he said. "Thank you for thinking of it, but no."

She wished him luck, voice only just under control, soft at the edges. All during the conversation Meneval, the cameraman, was talking to his wife on the next phone. Trying to calm her, saying that a cat who'd run away would surely return. But, Casson thought, it wasn't really about the cat.

Gabriella had approached the subject of *phone calls* with some delicacy, but she knew exactly what she was talking about. She knew he belonged to a certain level of society, and what that meant. That X would call Y, that Y would have a word with Z—that Casson would suddenly find himself with an office and a secretary and a job with an important title—honor preserved, and no need to die in the mud.

The column left Vincennes at dawn on the twelfth of May, a Sunday. Captain Degrave and Meneval in the Peugeot, Casson assigned to drive the truck—once again, somebody had disappeared.

At first he had all he could handle. The truck was heavy, with five forward gears, the clutch stiff, the gearshift cranky and difficult. You didn't, he learned quickly, shift and go around a corner at once. You shifted—ka, *blam*—then slowly forced the truck around the corner. It was hard work, but once he caught on to that, to approach it as labor, he started to do it reasonably well.

Strange to see Paris through the window of a truck. Gray, empty streets. Sprinkle of rain. Salute from a cop, shaken fist from a street cleaner—*give the bastards one for me.* A toothless old lady, staggering up the embankment after a night's sleep under a bridge, blew him a kiss. *I was pretty, once upon a time, and I fucked soldier boys just like you.* Up ahead, the commander of a tank—its name, *Loulou,* stenciled on the turret—waved a gloved hand from the open hatch.

They moved north, no more than twenty miles an hour because of the tanks, through the eastern districts of Paris. Nobody Casson knew came here—indeed there were people who claimed they lived an entire life and never left the 16th Arrondissement, except to go to the country in August. Here it was poor and shabby, not like Montparnasse; it had no communists or whores or artists, just working people who never got much money for their work. But the real Parisians, like Casson, made the whole city their home. The column crossed the rue Lagny, at boulevard d'Avout. Rue Lagny? My God, he thought, the Veau d'Or! Poor and shabby, yes, but there was always a way to spend a few hundred francs if you knew your way around. The *vin de carafe* was Brouilly, old Brouilly, from some lost barrel, almost black. And the Bresse chicken was hand-fed on the owner's mistress's mother's farm.

Strange how life turns, Casson thought. He suddenly felt the ecstasy of the unbound heart. Going to Belgium, to the war. Well then, he'd go. He'd never used the word *patriot,* but he loved this whore of a France, its narrow lanes, dark and twisted, where you smelled the bread and smelled the piss and bored women leaned on the windowsills— want a ride? The engine of the truck whined, Casson tried a lower gear. But now it grumbled, skipped a heartbeat or two, so he shifted back to the whine.

Rheims.

Again the crowds, and everywhere the tricolor. The women hung garlands on the tanks' cannon and handed the crews armloads of flowers, cigarettes, candy. Casson had a long pull from a bottle of champagne handed through the window and a wet kiss from a girl who jumped on his running board. A priest stood on the steps of Rheims cathedral and held up a crucifix, blessing the tanks as they rumbled past.

A few blocks ahead, the Peugeot was pulled over and Degrave waved at him to stop. "We'll want this," he said. Casson and Meneval loaded one of the cameras, set it up on a tripod on the back of the truck. Degrave took over the driving, Casson worked as the director. They circled around through the backstreets, rejoined the column, filmed the women kissing the tank crews and waving the tricolor. Of the priest, a close-up. Casson banged on the roof of the cab and Degrave stopped. A very French priest—rosy skin, fine hair, a certain refinement in the set of the lips. He held the crucifix with passion. They'd shut up in the

boulevard movie theatres when they saw this, Casson thought. It was
all well and good to screw the boss and hustle the girls, but they'd all
made first communion, and they would all send for the priest when
the time came. Cut to the faces of the tank commanders as their machines clanked past. Serious, courageous, going to war. Then a four-
teen-year-old girl, tears in her eyes as she ran alongside a tank and
handed up a branch of white lilac.

The column left the city on the RN 51. By the side of the road, the
stone markers said SEDAN–86. Eighty-six kilometers, Casson thought.
From here, you could drive to the border in an hour.

The crowd beside the road through Rethel was nothing like the one in
Rheims. This crowd was watchful, and silent, and there were no garlands for the tank guns. After that, the villages were empty. There was
no mayor, nobody waving, nobody. They had locked their houses and
gone away. When Casson turned off the engine, he could hear the distant rumble of artillery.

On the *Route Nationale* there were refugees who had come south
from Belgium. It looked the same, Casson thought, as the newsreels
he'd seen of Poland in September of 1939. Exactly the same. To the
question *what should be taken?* every family had its own answer—the
bed, the painting, the clock. But then, days later, it didn't matter. Exhaustion came, the treasures were too heavy, and into the fields they
went.

Rough faces. Flemish, reddened, coarse to French eyes—the thick-
handed cousins from the north, pikemen of a hundred armies in wars
that lasted a century. The column slowed, then stopped. A nun came
to Casson's truck and asked for water. He gave her what he had, she
took it away, shared it out among the refugees sitting by the roadside,
then brought back the empty bottle. "God bless you, monsieur," she
said to him.

"Where are you from, sister?"

"The village of Egheze." Then she leaned closer and whispered,
"They burned the abbey to the ground," her voice shaking with anger
while she held his arm in a steel grip. Then she said, "Thank you for
your kindness," and walked away, back to the people by the side of
the road.

❧

The column stopped at dusk. From the Ardennes forest, up on the Belgian border, the guns thundered and echoed. The tank crews sat on a stone wall, smoked cigarettes, and drank wine from a brown bottle. There was a reservist with them, a man with a double chin and a hopeful smile. For a long time nobody spoke, they just listened to the artillery. "Well," the man said, "it seems the Boche have come a long way south." The tank crewmen grinned and exchanged glances. "He's worried we won't win," one of them said. They all laughed at that. "Well," said another, "one never knows." That was even funnier. After a moment the first one said, "Ah, my little *patapouf*." *Fatty*, he'd called him, but gently, with the tenderness that very hard people sometimes show very soft people. "You have a day or two left to live," he said. "You better take a little more of this." He handed over the bottle. The man drank, then wiped his lips with the back of his hand and made an appreciative face to show how good the wine was.

A dispatch rider on a motorcycle picked up the day's film. Then Casson followed the Peugeot on a steep, narrow road that wound down to the banks of a river. A series of tight curves—it took Casson four moves to maneuver the truck through the final hairpin.

He turned off the ignition, then sat still for a long time. A tiny village, completely deserted, the people fled or sent away. A silent, cobbled street; on one side the river, on the other a few old buildings, crumbling, leaning together, ivy and wild geranium growing up the stone corners and over the tops of the doorways. In the silver moonlight the water and the stone were the same color. A low hill rose above the tile roofs to a wall masked by shrubbery, then Lombardy poplars rustled in the breeze. Then the stars.

Captain Degrave walked over from the Peugeot and appeared at the window of the truck. "There's a hotel up the street," he said. "The Hotel Panorama. We were supposed to billet there, but the colonial troops have it."

Casson had seen them on the road earlier that day; Algerian infantry and Vietnamese machine-gun squads. "I can sleep in the truck," he said.

"Yes," Degrave said. "You might as well."

Casson lay across the seat, listening to the river—the wash of the water moving along the stone embankment—and the cicadas. He turned on his side and fell asleep.

He had a powerful dream, a dream of lost love found again. His heart swelled with happiness. The woman sat across from him—their knees almost touched—and spoke in whispers, as though people were nearby and could hear them.

"That was love," she explained. "We were in love."

He agreed, nodded, their eyes met, they longed to hold each other but it was a public place. "We can't let it go again," she said.

"No."

"We can't."

He shook his head. If they let it go again it would be gone forever.

He woke up. The guns had stopped, there was just the river and the insects, loud on a summer night.

They worked hard the next day. Degrave started out just as the sun was coming up. They traveled along the river, through a burned village. Casson saw signs in Flemish, so they were actually over the border, in Belgium. They drove for a long time, the roar of the tank engines was deafening, the smell of gasoline and scorched oil hung thick in the morning air. At Degrave's signal he pulled to one side. Meneval cranked up the camera until the spring was tight, then they filmed the column—tanks coming over a hill, bouncing on their treads in a cloud of dust. They filmed the Algerians on the march, their faces dark and sweating, and the Vietnamese machine gunners, carrying spare barrels and steel boxes of ammunition. *Moving up to battle, somewhere in Belgium.*

They drove and filmed all day, then stopped in a forest, slept, ate some salted beef and lentils from ration tins. The officers waited for darkness, then ordered the column to move forward. The night was black and very warm. Casson bit his lip as he fought the wheel and shifted gears, dazed from the noise and the heat, close to exhaustion. To his left, on a wooded hillside, a flash lit up a grove of pine trees and the sound of a hollow thump came rolling down the hill, audible above the whine of the engine. What was it? But of course he knew what it was. Fascinated, he stared at the sideview mirror, a small fire flickered at the center of the dark glass, then the road curved and it was gone. Directly ahead of him, the silhouette of a tank's turret gun traversed back and forth.

A soldier ran in front of him and waved for him to slow down. A group of men, shadows, moved restlessly around something on the ground. Casson saw one white face turned suddenly toward him, the eyes were wide with fright. Then an officer with a swagger stick swept it violently in the direction the column was headed—*move, move*—and Casson stepped on the gas. Another flare on the hillside. Then a flash blinded him. He took a hand from the wheel and pressed his eyes. A loud crack. Followed by a gentle patter as twigs and dirt rained down on the metal roof of the cab. *They're trying to kill you, Jean-Claude.* The idea was an affront, he clenched his teeth and gripped the wheel harder. Two officers stood by a halted tank. After he'd gone past, one of them ran to catch up with him and banged on his door. "Stop! Is that gasoline in the back?"

"Yes, sir."

"Well then, back the truck up. We need it."

Casson shifted into reverse, rolled back until he was even with the tank. A commander climbed out of the hatch, then vaulted to the ground. "That's French fire!" he shouted. "Idiots! Clowns! What are they doing, shooting up here?"

"I assure you that it is not French fire, Lieutenant." From his insignia, Casson could seee he was a major.

"What, Belgian? English?"

"No."

Two soldiers wrestled a drum of gasoline to the edge of the truck, then Casson helped them to lower it onto its side. One of them attached a hose to the barrel and ran the other end into the tank's fuel pipe. Overhead, the sound of fabric ripping and the top of a tree whipped like a rag in a hurricane. Gasoline sloshed on Casson's shoes. The major had a lit cigarette in the corner of his mouth. "Careful there, you." An aristocrat, talking to his groom, Casson thought. The major stepped back, his high boots supple and glistening. This was still the cavalry, the hulking tanks were simply machines they were forced to use.

A staff car came speeding through the column and skidded to a stop.

A junior officer leaped out, ran up to the major and saluted. "Major Mollet, sir. The general's compliments. Why are we under fire?"

"It is German artillery."

"Sir."

The officer ran back to the car. The gasoline drum was empty, Casson started to screw the cap back on the opening as the soldiers coiled the hose. From the car, an angry shout. Then the back door flew open. The junior officer ran around to that side and was joined by the driver. Casson looked down, afraid to stare. At the car, a polite struggle was under way—a muttered curse, a loud whisper. At last they managed to extricate the general from the backseat. He was enormously fat, his breath sighed in and out as he walked over to the major. The major saluted. "General Lebois, sir."

"Mollet." The general touched the brim of his hat with a forefinger. "What's going on here?"

Two more explosions on the hillside. In the light, Casson could see the general's skin, a web of broken purple veins on his cheeks.

"The Wehrmacht, sir."

"They can't be this far south."

"Respectfully, sir, I believe they are."

"No, it's the damn English. All excited for no reason at all and shooting in the dark."

"Sir."

"Send a motorcycle courier over there. Somebody who speaks English."

"Yes, sir."

A shell landed on the road, about three hundred yards ahead of them. A truck had been hit. As it started to burn, there were shouts of "get water," and "push it off the road." Casson could see dark shapes running back and forth. The general growled, deep in his chest, like a dog that doesn't want to move from its place on the rug.

The major said, "Perhaps it would be faster if we fired back."

"No," the general said. "Save the ammunition. Waste not, want not."

"Very good, sir," the major said.

Casson returned to his truck. A glance in the mirror, he could see the two aides, trying to get the general back in his car. Casson moved up the column, working his way around tanks, tapping his horn when people got in the way. It was slow, difficult work, he never stopped shifting gears. He had to wait while one tank attempted to push a second off the road. It had been hit and was on fire, orange flames and boiling black smoke. By the light of the fire Casson could read the name *Loulou* stenciled on its turret.

Dawn. The sky pale, swept with the wisps of white scud that marked the high wind blowing in from the Channel.

The road to the fort on the heights of Sedan worked its way around the edges of the city, then climbed past plowed fields and old forest. At the gate to the fort, the Peugeot was waved through but Casson was stopped. The sentries were drunk and unshaven. "What brings you here?" one of them said.

"We're making movies."

"Movies! You know Hedy Lamarr?"

"Dog dick," said another. "Not those kinds of movies. *War* movies."

"Oh. Then what the hell are you doing up here?"

The second man shook his head, walked over to the truck and offered Casson a bottle through the window. "Don't let him get to you," he said. "Have some of this."

Casson raised the bottle to his lips and drank. Sharp and sour. The man laughed as he took the bottle back. "Come and see us, squire, after this shit's done with."

The hard Parisian sneer in the voice made Casson smile. "I will."

"You can find us up in Belleville, at The Pig's Ass."

"See you then," Casson said, shoving the clutch in.

"Red front!" they called after him.

Fortress at Sedan!
Raising and saluting the flag, morning reveille played on a bugle. Domestic life in the barracks—washing clothes, shining boots. Here are the cooks, preparing breakfast for the hungry poilus. A cannon, the famous French 75, is aimed out over the Meuse valley. A vigilant sentry keeps watch with binoculars—no Germans yet, but we're ready for them when they come.

Captain Degrave had an old friend serving with an artillery regiment and the gunners fed them breakfast. Casson ached from the driving, he was filthy with oily soot, and he wanted to shave more than anything else in the world, but the food seemed to bring him back to life. The gunners were countrymen from the Limousin. They'd stewed some hens in a huge iron kettle, added spring onions and wild garlic from the pastures outside the fort, found the last of the winter carrots in an "abandoned" root cellar, added Tunisian wine, a lump of fat, and a fistful of salt, then served it smoking hot in a metal soup plate. Afterward he sat back against a stone wall and had a hand-rolled cigarette stuffed with pipe tobacco. Maybe the world wasn't as bad as it seemed.

It was strange, he thought, to be suddenly pulled from one life and dropped down into another. In Paris it was a May morning, Marie-Claire and Bruno probably making love by the open window that looked out over the Bois de Boulogne. She was, he recalled, at best obliging about it, she really didn't like to do it in the morning; she had to be courted. And then—a little Marie-Claire punishment—she wouldn't take off her nightgown. She'd pull it up to her chin, then stick her tongue out, saying that if you insisted on making love like a peasant, well then by God you could just make love like a peasant. That was, at least, how she started out. As always with Marie-Claire, things got better later.

Of course it might be different with Bruno, but he doubted it. My God, he thought, it's like another world. Another *planet*. The lawyers, Arnaud and Langlade, would be going off to their offices in an hour or so, smelling like cologne, their ties pulled up just right, flirting with the women they passed in the street.

Casson stood, looked out over the wall at the early sun just lighting up the Meuse, burning off the valley mist. Bibi Lachette would still be asleep, he thought. She seemed like the type who slept late, dead to the world. Would she do it in the morning? Mmm—no, not it—but something. Generous, Bibi. He certainly did like her. Not love exactly, it was more like they were two of a kind, and, he thought, in some parts of the world that might be even better than love.

From the heights the river didn't look like much of a barrier, it was too pretty. Placid blue water that ran in gentle curves, you'd do better to paint it than to try and fight behind it. What had one of the gunners called it? Just a little *pipi du chat*—a cat pee. Christ, he thought, what the hell am I doing in a war?

Sunset. They'd filmed the commanding officer reviewing a company of infantry, backs stiff, thumbs on the seams of their trouser legs. Then Degrave had asked him to take the film over to the regimental headquarters building where the courier from Paris was due at seven to pick it up.

The road was made of cut stone and ran along a parade ground lined with cannon from Napoleon's time. He slowed down when a siren sounded, hoarse and broken, and heard a drone somewhere above him. The last of the orange sun was in his face—he let the truck roll to a stop, shaded his eyes, stared up into the early evening light.

A plane popped out of a cloud, abruptly slid sideways—Casson saw a black Maltese cross as the wing lifted—then dove at a sharp angle. For a moment he was a spectator, fascinated by the theatre of it, clearly it had nothing to do with him. Then the edges of the wings twinkled and the whine of the engine became a scream, rising over the rattle of the plane's machine guns. Casson jumped out of the truck and ran for his life. *Stukas*, he thought. Like the newsreels from Poland.

At the bottom of its dive, the Stuka released a bomb. Casson's ears rang, a puff of warm air touched his cheek, he saw, a moment later, black smoke tumbling upward, lazy and heavy. Just ahead of him, from the roof of the headquarters building, a spray of orange sparks seemed to float into the sky amid the drumming of antiaircraft cannon. Then more Stukas, whine after whine as they dove. Casson reached the building, fought through the shrubbery, then rolled until he got himself wedged between the ground and the base of a brick wall.

He looked up, saw a Stuka turn on its back, then slide into a shallow dive, rotating very slowly as it headed for the earth, a thin line of brown smoke streaming from its engine. Then a second Stuka exploded, a ball of yellow fire, flaming shards spinning through the air. Casson's heart was pounding. Thick smoke stood slow and ponderous above the fort and the wind reeked of gasoline. The fuel tanks, he realized, that was what they'd come for, gray domes that stood three stories high—the smell of burning petroleum was making him dizzy.

The drone of the airplanes faded into the distance, heading north into Belgium.

They moved to a little village outside the city of Sedan, the vehicles parked in a farmyard. Meneval slept in the car, Degrave and Casson stayed awake, sitting on the running board of the truck. A mile to the west, the fort was still burning, but directly above them the night was starry and clear.

Degrave had a heavy, dark face, dark hair, thinning in front—he was perhaps a little old to be a captain—and there was something melancholy and stubborn in his character.

"We'll film in the blockhouse tomorrow," he said. "Down near the river. Then we'll move on someplace else—the fort can't hold much longer."

Casson stared, not understanding.

"We've lost the air force," Degrave explained. "It's gone—eighty percent of it destroyed on the first morning of the war."

After a moment Casson said, "Then, they'll cross the border."

Degrave was patient. "The war is over, Corporal," he said gently.

Casson shook his head, "No," he said, "I can't accept that."

Degrave reached inside his coat and produced a crumpled, flattened packet of Gauloises Bleu. Two remained, bent and ragged. Degrave offered the packet, Casson pulled one free with difficulty. Degrave had a special lighter, made from a bullet cartridge, that worked in the wind. After several snaps they got both cigarettes lit.

"We're going to lose?" Casson said.

"Yes."

"What will happen?"

Degrave stared at him a moment, then shrugged. How could he know that? How could anybody?

3:30 A.M.

The blockhouse was long and narrow, built into the hillside, and very hot and damp. It smelled like wet cement. A squad of gunners lay on the dirt floor and tried to sleep, staring curiously at Casson and the others when they arrived. There were four embrasures, narrow firing slits cut horizontally into the wall. Meneval set up his camera at the far end of the blockhouse, wound the crank and inserted a new roll of film. The sergeant in charge handed Casson a pair of binoculars and said, "Have a look."

Casson stared out at the river.

"They tried twice, yesterday. A little way east of here. But they weren't serious. It was just to see what we did."

A field telephone rang and the sergeant went to answer it. "Fifteen seventy-two," he said, a map reference. "It's quiet. We've got the moviemakers with us." He listened a moment, then laughed. "If she shows up here I'll let you know."

A three-quarter moon. Casson made a slow sweep of the far bank of the Meuse, woods and a meadow in brilliant ashen light. He could hear crickets and frogs, the distant rumble of artillery. Thunder on a summer night, he thought. When it's going to storm but it never does.

Degrave was standing next to him, with his own binoculars. "Do you know François Chambery?" he asked.

"I don't think so."

"My cousin. He's also in entertainment—a pianist."

"He performs in Paris?"

"He tries."

Casson waited but that was all. "Where are you from, Captain?"

"The Anjou."

Casson moved the binoculars across the trees. The leaves rustled, nothing else moved. In the foreground, the river seemed phosphorescent in the moonlight. To the west, the artillery duel intensified. It wasn't thunder anymore, it sounded angry and violent, the detonations sharp amid the echoes rolling off the hillsides. "They're working now," somebody said in the darkness.

As Casson swept his binoculars across the forest, something moved. He tightened the focus until he could see tree trunks and leafy branches. Suddenly, a deer leaped from the edge of the woods, followed by another, then several more. They were colorless in the moonlight, bounding down the meadow to the bank of the river, then veering away into a grove of birch trees.

"What is it?" the sergeant said.

"Deer. Something chased them out of the woods."

4:10

The moon fading, the light turning toward dawn shadow. Casson was tired, ran a hand across his face. In the woods, a heavy engine came to life. It sounded like a tractor on a construction site—plenty of gas fed into it on a chilly morning. Then, others. Behind Casson the soldiers grumbled and got to their feet. There were three Hotchkiss guns aimed out the embrasures. The crews got busy, working bolts, snapping clips into the magazines. Casson could smell the gun oil.

One of the tanks broke cover, just the front end of the deck and the snout of the cannon. "Leave him alone," the sergeant said.

The French guns stayed silent. Meneval ran off a few seconds of film—they wouldn't get much, Casson thought, not for another hour. The blockhouse was quiet, Casson could hear the men breathing. The tank reversed, disappeared into the forest. Was it over, Casson wondered. The soldier next to him, gripping the handles of a machine gun, said under his breath, "And . . . now."

It was a close guess—only a few seconds off. A whistle blew, the Germans came out of the forest. The German tanks fired—orange flashes in the trees—and French antitank cannon fired back from the other blockhouses. The German infantry yelled and cheered, hundreds of them, running down the meadow carrying rubber boats and paddles. Clearly it was something they'd drilled at endlessly—it was synchronized, rehearsed. It reminded Casson of the news footage of gymnastic youth; throwing balls in the air or waving ribbons in time to music. Casson could hear the officers shouting, encouraging the soldiers. Some of the men reached the bank of the river and held the boats so their comrades could climb in.

The Hotchkiss guns opened up, tracer sailing away into the far bank and the troops boarding the rafts. German machine guns answered—fiery red tracer that seemed slow at first, then fast. Some of it came through the slits, fizzing and hissing in the blockhouse with the smell of burnt steel. The French gunners worked hard, slamming the short clips into the guns and ripping them out when they were done. On the far bank of the river, some soldiers bowed, others sat down, rolling on the ground or curling up.

Then it stopped. A few rubber boats turned in the current as they floated away, a few gray shapes floated along with them. The silence seemed strange and heavy. Casson let the binoculars hang on their strap and leaned against the lip of the gunport. Just outside, he heard twigs snapping and pounding footsteps on the dirt path. Two French soldiers ran past, then three more. The sergeant swore and hurried outside. Casson heard his voice. "Stop," he called out. "You cannot do this—go back where you belong."

The answering voice was cold. "Get out of the way," it said.

At dusk, a message on the field telephone: the unit had been ordered out. Degrave's allies in Paris, Casson suspected, knew the battlefield situation for what it was and had determined to save a friend's life. "We're being sent south," Degrave explained as they packed up the equipment. "To the reserve divisions behind the Maginot Line."

They tried. But in the darkness on the roads leading out of Sedan nobody was going anywhere. Thousands of French troops had deserted, their weapons thrown away. They trudged south, eyes down, among columns of refugees, most of them on foot, some pushing baby carriages piled high with suitcases. Casson saw artillery wagons—the cannon thrown off, soldiers riding in their place—pulled by farm horses; an oxcart carrying a harp, a hearse from Mons, a city bus from Dinant, the fire truck from Namur. Sometimes an army command car forced its way through, packed with senior officers, faces rigid, sitting at attention while the driver pounded on the horn and swore. *Let us through, we're important people, retreating in an important fashion.* Or, as a soldier riding on Casson's running board put it, "Make way, make way, it's the fucking king." Then, a little later, as though to himself, he said "Poor France."

Casson and the others moved slowly south, at walking speed. Back on the Meuse, the Wehrmacht was attacking again and whatever remained of the Forty-fifth Division was fighting back—floods of orange tracer crisscrossed the night sky above the river.

It was hard work, coaxing the truck forward among the refugees. They slept for an hour, then started up again. In first light, just after dawn, Casson spotted a road marker and realized they'd traveled less than twenty miles from Sedan. And then, prompt to the minute at 7:00 A.M., the Stukas came to work. They were very diligent, thorough and efficient, taking care to visit each military vehicle. Casson ran for the ditch and up went the truck—gasoline, cameras, film stock, canned lentils. He sat in the dirt and watched it burn, caught up in a fury that amazed him. It made no sense at all—they'd stopped him from making idiotic newsreels that nobody would ever see—but something inside him didn't like it.

But, whether he liked it or not, that was the end of the *Section Cinématographique* of the Forty-fifth Division, decommissioned in a cow pasture near the village of Bouvellement on a fine May morning in 1940. The Peugeot had also been a victim of the Stukas, though it had not burned dramatically like the truck. A heavy-caliber bullet had punched through the engine, which could do no more than cough and dribble oil when Degrave tried the ignition. "Well," he said with a sigh, "that's that."

He then gave Meneval and Casson permission to go, filling out official little slips of paper that said they'd been granted emergency leave. For himself, he would make his way to the military airfield at Vouziers, not all that far away, and request reassignment.

Meneval said he would leave immediately for home, just outside Paris. His family needed him, especially his wife, who'd been absolutely certain that he was gone forever.

"You understand," Degrave said, "that the fighting is going in that direction."

"Yes, probably it's not for the best," Meneval said gloomily. "But, even so." He shook hands and said good-bye and headed for the road.

Degrave turned to Casson. "And you, Corporal?"

"I'm not sure," Casson said.

"What I would recommend," Degrave said, "is that you make your way to Mâcon. There's a small army base north of the city—it's the Tenth Division of the XIV Corps. Ask for Captain Leduc, mention my name, tell him you are an *isolée*—a soldier separated from his unit. They'll give you something to eat and a place to sleep, and you'll be out of the way of, of whatever's going to happen next."

He paused a moment. "If the Germans ask, Corporal, it might be better not to mention that you were recalled to service. Or what you did. Other than that, I want to thank you, and to wish you luck."

Casson saluted. Degrave returned the salute. Then they shook hands. "We did the best we could," Degrave said.

"Yes," Casson said. "Good luck, Captain."

Casson headed for Mâcon. Sometimes, in a café, he heard the news on a radio. Nothing, he realized, could save them from losing the war. He left the roads, walked across the springtime fields. He ate bread he found in a bombed bakery in Châlons, tins of sardines a kind woman gave him in Chaumont. He was not always alone. He walked with peasant boys who'd run away from their units. He shared a campfire with an old man with a white beard, a sculptor, he said, from Brittany somewhere, who walked with a stick, and got drunk on some bright yellow stuff he drank from a square bottle, then sang a song about Natalie from Nantes.

As Casson watched, the country died. He saw a granary looted, a farmhouse burned by men in a truck, a crowd of prisoners in gray behind barbed wire. "We'll all live deep down, now," the sculptor said, throwing a stick of wood on the fire. "Twenty ways to prepare a crayfish. Or, you know, chess. Sanskrit poetry. It will hurt like hell, sonny, you'll see."

The villages were quiet, south of Dijon. The spaniel slept in the midday heat, the men were in the cafés at dusk, the breeze was soft in the faded light that led to evening, and the moon rose as it always had.

THE
JADE
PAGODA

T 20 August, 1940.

he silence of the empty apartment rang in his ears. The bed had been made—the concierge's sister coming in to clean as she always did—and the only sign of his long absence was a dead fern. Still, he felt like a ghost returning to a former life. And he had to put the fern outside the door so he wouldn't see it.

The heat was almost liquid. He opened the doors to the little balcony but it wasn't all that much better outside. Hot, and wet. And still—as though all the people had gone away. Which they had, he realized. Either fled before the advancing Wehrmacht in June, or fled to the seashore on the first of August. Or both. Practical people on the rue Chardin.

He sat on the edge of the bed, took a deep breath, let it out slowly. The man who had lived here, the producer Jean Casson, Jean-Claude to his friends, little jokes, small favors, a half-smile, *maybe we should make love*—what had become of him? The last attempt at communication was propped against the base of a lamp on the bedside table. A message written in eyebrow pencil on the inside cover of a matchbook from the bar at the Plaza-Athenée. *34 56 08* it said, a phone number. Signed *Bibi.*

He'd spent a long time walking the roads, a long span of empty days in the barracks of a defeated army, and he'd thought, every day, about what had happened up on the Meuse. The machine-gun duels across the river, the French soldiers running away, the refugees on the roads. It seemed strange to him now, remote, an experience that happened to somebody else, in some other country.

He shaved, smelled the lotion he used to wear, then put the cap back on the bottle. Went for a walk. Rue des Vignes. Rue Raffet. Paris as it always was—smelly in the heat, deserted in August. He came to the Seine and rested his elbows on the stone wall and stared down into the river—Parisians cured themselves of all sorts of maladies this way. The water was low, the leaves on the poplars parched and pale. Here came a German officer. A plain, stiff man in his mid-thirties, his Wehrmacht belt buckle said *Gott Mit Uns,* God is with us. Strange God if he is, Casson thought.

The Métro. Five sous. Line One. Châtelet stop, Samaritaine department store, closed and dead on a Sunday. He would survive this, he thought. They all would, the country would. "Peace with honor," Pétain had called the surrender. Peace with peace, at any rate, and not to be despised. Just another *débâcle,* the lost war. And French life had plenty of those. There goes the electricity, the Christmas dinner, the love of one's life. *Merde.*

In the back streets of a deserted commercial district he found a little café open and ordered an *express.* The price had doubled, the coffee was thin, and the proprietor raised a cautionary eyebrow as he put the cup down—*this is how things are, I don't want to hear about it.* Casson didn't complain. He was lucky to be alive, paying double for a bad coffee was a privilege.

On the flight south from Sedan he'd been lucky twice. The first time, he was with a company of French infantry, half of them still armed, when they were overtaken by a German column. An officer stood on a tank turret, announced the *Panzerkorps* had no time to deal with prisoners, and directed them to lay their weapons down on the road. When that was done a tank ran over them a few times and the column went on its way. Others had not been so fortunate—they'd heard about whole divisions packed into boxcars and shipped off to camps in Germany.

The second time, Casson was alone. Came around the curve of a road outside Châlons to find three Wehrmacht officers on horseback. They stared at him as he walked past—a lone, unarmed soldier in a shabby uniform. Then he heard a laugh, glanced up to see a young man with the look of a mischievous elf, or perhaps, if some small thing annoyed him, a murderous elf. "You halt," he said. He let Casson stand there a moment, then leaned over, worked his mouth, and spit in his face. His friends found that hilarious. Casson walked away, head down, and waited until he was out of sight before wiping the saliva off.

So what? he told himself. *It didn't mean anything.*

A woman came into the café and caught his eye. She was tall, had a big, soft face, net stockings, short skirt. Casson stood and gestured at an empty chair. "A coffee?" he said.

"Sure, why not."

The proprietor brought it over and Casson paid.

"Been out in the country?" she said.

"You can tell?"

She nodded. "You have the look. Too many healthy Frenchmen around, all of a sudden." She took a sip of coffee and scowled at the proprietor but he was busy not noticing her. She snapped her purse open, took out a small mirror, poked at a beauty mark pasted on her cheek. "Care for a fuck?" she said.

"No, thanks."

She closed the mirror and put it back in her purse. "Something complicated, it'll cost you."

"What if I just buy you a sandwich?"

She shrugged. "If you like, but I hate to see this louse have the business."

Casson nodded agreement.

"Oh, it's going to get real shitty here," she sighed. "Before, I was just about managing. Day to day, you know. But now . . ."

Casson took out a packet of cigarettes and they both lit up. The woman blew a long plume of smoke at the café ceiling. "Trick is," she said, "with these times, is don't let it ruin your life."

"My mother used to say that."

"She was right."

They smoked. A fat little man, commercial traveler from the suitcase he was carrying, looked into the café and cleared his throat. The woman turned around. "Well hello," she said.

"Are you, uh . . ."

The woman stood up. "I have to go," she said.

"Luck to you."

"Thanks. And you."

Monday morning, 7:00 A.M. The concierge knocked on his door. It took him a long time to unwind himself from sleep, dreams, the safety of his very own bed. He staggered to the door.

"Welcome home, Monsieur Casson."

He stood, swaying slightly, his shirt pulled together in one hand, his pants held up with the other. "Madame Fitou," he mumbled.

She was sweating with anxiety.

"What is it?"

"The car, monsieur."

"Yes?" He rarely drove it—it mostly stayed in the little garage off the courtyard.

The words came in a rush. "Well, of course we waited until you returned, and we worried about you so, but of course you know the authorities have made a requisition of all private automobiles, so, ah, it must be turned in. Of course there were posters, while you were away, monsieur. My husband made sure to write down the address, out in Levallois, because we thought, you'd have to be informed, you'd want to be, when you came home . . ." She ran down slowly.

"Oh, yes, of course."

Now he understood. The poor woman was afraid he'd refuse, that she would be dragged into disobedience, made to suffer for his casual attitude toward authority. "I'll take care of it this morning, madame," he said.

She thanked him, he could see the relief in her eyes. She'd lain awake all night, he supposed. In her imagination he had scoffed, jeered at her. Then, disaster. Police.

"I'd better get dressed," he said brightly, and managed a smile as he closed the door.

Madame Fitou and her sister held the doors open and Casson backed out carefully into the rue Chardin. No point in scratching the bodywork, he thought. He let the car idle a moment, then shifted into first gear. He didn't particularly share the national worship of automobiles, but this one had been very hard to get hold of and he was sorry to lose it.

A Simca 302. A model last manufactured in 1934, so those seen around Paris were all of a certain age. A sedan convertible, built low to the ground, always forest green. Walnut dash, rag top, throaty engine. Just the sort of car the producer Jean Casson might be expected to drive. Actually, just the sort of car the producer Jean Casson might be expected to drive—Jensen, Morgan, Riley—the producer Jean Casson couldn't afford.

The 302 was nice enough to look at, but it wasn't at all nice to its owner. It was a sulky, spoiled car that drank gas, that sputtered and died at traffic lights, that whined if made to go at high speeds, that wanted nothing to do with the weather after October. Still, it was a credible showpiece, and if it misbehaved with an important personage—it knew who was sitting in its passenger seat—Casson would smile and shake his head, helpless. A depraved passion, what could one do.

Of course it drove like an angel on its way to the garage. Out avenue Malakoff on a cloudy August morning, a few sprinkles of rain. Casson worked his way patiently through swarms of bicyclists; clerks and factory workers, young and old, everyone peddling along together, most of them sour-faced and grim, ringing their bicycle bells when some idiot went too slow or too fast.

The light was red at the intersection of Malakoff and the busy avenue Foch. A black sedan pulled up next to him and Casson and the passenger glanced at each other. German soldiers. Casson turned away. They were junior officers, probably lieutenants. They had the look of young men going to work at a bank or a law office—perhaps the military version, paymaster or judge advocate. Something administrative, he thought, and probably technical.

They were staring at him. He glanced back—*yes?*—but it didn't make them stop. They both wore glasses, one of them had round, tortoiseshell frames, the other silver rims. Their faces were pink, freshly shaved, their hair cut to military length and combed into place with hair tonic, and the way they were staring at him was rude. The light went green. The bicyclists moved off, Casson resisted an urge to speed ahead, hesitated so the sedan could go first.

But it didn't. They were waiting for him. *Conards!* he thought. Jerks. What's your problem? He eased the car into gear and inched forward. I'm not supposed to be driving, he thought. They can see I'm French, and that means I'm supposed to be pedaling a bicycle while they drive a car. His stomach turned over—he didn't want a confrontation, he wasn't sure exactly what that would mean. He let the Simca fade a little, waiting an extra beat between second and third. The sedan's door moved ahead of his, and he saw the two were talking, urgently, then the passenger looked out the window again. Clearly he was concerned, perhaps slightly annoyed.

Porte Maillot. A large, busy traffic circle with avenues radiating like spokes in all directions. A horn blasted behind Casson and he swerved over into the right lane as a Wehrmacht truck tore past him, swaying as it lurched around the circle. Then the sedan was back, the passenger not a bit less irritated. Casson began to feel sick. *What's the problem, Fritz? You think somebody peed in your soup?* He knew the look on the lieutenant's face—righteous indignation, a German religion.

Up ahead, another traffic light at the avenue des Ternes. Now green, but not for long. If they stopped side by side, the Germans were going to get out of their car and make an issue of it. And he wasn't legal, he wasn't supposed to be driving this car. He didn't know exactly what they'd do about it but he didn't want to find out. *You have not behaved correctly, now you must suffer the consequences.* A side street came up on his left, he threw the wheel over and stepped on the gas.

Rue du Midi. He didn't remember ever being here but he thought he was just at the edge of Neuilly. He stopped in the middle of the block, in front of a villa with an elaborate iron gate in its wall, and lit a cigarette. His hands were shaking. He glanced out the window at the view mirror. There they were. Up the street he could just see the black sedan, out on the avenue, backing up slowly in order to turn into the rue du Midi. They were going to come after him.

The sweat started at his hairline, he jammed the gear shift into first and took off. On his left, a tiny cobbled lane, something dark and lost about it. A place to hide. He turned in, gray plaster walls rose on both sides, there was barely room for a car. He followed a long curve, past an old-fashioned gas lamp, an even narrower alley that opened to his left, a row of shuttered windows. Where was he? It was perpetual twilight in here, the walls so close they amplified the car engine and he could hear every stroke of the pistons.

The street ended at a wall.

Covered with vines and moss, crumbling, twenty feet high. Over the oak and iron doors the chiseled letters on the capstone had been worn almost flat by time—the Abbey of Saint Gervais de Toulouse. Casson turned off the ignition then had to work his way free of the Simca because the walls were so close. He ran to the entry—he thought he could hear the sedan back in the rue du Midi. There was a chain hanging down the portal, he pulled it, heard the clang of an iron bell within the walls. He tried again, then again, glancing back over his shoulder and expecting the Germans at any second.

"Hello!" he called.

From the other side of the door: "What do you want?"

"Let me in. The Germans are after me."

Silence. Now he was sure he could hear the sedan—the whine of reverse gear, then the sound of idling where the lane opened to the street. "Please," he said. "Open the door."

He waited. Finally, a voice: "Monsieur, you cannot come in here."

"What?"

The silence seemed to last a long time. "Please go away, monsieur."

For a moment, Casson tried to explain it away—it was a Coptic order, or Greek, something exotic. But the man on the other side of the wall was French. "You should be ashamed of yourself," Casson said.

Silence.

Casson turned away from the door and ran back down the cobbled lane, in the direction of the rue du Midi, looking for the alley he'd seen. He found it, sprinted into the darkness and right into an iron grille. The shock made him cry out and a trickle of blood ran from his nose. He squatted down, his back against an icy stone wall, and held his hand against his face to stop the blood from getting on his shirt. He was perhaps ten feet down the alley. Out in the lane he heard footsteps, then two shadows moved quickly past the opening where Casson was hidden only by darkness. He forced himself against the wall. One of the soldiers said something, he was short of breath, and his whispered German was excited, perhaps a little frightened. Then the footsteps moved away, and Casson heard a shout as they found the car parked facing the Abbey wall. He could just hear them as they talked it over, then footsteps came back toward the alley, paused, and moved away toward the rue du Midi.

Too French for them in here, Casson thought. It was dark and damp and it smelled of old drains, burnt wood, cat piss, and God knew what else. It was too ancient, too secret. Sitting against the wall and wiping at his bloody nose, Casson felt something like triumph.

He counted to a hundred, then got the Simca backed down the lane and out into the street as quickly as he could. Because if the Germans had lacked the courage to search the alley—and Casson sensed they'd known he was in there—they were certainly brave enough to pick up a telephone once they got to work, and report the Frenchman and his car to the Gestapo, license plate and all.

As for the feeling of triumph, it didn't last long. In the winding streets of Levallois-Perret—the industrial neighbor of luxurious Neuilly—he stopped the car so a young woman carrying a bread and a bag of leeks could cross the street. A blonde, country-girl-in-Paris, big-boned, with spots of red in her cheeks and heavy legs and hips beneath a thin dress.

Their eyes met. Casson wasn't going to be stupid about it, but his look was open, *I want you.* When her lip curled with contempt and she turned away pointedly it surprised him. Eye contact in Paris was a much-practiced art, a great deal of love was made on the streets, some of it even made its way indoors. But she didn't like him. And she was able, her face mobile and expressive, to tell him why. Anybody driving a car since the requisition was a friend of the Occupier, and no friend of hers. Let him seek out his own kind.

A few minutes later he found the garage. It was enormous, packed with row on row of automobiles, all kinds, old and new, banged-up and shiny, cheap little Renaults and Bugatti sports cars. The German sergeant in charge never said anything about *where were you,* he simply took the keys. Casson wondered out loud about a receipt, but the sergeant merely shrugged and nodded his head at the door.

Later that morning he went to his office, but the door was padlocked.

Casson went home and called his lawyer.

Bernard Langlade—whose anniversary he'd celebrated at Marie-Claire's—was a good friend who happened to be a good lawyer. A personal lawyer, he didn't represent CasFilm or Productions Casson. Sent a bill only when he was out of pocket and, often enough, not even then. He looked at papers, listened patiently to Casson's annual tax scheme—taking off his glasses and rubbing his eyes—wrote the occasional letter, made the occasional phone call. In fact Langlade, though trained at the Sorbonne, spent his days running a company that manufactured lightbulbs, which his wife had inherited from her family.

"At least you're home, safe and in one piece," he said on the phone. "So let's not worry too much about locked doors. I have a better idea—come and have lunch with me at one-thirty, all right? The Jade Pagoda, upstairs."

A fashionable restaurant, once upon a time, but no more. It had fallen into a strange, soft gloom, deserted, with dust motes drifting through a bar of sunlight that had managed to work its way between the drapes. The black lacquer was chipped, the gold dragons faded, the waiter sat at a corner table, chin propped on hand, picking horses from the form sheet in the Chinese newspaper.

"Well, Jean-Claude," Langlade said, "now we're really in the shit."

"It's true," Casson said.

"And I worry about you."

"Me?"

"Yes. Life under German rule is going to be bad, brutal. And it's going to demand the cold-blooded, practical side of our nature. But you, Jean-Claude, you are a romantic. You sit in a movie theater somewhere, wide-eyed like a child—it's a street market, in ancient Damascus! A woman takes off her clothes for you—she's a goddess, you're in love!"

Casson sighed. His friend wasn't wrong.

"That must change."

Langlade took a sip of the rosé he'd ordered with lunch and scowled. He was ten years older than Casson, tall and spare and extremely well-dressed, with iron-colored hair going white over the ears, large features, dark complexion, and a mouth set in perpetual irony—life was probably not going to turn out all that well, so one had better learn to be amused by it. He raised an eyebrow as he said, "You have a bicycle?"

"No."

"We'll get to work on it. Immediately. Before all the world realizes it's the one thing they absolutely must have."

"Not for me, Bernard."

"Ah-hah, you see? That's just what I mean."

Casson poked his fork at a bowl of noodles. It needed sauce, it needed something. "All right, I'll ride a bicycle, I'll do what I have to do, which is what I've always done. But what worries me is, how am I going to earn a living? What can I do?"

"What's wrong with what you've always done?"

"Make films?"

"Yes."

"What—*The Lost Rhine Maiden*? *Hitler Goes to Oxford*?"

"Now Jean-Claude . . ."

"I'm not going to collaborate."

"Why would you? I'm not. I'm making lightbulbs. Your lights will burn out, you'll need replacements. But they won't be Nazi lightbulbs, will they?"

Casson hadn't thought of it quite that way.

"Look," Langlade said, "your barber—what's he going to do under the Occupation? He's going to cut hair. Is that collaboration?"

"No."

"Well, then, what's the difference? The barbers will cut hair, the writers will write, and the producers will make films."

Casson gave up on the noodles and put his fork down by the plate. "I won't be able to make what I want," he said.

"Oh shit, Jean-Claude, when did any of us ever do what we wanted?"

The waiter appeared with two plates of diced vegetables. Langlade rubbed his hands with pleasure. "Now this is what I come here for."

Casson stared at it. A carrot, a mushroom, a scallion, something, something else. As Langlade refilled their glasses he said, "I'll tell you a secret. Whoever can discover a wine that goes with Chinese food will be very rich."

They ate in silence. The Chinese waiter gave up on the racing form, and his newspaper rattled as he turned the page. "What was it like here?" Casson said.

"In May and June? Terrible. At first, a great shock. You know, Jean-Claude, the Gallic genius for evasion—we will not think unpleasant thoughts. Well, that's fine, until the bill comes. What they believed here I don't know, perhaps it wouldn't matter if the Germans won. There were women to be made love to, bottles of wine to be opened, questions of life and the universe to be discussed, *important* things. If we lost a war, well, too bad, but what would it matter? The politicians would change the color of their ties, possibly one would have to learn a new sort of national anthem. After all, the shits that run the country are the shits that run the country—how bad could it be to have a new set?

"Ah but then. We sat here in Paris the second week in May, reading the departmental numbers on the license plates. It started in the extreme north—one day the streets were full of 10s from the Aube. By midweek we had the 55s from the Meuse and, a day or two later, the 52s from the Haute-Marne. And no matter what the radio said, it began to dawn on us that something was moving south. And so on a Thursday, the first week in June, a great mob—can you guess?"

"Marched on the Elysée Palace."

"Descended on the luggage department at the Galéries Lafayette."

Casson shook his head, ate some of the diced vegetables, poured himself some more rosé. By the end of the second glass it wasn't too bad. "Tell me, Bernard, in your opinion, how long is this going to go on?"

"Years."

"Two years?"

"More like twenty."

Casson was stunned. If that were true, life could not be suspended, left in limbo until the Germans went home. It would have to be lived, and one would have to decide how. "Twenty years?" he said, as much to himself as Langlade.

"Who is going to defeat them? I mean really defeat them—throw them out. The answer hasn't changed since 1917—the Americans. Look what happened here, a German army of five hundred thousand attacked a nation with armed forces of five and a half million and beat them in five days. Only the Americans can deal with that, Jean-Claude. But you know, I don't see it happening. Even if Roosevelt decided tomorrow that America had to be involved, even if the senators saw any point in spilling Texas blood for some froggy with a waxed mustache, even *then,* it's years to build the tanks. And get them here—how? Flown by Babar? No, everything has changed, the rules are different. Your life is your country now, my friend. You are a citizen of the nation Jean-Claude, and you will have to learn to live on those terms or you will not survive."

Langlade had shaken his fork at Casson as he was making his point, now he caught himself doing it and put it down on his plate. Cleared his throat. Took a sip of wine. The waiter turned another page of the newspaper. Casson looked up to see one corner of Langlade's mouth twist up in a sudden smile. "*Hitler Goes to Oxford* indeed!" he said under his breath, laughing to himself.

"And there he meets Laurel and Hardy," Casson said. "The college servants."

It was not the first time he'd had to glue his life back together.

The banks had resumed operations in July, but there had been problems, confusion, and for some reason the checks to the landlord for the office on the rue Marbeuf had not gone through. The landlord, a fat little creature, shoulders back, tummy sucked in, said "Such difficult times, Monsieur Casson, how was one to know . . . anything? Perhaps now, life will become, ah, a little more *orderly.*"

He meant: you attempted to take advantage of war and Occupation by not paying your rent promptly, but I'm smarter than that, monsieur! And he also meant: *Orderly.*

Which was to say, Pétain and everything he believed in—by September Casson had learned to recognize it from the slightest inflection. France, the theory went, *deserved* to be conquered by Germany because it was such a corrupt, wicked nation, with a national character so degenerate it had stormed the Bastille in 1789, a national character deformed by alcohol, by promiscuity, by loss of the old moral values.

❖

He's right, Casson thought, one September evening, gently improving the angle of a pair of legs in silk stockings. The radio was playing dance music, then Pétain came on, from Vichy. The usual phrases: "We, Philippe Pétain," and "France, the country of which I am the incarnation."

"Ah, the old general," she said.

"Mmm," Casson answered.

They waited, idling, while Pétain spoke. Waiting was a style just then—*it will all go away, eventually.*

"You have warm hands," she said.

"Mmm."

Lazy and slow, just barely touching each other. Could there be a better way, Casson wondered, to get through a speech? When the dance music returned—*French* dance music, plinky-plinky-plink, none of this depraved "jazz," but upright, honest music, so *Maman* and *Papa* could take a two-step around the parlor after dinner—he was almost sorry.

He missed Gabriella. Once the padlock was removed he'd found the note she'd left for him. It was dated 11 June—the day after Italy had declared war on an already defeated France. "I cannot stay here now," she'd written. Casson remembered the barracks where he'd heard the news. The soldiers were bitter, enraged—what cowardice! The Germans had brutal souls, they did what they did, but the Italians were a Latin people, like them, and had rushed in to attack a fallen neighbor.

"I will miss you, I will miss everything," Gabriella wrote. She would always remember him, she would pray for his safety. Now she would go back to Milan. The Paris she had longed for, it was gone forever.

Otherwise there was nothing. Mounds of pointless mail, the rooms dusty and silent. Casson sat at his desk, opened files, read papers. What to do next?

Late September it began to rain, he met a girl called Albertine, the daughter of the concierge of a building on the rue Beethoven. On market day, Thursday in Passy, he'd stood at the vegetable cart, staring balefully at a mound of broad yellow beans—there was nothing else. A conversation started, he wondered what one did to prepare these things, she offered to show him.

The affair floated in the broad gray area between commerce and appetite. Albertine was not beautiful, quite the opposite. Some day, perhaps, she would glow with motherhood, but not now. At nineteen she was pinched and red, with hen-strangler's hands and the squint of an angry farmwife. That was, Casson thought, the root of the problem: there was a good deal of Norman peasant blood in the population of Paris and in big Albertine it ran true to type. She came to his apartment, revealed the mystery of the yellow beans—one boiled them, *voilà!*—took off her dress, sat on the edge of the bed, folded her arms, and glared at him.

The time with Albertine was late afternoon, usually Thursday. Then, before she went home, she would make them something to eat. In the old days his dinners had drifted down from heaven, like manna. Life was easy, attractive men were fed. There were dinner parties, or a woman to take to a restaurant, or he'd go to a bistro, Chez Louis or Mère Louise, where they knew him and made a fuss when he came in the door.

That was over. Now the Germans ate the chickens and the cream, and food was rationed for the French. The coupons Casson was issued would buy 3 1/2 ounces of rice a month, 7 ounces of margarine, 8 ounces of pasta, and a pound of sugar. The sugar he divided—most to Albertine, the remainder for coffee. One had to take the ration stamps to the café in the morning.

So mostly it was vegetables—potatoes, onions, beets, cabbages. No butter, and only a little salt, but one survived. Of course there *was* butter, what the Germans didn't want—one sometimes saw a soldier eating a stick of it, like an ice-cream cone, while walking down the street—could be bought on the black market. He would give Albertine some money and she would return with cheese, or a piece of ham, or a small square of chocolate. He never asked for an accounting and she never offered. What she kept for herself she earned, he felt, by thrift and ingenuity.

The women he usually made love to were sophisticated, adept. Not Albertine. A virgin, she demanded to be taught "all these things" and other than an occasional *What?!!* turned out to be an exceptionally diligent student. She had rough skin and smelled like laundry soap, but she held nothing back, gasped with pleasure, was irresistibly shameless, and hugged him savagely so that he wouldn't drift up through the ceiling and out into the night. "Only in war," she said, "does this happen between people like us."

Casson went to the office but the phone didn't ring.

It didn't ring, and it didn't ring, and it didn't ring. The big studios were gone, there was no money, nobody knew what to do next. Weddings? The director Berthot claimed to have filmed three since July. Rich provincials, he claimed, that was the secret. Watch the engagement announcements in places like Lyons. The couple arrive separately. The nervous papa looks at his watch. The flowers are delivered. The priest, humble and serious, greets the grandmother. Then, the kiss. Then, the restaurant. A toast!

Casson glued two papers together by licking the edges and rolling tobacco into a cigarette. Working carefully, he managed to get it lit with a single match. "Can you make me one of those?" Berthot asked hungrily.

Casson, that devil-may-care man-about-town, did it. When it took two tries to light the ragged thing, Casson smiled bravely—matches were no problem for him. "I had an uncle," Berthot said, "up in Caen. Wanted to turn me into a shoemaker when I was a kid." He didn't have to go on, Casson understood, the shoemakers had plenty of work now.

The October rains sluiced down, there was no heat on the rue Marbeuf. He had enough in the bank to last through November's rent, then, that was that. What was what? Christ, he didn't know. Sit behind his desk and hold his breath until someone ran in shaking a fistful of money or he died of failure. He went to the movies in the afternoon, the German newsreels were ghastly. A London street on fire, the German narrator's voice arrogant and cocksure: "Look at the destruction, the houses going up in flames! This is what happens to those who oppose Germany's might." Going back out into the gray street in midafternoon, the Parisians were morose. The narrator of the newsreel had told the truth.

He answered an advertisement in *Le Matin*. "Distribute copies of a daily bulletin to newsstands." It was called *Aujourd'hui à Paris* and listed all the movies and plays and nightclubs and musical performances. The editor was a Russian out in Neuilly who called himself Bob. "You'll need a bicycle," he said. Casson said, "It's not a problem," remembering his conversation with Langlade. But he never went back—inevitably he would encounter people he knew, they would turn away, pretend they hadn't seen him.

Langlade. Of course that was always the answer, one's friends. He'd heard that Bruno and Marie-Claire were doing very well, that Bruno had in fact received delivery of the MGs left on the Antwerp docks, that he now supplied French and Italian cars to German officers serving in Paris. But something kept him from going to his friends—not least that they were the sort of friends who really wouldn't have any idea how to help him. They'd always looked up to him. They did the most conventional things: manufactured lightbulbs, imported cars, wrote contracts, bought costume jewelry, while he *made movies.* No, that just wouldn't work. They would offer him money—*how much?* they'd wonder. And, after it was gone, what then?

28 October, 1940.
He'd brought his copy of *Bel Ami* to the rue Marbeuf as office reading—he'd always wanted to make a film of de Maupassant, everyone did. Then too, he simply had to accept the fact that one didn't find abandoned newspapers in the cafés until after three.

11:35. He could now leave the office, headed for a café he'd discovered back in the Eighth near the St.-Augustin Métro, where they had decent coffee and particularly good bread. Where he could pretend—until noon but not a minute later—that he was taking a late *casse-croûte,* midmorning snack, when in fact it was lunch. And the waiter was an old man who remembered *Night Run* and *The Devil's Bridge.* "Ah, now those," he'd say, "were movies. Perhaps a little more of the bread, Monsieur Casson."

Casson's hand was on the doorknob when the telephone rang.

He ran to the desk, then forced himself to wait for the end of the second ring before he picked it up and said "Hello?" Not disturbed, exactly, simply unable to hide the fact that his concentration had been elsewhere, that he'd been busy—perhaps in a meeting, perhaps in mid-sentence as he reached back for the receiver.

"Jean Casson?"

"Yes."

"Hugo Altmann." The line hummed for a moment. "Yes? Hello?"

"Altmann, well, of course."

"Perhaps you don't—remember me."

"No, no. I was just . . ."

"Tell me, Casson, can you possibly cancel your lunch today?"

"Well. Yes, I could. It's not anything I can't reschedule."

"Perfect! You're still on the rue Marbeuf?"

"Yes. Twenty-six, just off the boulevard."

"Save me parking, will you? And wait for me downstairs?"

"All right."

"Good. Ten minutes, no more."

"See you then."

He ran into the bathroom down the hall and stared into the mirror above the sink. Shit! Well, not much he could do about it now—his shirt was tired, his jacket unpressed. But he'd shaved carefully that morning—he always did—his hair simply looked vaguely arty when he avoided the barber, and his shoes had been good long ago and still were. It was, he thought, his good fortune to be one of those men who couldn't look seedy if he tried.

Altmann he remembered well. He worked for Continental, the largest of the German production companies, with offices out by Paramount in Billancourt. A film executive, typical of the breed. The practical, plodding French of the long-term expatriate—nothing fancy but nothing really wrong. Smooth manners, smooth exterior, but not sly. He was, one felt, constitutionally neat, and courtly by upbringing. Well-dressed, favoring muted tweed suits and very good ties in rich colors. The kind of hair that faded from blond to no color at all in the mid-forties, combed back at the age of seven and still in place. Scandinavian complexion, blue eyes—like a frozen lake—and a smile. Always a second drink, always enthusiastic—even about the most godawful trash because you just never knew what people were going to like—always at work. Casson had been at several meetings with him out at Continental, a lunch or two a few years ago, it was all a little hazy.

A last look in the mirror; he ran his fingers through his hair, splashed water on his face, that was the best he could do. Glancing at his watch he hurried out of the bathroom and down the stairs.

Outside, the sun was just fighting its way out of the clouds. Omen? An exquisite Horch 853 swept to the curb, Altmann waved from behind the wheel. Casson wasn't impressed by cars, but still . . . Silvery-green coachmaker's body, graceful lines, spare tire—silvery-green metal center—snugged into the curve of the running board just forward of the driver's door. Casson slid into the leather seat, they shook hands, said hello.

They sped up the rue Marbeuf, then out onto the Champs-Elysées. The Horch had twelve cylinders, five forward gears, and the voice of a sports car, muttering with suspended power every time the clutch was depressed. "We'll go eat somewhere in the country," Altmann said. "Some days I just can't stand the city, even Paris."

Out through Neuilly in light traffic; a few military vehicles, a few bicycles, the occasional horse and cart. Next came Courbevoie; empty, winding streets. Then left, following the Seine: Malmaison, Bougival, Louveciennes. The little restaurants facing the water had been for painters and dancers, once upon a time, but the money had always followed the kings, west from Paris and along the river, and eventually the cooks followed the money—the lobsters came and the artists went.

"So," Altmann said, "are you doing anything special?"

"Not much. You're still with Continental?"

"Oh yes. Just the same as always. Everything changes, you know, except that it all stays the same."

Casson laughed. Altmann took a pack of cigarettes out of his pocket, shook it adeptly so that several popped up, and held it across the seat. Casson took one, Altmann lit it, then his own, with a polished lighter.

"We're bigger now," Altmann continued. "There's that difference. A good deal bigger, in fact." A town fell away and they were in the countryside. Corot, Pissarro, they'd all painted up here. Autumn valleys, soft light, white clouds that rolled down from Normandy and lit up the sky. The most beautiful place on earth, perhaps. It struck Casson in the heart, as it always did, and he opened the window to get the glass out of his way. The car drifted to a stop as Altmann prepared to turn. There were yellow leaves on the road, little swirls of them when the wind blew, Casson could hear them scratching along over the rumble of the engine.

They turned right, came back out on the river and headed west. Altmann drew on his cigarette, the exhaled smoke punctuated his words as he talked.

"I hope you're not waiting for me to discuss politics, Casson, because frankly it's all gotten beyond me." There was a man carrying a basket on a wooden footbridge that crossed the river. He turned to look at the glorious car, shifting the weight of the basket on his shoulder. "The things I've seen," Altmann continued, "in Germany *and* France, the last five years, I really don't know what to say about it." He paused, then said, "It didn't even occur to me that my phone call might offend you—but it does now, and if you like I'll turn around and take you back to Paris. It's just that I came back from Berlin and thanked God that Paris was as it always was, that nothing was burned or blown up, that I was going to be able to live here, on some kind of terms anyhow, and to make films. The truth is, you and I are lucky—we can simply get out of the world's way while it destroys itself, we don't have to be crushed by it. Or, maybe, I should turn around. It's up to you, I'll understand one way or the other."

"It's too nice a day to go back to the city," Casson said.

"There's bad blood between our countries, it's no good, but it doesn't have to be between us, does it?"

"No, no, not at all."

Altmann nodded, relieved. On the left a cluster of houses, almost a village. Just on the other side, where the fields began, a restaurant, Le Relais. "Why not?" Altmann said. The tires crunched over the gravel by the entry as the Horch rolled to a stop.

Inside it was quiet and it smelled good. A few local people were having lunch, they glanced up as Casson and Altmann came in, then looked away. The *patron* seated them in the bay by the front window, looking out over the flowers in the windowbox. Casson studied the handwritten menu, but there wasn't much choice—basically the *plat* they'd cooked that day and a few substitutes, like an omelet that the kitchen could produce if you just had to have something else. So they ordered what there was—Altmann had a fistful of ration coupons—a

platter of warm *langouste,* crayfish, not long out of the river, followed
by an *andouille,* the Norman sausage the butchers made from the very
bottom of the tub of leftovers, cooked in cider vinegar. All of it so good,
in an off-hand way, that it made Casson lightheaded. For wine, what
Le Relais offered was the color of raspberry jam, dry as a bone and
sharp as a tack, in liter bottles without label or cork; and when the
first was gone a second appeared. All this accompanied by small talk—
business was never discussed with food—until the coffee arrived. Then
Altmann said "Let me lay the situation out for you as it stands today."

"Good," Casson said, taking yet another of Altmann's cigarettes.

"The major difference is, they're going to set up a committee called
a *Filmprüfstelle,* Film Control Board, that will answer to Goebbels's
people in the *Propagandastaffel* up in the Hotel Majestic. Now UFA-
Continental is going to have to deal with them, I would not try to tell
you otherwise, and they are who they are, enough said. On the other
hand, *they* have to deal with *Continental,* and it's not at all clear who's
the bigger dog in this yard. Our capitalization has increased to ten million reichsmarks—two hundred million francs. With the cost of making a film in France averaging out to about three and a half million
francs, you can see what's going to happen. Certainly there will be quite
a lot of waltzing—powdered boobs in ball gowns and all the rest of it,
there's always that, but they can't have ten million reichsmarks' worth
even if that's what they think they want. We've acquired thirty-nine
movie theatres, and we have the laboratories and the processing—once
you get to that stage there must be more than Old Vienna, and that's
going to come from independent producers and directors. Do you
see?"

Casson nodded. He saw. The thirty-nine theatres came in large part
from the confiscation of property belonging to Siritsky and Haik, Jewish film exhibitors.

"So when I say," Altmann continued, "that the Nazis have to deal
with Continental, I mean it. It's felt in Berlin that if French culture is
destroyed then we've failed to resolve the difficulties between us. This
is *not* Poland, this is one of the greatest cultures the world has ever
produced—Hitler himself dares not claim otherwise." He drank a sip
of coffee, then another.

"Now look," he said, voice lower. "We're not sure ourselves exactly
what they're going to let us do. Obviously a celebration of the French

victory in 1918 won't work at the Control Board, but a hymn to Teutonic motherhood won't work at Continental. Between those extremes, if you and I are going to work together, is where we'll work."

"I won't make Nazi propaganda," Casson said.

"Don't. See if I care." Altmann shrugged. "Casson, you couldn't if you wanted to, all right? Only a certain breed of swine can do that—German swine or French swine. Perhaps you know that a German film, *The Jew Süss,* has broken box-office records for the year in Lyons, Toulouse, and, of course, Vichy."

"I didn't know that."

"It's true. But, thank God, Paris isn't Lyons or Toulouse."

"No."

"Well?"

"It's a lot to think about," Casson said.

"You know Leveque?"

"Of course. *The Emissary.*"

"Raoul Mies?"

"Yes."

"They've both signed to do projects—no details, but we're working on it."

Casson looked out the window. The Seine was high in its banks, as it always was in autumn, and gray. It was going to rain, the weeds on the river bank bent over in the wind. *Life goes on,* he thought. "I don't know," he said quietly.

"Good," Altmann said. "An honest answer." He leaned closer to Casson. "I have to get up every morning and go to an office, like everybody else. And I don't want to work with every greasy little pimp who wants to be in movies. I want my day to be as good as it can—but I'm flesh and blood, Casson, just like you, and I'll do what I have to do. Just like you."

Casson nodded. Now they'd both been honest. Altmann started to pour the last of the wine, then put the bottle down and signaled the *patron.* "What do you have for us—something good."

The patron thought a moment. "Cognac de Champagne?"

"Yes," Altmann said. "Two, then two more." He turned back to Casson. "They'll pay," he said. "Believe me they will."

Casson wasn't sure what he meant. Expensive Cognac? Expensive film? Both, very likely, he thought.

◆◆◆

This one cried. Nothing dramatic, shining eyes and "Perhaps you have a handkerchief." He got her one, she leaned on an elbow and dabbed at her face. *"Bon Dieu,"* she said, more or less to herself.

He reached down and pulled the sheet and blanket up over them, it was cold in November with no heat. "You're all right?"

"Oh yes."

He rolled a cigarette from a tin where he kept loose tobacco and burnt shreds. They shared it, the red tip glowing in the darkness.

"Why did you cry?"

"I don't know. Stupid things. For a moment it was a long time ago, then it wasn't."

"Not a girl anymore?"

She laughed. "And worse."

"You are lovely, of course."

"La-la-la."

"It's true."

"It was. Maybe ten years ago. Now, well, the old saying goes 'nothing's where it used to be.' "

From Casson, a certain kind of laugh.

After a moment, she joined in. "Well, not *that*."

"You're married?"

"Oh yes."

"In love?"

"Now and then."

"Two kids?"

"Three."

They were quiet for a moment, a siren went by somewhere in the neighborhood. They waited to make sure it kept going.

"In the café," she said, "what did you see?"

"In you?"

"Yes."

"Truth?"

"Yes."

"I don't know. I was, attracted."

"To what?"

"To what. Something, maybe it doesn't have a name. You know what goes on with you—deep eyes, and the nice legs. Right? Try to say more than that and you're chasing desire, and you won't catch it. 'Oh, for me it's a big this and a little that, this high and that low, firm, soft, hello, good-bye.' All true, only next week you see somebody you have to have and none of it is."

"That's what attracted you?"

Casson laughed, his face warm. "You came in to buy cigarettes, you glanced at me. Then you decided to have a coffee. You crossed your legs a certain way. I thought, I'll ask her to have a coffee with me."

She didn't answer. Put the bottom of her foot on top of his.

"You like this, don't you?" he said softly.

"Yes," she sighed, bittersweet, "I do like it. I like it more than anything else in the world—I think about it all day long."

That fall the city seemed to right itself. Casson could feel it in the air, as though they had all looked in the mirror and told themselves: you have to go on with your life now. The song on the radio was from Johnny Hess. *"Ça revient,"* he sang—it's all coming back. *"La vie recommence, et l'espoir commence à renaître."* Life starts again, and hope begins to be reborn.

Well, maybe that was true. Maybe that had better be true. Casson went to lunch with an editor from Gallimard, they had a big list that fall, people couldn't get enough to read. One way to escape, though not the only one. There were long lines at the theatres—for *We Are Not Married* at the Ambassadeurs, or the *Grand Revue* at the Folies-Bergère. The Comédie-Française was full every night, there was racing at Auteuil, gambling at the Casino de Paris, Mozart at Concert Mayol. *The Damnation of Faust* at the Opéra, *Carmen* at the Opéra-Comique.

"What are you looking for?" the Gallimard editor asked. "Anything in particular?"

Casson talked about *Night Run* and *No Way Out*. What the rules were when the hero was a gangster. The editor nodded and said "Mm," around the stem of his pipe. Then his eyes lit up and he said, "Isn't it you who made *Last Train to Athens*?"

That he loved. Well, Casson thought, at least something. "Come to think of it," the editor said, polishing his glasses with the Deux Magots' linen napkin, "we may have just the right thing for you. Publication not scheduled until winter '42, but you certainly understand that that isn't far off."

"Too well."

"*The Stranger*, it's called."

Casson nodded appreciatively. No problem putting that on a marquee.

"By a writer named Albert Camus, from Algiers. Do you know him?"

"I've heard the name."

The editor talked about the plot and the setting, then went on to other things. Casson wrote the title on a scrap of paper. It wasn't what he'd made, more like what he'd always wanted to make, maybe would have made if the human-predicament stuff hadn't been thrown overboard during the hunt for money.

"Now I don't know if this is for you," the editor said, "but there's a writer named Simone de Beauvoir—she has the cultural program on Radio Nationale—and she's working on a novel . . ."

Now he had the scent. The next day he spent at the Synops office, where synopses of ideas for films—from novels, short stories, treatments—were kept on file. It was busy; he saw Berthot, hunting eagerly through a stack of folders. "How's the wedding business?" he asked. Berthot looked sheepish. "I'm out of it," he said quietly. "For the moment." What the hell, Casson thought. Was he the last one to catch on? The war was over, it was time to go back to business.

"Hello, Casson!" Now there was a voice that caught your attention—foreign, and, by way of compensation, much too hearty. Casson looked up to see Erno Simic, the Hungarian. Or, if you liked your gossip, the "Hungarian." A tall man, slightly stooped, a head too large for a pair of narrow shoulders, hooded eyes, a smile, meant to be ingratiating, that wasn't. A French citizen of complex Balkan origins—no matter how many times he told you the story you could never keep it straight. Simic ran a small distribution company called Agna Film, which operated in Hungary and Romania.

"Simic," he said. "All going well?"

"Today it is. Tell me please, Jean-Claude, we can eat together sometime soon?"

"Of course. Call me at the office?"

"I will, naturally. There is a Greek place, in the Tenth . . ."

Better every day, his world coming back to life.

Cold at night. None of that your side/my side diplomacy in the bed. Maybe he didn't know her name and maybe the name she told him was a lie and maybe he did the same thing, but three in the morning found them curled and twisted and twined together in the chill air, hugging like long-lost lovers, riding each other's bottoms through the night, arms wrapped around, hanging on to anything they could get hold of.

Cold at night, and cold in the daytime. They had everything rationed now—coal and bread and wine and cigarettes. Only work kept him from thinking about it. Somewhere out in the lawless borderlands of the 19th Arrondissement he found Fischfang, as always at the center of incredibly complicated domestic arrangements. There were children, there were wives, there were apartments—mistresses, comrades, fugitives. Fischfang was never in one place for very long. Late one afternoon he sat with Casson in a tiny kitchen where a young woman was boiling diapers in a kettle. The coal stove smoked, mildew blackened the walls.

Casson explained that he was back in business, that he was looking for a project, and how the rules had changed.

Fischfang nodded. "Not too much reality—is that it?"

"Yes. That's how it has to be."

Fischfang stared out the window, the sky gray with winter coming. "Then what you might be able to do," he said, "is a Summer Night movie. You know what I mean—the perfect night of summer in the full moon. A certain group of people have gathered in a castle, a country house, a liner on the high seas. A night of love, *the* night of love. Just once, dreams come true. By the end, one couple has parted, but we see that, ah, Paul has always loved Marie, no matter how life has tried to drive them apart. The crickets chirp, the moon rises, the music of the night is sublime. Hurry—life will soon be over, time is short, we have only this night, we must live out our loveliest dream, and it's only a few hours until dawn."

He wound down. They were both silent. At last Fischfang cleared his throat, lit a cigarette. "Something like that," he said. "It might work."

On the way back to his office, Casson saw a girl, maybe sixteen or so, wearing a school uniform, arms wrapped around her books. It was dusk. She looked directly into his eyes, an intimate look, as they moved toward each other on the crowded boulevard. "Monsieur," she said. Her voice was urgent, emotional.

He stopped. Yes? What? The usual Jean-Claude, the usual half-smile, whatever you want, I'm here. She thrust a folded paper into his hand, then was off down the street, disappearing into the shadows. He stepped into a doorway, unfolded the paper. It was a broadsheet, a one-page newspaper. *Résistance,* it was called. WE MUST FIGHT BACK, the headline said.

On 17 December, Jean Casson signed with Continental.

HOTEL
DORADO

*J*9 December, 1940.

ean Casson sat at his desk at four in the afternoon. He wore an overcoat, a muffler, and gloves. Outside, a winter dusk—thick, gray sky, the lines of the rooftops softened and faded. Looking out his window he could see a corner where the rue Marbeuf met the boulevard. People in dark coats on the stone-colored pavement, like a black-and-white movie. Once upon a time they'd loved this hour in Paris; gold light spilling out on the cobbled streets, people laughing at nothing, whatever you meant to do in the gathering dark, you'd be doing it soon enough. On these boulevards night had never followed day—in between was *evening,* which began at the first fading of the light and went on as long as it could be made to last. *Sometimes until dawn,* he thought.

He went back to his book, *Neptune's Daughter,* turning the pages awkwardly with his glove, making notes in soft pencil. Work, *work.* The telephone rang, it was Marie-Claire, organizing a dinner. They were trying hard, his little group of friends, he was proud of them.

Rolling the holiday boulder up a long and difficult slope—but at least working together. Christmas in France was not the ritual it was in England, but the New Year *réveillon* was important, and you were supposed to eat fine things and feel hopeful.

They talked for a time, the same conversation they'd had for years—they must, he thought, somehow or other like having it. And it ended as it always did, with another telephone call planned—a Marie-Claire crisis could not, by definition, be resolved with a single telephone call.

Neptune's Daughter. Veronica and Perry drinking sidecars in Capri and watching the sun set. "Where do you suppose we'll be on this day next year?" Veronica asks. "Will we be happy?" The telephone rang again. Marie-Claire, Casson thought, a forgotten detail. "Yes?" he said.

"Hello? Is this Jean Casson?" An English voice, accenting the first syllable of *Ca*sson. A voice he knew.

"Yes. Who is this, please?"

"James Templeton."

The investment banker from London. "It, it's good to hear from you." Casson's English worked at its own pace.

"How are you getting on, over there?" Templeton asked.

"Not so bad, thank you. The best that we can, you know, with the war . . ."

"Yes, well, we haven't forgotten you."

Casson's thoughts were flying past. Why was this man calling him? Could it be that some incredibly complicated arrangement was going to allow British banks to invest in French films? There was a rumor that England and Germany continued to trade, despite the war, using middlemen in neutral nations. Or, maybe, a treaty had been signed, and this was a protocol sprung suddenly to life. Maybe, he thought, his heart quickening, the fucking war is over! "Thank you," he managed to say. "What, uh . . ."

"Tell me, do you happen to see much of Erno Simic? The Agna Film man?"

"What? I'm sorry, you said?"

"Simic. Has distribution arrangements in Hungary, I believe. Do you see him, ever?"

"Well, yes. I mean, I have seen him."

"He can be extremely helpful, you know."

"Yes?"

"Definitely. Certain business we're doing now, he is somebody we are going to depend on. And since you're a friend of ours in Paris, we thought you might be willing to lend a hand."

"Pardon?"

"Sorry. To help, I mean."

"Oh. Yes, I see. All right. I'll do what I can."

"Good. We *are* grateful. And we'll be in touch. Good-bye, Casson."

"Good-bye."

He knew. And he didn't know. He could decide, at that point, that he didn't know. He fretted, waiting until six to walk over to Langlade's office. "Jean-Claude!" Langlade said. "Come and have a little something." From a bottom drawer he produced an old wine bottle refilled with calvados. "We went to see the Rouen side of the family on Sunday," Langlade explained. "So you'll share in the bounty."

Casson relaxed, sat back in his chair, the calvados was like soothing fire as it went down.

"This is hard-won, I hope you appreciate it," Langlade continued. "It took an afternoon of sitting on a couch and listening to a clock tick."

"Better than what you get in a store," Casson said.

Langlade refilled the glass. "My good news," he said, "is that suddenly we're busy. Some factory in Berlin ordered these tiny little lightbulbs, custom-made, grosses of them. God only knows what they're for, but, frankly, who cares?" He gave Casson a certain look—it meant he'd been closer to disaster than he'd been willing to let on. "And you, Jean-Claude? Everything all right?"

"A very strange thing, Bernard. Somebody just telephoned me from London."

"What?"

"A call, from a banker in London."

Langlade thought hard for a moment, then shook his head. "No, no, Jean-Claude. That's not possible."

"It happened. Just now."

"They've cut the lines. There isn't any way that somebody could call you from London."

"You're certain?"

"Yes. Who did you say?"

"An English banker."

"Not from London, *mon ami*. What did he want?"

"He wasn't direct, but he suggested that I do business with a certain distribution company."

Langlade stared at the ceiling for awhile. When he spoke again, his tone of voice was subtly altered. "He called from France." Then, "What are you going to do?"

"I don't know," Casson said. "He's in France, you think?"

"Possibly Spain, or Switzerland, but definitely on the Continent— because the lines under the Channel were cut last June."

"Well," Casson said.

"You better think it over," Langlade said.

Someone knocked discreetly on the office door. Langlade, it seemed to Casson, was not sorry to be interrupted.

The apartment was across a courtyard from a dress factory, through a cloudy window Casson could see women working at sewing machines. Fischfang sat at a table in the tiny kitchen, wearing an old sweater, and a blanket around his shoulders. He'd shaved his beard and mustache, the skin looked pale and tender, and his eyes were red, as though he hadn't slept the night before. Outside, a few snowflakes drifted past the window.

"Do you need anything?" Casson asked.

Fischfang shrugged—everything, nothing. The apartment belonged to his aunt. When she'd opened the door, Fischfang had taken a moment to make sure it was Casson, then used an index finger to close a drawer in the kitchen table. But not before Casson had caught sight of a revolver.

Casson sat at the table, the aunt served them some strange drink— not exactly tea—but at least it was hot. Casson held the cup with both hands to keep warm. "Louis," he said, "why do you have a gun? Who's coming through the door?"

Fischfang looked out the window, a muscle in his jaw ticked. Casson had never seen him like this. Angry, of course, but that was nothing new. A communist, he lived on injustice, a vitamin crucial to daily life, and he was always fuming about what *X* said or *Y* wrote. But now, something else. This was nothing to do with Marxist fury. Fischfang was scared, and bitter.

"I have been denounced," he said, as though the words were strange to him.

Casson's face showed sympathy, but in his heart he wasn't surprised. The kind of life Fischfang lived, seething with politics—the Association of Revolutionary Artists and Writers, *left deviation, rotten liberalism,* Stalinists, Trotskyites, Spartacists, and God only knew what else. Denunciation must have been a daily, perhaps hourly, event.

"Maybe you remember," Fischfang went on, "that last August the Germans demanded that all Jews register."

"I remember," Casson said.

"I didn't."

Casson nodded once—of course not.

"Someone found that out, I don't know who it was. They turned me in. For money, perhaps. Or some advantage. I don't know."

The aunt closed a bureau drawer in the other room. From across the courtyard Casson could hear the clatter of sewing machines. The women were hunched over their work, their hands moving quickly. "Now I understand," he said. "You're certain?"

"No, not completely. But things have happened."

Casson took a breath. "So then, we'll have to get you away somewhere."

Fischfang stared at him for a moment. Will you really? When the time comes? Then he looked down, squared a tablet of lined paper on the table in front of him, laughed a little. "Life goes on," he said, in a tone that meant he didn't particularly care if it did or not. Then he passed the tablet across to Casson. "Have a look," he said.

Spidery writing in blue ink, floating from margin to margin. *Hotel Dorado* it said on top. A sort of miracle, Casson thought, the way these things started from nothing. Just a few words on a piece of paper. For an instant he could smell movie theatre—figures flickering on the screen, the pitch of the voices, the sound of the projector when there was a pause in the dialogue. He pictured the title. On the marquee of the Graumont, just off the place de l'Opéra. He didn't know why there, it was just the theatre he always imagined.

He read on. A little village in the south of France, on the Mediterranean. A fishing village, where a few Parisians come every August to stay at the Hotel Dorado. Autumn, the season over, the hotel deserted. The owners, an old couple, about to retire. The hotel has been sold to a large combine, they're going to tear it down and build a new one, modern and expensive. The couple decides to write to their oldest, most faithful clients. "The hotel is going out of business, but come and stay with us the last weekend in October, we'll have a glass of wine, a few memories."

Casson looked up. "All in one weekend?"

"Yes."

"That's good."

"A night when they arrive. A day when we meet them, a long night when everything happens, then a little scene where they get on the train to go back to Paris—except for the ones who are going to run off together and start a new life."

Casson went back to reading. The characters you'd want—the *Corps Humaine*, the human repertory company—were all there. The banker, the confidence man, the actress, the postal clerk and his wife who scrimp and save all year so they can pretend to be upper class for two weeks, the lovers—their spouses left in Paris—the widow, the couple about to separate, giving it one last chance.

"Who's the star, Louis?"

"I thought—one of those ideas that's either a love letter from the gods or a little patch of quicksand meant just for you—it should be a young woman. Lonely, mysterious. Who misses her train and comes there by accident. Not a member of the sentimental company but, finally, its heart. Or, I don't know, maybe that's overdoing it."

Casson waved him off. "No, that's what I like about this kind of movie, you can't really overdo it."

"Who would you want to star?"

Casson watched the falling snow for a time. "Last May, a hundred years ago if you know what I mean, I had lunch with old Perlemère, who used to represent Citrine, and her name came up in the conversation."

Fischfang's eyes sparkled. "That's good. More than one way, if you think about it."

"Beautiful—not pretty. Mysterious. No virgin. She's been to the wars, she's battle-scarred, but maybe she can try one last time, maybe she can love again, but we don't know until the final scene. It should be—will life let her?"

"A character trying to come back," Fischfang said. "Played by an actress trying to come back."

Casson nodded. "Something like that."

They both smiled. Maybe it would work, maybe it wouldn't, like everything else. But they were trying, at least. They could see their breath when they talked in the cold kitchen, outside the snow drifted past. "I'll get it typed up," Casson said.

Hugo Altmann tilted his chair back and blew a long, slow, meditative plume of smoke at the ceiling of his office. "Citrine, Citrine," he said. "Do you know, Casson, that she always seemed to me the most elementally *French* actress. The sort of woman, in bed she gives everything. Yet there is something inside her, a bitterness, a knowledge of the world, that spoils it all—you get everything, but it isn't what you wanted." He paused a moment. "You've worked with her before?"

"*Night Run.*"

"Ach, of course. And to direct?"

"Don't really know yet."

"Well, let's find you some development money, and get a screenplay on paper. Who do you have in mind there? Cocteau's working, lots of others."

"Louis Moreau, perhaps."

"Who?"

"Moreau."

"Never heard of him."

"He's new."

"Hm. Well, all right, give him a try." He leaned over toward Casson, his expression shrewd and confidential. "So, between us, who saves the hotel at the end, eh? I'm betting on the confidence man," he said with a wink.

It took two weeks to find Citrine. He trudged across the city, office to office, the world of small-time talent agents, booking agents, press agents—everybody knew somebody. Perlemère helped, offering the

names of a few friends. In the end, it turned out that she was per-
forming at a cabaret amid the working-class dance halls on the rue de
Lappe, out by Bastille. Le Perroquet, the parrot, it was called. Casson
pulled his coat tight around him and kept his eyes down—this was not
his district, he didn't belong here, and he didn't want a punch in the
nose to remind him of it.

Closed, the first time he went. No reason, just closed. The blue neon
parrot on a red branch was dark. The next time he tried was on Christmas Eve, and it was open. There was a poster by the door, the name
Loulou across the bottom. Citrine—though it took him a moment to
recognize her—Citrine on a high stool. Top hat, net fabric with rhine-
stones on top, bare legs crossed down below, spike heels with satin
bows, a cabaret smile. *Well, what about you, big boy?*

A Christmas Eve blizzard. The white flakes swirled and hissed and
made drifts in the doorways. Now and then a car came sliding down
the street, tires spinning, engine whining as it worked its way around
a corner. The blue-painted glass on the street lamps cast Hollywood
moonlight on the snow.

Hot inside, steamy, and packed. He tried the stage door, but a doorman dressed like an apache—black sweater and beret and cigarette
dangling from the corner of the mouth—ran him off. "You'll pay. Like
the rest of the world, *conard.*"

He paid. To join a hundred German officers jammed together in a
small room, reeking of shaving lotion and stale sweat and spilled wine
and all the rest of it. There was a master of ceremonies in a tuxedo,
sweating and telling jokes, then zebras, naked girls in zebra masks,
bucking and prancing, hoisting their knees up to their foreheads and
singing "Paris smells so sweet." Saluting British style—whistles from
the crowd—then turning around and grabbing their ankles—roars of
approval. A fat major next to Casson almost died of pleasure, laughed
as tears ran down his cheeks, gave Casson a best-pal whack between
the shoulder blades that sent him flying into the crowd.

Then the room went dark, the curtain creaked open, a violet spotlight popped on, and there was Loulou. By then he'd worked his way
to a position near the stage where he knew she would be able to see
him, and, after the second number, she did. He could tell. At first,
Jesus it's Casson, what's he doing here? Then the corner of her mouth

lifted, not much, but a little: he was there to see her, it was no accident.

But he wasn't going to see her anytime soon. A table of colonels, prominent in the front of the room, demanded the presence of the beautiful Loulou and she was produced, guided to the table by the owner of the Perroquet, an eel in a checked suit. They were merry colonels, they touched her shoulder and told her jokes and tried to speak French and gave her champagne and had quite a time for themselves. Question was, would Hansi be the one to fuck her, or was she going to favor Willi? The battle raged, the competing armies surged back and forth as Casson looked at his watch and realized that the last Métro of the night had left Bastille station.

Finally the owner came around, bowed and scraped and tried to get his *chanteuse* back. Hansi and Willi were in no mood for that, but the owner had a trick up his checked sleeve and sent a phalanx of zebras into action. They arrived neighing and whinnying, sat on the colonels' laps and wiggled about, tickled their chins, stole their eyeglasses and fogged them with their breath.

The colonels roared and turned red. Champagne was poured into glasses and everywhere else—to the colonels it seemed that champagne had found its way to places where champagne had never been before. One ingenious soul filled his mouth until his eyes bulged, then punched his cheeks with his index fingers—*pfoo!*—showering Hansi and Willi, assorted zebras, and Loulou, who wiped her face with her hand as she made her escape and climbed up on the tiny stage.

Most actresses could carry a tune if they had to and Citrine was no different. She simply played the role of a cabaret singer, and she was good at it. The throaty voice, hoarse from cigarettes and drinks in lonely cafés. *I always knew you'd leave me, that I'd be alone.* You could see her man, the little cockerel with a strut. *And there you were, with her, at the table where we used to sit.* Of course there was a kid, in military school somewhere. *Oh well, perhaps once more, for old times' sake.* The eyes, slowly cast down, a few notes from the battered old piano, the spotlight dimming out. Ahh, Paris.

She sent the doorman in the black sweater to get him and they hurried away down an alley, indignant German shouts—"Loulou! Loulou!"—

growing faint as they turned a corner. Which left them in the middle of a blizzard on the wrong end of Paris and no Métro with the curfew hour, one in the morning, long gone.

"We'll walk," she said with determination. "It will keep the blood moving. And something will occur."

"Walk where?"

"Well, Jean-Claude, I stay at a sort of a not-so-good hotel these days—and even not-so-good as it is, they close it down like the Forbidden City after one-thirty. It usually works to sleep on a couch at the club, but not tonight, I think."

"No."

"So, we walk."

"Passy . . ."

She took his arm with both of hers, her shoulder firmly against him, and they walked through the blizzard. He was happy to be held this way, he really didn't care if they froze to death; a set of fine ice statues, one with a smile. *Citrine, Citrine,* he thought. She wore a long black coat and a black beret and a long muffler wound around her neck.

"I want you to be in a movie," he said.

"Tell me about it."

"You will star."

"Ah."

"You'll be in most of the scenes. It's about an old hotel in a little village, somewhere in the Midi. It's been sold, and people come down from Paris one last time, and you wander in from, ah, from the land of the lost strangers."

"Ah yes, I know this place, I have lived there. We are forever wandering into movies."

He laughed, she held his arm tight. Somewhere out in the swirling snow, a car, the engine getting louder. They rushed into the first doorway. Lights cut the dark street—police on the prowl. "Pretend to kiss me," she said.

They embraced, star-crossed lovers in a doorway. The car—French, German, whoever it was—passed them by. Casson's heart was hammering, it was all he could do not to press his hand against his chest. And nothing to do with the police. *My God, I am fourteen,* he thought. When the car was gone they walked in silence, heads down against the wind.

She'd come to Paris from Marseilles at sixteen—it would have been running away if anybody had wanted her to stay there. Her mother had kept a boardinghouse for merchant seamen, mostly Turks and Greeks, and, the way Citrine put it, "one of them was probably my father." Thus her skin was pale, with a shadow beneath it, she had hair the color of brown olives—worn long—with glints of gold in it, almond-shaped eyes, and to him she'd always smelled like spice—*Byzantine,* whatever that meant. It meant his fantasy side ascendant, he knew, but he thought about her that way anyhow. Across a room she was tall and slim, distant, just the edge of cold. And she was in fact so exotic, striking—a wide, heavy-lipped mouth below sharp cheekbones, like a runway model—that she looked lean, and hard. But the first time he'd put his arms around her, he had understood that it wasn't that way; not outside, not inside.

In the course of the love affair she had only once told secrets about her past, about the boardinghouse where she'd grown up. "How much they loved and respected my mother," she'd said. "They waited with me until I was fourteen, and then there were only two of them, and they made sure I enjoyed it."

"Did they beat you?"

"Beat me? No, not really."

That was all. They were on a train, she turned away and looked out the window. She had said what she wanted to: *yes, I knew too much too young, you'll have to go on from there.*

He had tried—he thought he'd tried, he remembered it that way. She had, too. But they drifted. A day came, and whatever had been there before wasn't there anymore. Another Parisian love affair ended, nobody could really explain it, and nobody tried.

They angled away from the river, into the 7th Arrondissement, toward Passy, hurrying across the Pont de Solférino, where white snow spun over the black river and the wind sang in the arches of the bridge. "Jean-Claude?" she said, and he stopped.

She looked up at him, there were white crystals of ice in her eyelashes, frozen tears at the corners of her eyes, and she was shivering. "I think I need to rest for a moment," she said.

They found a little shelter, in the shallow portal of an ancient building. She burrowed against his chest. "How can there be nothing?" she said plaintively. She was right, the streets were deserted, no bicycle cabs, no people.

"We're halfway," he said.

"Only that?"

"A little more, maybe."

"Jean-Claude, can I ask you a question?"

"Of course."

"Is there really a movie? Or is it, you know."

"A movie. *Hotel Dorado,* we're calling it. For Continental, maybe. Of course like always, it's pure air until the great hand from the sky comes down and writes a check."

"I wondered. Sometimes, I think, men want to run their lives backward."

"Not women?"

"No."

Not women? Not ever? It was warm where he held her against him. Slowly he unwound the long muffler, ran it under her chin and around so that her ears were covered.

"Thank you," she said. "That's better."

"Shall we start out again? Sooner we do . . ."

"Listen!" she whispered.

A car? She canted her head, held the muffler away from one ear. He could hear only the hiss of falling snow, but then, faintly, a violin. And then a cello. He looked up the side of the building, then across the street. But the snow made it hard to locate.

"A trio," she said.

"Yes."

He looked at his watch. *Oh, France!* 3:25 on the morning of Christmas, in an occupied city, three friends determine to stay up all night and play Beethoven trios—in a cold, dark apartment. She looked up at him, mouth set hard as though she refused to cry.

Rue de Grenelle, rue Vaneau, tempting to take Invalides, but better to swing wide of the Ecole Militaire complex. Military and security offices had been there before and they would still be in operation, with new tenants. Plenty of Gestapo and French police in the neighborhood.

So, find Grenelle again, and take the next small street, less important, in the same direction.

They never heard the car until they were almost on top of it, then they hugged a wall and froze. It was a Citroën Traction Avant, always a Gestapo car because the front-wheel drive worked on nights like these, with chains on the tires. It was idling—perfectly tuned, it hardly made a sound—the hot exhaust melting the snow behind the rear wheel. Through the back window they could see the silhouette of a man in the passenger seat. The driver had left the car and was standing in front of an apartment building, urinating on the front door.

Casson held his breath. The Germans were only fifty feet from them. The driver had left the Citroën's door ajar, and the passenger leaned over and called out to him. The driver laughed, said something back. Banter, apparently. Taking a piss in a snowstorm, that was funny. Doing it on some Frenchman's door, that was even funnier. Jokes, back and forth, guttural, thick, incomprehensible. To Casson, it sounded as though somebody was grinding language into broken words that could never be used again. But, he thought, they are in Paris, we are not in Berlin.

The man at the doorway started buttoning up his fly, then, as he hurried toward the car, he said the words "rue de Vaugirard"—an island of French in the German sentence. So, Casson thought, they were going to the rue de Vaugirard, to arrest somebody on Christmas Eve. Citrine's hand found his, she'd heard it too.

Suddenly the car moved—*backward*. Casson pressed frantically against the wall, Citrine's hand closed like a steel claw. Then the wheels spun, caught, and the car drove off down the street. The Germans hadn't known they were there, they were just making sure they didn't get stuck in the snow.

An hour later, the apartment on the rue Chardin. There was no heat, and Casson preferred not to turn on the lights, often faintly visible at the edges of the blackout curtains. They shed their outer clothes in the bathroom, hanging them over the bar that held the shower curtain so they could drip into the tub as the snow and ice melted.

"Bed is the only place," he said. He was right, they were both trembling with the cold, and they climbed into bed wearing their underwear.

At first the sheets were as cold as they were, then the body heat began to work. She took a deep breath and sighed, coming gently apart as the night's adventure receded.

"Are you going to sleep?" he said.

"Whether I want to or not." Her voice was faint, she was barely conscious.

"Oh. All right."

She smiled. "Jean-Claude, Jean-Claude."

"What?"

"Nothing. Go to sleep."

He couldn't—he ached for her.

She sensed what he was going to do, moved close in a way that made it impossible. "I can't, Jean-Claude. I can't. Please."

Why?

As though she'd heard: "You're going to think a dozen things, but it's that I can't feel that way again, not now. If we were just going to amuse ourselves, well, why not? But it isn't that way with us, you get *inside* me, that's no play on words, I mean to say it. Do you understand?"

"Yes."

"If it wasn't a war, if I had money. If I just had it in me, the strength to live . . ."

"You're right, I'm sorry. It's just me, Citrine."

"I know. I know you—you fuck all the girls." But the way she said it was not unkind.

And even before the sentence ended, she was slipping away. Her breathing changed, and she fell asleep. He watched her for a time. Strange, the way her face worked, she always looked worried when she slept. Sometimes her breathing stopped, for a long moment, then it would start again. *She dies,* he'd thought years ago. *She dies, then she changes her mind.*

They woke up in the middle of Christmas Day. The snow had stopped. She wrote the name of a hotel on a scrap of paper, kissed him on the forehead, said "Thank you, Jean-Claude," and went out into the cold.

29 December, 1940.

He left the office at six-thirty. He had a little money now, from Altmann, and a secretary. A cousin of his named Mireille, from the Morvan, his mother's side of the family. She was a dark, unhappy woman with three children and an eternally useless husband. She showed up just about the time the money did, so he hired her—it was simply life's way, he figured, of telling you what you ought to do.

The coldest winter of the century. The price of coal climbed into the sky, the old and the poor got into bed with every scrap of wool they owned and there they found them a week later. German soldiers flooded into Paris, from garrison duty in Warsaw and Prague, and Paris entertained them. Are you tense, poor thing? Have a little of this, and a little of that. England wouldn't give up. The submarine blockade was starving them, but they had never been reasonable, and they apparently weren't going to be now. Well, the French would also survive. More or less.

Out on the street, Casson pulled his coat tight around him and turned toward the Métro station at avenue Marceau. Two stops, Iéna and Trocadéro, and he could walk the rest of the way. The Passy station was closer to the rue Chardin, but that involved a *correspondance,* a change of lines, so if he stayed on the Line 9 train he'd be home in a few minutes. Albertine, tonight. His big, ugly treasure of a farm girl. Something good to eat. Vegetables, cow food—but garlic, salt, a drop of oil, and the cunning way she chopped it all up. Jesus! Was it possible that he'd reached that ghastly moment in life when the belly was more important than the prick? No! Never that! Why, he'd take that Albertine and spread her . . .

"Hey, Casson."

That voice. He turned, annoyed. Erno Simic, waving his arm and smiling like a well-loathed schoolmate, was trotting to catch up with him. "Wait for me!"

"Simic, hello."

"I never called—you're angry?"

"No. Not at all."

"Well, I been busy. Imagine that. Me. I got phone calls and messages, meetings and telegrams. Hey, now we know the world is upside down. Still it means a few francs, a few *balles,* as they say, eh? So we'll have a drink, on me. I promised a lunch, I'm gonna owe it to you, but now it's a drink. Okay?"

Paris hadn't surprised Casson for twenty years but it did now. Simic took him down the Champs-Elysées to avenue Montaigne, one of the most prestigious streets in the city, then turned right toward the river. They worked their way through a busy crowd in front of the Plaza-Athenée, mostly German officers and their plump wives, then walked another block to a residential building. On the top floor a grand apartment with a view to the river had been converted to a very private bar.

Seated at a white piano, an aristocratic woman wearing a black cocktail dress and a pillbox hat with a veil was playing "Begin the Beguine." Simic and Casson were shown to a table by a fat man in a sharkskin suit draped to hide both him and some sort of weapon. The tables on the teak parquet were set far apart, while the walls were covered with naughty oil paintings of naughty, and exceptionally pink, women. The room was crowded; a beautiful woman at the next table drinking tea, on second glance perhaps a prostitute of the most elevated class. By the window, two French colonels of cavalry. Then a table of dark, mustached men, Armenian or Lebanese, Casson thought. There was a famous ballet master—Russian émigré—sitting alone. In the corner, three men who could have been gangsters or black-market butchers, or both. Simic enjoyed Casson's amazement, his big smile broadening from ingratiating to triumphant.

"Hah! It's discreet enough for you, Casson?"

"How long—?"

Simic spread his hands. "Summer, as soon as everything settled down. It belongs to Craveur, right?"

Craveur was a famous restaurant owner, his family had been in the business since 1790, when the first restaurants were opened. Simic signaled to a waiter, a plate of petits fours salées—herring paste, oysters, or smoked salmon on puff pastry—appeared along with two large whiskey-and-sodas.

"It's what I always have," Simic confided. "Mm, take all you want," he said, mouth full.

Casson sipped the whiskey-and-soda, lit up one of Simic's Camel cigarettes, and sat back on a little gold chair with a gold cushion.

"Your name came up in a conversation I had," Simic said. "With a man called Templeton. You know him, right? Works in a bank?"

"Yes."

"He vouches for you."

"He does?"

"Yes. And that's important. Because, Casson, I still got Agna Film, but now I'm also a British spy."

"Oh?"

"That's how it is. You're surprised?"

"Maybe a little." Casson ate an oyster petit four.

"I'm a Hungarian, Casson. Not exactly by birth, you understand, but by nationality at birth. Still, *Mitteleuropa,* central Europe, is the world I understand, just like Adolf—so I see clearly certain things. Some people say that Adolf is a devil, but he's not, he's the head of a central European political party, no more, no less. And what he means to do in France is to destroy you, to ruin your soul, to make you despise yourselves, that's the plan. He wants you to collaborate, he makes it easy for you. He wants you to denounce each other, he makes it easy for you. He wants you to feel that there's no nation, just you, and everybody has to look out for themselves. You think I'm wrong? Look at the Poles. He kills them, because they come from the same part of the world that he does, and they see through his tricks. You understand?"

Casson nodded.

"So we got to stop that—or else. Right? Myself, I'm betting on the English, and I am going to work with them, and I want you to work with me, to help me do what I have to do."

"Why me?"

"Why you. You're known to the English—James Templeton has spoken for you, he knows you don't have sympathy with the Germans. It also helps that you're a film producer. You can go anywhere, you can meet anybody, of any class. You handle money, sometimes in large amounts, sometimes in cash. You might take ten people on a train. You might charter a freighter. You might use several telephone numbers, bank accounts—even in other countries. For us, it's a good profession. Do you see?"

"Yes."

"Want to help?"

Casson thought a moment, he didn't really know what to say. He did want to help. Left to himself he would never have done anything, just gone on trying to live his life as best he could. But he hadn't been left to himself, so, now, he had to decide if he wanted to become involved in something like this.

Yes, he said to himself. But it was what they called *un petit oui*—a little yes. Not that he was afraid of the Germans—he was afraid of them, but that wouldn't stop him—he was afraid of not being any good at it.

"I will help you, if I can," he said slowly. "I don't know exactly what it is you want me to do, and I don't know if I'd do it right. Maybe for myself that wouldn't matter, but there would be people depending on me, isn't that true in something like this?"

A backhand sweep of the arm, Simic knocked the uncertainty across the room. "Ach—don't worry! The Germans are idiots. Not in Germany, mind you—there you can't spit on the street, because they got everybody watching their neighbor. But here? What they got is a counterespionage service, which is lawyers, that's who they hire. But not the Jewish lawyers, they're all gone. And not the top lawyers, they're high up, or they're hiding. Found themselves a little something in this bureau or that office—hiding. So, you don't have to worry. Of course, you can't be *stupid,* but we wouldn't be talking if you were. And, oh yes, you'll make some money in this. We can't have you poor. And you'll get all the ration coupons you need, the British print them in Tottenham."

"Where?"

"A place in London. But they're very good, never a problem. Suits, food, gasoline, whatever you want."

In a dark corner, the piano player was hard at work: "Mood Indigo," "Body and Soul," "Time on My Hands." Cocktail hour in Paris— heavy drapes drawn over the windows so the world outside didn't exist. The bar filled up, the hum of conversation getting louder as the drinks arrived. The expensive whore at the next table was joined by a well-dressed man, Casson had seen him around Passy for years, who wore the gold seal ring that meant nobility. He was just out of the barber's chair, Casson could smell the talcum powder. The woman was stunning, in a gray Chanel suit.

The waiter brought two more whiskey-and-sodas. "Chin-chin," Simic said and clinked Casson's glass.

"Tell me what," Casson said, "*exactly* what, it is that you want me to do."

Simic looked serious, the big head on the narrow shoulders nodding up and down. "A proper question, Casson. It's just, I have to be cautious."

Casson waited.

"Well, to those who know, the place that matters most in this war is Gibraltar. Sits there, controls the entrance to the Mediterranean, means that the British can go into North Africa if they want, then up to Sicily, or Greece. Or Syria. That means Iraqi and Persian oil—you can't fight without that—and the Suez Canal. Can Adolf take Gibraltar? No. Why not? Because he'd have to march across Spain, and for that he needs Franco's permission because Franco is his ally. A neutral ally, but an ally. Don't forget, Adolf helped Franco win his civil war. So, what will Franco do?"

"I don't know," Casson said.

"You're right! The British don't know either. But what you want, for your peace of mind, is your own man guarding the back door to your big fortress, not the ally of your enemy. Understand?"

"Yes."

"So, what I'm working on." Simic lowered his voice, leaned closer to Casson. "What I'm working on is a nice private Spaniard for the British secret service. A general. An important general, respected. What could he do? What couldn't he do! He could form a guerrilla force to fight against Franco. Or, better, he could assassinate Franco. Then form a military junta and restore the monarchy. Prince Don Juan, pretender to the Spanish throne, who is tonight living in exile in Switzerland, could be returned to Catalonia and proclaimed king. See, Franco took the country back to 1750, but there's plenty of Spaniards who want it to go back to 1250. So the junta would abolish the Falangist party, declare amnesty for the five hundred thousand loyalist fighters in prison in Spain, then declare that Spain's strict neutrality would be maintained for the course of the war. And no German march to Gibraltar."

Slowly, Casson sorted that out. It had nothing to do with the way he thought about things, and one of the ideas that crossed his mind was a sort of amazement that somewhere there were people who considered the world from this point of view. They had to be on the cold-hearted side to think such things, very close to evil—a brand-new war in Spain, fresh piles of corpses, how nice. But, on the other hand, he had been reduced to crawling around like an insect hunting for crumbs in the city of his birth. It was the same sort of people behind that—who else?

The man and the woman at the next table laughed. She began it, he joined in, one of them had said something truly amusing—the laugh was genuine. *You think you know how the world works,* Casson thought, *but you really don't. These people are the ones who know how it works.*

Several times, over the next few days, he put one hand on the telephone while the other held his address book open at the S–T page. *Sartain Frères. Ingrid Solvang. Simic, Erno—Agna Film.* Not a complicated situation, he told himself. Very commonplace. Sometimes we believe we can make a certain commitment but then we find that, after all, we can't. So then, a courteous telephone call: sorry, must decline. *It's just the way things are right now.* Or, maybe, *It's just not something I can do.* Or, *It's just*—in fact, who the hell was Erno Simic that he deserved any kind of explanation at all? So, really, it was Casson explaining to himself.

Out on the boulevard, from the building they'd requisitioned in the first month of the Occupation, the young fascists of the *Garde Française* and the *Jeune Front* goose-stepped on the packed snow. Across the street, the optician Lissac displayed a sign that said WE ARE LISSAC, NOT ISAAC. A few doors down, broken windows, where an umbrella-and-glove shop had been forced to advertise itself as an *Enterprise Juive.*

Would murdering Franco stop that?

His heart told him no.

Then do it for France.

Where?

France—was that Pétain? The *Jeune Front?* Those pinched, white, angry little faces, scowling with envy. The patrons of the bar on the avenue Montaigne? The soldiers running away from the battle on the Meuse?

But he didn't dial the telephone. At least, not all the numbers.

And so, inevitably, he arrived at his office one morning to find that a message had been slipped beneath the door. Hocus-pocus, was how he thought about it. An uncomfortable moment, then on with his day.

Hotel Dorado. That was better medicine than Spanish murder, right?

And so, inevitably, the hocus-pocus itself.

Maybe not the best time for it, an icy night in the dead heart of January. Something that day had reached him, some sad nameless thing, and the antidote, when he found her, was blonde—a shimmering peroxide cap above a lopsided grin. Older up close than she'd first seemed—at a gallery opening—and not properly connected to the daily world. Everything about her off center, as though she'd once been bent the wrong way and never quite sprung back.

They sat on the couch and nuzzled for a time. "There is nobody quite like me," she whispered.

He smiled and said she was right.

She undid a button on his shirt and slid a hand inside. The telephone rang once, then stopped. It bothered her. "Who is it?" she said, as though he could know that.

But, in fact, he did know. And a minute later, sixty seconds later, it did it again. "What's going on?" she said. Now she was frightened.

"It's nothing," he said. Then, to prove it was nothing, "I have to go out for a while."

"Why?" she said.

He'd always thought, not all that proud of it, that he was a pretty good liar. But not this time. He'd been caught unprepared, no story made up just in case, so he tried to improvise, while she stared at him with hurt eyes and pulled her sweater back down. In the end, she agreed to wait in the apartment until he returned. "Look," he said, "it's only business. Sometimes, the movie business, you need to take care of something quietly, secretly."

She nodded, mouth curved down, wanting to believe him, knowing better.

In the street, it was ten degrees. He walked with lowered head and clenched teeth, the wind cutting through his coat and sweater. He swore at it, out loud, mumbling his way along the rue Chardin like a madman hauling his private menagerie to a new location.

At last, half-frozen, he crept down the ice-coated steps of the Ranelagh Métro and installed himself in front of a poster for the Opéra-Comique, a Spanish dancer swirling her skirt. A few minutes later, he heard the rumble of a train approaching through the tunnel. The doors slid open, out came a little man with a briefcase of the type carried under the arm. Casson could have spotted him five miles away, but then, the Germans were "idiots." And he, Casson, was so brilliant he'd believed *Erno Simic* when he'd called them that.

The contact was a small man, clearly angry at the world. Peering up and down the station platform he reminded Casson of a character in an English children's story. *The Wind in the Willows?* Waxed mustache, derby, fierce eyebrows, ferocious glare above an old-fashioned collar. Following instructions, Casson turned to the wall and stared at the poster. For a time, nothing happened. The dancer smiled at him haughtily and clicked her castanets in the air.

Finally, the man stood beside him. Cleared his throat. "An excellent performance, I'm told."

That was part one of the password. Part two was the countersign: "Yes. I saw it Thursday," Casson said.

The contact leaned the briefcase against the wall at his feet and began to button his coat. Then, hands in pockets, he hurried away, his footsteps echoing down the empty platform as he headed into the night. Casson counted to twenty, picked up the briefcase, and went home.

His blonde was bundled in a blanket, snoring gently on the couch. He went into the bedroom and closed the door. Before he put the briefcase on the shelf that ran across the top of his closet—under the bed? behind the refrigerator?—he had a look inside. Three hundred thousand pesetas—about $35,000 in American money—in thirty bundles of hundred-peseta notes, each packet of ten pinned through its upper right-hand corner.

Back in the living room, the blonde opened one eye. "You don't mind I took a nap," she said.

"No," he said.

"Keep me company," she said, raising the blanket. She'd taken off her skirt and panties.

Casson lay down next to her. It wasn't so bad, in the end. Two castaways, adrift in the Paris night, three hundred thousand pesetas in a bedroom closet, air-raid sirens at the southern edge of the city, then a long flight of aircraft, south to north, passing above them. On the radio, the BBC. A quintet, swing guitar, violin—maybe Stephane Grappelli—a female vocalist, voice rough with static. The volume had to be very low: radios were supposed to be turned over to the Germans, and

Casson was afraid of Madame Fitou—but he loved the thing, couldn't bear to part with it. It glowed in the dark and played music—he sometimes thought of it as the last small engine of civilization, a magic device, and he was its keeper, the hermit who hid the sacred ring. Some day, in times to come, the barbarians would break camp and trudge away down the dusty roads and then, starting with a single radio, they would somehow put everything back the way it had been.

Very sensitive to the touch, this blonde. Thin, excitable—she sucked in her breath when something felt good. Still, she was quiet about it. That was just common sense. They even pulled the blanket up over their heads, which made everything seem dark and secret and forbidden. Probably he'd laugh at that some day, but just then it wasn't funny, because they really *were* out there, the secret police and their agents, and this was something they probably didn't approve of. It wasn't spelled out—just better to be quiet.

When they were done with one thing, and before they moved on to the next, Casson went to the phone, dialed Simic's number, let it ring once, and hung up. Then he counted to sixty, and did it again. He wondered, as he was counting, if it was a good idea to keep Simic's number in his address book. In fact, where did Simic keep his number?

He crawled back under the blanket, the blonde yawned and stretched, and they began to resettle themselves on the narrow couch. By his ear she said, "You had better be careful, my friend, doing that sort of thing."

"Perhaps you prefer I do this sort of thing?"

"I do, yes. Anybody would." A few minutes later she said, "Oh, you're sweet, you know. Truly." Then: "A pity if you invite them to kill you, *chéri*."

Lunch, Chez Marcel, *rognons de veau,* a Hermitage from Jaboulet, 1931.

Hugo Altmann held his glass with three fingers at the top of the stem, canted it slightly to one side, poured it half full, then twisted the bottle as he turned it upright. He looked at the wine in his glass, gave it just a hint of a sniff and a swirl before he drank. "I like the script," he said. "Pretty damn smooth for a first draft. Who is this Moreau?"

"Comes out of the provincial theatre, down by Lyons somewhere.

Strange fellow, afraid of his own shadow, keeps to himself pretty much. Has a little cottage out past Orly—lives with his mother, I think. No telephone."

"Maybe I could meet him, sometime. A very sure hand, Jean-Claude, for the 'provincial theatre, down by Lyons.' "

Casson shrugged and smiled, accepting the compliment, proud of his ability to unearth a secret talent. He suspected Altmann knew how much he'd depended on Louis Fischfang for his scripts, and he'd intended "Moreau" as a fiction convenient for both of them. Altmann, however, seemed to think Moreau actually existed.

"Maybe some day," he said. "Right now, Hugo, I need him to think about *Hotel Dorado* and nothing else. If he meets you, he might start having *ambitions*."

"Well, all right." Altmann chased the last of the brown sauce around his plate with a piece of bread. "That banker in the first scene—Lapont? Lapère? Don't let anything happen to him. He's magnificent, truly loathsome—I can just see him."

"I'll tell Moreau he's on the right track. Now, make it *really* good."

Altmann smiled and took a sip of wine.

"I've been thinking," Casson said. "Maybe we should consider a different location."

"Not the Côte d'Azur?"

"It's commonplace, everybody's been there."

"That's the point, no?"

"Mmm—I think we have the plot, Hugo. But it's the setting I worry about. The feel of a place that's not the everyday world—come August, you leave your work, you leave the daily life, and you go there. Something special about it. I don't want anybody thinking, 'Well, *I* wouldn't sell that hotel—I'd put in a damn fine restaurant and put some paint on the façade.' "

"No, I guess not."

The waiter came to take the plates away. "There's a *reblochon* today, gentlemen," he said. "And pears."

"Bring it," Altmann said.

"I've been thinking about Spain," Casson said.

"Spain?"

"Yes. Down on the Mediterranean. Someplace dark, and very quiet.

The *propriétaires* are still French. Expatriates. But the clients are a little more adventurous. They go to Spain for their holidays."

"Hm."

"Anyhow, I'd like to go and have a look. Scout locations."

"All right, it shouldn't be a problem. But, I don't know, it doesn't, somehow—Spain?"

"Could be the key to it all, Hugo."

Altmann began preparing a cigar, piercing the leaf at the end with a metal pick he took from his pocket. He looked up suddenly, pointed the cigar at Casson. "You're a liar," he said. Then he broke out in a wide grin. "Have to take, uh, somebody down there with you, Jean-Claude? Just in case you need help?" He laughed and shook his head—*you scoundrel, you almost had me there.*

Casson smiled, a little abashed. "Well," he said.

Altmann snapped his lighter until it lit, then warmed the cigar above the blue flame. "Romantic in Spain, Jean-Claude. Guitars and so forth. And one doesn't run into every damn soul in the world one knows. You don't really want to move the story there, do you?"

"No," Casson said. "There's a lady involved."

Altmann nodded to himself in satisfaction, then counted out a sheaf of Occupation reichsmarks on top of the check. For a German in an occupied city, everything was virtually free. "Come take a walk with me, Jean-Claude," he said. "I want to pick up some cashmere sweaters for my wife."

The following afternoon Altmann sent over a letter on Continental stationery and, after a phone call, Casson took it to the Gestapo office in the old Interior Ministry building on the rue des Saussaies. The officer he saw there occupied a private room on the top floor. *SS-Obersturmbannführer*—lieutenant colonel—Guske wore civilian clothes, an expensively tailored gray suit, and had the glossy look of a successful businessman. A big, imposing head with large ears, sparse black hair—carefully combed for maximum coverage—and the tanned scalp of a man who owns a sailboat or a ski chalet, perhaps both.

His French was extremely good. "So, we are off to sunny Spain. Not so sunny just now, I suppose."

"No. Not in January."

"You've been there before?"

"Several times. Vacations on the beaches below Barcelona, in the early thirties."

"But not during the civil war."

"No, sir."

"Are you a Jew, Casson?"

"No. Catholic by birth. By practice, not much of anything."

"I regret having to ask you that, but I'm sure you understand. The film business being what it is, unfortunately . . ."

A knock at the door, a secretary entered and handed Guske a dossier. Casson could see his name, lettered across the top of the cardboard folder, and the official stamp of the Paris Préfecture de Police. Guske opened it on his desk and started reading, idly turning pages, at one point going back in the record and searching for something, running an index finger up and down the margin. Ah yes, there it was.

He moved forward again, making the sort of small gestures—rhythmic bobbing of the head, pursing of the lips—that indicated irritation with petty minds that noted too many details, an inner voice saying *yes, yes, then what, come on.*

At last he looked up and smiled pleasantly. "All in order." He squared the sheets of paper, closed the dossier, and tied it shut with its ribbon. Then he took Altmann's letter and read it over once more. "Will your assistant be coming to see us?" he asked.

"No. Change of plans," Casson said. "I'm going alone."

"Very well," Guske said. He drew a line through a sentence in Altmann's letter and initialed the margin, wrote a comment at the bottom and initialed that as well, then clipped the letter to the dossier and made a signal—Casson did not see how it was done—that brought the secretary back. When she left he said, "Come by tomorrow, after eleven. Your *Ausweis* will be waiting for you at the downstairs reception."

"Thank you," Casson said.

"You're welcome," Guske said. "By the way, what did you do during the May campaign? Were you recalled to military service?"

"No," Casson said. "I started out to go south, then I gave it up and stayed in Paris. The roads . . ."

"Yes. Too bad, really, this kind of thing has to happen. We're neighbors, after all, I'm sure we can do better than this." He stood, offered a hand, he had a warm, powerful grip. "Forgive me, Herr Casson, I must tell you—we do expect you to return, so, please, no *wanderlust*. Some people here are not so understanding as I am, and they'll haul you back by your ears."

He winked at Casson, gave him a reassuring pat on the shoulder as he ushered him out of the office.

Casson couldn't reach Citrine by telephone. A clerk answered at the hotel desk, told him that guests at that establishment did not receive phone calls—maybe he should try the Ritz, and banged the receiver down. So Casson took the Métro, out past the Père-Lachaise cemetery, walked for what seemed like miles through a neighborhood of deserted factories, finally found the place, then read a newspaper in the dark lobby until Citrine came sweeping through the door.

When he suggested they go to his apartment she gave him a look. "It's work," he said. "I'm going to Spain tomorrow, and you know what an office is like at night."

They took a bicycle taxi up to the Passy shopping district, by the La Muette Métro and the Ranelagh gardens. It was just getting dark. "We'll want something to eat, later on," he explained.

Her eyes opened wide with feigned innocence. "And look! A bottle of wine. Someone must have left it here."

"Work and supper, my love. Home before curfew."

Truce. She walked with him in the way he'd always liked, hand curled around his arm, pressed tight to his side, yet gliding along the street like a dancer. That was good, but not best. Best was how she used to slip her hand in his coat pocket as they walked together. That would make him so happy he would forget to talk, and she would say, innocent as dawn, "Yes? And?"

For a winter evening La Muette wasn't so bad. The little merry-go-round wouldn't be back until the spring, but there was an organ-grinder, a blind man who smiled up at the sky as he turned the handle. Casson gave him all his change. The snow drifted down, a flake at a time, through the blue lamplight.

He'd stored up a hoard of ration coupons, even buying some on the black-market bourse that now functioned at a local café. So, for a half-hour, he could once again be the provident man-about-town. "The smoked salmon looks good, doesn't it." They decided on a galantine of vegetables. "A little more, please," he said as the clerk rested her knife on the loaf and raised an eyebrow. For dessert, two beautiful oranges, chosen after long deliberation and a frank exchange between Citrine and the fruit man. Also, a very small, very expensive piece of chocolate.

There was a long line in front of the boulangerie. The smell of the fresh bread hung in the cold air, people stamped their feet to keep the circulation going. This line was always the slowest—portions had to be weighed, ration coupons cut out with a scissors—and sometimes a discussion started up. "Has anybody heard about North Africa?" Casson looked around to see who was speaking. A small, attractive woman wearing a coat with a Persian-lamb collar. "They say," she continued, "an important city has been captured by the English." She sounded hopeful—there'd been no good news for a long time. "Perhaps it's just a rumor."

It was not a rumor. Casson had heard the report on the French service of the BBC. The city was Tobruk, in Libya. Twenty-five thousand Italian troops taken prisoner, eighty-seven tanks captured by Australian and British soldiers. He started to answer, Citrine gave him a sharp tug on the arm and hissed in his ear, *"Tais-toi!"* Shut up.

Nobody on the line spoke, they waited, in their own worlds. On the way home to the rue Chardin, Citrine said, "You must be born yesterday. Don't you know there are informers on the food lines? They get money for each radio the Germans find, they have only to persuade some fool to say he heard the news on the BBC. Jean-Claude, please, come down from the clouds."

"I didn't realize," he said.

He had almost spoken, he had actually started to speak when Citrine stopped him. They would have searched the apartment. Looked in the closet.

"You must be careful," she said gently.

On the rue Chardin, a gleaming black Mercedes was idling at the curb. The radio! *No,* he told himself. Then the door opened and out came the baroness, smothered in furs, who lived in the apartment below him. "Oh, monsieur, good evening," she said, startled into courtesy.

The man who'd held the door for her, a German naval officer, stepped to her side and made a certain motion, a slight stiffening of the posture, a barely perceptible inclination of the head; a bow due the very tiniest of the petit bourgeois. He was pale and featureless, one of those aristocrats, Casson thought, so refined by ages of breeding they are invisible in front of a white wall. There was an awkward moment— introduction was both unavoidable and unthinkable. The baroness solved the problem with a small, meaningless sound, the officer with a second stiffening, then both rushed toward the Mercedes.

"What was that?" Citrine asked, once they were in the apartment.

"The baroness. She lives down below."

"Well, well. She's rather pretty. Do you—?"

"Are you crazy?"

They took off their coats. Citrine walked around the small living room, moved the drape aside and stared out over the rooftops. The Eiffel Tower was a dim shape in the darkness on the other side of the river. "It's all the same," she said. "Except for the lights."

"Oh look," he said. "A bottle of wine. Someone must have left it here."

For the occasion, a pack of Gauloises. They smoked, drank wine, played the radio at its lowest volume. Citrine paged through the script, following the trail of SYLVIE as it wound from scene to scene. Casson watched her face carefully—this was Fischfang's first real test. Altmann could be fooled, not Citrine. She scowled, sighed, flipped pages when she grew impatient. "How old is this Sylvie, do you think?"

"Young, but experienced. In the important moments, much older than her years. She wants very much to be frivolous—her life carried her past those times too quickly—but she can't forget what she's seen, and what she knows."

Citrine concentrated on a certain passage, then closed the script, keeping the place with her index finger. She met Casson's eyes, became another person. " 'My dreams? No, I don't remember them. Oh, some-times I'm running. But we all run away at night, don't we.' "

Casson opened his copy. "Where are you?"

"Page fifty-five, in the attic. With Paul, we're . . ." She hunted for a moment. "We're . . . we've opened a trunk full of old costumes."

"For the carnival, at Lent."

"Oh." She turned to the wall, crossed her arms. " 'My dreams.' "
She shook her head. " 'No. I don't remember them.' " *I don't want to
remember them*. And somehow she bent the word *dreams* back toward
its other meaning. She relaxed, dropped out of character. "Too much?"

"I wish Louis were here. He'd like it that way."

"You?"

"Maybe."

"You want to direct this, don't you."

"I always want to, Citrine. But I know not to."

8:30. A second bottle of wine. Scarlatti from the BBC. The room
smelled like smoke, wine, and perfume. "Did you know," she said, "I
made a movie in Finland?"

"In Finnish?"

"No. They dubbed it later. I just went ba-ba-ba with whatever feeling they told me to have and the other actors spoke Finnish."

"That doesn't work," Casson said. "We did a German version that
way, for *The Devil's Bridge*."

Citrine's eyes filled with soft passion, she leaned forward on the
couch, her voice a whisper. "Ba, ba-ba. Ba-ba-ba?"

Casson extended the wine bottle, holding it over Citrine's glass. "Ba
ba?"

"Don't," she said, laughing.

He smiled at her, poured the wine. Happiness rolled over him, he
felt suddenly warm. Perhaps, he thought, paradise goes by in an instant. When you're not looking.

"I'm almost asleep," she said.

Or was it? Warmth rolled over him, he felt suddenly happy. He went
to the radiator and put a hand on it. "A miracle," he said. The apartment hadn't been like this for months. From somewhere, coal, apparently abundant coal, had appeared, and Madame Fitou had decided,
against all precedent, to use a great deal of it. This was, he realized, a
rather complicated miracle.

"Suddenly," he said, "there's heat."

Citrine spread her hands, meaning obvious conclusion. "Don't you see?"

"No."

"A beautiful baroness, a dashing German officer, coal is delivered."

It felt good in the apartment, they were in no hurry to leave. The Occupation authority, grateful for a compliant population, had given Paris a Christmas present: extension of curfew to 3:00 A.M. Casson and Citrine talked—*Hotel Dorado,* life and times, the way of the world. They'd never disagreed about big things, it had gone wrong between them somewhere else. They liked eccentricity, they liked kindness, coincidence, people who lost themselves in the study of planets or bugs. They liked people with big hearts. They wanted to hear that in the end it all turned out for the best.

Just after midnight she wandered into the kitchen, dabbed her finger in some galantine gelatin left on a plate and licked it off. A moment later Casson came in to see what she was doing, found her standing by the pipe that ran, mysteriously, through the corners of all the kitchens in the building. She was listening to something, hand pressed over her mouth, like a schoolgirl, to keep from giggling.

"What—?" he said.

She touched a finger to her lips, then pointed to the pipe. He listened, heard faint sounds from below. It made no sense at first.

"Your baroness?" she whispered.

"Yes?"

"Is getting a red bottom."

Sharp reports—slow and deliberate, demure little cries. There was only one thing in the world that sounded like that.

"*Tiens,*" Casson said, amazed. "And in the kitchen."

Citrine listened for a time. "Well," she said, "I predict you'll have a warm winter."

Later he walked her to the Métro—she wouldn't let him take her back to the hotel. "Good night," he said.

She kissed him on the lips, very quickly and lightly, it was over be-fore he realized it was happening. "Jean-Claude," she said. "I had a good time tonight. Thank you."

"I'll call you," he said.

She nodded, waved at him, turned and went down the stairs of the Métro. *She's gone,* he thought.

A CITIZEN
OF THE
EVENING

Night train to Madrid.

The air was ice, the heavens swept with winter stars, white and still in a black sky. Jean Casson had done what he'd done, there was no going back. The train pulled slowly from the Gare de Lyon, clattered through the railyards south of the city, then out into the night.

A first-class compartment; burgundy velveteen drapes, gleaming brass doorknobs. Casson pressed his forehead against the cold window and stared out into the dark countryside. Looking out train windows was good for lovers. *Citrine, Citrine.* They'd made love in a train once; lying on their sides in a narrow berth, looking out at the backyards of some town, sheets hanging on wash lines, cats on windowsills, smoke from chimneys on tile roofs. It was a long autumn that year and nobody thought about war.

Staring out train windows good for lovers, not so bad for secret agents. *We are all adrift in the world, we do what we have to do.* Casson turned out the lamps so he could see better. Outside, the Beauce.

Old, deep France—*France profonde,* it was said. A flat plain where they grew wheat and barley, sometimes a forest where long ago they'd hunted bear with Beauceron dogs. A knock at the door, his heart hammered. "Monsieur?" Only a steward in a white jacket, peering at a list.

"Monsieur Dubreuil?"

"No, Casson."

"Monsieur Casson, yes. Would you wish the first or second seating?"

"Second."

"Very good, sir."

He closed the door, the rattle of the train subsided. A man with eyes shadowed by the brim of a fedora came down the corridor, glanced into Casson's compartment. *Calm down,* Casson told himself. But he couldn't. The tanned, smiling Colonel Guske kept forcing himself to the front of Casson's attention. He wasn't a smart lawyer—Simic had been right there, Casson thought—but he was the sort of man who got things done. Worked hard, full of vigor and stupefying optimism about life. *Must get that spinnaker rigged! Must keep the racquet straight on my backhand! Must get to the bottom of that Casson business!*

He closed his eyes for a moment, took a deep breath. Forced himself to take comfort from the dark countryside beyond the window. The French had fought and marched across these plains for centuries. They'd fought the Moslems in the south, the Germans in the east, the British in the west. The Dutch in the north? He didn't know. But they must have, some time or other. The War of the Spanish Succession? The Thirty Years' War? Napoleon?

Calm down. Or they'd find him dead of fear, staring wide-eyed at the scenery. Then it would be their turn to worry about the three hundred thousand pesetas. Of course, he thought, they wouldn't worry very long. Or, perhaps, it would just stay where it was—God only knew what would be lost forever in this war. The train slowed, and stopped. Outside, nothing special, a frozen field.

Compartment doors opening and closing, the sound of a slow train rumbling past. Something to do, anyhow. He got up and joined the other passengers, standing at the windows in the corridor. A freight train, flat cars loaded with tanks and artillery pieces under canvas tarpaulins, gun barrels pointing at the sky. He counted thirty, forty, fifty, then stopped, the train seemed to go on forever. His heart fell—what could he, what could any of them do against these people? Lately it was fashionable in Paris to avert one's eyes when seated across from Germans in the Métro. Yes, he thought, that would do it—the French won't look at us, we're going home.

His fellow passengers felt it too. Not the German aviators at the end of the car, probably not their French girlfriends, drunk and giggling. But the man who looked like a butcher in a Sunday suit, and Madame Butcher, they had the same expression on their faces as he did: faintly introspective, not very interested, vague. Strange, he thought, how people choose the same mask. Tall man, head of an ostrich, spectacles. A professor of Greek? A young man and his older friend—theatre people, Casson would have bet on it. The woman who stood next to him was an aristocrat of some sort. Late forties, red-and-brown tweed suit for traveling, cost a fortune years ago, maintained by maids ever since.

She felt his eyes, turned to look at him. Dry, weatherbeaten face, pale hair cut short and plain, eight strokes of a brush would put it in place. Skin never touched by makeup. Faded green eyes with laugh wrinkles at the corners her only feature. But more than sufficient. She met his glance; gave a single shake of the head, mouth tight for an instant. *How sad this is,* she meant. And I don't know that we can ever do anything about it.

He acknowledged the look, then by mutual agreement they turned back toward the windows. Tanks on flat cars crept past, canvas stiffened by white frost, at that speed the rhythm of the wheels on the rails a measured drumbeat. Then it was over, a single red lantern on the last car fading away into the distance. Casson and his neighbor exchanged a second look—*life goes on*—and returned to their compartments.

The train got under way slowly, dark hills on the horizon just visible by starlight. The woman reminded him of someone, after a moment he remembered. A brief fling, years ago, one of his wife's equestrienne pals—whipcord breeches and riding crops. A long time since he'd thought of her. Bold and funny, full of prerogatives, afraid of neither man nor beast, rich as Croesus, cold as ice, victor in a thousand love affairs. She had a white body shaped by twenty years of bobbing up and down in a saddle, hard and angular, and in bed she was all business, no sentimental nonsense allowed. She did, on the other hand, have delicious, fruit-flavored breath, particularly noticeable when she had him make love to her in the missionary position.

He'd wondered about her—connections with diplomats, months spent abroad, nights in exotic clubs one heard about from friends—wondered if she wasn't, perhaps, involved with the secret services. Just as he'd wondered what sort of hobbies she pursued with the riding crop. But he never asked, and she never offered. Her life belonged only to her; no matter if she spied, whipped, made millions, she didn't talk about it.

Now, stupidly, he felt better—*just being near a woman*. But it was true. He dozed, woke up at Auxerre station. The blackout made the station ghostly, the waiting passengers shapes in the darkness. The doors opened, just enough time for people to get on the train, then closed. The locomotive vented white steam that hung still in the freezing air. He waited for the coach to jerk forward as the engine got under way.

Instead: the door at the end of the corridor was thrown open and a voice called out *"Kontrol."* Casson sat up so suddenly it hurt his back. In the corridor, German voices, shouting instructions. What? This couldn't happen. *Once the train leaves Paris, nobody bothers you, the Germans can't be everywhere.* In panic, he twisted to look out on the platform: pacing shadows, silhouettes of slung rifles just visible in the darkness. *The darkness.* He tested the window, no give. Of course, windows in a railway coach, you had to be strong. *Strong enough.* A door slammed in the passageway, another opened. *Jump out the window, crawl under the train.* Across the track. Running full speed. Out into the street. Auxerre. Who did he know? Where did they live? Someone, there was always someone, someone would always help you. The door to his compartment opened. *"Kontrol."*

He stood up.

Something in German, a wave of the hand. *Sit down.* He sat. There were two of them, SS officers, leather coats open to black uniforms with lightning insignia, steel-handled Lugers in high-riding leather holsters. They hadn't been in the train very long—he could feel the cold air on them.

"Papieren."

A gloved hand extended. Casson fumbled for his identification in the inside pocket of his jacket. His fingers had gone numb. The passport, the *Ausweis,* the envelope. He took them out. *No, not the envelope.* Clumsy, maladroit. His arm had no feeling in it, the hand thick and

slow. *Take back the envelope.* He swallowed, there was something
caught in the center of his chest.

"*Was ist los?*"

No, not this, this doesn't concern you. He placed passport and travel
permit on the glove, started to put the envelope back in his pocket. His
hand wouldn't work at all. He folded the envelope in half and stuffed
it in, spreading his lips in what he hoped looked like a smile. Sorry to
be so stupid, sorry to be trouble, sorry sir, regret, excuse.

Didn't work.

Something interesting here. The officer now looked closely at him
for the first time. Not very old, Casson thought, in his thirties, perhaps. A fleshy face—fat later on—small eyes, cunning. This job was
the most important thing that had ever happened to him. *Not* in a shop.
Not in a garage. Casson looked down. The man hooked a gloved
index finger under his chin and raised his head to where he could see
Casson's eyes. What are you? What are you to *me*? Just one more pale
Frenchman? Or a fatal error?

Lazily, the German inclined his head toward the luggage rack.
"*Valise,*" he said softly.

Casson's hands were shaking so badly he had a hard time getting his
suitcase down from the luggage rack. The Germans waited, the heavy-
faced one taking a second look at his papers and making a casual re-
mark to his colleague. Casson recognized only one word—*Guske.* As
in, *It's Guske who signed the travel permit, the dossier must be han-
dled in his office.* The response was brief, neutral—and something
more. Respectful? As in, *Well, sometimes you come across these things.*

The officer turned on the lamps in the compartment. Whatever was
caught in Casson's chest now swelled, and made it hard to breathe.
He fumbled with the lock, finally laying the suitcase open on the seat.
It looked harmless enough; two shirts, side by side, one of them fresh
from the *blanchisserie,* the other worn, then folded for packing. There
was a nice leather case that held razor and shaving soap. Socks, shorts.
The copy of *Bel Ami* that he'd meant to read on the train.

The heavy-faced officer picked up the book. Held it by the spine and
shook it, a slip of paper used as a bookmark fell out and drifted to the
floor. Next he felt the front and back covers, riffled the pages, worked

a finger down between the spine and the binding and ripped it off, holding it up to the light, checking one side, then the other, then tossing it and the book onto the seat. He reached over, lifted one corner of a shirt, saw nothing very interesting beneath it—a newspaper, perhaps—and dropped it back into place.

They handed Casson back his identity papers and left. He heard them—opening the next door in the passageway, shouting orders—as though they were men in a dream. Very slowly, he slid the papers back into the inside pocket of his jacket. Next to the envelope. His fingers rested on the envelope for a moment. *What they would have done to me.*

In the dining car, the second seating, 10:30. The only light, flickering candles on the white tablecloths. The woman in the tweed suit was shown to his table. "Monsieur, I hope you don't mind." No, not at all, he was glad for the company. The waiter brought a bottle of wine, cold vegetable salad with an oily mayonnaise, nameless fish in railroad sauce—to Casson it barely mattered.

"I am called Marie-Noëlle," she said. "Meeting on a train, you see, we don't have to wait ten years for first names."

He smiled, introduced himself. He would be happy to call her Marie-Noëlle, but he did wonder what the rest might be.

She sighed—it always came to this. There was, she confessed, "a thoroughly disreputable person sometimes addressed as Lady Marensohn," but it wasn't really her. The title was by marriage—a husband who had died long ago, something in the small nobility of Sweden, a diplomat of minor status. "Terribly concerned with jute," she said grimly. "Morning and night." She herself had been born into a family called de Vlaq, from the Dutch–Belgian border, "even smaller nobility, if that's possible," and grown up on family estates in Luxembourg—"they called it wine, but, you know, really . . ."

She smoked passionately—Gitane followed Gitane, lit with strong fingers stained yellow by nicotine—and laughed constantly, a laugh that usually ended in a cough. "To hell with everything," she said, "that's what it says on my family crest. Citizen of the evening, resident of Paris since time began, and the only nobility I acknowledge is in good works for friends."

A German officer covered with medals moved down the aisle between tables, his girlfriend followed along behind, vividly rouged and lipsticked, wearing a tight cap of glossy black feathers. When they'd gone by, Marie-Noëlle made a face.

"Don't care for them?" Casson said.

"Not much."

"But you can leave, can't you?"

She shrugged. "Yes. Maybe I will, but, where to go?"

"Sweden?"

"Brr."

"Switzerland, then."

"Switzerland, Switzerland. Yes, there's always that. Geneva, gray but possible. On the other hand, the visa. I mean, you have to know . . . God. *Well.* Not just to nod to. Last September, a friend of mine went through it. She tried the embassies, the Americans, the Portuguese, and the Swiss. Spent hours on the lines but in the end all she could get was a Venezuelan resident card, which cost her a fortune, and, worse yet, the only place she could go with it was Venezuela."

She stubbed out a Gitane, lit another. "Well, she tries. She does try. She's positive, she's cheerful. She's all the things you're supposed to be. 'So different,' she writes. 'The Latin culture—sunny one minute, stormy the next. And Caracas—intrigue!' Of course it's ghastly, and she's miserable. It isn't Paris, it's a kind of horrid not-Paris. She sees the other émigrés, most of them grateful to be alive, but all they can talk about is when will it end, when can we go back, when can life be what it always was."

The train slowed, they peered out the window, trying to see past the reflection of the candle flame in the black glass. They were at the edge of a small city, passing the cottages that lined the track. Then came the dark cathedral with tall spires, winding streets, the railway station brasserie, and finally the platform. BOURGES, the sign said. Now a port of entry for the unoccupied part of France governed by Vichy.

The French border police were waiting on the platform, holding their capes tight around them and stomping their feet to keep warm. "More police," Marie-Noëlle said acidly.

"French, this time."

"Yes, there's that to be said for it." She exhaled smoke through her nose and mouth when she talked. "Tell me," she said, leaning over the table, her voice lowered, "they didn't give you too bad of a time, did they? The SS? I was listening, next door, but I couldn't hear much."

"Not too bad," he said.

The train jerked to a stop with a hiss of steam. The gendarmes came down the aisle, asking politely for papers. They knew they were in the first-class dining car, rolled the *Madames* and *Monsieurs* off their tongues, had a desultory glance at each passport, then left with a two-fingered salute to the visor of the cap. *Only a formality, of course you understand.*

"Remarkable," Marie-Noëlle said, when the police had gone to the next table. "You are perhaps the only person I know who's ever had a decent photograph in a passport."

Casson held it up and said "What, this? I wouldn't let him in my country."

"Yes, but look here—is this not the aunt kept locked up in the attic?"

He smiled, it was even worse than that.

"Now, monsieur," she said, a mock-serious note in her voice, "how am I going to persuade you to allow me to buy us a brandy?"

He would not allow it. He insisted on paying for the brandies, and for those that followed. Meanwhile they smoked and talked and made the dinner last as long as they could. Very late at night, after the stop at Lyons, the train started the long run down the Rhône valley, the sky cleared and the moon ran beside them, a yellow disc on the still river.

She grew tired, and reflective, not so sure about the world. "What do you think," she asked, "in your heart. Must I leave this country?"

"Perhaps," he said. *Peut-être*, could be. In diplomacy it meant yes— yes with regret. "Of course," he went on, "it's not something I can do, so maybe I shouldn't be giving advice."

"Not something you can do?"

"No."

"What stops you?"

He looked puzzled.

"In a few hours," she said, "you'll be in Spain. Sunny Spain, *neutral* Spain. From there, ships leave daily, to every port in the world. But why wait for a booking on a ship? There is a ferry, in Algeciras, it goes across to Ceuta. One simply pays and walks on. Then, it takes less than an hour, you are in Spanish Morocco. Once there, well . . ."

It was true. Why hadn't it occurred to him? He had three hundred thousand pesetas in a suitcase, a travel permit for Spain. A thousand stories began this way—an opportunity, a sudden decision, then freedom, a new life. It took courage, that was all. He saw himself doing it: walking off the ferry with raincoat tossed over one shoulder, hat brim turned down, valise in hand, turning to look back one last time at the dark mass of Europe. Why not? What would he be giving up— a movie that would never be made? A woman who was never going to love him again? A city that would never be the same?

But then, from somewhere deep inside, the sigh of common sense. The man with the raincoat and the hat brim turned down wasn't him. "Perhaps," he said, "you will join me for a drink, Madame Marie-Noëlle. At Fouquet's, one of the tables on the boulevard."

A corner of her mouth turned up in a grin, she flirted with him a little. "Chilly for the outdoor tables, monsieur. No?"

"I meant, in the spring."

"Ah." She considered it. "Probably, I will meet you there," she said, then shook her head slowly, in gentle despair for both of them. "Charming. The last romantic."

He sat back in the chair; it was very late at night. "It is the only trick I know," he said. Then, after a moment, "You're one too."

"No, no," she said. "I'm something else."

Port Bou, the Spanish frontier, 4:40 P.M.

Here the passengers had to leave the train and wait on lines; customs, border formalities. Casson had been through it before, years earlier, and when he'd thought about the crossing it had seemed to him the second most likely place he might be arrested. The passengers stood quietly, nobody made jokes. Cold, thin air in the Pyrenees, jagged ridges, white mist, snowfields fading in the last light. The *Guardia* sentries pacing up and down the lines were like ghosts from Napoleon's wars; leather tricorn hats, greatcoats, long, thin rifles that looked like muskets. He searched everywhere for Marie-Noëlle, but she had disappeared. Left the train, apparently. Where—Narbonne? Perpignan? Would she have said? No, probably not. But it was a loss. He'd planned on going through the frontier with her, somebody to talk to, easier to pretend that you weren't scared.

The line marked *Entrada*. Two uniformed officers and a civilian sat at a plank table in a shed heated by a smoky wood stove. The line of passengers was kept back twelve feet from the table—a distance where the tension of the examination could be felt but the questions, and the follow-ups, could not be heard. The final line, *Entrada*. From here the passengers drifted away, in twos and threes, to a coach on the south-bound local, idling at the far end of the station, that ran on the Spanish-gauge track. They walked briskly—really, how had they allowed themselves to worry like that—and made a point of not looking back. There was one couple, elderly, well-dressed, being returned to the French train, and a young woman, being led away by two men in overcoats, but that was all. The young woman looked at Casson, trying to tell him something with her eyes. The men at her side followed the glance—an accomplice, perhaps?—and Casson had to look away. He hoped she'd had time to see that he understood, that he would remember what had happened to her.

Casson got through. They studied his papers, running an index finger under the important phrases. The civilian wore a coat with a fur collar and a pince-nez. "The reason for your visit, señor?"

"For a film, to look at possible locations."

"What kind of film?"

"A romantic comedy."

The man passed his papers to one of the *Guardia*, who stamped *Entrada-27 Enero 1941* in his passport and initialed it.

The Spanish train was old and dirty, cold air flowed up through the floorboards. All the way to Barcelona he stared out the window, seeing nothing. His mouth was dry, he swallowed but it did not seem to help. The compartment was crowded; two Luftwaffe officers, two women who might have been sisters, a fat, unshaven man who slept for most of the journey. Casson told himself that nothing would happen. He simply had to believe in himself—the world would always respect a self-confident man, and nothing would happen. He was sweating, he could feel it under his arms, even in the chilly compartment, and he tried to be surreptitious about wiping it away from his hairline.

The outskirts of Barcelona. There had been fighting here in 1937. The track was elevated and he could see into apartments; rooms with black flash marks on the walls, charred beams, dressers with drawers pulled out, a bed standing on end. The passengers stared in silence as the train crawled past. Then the fat man woke up and abruptly pulled the curtains closed. Why did he do that? Casson wondered. Was he Spanish? French? Republican? Falangist? Casson swallowed. The man stared at him, daring him to say something. Casson looked at his feet, his fingers touched the envelope in his pocket.

Barcelona station, 8:10 P.M.

The train to the southern coast wasn't due to leave until 10:20. Casson went to the station buffet, took a dry bun with a crust of pink icing and a tiny cup of black coffee, and found a table by the back wall. Of course he was watched.

For their eyes, he played the traveler. Dug into his valise, retrieved his copy of *Le Matin* and spread it out on the table—JAPANESE FOREIGN MINISTER WARNS U.S.A. NOT TO INTERFERE IN ASIAN AFFAIRS. Took traveler's inventory, checking his railway ticket and passport, putting French francs in this pocket, pesetas in that pocket. In fact, he needed to change money, and reminded himself to keep the receipt from the *cambio*. The border police had recorded the amount of French francs he'd brought into the country and they'd want a piece of paper when he went back out.

And he was going back out.

He'd studied what he intended to do, walked through it in his mind, hour by hour, step by step. So that, if it suddenly felt wrong, he could walk away. A patriot, he reminded himself, not a fool. There would be hell to pay if he abandoned the money. But then, he was a film producer, there'd been hell to pay before in his life, and he'd paid it.

Better now, he calmed down. This was something he could do. *Go out the door, if you like,* he told himself. He liked hearing that, he could answer by saying *no, not yet, nothing's gone wrong.*

He refolded the newspaper and returned it to his valise, next to the torn copy of *Bel Ami.* Made sure, one last time, of passport, money, and all the rest of it, and, oh yes, a certain envelope in the inside pocket of his jacket. He tore it open, took out a receipt with *Thos. Cook Agency* printed across the top, and a first-class railway ticket, Paris/Barcelona.

The watchers were probably watching—after all, that's how they made their living—but there wasn't very much for them to watch at Casson's table. Just another traveler, nervous as the rest, fussing with his papers before resuming his journey. He stood, drained the last little sip of coffee, and picked up his valise. On the way out of the buffet he balled up the envelope and tossed it in the trash.

The baggage room was off by itself, at the end of a long corridor with burned-out lamps and NO PASARÁN daubed on the walls with red paint. Casson stood at the counter and waited for thirty seconds, then tapped the little bell. For a moment, nothing happened. Then he heard the deliberate, uneven rhythm of somebody walking with a pronounced limp. It went on for a long time, the office was at the other end of the room and the clerk walked slowly, with great difficulty. A short, dark man with a pencil-thin mustache, an angry face, and an eight-inch heel on a built-up shoe. On the breast pocket of his smock was a lapel pin, bright silver, a signal of membership in something, and Casson sensed that this job came from the same place the pin did, it was a reward, given in return for faith and service. To a political party, perhaps, or a government bureau.

Be normal. Casson handed over the receipt. "Baggage for Dubreuil."

The clerk peered at the number, then said it aloud, slowly. Standing on the other side of the counter, Casson could smell clothes worn for too many days. The clerk nodded to himself; yes, he knew this one, and limped off, disappearing among the rows of wooden shelves piled to the ceiling with trunks and suitcases. Casson could hear him as he searched, up one aisle, down the next, walking, then stopping, walking, then stopping. Somewhere in the back, a radio played faintly, an opera.

It was going to work. He could feel it, and permitted himself just a bare edge of relief. It was going to work because it wasn't complicated. He had simply gone to his customary travel agent at the Thomas Cook office on the rue de Bassano, told him an associate named Dubreuil was accompanying him to Spain, and purchased two first-class, round-trip tickets, checking Dubreuil's suitcase through to Barcelona. The standard procedure would have been for the agent at Cook's to demand Dubreuil's passport, but Casson had done a great deal of business there over seven or eight years and the travel agent wasn't going to get fussy over details with a valued customer.

Prevailing opinion in Paris had it that checked baggage, stacked high in icy freight cars, was not searched very seriously at the Spanish frontier. If the worst happened, however, and a Spanish customs guard discovered a suitcase full of pesetas and turned it in instead of stealing it, they could look for Dubreuil all they wanted; they'd never find him because he didn't exist. There was, for Casson, a brief moment of exposure, when he had to pretend to be Dubreuil in order to claim the suitcase, but that was going to be over in a few seconds and he would be on his way.

The clerk returned to the counter, his face bland and satisfied. He handed Casson a slip of paper, and said "Not here," in Spanish. Casson looked at his hand, he was holding the baggage receipt.

"Pardon?" He hadn't understood, he'd thought—

"Not here, señor."

Casson stared at him. "Where is it?"

A shrug. "Who can say?"

Casson heard train whistles in the distance, the clash of couplings, the opera on the clerk's radio. They would kill him for this.

"I don't understand," he said.

The clerk stepped back a pace. His next move, Casson realized, would be to roll down the metal shutter. The man's face was closed: a suitcase didn't matter, a passenger didn't matter, what mattered was the little silver pin on his blue smock. Against that magic, this insistent Señor Dubreuil was powerless.

"The train from Port Bou . . ." Casson said.

The hand started to reach for the shutter, then decided that the moment had not quite arrived and contented itself with sliding casually into a pocket. "Good evening, señor," the clerk said.

Casson turned away quickly. He didn't know where to go or what to do but he felt he had to put distance between himself and the baggage room. He trotted back up the corridor, the valise bouncing in his hand, footsteps echoing off the cement walls. Breathing hard, he made himself slow down, then walked through the station buffet and found the platform where the Port Bou train had come in. The track was empty.

"Missed your train?"

English. A huge man with a huge gray beard, sitting on a baggage cart surrounded by two battered wooden boxes, an old carpetbag, and a collapsed easel tied with a cord. "Have you missed your train, monsieur?" Phrasebook French this time, plodding but correct.

Casson shook his head. "Lost baggage." *Perdu*. Meant lost, all right, much more so, somehow, than in any other language. That which was *perdu* joined lost time, lost love, lost opportunity and lost souls in a faraway land where nothing was ever seen again.

"Damn the luck."

Casson nodded.

"Speak English?"

"Yes."

"Just come in from the border?"

"Yes."

"Hm." The man looked at his watch. "Only left thirty seconds ago. Did you leave it on the train?"

"No. It was checked baggage."

"Ah-hah! Then there's hope."

"There is?"

"Oh yes. Sometimes they don't take it off. They forget, or they just don't. They're Spanish, you see. Life's so bloody, *conditional*."

"It's true," Casson said gloomily.

"You might catch it, you know, if you don't dawdle. It stops at a village station just south of Barcelona, that train. The 408 local." The man glowered with conviction and took a much-thumbed little booklet from his coat. Among the English, Casson knew, were people who suffered from a madness of trains. Perhaps this was one of them.

"Yes," the man said. "I'm right. Here it is, Puydal. A Catalonian name. Arrival, 9:21." The man looked up. "Well," he said, "for God's sake hurry!"

Casson moved quickly. This didn't happen only in Spain. In France too, your baggage popped up here, disappeared there, sometimes reappeared, sometimes was never heard from again. At the corner of the station, a long line of taxis. He jumped in the first one and said "Puydal station. Please hurry."

The driver turned the key in the ignition. And again. Finally, the engine caught, he gave it a few seconds, then swung slowly out into the street, and accelerated cautiously. Casson glanced at his watch. 9:04. At this rate they would never get there in time.

"Please," Casson said. *Por favor.*

"Mmmm—" said the driver: yes, yes, a philosopher's sigh. Vast forces of destiny, stars and planets, the run of time itself. A candle flickered, the course of life drifted one point south. "—Puydal, Puydal." Clearly, this was not his first trip to Puydal railroad station.

In the event, the sigh was accurate.

Puydal was where you went when all was lost, Puydal was where fate got a chance to mend its ways and the stationmaster's spaniel bitch was sitting on the Dubreuil suitcase. Casson had gone to the Galéries Lafayette to buy one, then discovered an Arab in business on a side street selling the homely classic—pebbled tan surface with a dull green and red stripe that half the world seemed to own.

"Ah, so this is yours?" said the stationmaster. "May I just, Señor Dubreuil, have the briefest glance at your passport?"

They don't ask for the passport, they ask for the ticket.

Casson handed over his passport. "I am Señor Casson," he said. "The friend of Señor Dubreuil. He is sick, *enfermo,* I am to collect his baggage." He dug into his pocket, took out a handful of francs, pesetas, coins of many lands. "He told me, 'a gratuity,' in appreciation, he is sick, it's cold . . ."

The stationmaster nodded gravely and took the money, shooed his dog off and saluted. *"Mil gracias."* Casson grabbed the suitcase and trotted out the door to find the same taxi. "Barcelona station," he said to the driver, looking at his watch. The express to the southern coast was due to leave in seventeen minutes, they would never make it. "Please hurry," he said to the driver.

There were no other cars, the taxi bumped along the cracked surface of the old macadam road, one headlight aimed up in the pine trees, the other a faint glow in the darkness. The engine missed, the gears whined, the driver sang to himself under his breath. Casson hoisted the suitcase onto his lap and opened it a crack. Yes, still in there. Thank God. Folded up in threadbare shirts and pants he'd bought at a used-clothes cart out in Clignancourt. He leaned back, closed his eyes, felt clammy and uncomfortable as the sweat dried on his shirt in the cold night air. It was time to admit to himself he had no idea what he was doing—he'd read Eric Ambler, he had a general idea of how it was all supposed to work, but this wasn't it.

28 January, 1941. The Alhambra Hotel, Málaga.

A Spanish casino in winter. Cold gray sea, storms that blew rain against the window and sang in the stucco minarets. In the dining room, a string orchestra, a thé dansant, the songs Viennese, the violins flat. Still, the guests danced, staring into the private distance, the women wearing jewels and glass and Gypsy beads, the men in suits steamed over the green-stained bathtubs. Refugees, fugitives, émigrés, immigrants, stateless persons, wanted by this regime or that, rich or shrewd or lucky enough to get this far but no farther, washed up at the end of Europe, talking all night—in Bessarabian Yiddish or Alsatian French—stealing rolls from breakfast trays in the halls, trying to tip the barman with Bulgarian lev.

In the courtyard, a Moorish garden; rusty fountain, archway hung with dead ivy that rustled in the wind. Casson walked there, or by the thundering sea, ruining his shoes in the gray sand. But, anything not to be in the room. He'd placed an advertisement in *ABC*, the Monarchist daily, in the *Noticias* section. SWISS GENTLEMAN, COMMERCIAL TRAVELER, SEEKS ROOM IN PRIVATE HOME FOR MONTH OF FEBRUARY. Then, he waited. Three days, four days, a week. Nothing happened. Perhaps the operation had been canceled, and they'd just left him there. On his walks he composed long letters to Citrine, things he would never be able to write down—very beautiful things, he thought. In the casino he gambled listlessly, betting red and black at the roulette table, sticking at seventeen in blackjack, breaking even and walking away. A woman slipped a note in his pocket—*Would you like to visit to me? I am in the Room 34.* Maybe he would have liked to, but now he didn't know who anybody was or what they were after.

He was shaving when the telephone rang, two long notes. He ran into the bedroom. "Yes?"

"Are you the gentleman who advertised in the newspaper?"

The number given in the newspaper had not been for the Alhambra.

"Yes," he said.

"I wonder, perhaps we could meet."

French, spoken well by a Spaniard.

"All right."

"In an hour? Would that be convenient?"

"It would."

"The hotel has a bar . . ."

"Yes."

"It's three-twenty. Should we say, four-thirty?"

"Good."

"I'll see you then."

"Good-bye."

Casson took a table in the corner, ordered a dry sherry. Beyond the curtained window the rain drummed down. At the next table a couple in their thirties was having a conspirators' argument. *He* should make the approach, say *this*, and tomorrow evening was the very last moment they could wait to do it. She was afraid, there was only this one chance, what if they tried and failed. Maybe it would be better not to give themselves away, not just yet.

A bellhop in hotel uniform, silver tray with an envelope on it. "A message for you, sir."

Casson tipped him, opened the envelope. Expensive notepaper, elegant handwriting. "Please forgive the inconvenience, but the meeting has been moved. To the yacht *Estancia*, last slip, C dock, in the harbor. Looking forward to meeting you." Signed with initials.

"May I send a message back?" Casson asked the boy.

"The gentleman has left, sir."

So be it. They had looked him over in the bar, checked to see if he was alone, and now they were going to do business. He folded the note and put it in his pocket, paid for the sherry, and walked out the front door of the hotel. The rain was running brown in the cobbled street. Well, he'd get wet. No, that wouldn't work. He'd have to go back upstairs and get a raincoat.

He'd learned to be sensitive to sudden changes of direction—he'd come back to the room unexpectedly one night and heard, thought he heard, some commotion on the balcony just as he got the door unlocked and open. There was nothing to see, the balcony door was locked when he tried it. But somebody had been in the room, then left when they heard him at the door. How did he know? He didn't know how, he just did. And, more, it was somebody he didn't want to catch, because he wasn't exactly sure where that might lead.

He got off the elevator, then paused at the door. Put the key in, turned it, entered. Silent. The damp, still air undisturbed.

Outside it was dusk, low clouds scudding east, patches of yellow sky over the water out toward the African coast. The palm trees lining the *Paseo* were whipping in the gale, loose fronds blown up against the seawall. Casson put his head down, held on to his hat, and hurried toward the harbor. Two women in black shawls ran past, laughing, and a man in a cloth cap rode by on a bicycle, a straw basket hung on one arm.

The harbor, C dock; in the last slip, the *Estancia*. A small, compact motor yacht, elegant in the 1920s, then used hard over the years and now beginning to age—varnish worn off the teak in places, brasswork showing the first bloom of verdigris. The portholes were shuttered, the boat seemed deserted, bobbing up and down on the harbor swell amid the orange peels and tarred wood. Casson stood for a moment, rain dripping off the brim of his hat. Somewhere in his heart he turned and went back to Paris, a man who'd lived, for a moment, the wrong life. A wave broke over the end of the dock, white spray blown sideways by the wind. He took a deep breath, crossed the gangplank, rapped sharply on the door to the stateroom.

The door swung open immediately, he stepped inside and it closed behind him. The room was dark, and silent, except for creaking planks as the *Estancia* strained against its moorage. The man who had opened the door watched him carefully, his fingers resting on a table by a large revolver. Apparently this was Carabal—described to Casson as a Spanish army officer, a colonel. But no braid or epaulets. Pale gray suit and spectacles; sparse, carefully combed hair, and the bland face of a diplomat, reddened by excitement and winter weather. In his forties, Casson thought.

"I'm to say to you that we met, at the Prado, last April," Casson said.

Carabal nodded, acknowledging the password. "It was July"—countersign—"in Lisbon."

There was someone else on the boat—he changed position, and Casson could feel the shift of weight in the floorboards. Casson reached into the pocket of his raincoat, took out a key, handed it to Carabal. "It's on the sixth floor," he said. "Room forty-two. The suitcase is in the closet."

Carabal took the key. "Three hundred thousand?"

"Yes."

"Good. General Arado will contact your principals."

"How will that happen?"

"By letter. Hand-delivered in Paris on the fifteenth of February."

"All right."

"We will go forward."

"Yes."

"Good luck to all of us," Carabal said, opening the door.

Casson turned and left. On the dock, he raised his face to the wind-blown rain. *Thank God that's over.*

The walk back along the *Paseo* was glorious. Shattered cloud over the sea, puddles like miniature lakes—surface water ruffled by the gusting wind, a priest on a mule, the street lamps coming on in first darkness. Golden light, fluttering palm trees. *"Buenas noches,"* said the priest.

Back in the Alhambra, he felt the weight lift. Thank God it was over, now he could go back to his own life. After the war, a good story. *A revolver!* He took his wet shoes off, jacket and pants and shirt and socks, crawled into bed in his underwear. The pillow felt cool and smooth against the skin of his face. What was it, seven in the evening? So what. He didn't care. He would order from room service if he felt like eating.

An omelet. They could manage that. He had captured, by means of lavish tips, the allegiance of the room-service waiter, a man not without influence in the kitchen. That meant the omelet did not have to swim in oil and garlic and tomato sauce, it could be dry, with salt and parsley. He needed something like that now.

Oatmeal! He'd discovered it during a trip to Scotland. Steel-cut, they'd say, meaning the best, with yellow cream from an earthenware pitcher. He'd ordered it every morning; dense, gooey stuff—delicious, soothing. Of course down here they would never have such a thing.

Who had put the little slip of paper in his pocket? The redhead, he was almost sure of it. Pearl earrings, dancer's legs. Haughty, the chin tilted up toward heaven. Passionate, he thought, that kind of a sneer could turn into a very different expression, an O—surprised by pleasure. Or playful indignation. How dare you. He liked that, an excellent trick. Jesus, women. They thought up all these things, a man had no chance at all. And then, like Citrine, they turned away from you. How long could he mourn? It wasn't good not to make love. Unhealthy, there were all sorts of theories.

Tired. It scared him, what this little enterprise had taken from him in strength and spirit. Oh Lord, he was so tired. No redhead for him, not tonight. She wouldn't do it anyhow, not now, not after he'd ignored the note. *What? Monsieur! How dare you presume.* Ah, but, even better, the redhead says yes, they go to his room. She likes to kiss, that hard mouth softens against his. White skin, blue veins, taut nipples. Then later he admits the note excited him. "Note?" she says.

For a moment he was gone, then he came back. A strange little dream—a hallway in a house. Somebody he'd known, something had happened. It meant nothing, and he could not stay awake any longer. He took a deep breath and let it out very slowly to tell himself that the world was slipping back into place.

Oatmeal.

The phone. Those two sustained notes, again and again. He clawed at it, knocked the receiver off the cradle, groped around the night table until he found it, finally mumbled "What? Hello?"

"Jean-Claude! Hey it's me. I'm here. I owe you a drink, right? So now I got to pay up. Hello?"

Simic.

"Jean-Claude? What goes on there? Not *asleep*. Hey, shit, it's nine-thirty. Wait a minute, now I see, you're getting a little, right?"

"No, I'm alone."

"Oh. So, well, then, we'll have a drink. Say, in twenty minutes."

Casson's mind wasn't working at all. All he could say was yes.

"In the bar downstairs. Champagne cocktail—what about it?"

"All right."

"*A bientôt!*" Triumphant, Simic very nearly sang the words.

Don't be a rat, Casson told himself. He's happy, you be happy too. Not everything needs to fit in with your mood about it.

He staggered into the bathroom. What was Simic doing in Málaga? If he'd been intending to come, why hadn't he brought the money himself? Well, there was, no doubt, a reason, he would know it soon enough. He stood in the tub, pulled the linen curtain closed, inhaled the damp-drain odor of Spanish beach hotels. Five showerheads poked from the green tile—maybe in summer you'd be splendidly doused from every side. Not now. Five tepid drizzles and the smell of sulphur. *Putain de merde*. He threw handfuls of water on himself, then rubbed his face with a towel.

He got dressed, tied his tie, brushed his hair. Simic wasn't going to make a night of it, please God. Whorehouses and champagne and somebody with a bloody nose bribing a cop at dawn.

Down the hall, checked his watch, he was right on time. Pressed the bell for the elevator. It started up, humming and grinding, then stopped with a squeak. *Maybe if they left some oil out of the food and put it on the elevator*. All right, victory for the Alhambra, he would walk downstairs. No, here it came, slow and noisy. The door slid open, the elevator boy, about fifteen, in hotel uniform, mumbled good evening. Strange, he was pale, absolutely white. He slid the door closed. Everything smelled in this hotel, that included the elevator. Stopped on three. Bulky man in a tuxedo, who stood back against the wall and cleared his throat. Finally, the lobby.

The bar dark and very active, Spaniards having a drink before their eleven o'clock dinner hour. Fifteen minutes, then a table came open, next to a rubber plant. Casson tipped the waiter, sat down. Now, what could he order that would not do battle with the gruesome champagne cocktail he was going to be forced to drink? A dry sherry, and a coffee. A dish of salted almonds arrived as well. There was a string trio in the lobby, three elderly Hungarians who played their version of Spanish music. 10:10. Simic, where are you?

He sent the waiter to the bar for cigarettes. A brand called Estrella. Very good, he thought. Strong, but not too dry. He smoked, drank some sherry, ate an almond, took a sip of coffee. Why, he wondered, did he have to be the one to fight Hitler? Langlade was making lightbulbs, Bruno was selling cars. He ran down a list of friends and acquaintances, most of them, as far as he knew, were doing what they'd always done. Certainly it was harder now, and the money wasn't so good, and you had to go to the *petits fonctionnaires* all the time for this permission and that paper, but life went on. His father used to say to him—Jean-Claude, why do you have to be the one? 10:20.

Simic hadn't meant tomorrow night, had he? Was he in the hotel when he called? It had sounded that way, but as long as the call was local you couldn't really tell. By now, Casson had decided that maybe a celebration was a good idea. After all, they'd done it, hadn't they. Run money over the border, bribed a Spanish general. Despite the Gestapo and the vagaries of Spanish railroads. Strange—what was an English artist doing at Barcelona station?

10:22. Casson stood up, peered around at the other tables. That had happened to him once at Fouquet—his lunch appointment waiting at one table, he at another, both of them very irritated by the time they'd discovered what they'd done.

Well then, all right. A few minutes more and he was going back upstairs. The war was over for the night. Let the Germans rule the French for a thousand years, if they could stand it that long, he was going back to the room. Now, of course, he was hungry, but he wasn't going to sit alone in the dining room. He ate another almond. 10:28. He watched the second hand crawl around the face of his watch, then he stood up. Just as somebody was coming toward him, weaving among the tables. Well, finally. But, not Simic. Marie-Noëlle—of all people.

What a coincidence.

She sat across from him, ordered a double brandy with soda, got a Gitane going.

"I do have somebody joining me," he said apologetically. "A man I know from Paris."

"No," she said, "he isn't coming."

"Who isn't?"

"Your friend. Simic." She wasn't joking. He tried to make sense of that but couldn't.

She stared at him; worried, angry, tapped her index finger against the table, looked at her watch. "I'm leaving tonight," she said. "But, before I go, it's my job to decide about you, monsieur. As to whether you are a knave, or just a fool."

He stared at her.

"So," she said.

He didn't know what to say. His first instinct was to defend himself, to say something reasonably witty and fairly sharp. But he didn't. She wasn't joking, to her the choice was precisely described, insulting, but not meant as an insult. And, he somehow knew, it mattered. At last he said quietly, "I am not a knave, Marie-Noëlle."

"A fool, then."

He shrugged. Who in this life hasn't been a fool?

She canted her head to one side. Was this something she could believe? She searched his face. "Used?" she said. "Could be."

"Used?"

"By Simic."

"How?"

"To steal from us."

"Who is 'us'?"

"My employers. The British Secret Intelligence Service. In London."

This was a lot to take in but, somehow, not completely a shock. At some level he had understood that she wasn't just somebody met on a train. "Well," he said. "You mean, the people in the business of bribing Spanish generals."

"They thought they were, but it was a fraud. A confidence scheme—seven hundred thousand pesetas before your delivery, another million to come after that."

Casson lit a cigarette, shook his head as if to clear it.

"Simic was an opportunist," Marie-Noëlle said. "Apparently he'd dabbled with intelligence services before. In Hungary? Romania? France, perhaps. Who knows. He had a good, instinctive sense of how the game is played, of how money changes hands, of what kinds of things people like to hear. When the Germans took over he saw his chance—he could get rich if he came up with an operation that felt really authentic."

"And Carabal? Is he a colonel in the Spanish army?"

"Yes. Also a thief, one of Simic's partners."

"General Arado?"

"A monster, but not a traitor. Credible—for Simic's purpose. A history of support for the Bourbon monarchy. But, no inclination to overthrow the Falange. No inclination for politics at all."

Casson scowled, stared down at the table. He had assumed he was smarter than Simic, but maybe it was simply that he was above him, socially, professionally. He'd been worse than a fool, he realized. "And me?" he said.

"You. We are treating that as an open question. You'd been mentioned by a former business associate, and when Simic asked for a name we gave him yours. But then, after that, who knows. Under occupation, people do what they feel they have to do."

"You think I took your money."

"Did you take it?"

"No."

"Somebody did. Not what you brought down, we have that back, but there was an earlier payment, and some of that is missing."

"What happens to Carabal?"

"Can't touch him. There's an office theory that General Arado found the whole business amusing, and that Carabal's career will not suffer at all."

"And Simic?"

She spread her hands, palms up. *What do you think?*

"We went and had a drink," Casson said. "He explained to me the importance of Gibraltar, it was very persuasive."

"It is important."

"But they won't attack it."

"No," she said. "Because of the wind."

Casson didn't understand.

"It blows hard there, changes direction—it's tricky. You've seen those Greek amphoras in hotel lobbies, they plant geraniums in them.

Sometimes they wash up on the beach, from the ocean floor. Well, think how they happened to be down there in the first place—obviously somebody got it wrong. A wind like that, the Germans can't do what they did with the Belgian forts, they can't use paratroops, or gliders. As for an attack over land, the peninsula is narrow, and heavily mined from one side to the other. The roads are terrible, and the Spanish-gauge railroad track is different, which means the Wehrmacht can't run trains through France—they'd have to change over, and we'd know about it right away. That leaves an attack from the sea, which would have to be staged from Spanish Morocco, and the cranes at the port of Ceuta aren't big enough to lift heavy tanks and artillery onto ships."

"So then, why pay Spanish generals to overthrow Franco?"

"You have to understand the nature of the business. It has, like everything else, fashion, what the hemline is to the prêt-à-porter. So once an idea is, ah, born—memos written, meetings held—it takes on a life of its own. For a time, it's the local religion, and nobody wants to be the local atheist. Erno Simic understood that, understood how vulnerable we were to big, nasty schemes, and he decided to make his fortune. He would have played us along; the general is thinking, the general is nervous, the general has decided to go ahead, send a sniper rifle and a box of exploding candy. And on, and on. But, you know, somebody found a way to see if General Arado was actually in on it, and he wasn't."

"So everything I did . . ."

"Meant nothing. Yes, that's right. On the other hand, if the Seguridad or the Gestapo had caught you with the money . . ."

Casson sat back in the chair, the life in the bar was growing brighter and louder. The Spanish brandy wasn't very expensive, after a while it inspired a certain optimism. "Tell me something," he said. "Are you really Lady Marensohn?"

"Yes. I am pretty much who I said I was. There's just this one little extra dimension. Of course, I'd *prefer* you not to talk about it. As in, not ever."

"No, I won't." He thought a moment. "I hope you understand—Simic was what he was, but I believed in the scheme, I really thought it would damage Germany."

Marie-Noëlle nodded. "Yes, probably you did. It was my job, on the train, to find out who you were. As far as I can tell, you were drawn in, used. The people I work for, on the other hand . . ."

She paused a moment, she wanted to be accurate. "The people I work for," she said. "You have to understand, Britain is living on the edge of a cliff—and these people were never very nice people in the first place. Now the issue is survival, national survival. So they are, even more—difficult. Cold. Not interested in motive—words don't matter, what matters is what's done. So, perhaps, they feel it isn't over between you and them. Because if you sat down and joined, knowingly, with Simic, what, frankly would be different in your explanation? You'd say exactly what you've said."

Casson thought about it for a time, to see how that wasn't actually the case, but it was. "What can I do?" he said.

"Go back home, Monsieur Casson. Live your life. Hope for British success in 1941, and German failure. If that happens, there is every possibility that, for you, life will simply go back to being what it always was."

NEW
FRIENDS

Casson stood in Marie-Claire's living room, talking to Charles Arnaud, the lawyer. Everyone in the room was standing—one didn't sit down at a *cocktail Américain.* Casson sipped at his drink. "A cuba libre, they called it. It has rum in it."

Arnaud rapped a knuckle twice against his temple and made a knocking noise with his tongue. It meant strong drink, and a headache in the morning. Casson offered a sour smile in agreement. "Always the latest thing, with Bruno," he said.

"Have I seen you since I came back from Belgrade?" Arnaud said.

"No. How was it?"

Arnaud grinned. He had the face, and the white teeth, of a matinee idol, and when he smiled he looked like a crocodile in a cartoon.

"Bizarre," he said. "A visit for a week, a month of stories. At least. I went down there for a client, to buy a boatload of sponges, impounded in Dubrovnik harbor under a Yugoslav tax lien. Actually, at that point, I'd become a part owner." Arnaud was even less a conventional lawyer than Langlade—had for years been retained by shipping companies, but had a knack for becoming a principal, briefly, in crisis situations where a lot of money moved very quickly.

"I always stay at the Srbski Kralj. You know it?" Arnard said.

"I don't."

"King of Serbia, it means. Best hotel in town, wonderful food, if you can eat red peppers, and they'll send girls up all night. The bartender is a pimp, also a marriage broker—something interesting there if you think about it. Anyhow, what I have to do down there is clear, I have to hand over a certain number of dinar, about half the bill, directly to the tax collector, then they'll let the ship go, the sponges belong to us, and we know some people who buy sponges. Takes all kinds, right? So, I'm waiting around in the bar one night—these things take the most incredible amount of time to arrange—and I start talking to this fellow. You *have* to put this in a movie, Jean-Claude—he's, mmm, enormous, heaven only knows what he weighs, shaved head, mustache like a Turkish wrestler. A munitions dealer, won't say exactly where he's from, only that he's a citizen of Canada, in legal terms, and would love to go there some day."

Casson smiled, things happened to Arnaud.

"But, what really struck me about this man was, he was wearing an extraordinary suit. Some kind of Balkan homespun material, a shimmering green, the color of a lime. Vast, even on him, a tent. On his feet? Bright yellow shoes—also enormous. He could barely walk. 'Pity me,' he says, 'looking like I do. An hour ago I met with Prince Paul, the leader of Yugoslavia, on the most urgent matters.'

"And then he explains. A day earlier he'd been in Istanbul, closing a deal for Oerlikons, Swedish antiaircraft cannon, with the Turkish navy. Now he's done with that, and he has to get to Belgrade, but the choice of airlines isn't very appetizing, so he books a compartment on the Orient Express, Istanbul to Belgrade, should arrive just in time for his meeting. That night he goes to the dining car, sits across the table from a Hungarian actress—she says. A stunner, flaming red hair, eyes like fire. They drink, they talk, she invites him to come to her compartment. So, about ten o'clock our merchant, wearing red pajamas and bathrobe, goes to the next sleeping car and knocks on the lady's door. Well, he says, it's even better than advertised, and they make a night of it. He gets up at six the next morning, kisses her hand, and heads back to his room. Opens the door at the end of the car, and what do you think he sees?"

"I don't know. His, ah, his wife's mother."

"Oh no. He sees *track*. The train had been divided into two sections at the Turkish border, and now his wallet, his money, his passport, and his suitcase are heading for Germany—where he does not want them to go—and he's off to see Prince Paul in red pajamas. Well, the next stop is in Bulgaria, Sofia, and he gets off. In the station he manages to borrow a coin, and telephones his Bulgarian representative. 'Buy me a suit!' he says. 'The biggest suit in Sofia! And get down to the railroad station in a hurry!' Also a shirt, and a pair of shoes. Pretty soon the agent shows up and there's the boss, all three hundred pounds of him, sitting on a bench, surrounded by a crowd of curious Bulgarians. The fellow puts on the suit, drives to the Canadian legation, demands they call the next station, have the baggage taken off the train before it reaches Germany, and have it put on the next train to Belgrade.

"And they did it."

"He said they did. But he had his meeting in the big suit."

"The Balkans," Casson said. "Somehow it's always—did you ever meet the man who ate the Sunday paper?"

"Savovic! Yes. He ate also a Latin grammar, and a fez."

Véronique, Marie-Claire's sister who bought costume jewelry for the Galéries Lafayette, came over with a German officer on her arm. "You two are having a good time," she said. "I would like to present *Oberleutnant* Hempel."

"*Enchanté,*" Hempel said.

"*Oberleutnant* Hempel is in transport."

Hempel laughed. He seemed a good-natured man, quite heavy, with thick glasses. "My friend Bruno and me, we are in the automobile business." His French was ghastly and slow, a comma after every word. "Every kind of automobile, we got garages full of them, out in Levallois."

Casson smiled politely. Was he going to be offered an opportunity to buy his own car back from Bruno and the Germans? Bruno already had the apartment and the wife—not that Casson begrudged him the latter—but having the car as well seemed excessive.

Arnaud never stopped smiling. One had a few friends, but mostly people were meant to be used, one way or another, and if you weren't born knowing that you had better learn it somewhere along the way. He nodded encouragement as Hempel spoke, *yes, that's right,* even said a few words in return, the Horch, the Audi, Bavarian Motor Works. Now he had a lifelong friend. *"Ja! Ja!"* the officer said. He was sweating with gratitude. Véronique chose that moment to escape, smiling and backing away. Arnaud caught Casson's eye—glanced up at the ceiling. *Quel cul.*

Casson drank some more of the cuba libre. He'd be taking off his clothes and dancing on the table in no time at all. *Olé!* This was his third concoction and it was getting him good and drunk, perhaps that was acceptable at a real American cocktail party, but not in Passy. Still, maybe it didn't matter. Hempel laughed at something Arnaud said. Casson looked closer. Had he actually understood the joke? No—a German stage laugh. Very hearty. And this idiot had his car.

A hand took his elbow in a hard grip. "Come with me," Marie-Claire hissed in his ear. He smiled and shrugged as he was towed away. They wound their way through the chattering crowd in the smoky living room, around the corner, into the bedroom—a kidding *tiens!* from Casson, Marie-Claire whispering "I have to talk to you." She hauled him into the bathroom and shut the door firmly behind them. He peered around drunkenly. This had once been his, he'd shaved here every morning.

"Jean-Claude," she said, still whispering, "what am I going to do about this?"

"What?"

"What. This *boche,* this *schleuh.* He brings them home, now."

"I don't know," he said. "Maybe it's the wise thing to do."

"You don't believe that!" A fierce whisper. Then she moved closer to him, an aura of whiskey and perfume hung around her. Suddenly she looked worried. "Do you?"

"No." After a moment he said, "But," then sighed like a man who was going to have to tell more of the truth than he wanted to, "I'm afraid that it will turn out that way."

She looked grim—bad news, but maybe he was right. Someone

laughed in the living room. "After all," he said, "what matters to Bruno is that he *does well*. Right?"

She nodded.

"Well, that's how it is with him. If you take that away—what's left?"

She was going to cry. He set his glass carefully on the rim of the sink and put his arms around her. She shuddered once and leaned into him. "Come on," he said softly. "It's just the life we live now."

"I know."

"So, the hell with it."

"I'm scared," she said. "I can't do it—I'm going to make a mistake." A tear started at the corner of her eye. "Oh no," she said, stopping it with her finger.

"We're all scared," he said.

"Not you."

"Yes, me." He reached over her shoulder, took a washcloth off a peg and, hand behind his back, let cold water run on it. He squeezed it out and gave it to her, saying "Here," and she held it on her eye.

She looked up at him, shook her head. "What a circus," she said. She put her free hand on his chest, gave him a wry smile, then kissed him on the mouth, a moment, a little more, and warm. Casson felt something like an electric shock.

A discreet knock on the door. Véronique: "There are people here, Marie-Claire."

"Thank you."

In the living room, taking her coat off by the door, Bibi Lachette. "Jean-Claude!" she called out, eyes bright, mouth red and sexy. "This is Albert."

Fair-haired, pink-cheeked from the cold, a perfectly groomed mustache and goatee. "Ah yes," he said, unwinding himself from a complicated, capelike overcoat. "The film man."

10 March, 11 March, 12 March.

Please be spring. If nothing else, that. The trees at the entrances to the Métro, where warm air vented from down below, always bloomed first. Yes, said the newspapers, it had been the coldest winter in a hun-

dred years. Privately, more than one person in Paris—and in Prague
and in Warsaw and in Copenhagen—thought that God had punished
Europe for setting itself on fire, for murdering the innocent, for evil.
But then too there was, particularly in that scheme of things, redemp-
tion. And *now* would be a good time for it. The wind still blew, getting out of bed in the morning still hurt, the skin stayed rough and
cracked, but the winter was breaking apart, collapsing, exhausted by
its valiant effort to kill every last one of them.

Fischfang had barely survived; no coal, too many women and children, never enough to eat. He stared at himself in a mirror hung on a
bare wall, his face thin and angry. "Look what they have done to me,"
he said to Casson. "They ate all the food while we starved. Sometimes
I see one, plump and happy, strutting like a little pigeon. This is the
one, I tell myself. This one goes in an alley and he doesn't come out.
I've been close, once or twice. I think if I don't do something my head
will explode."

Casson nodded that he understood, taking wheat flour and milled
oats and a can of lard from a sack and setting it on the table. All he
could manage but, he thought, probably not enough. He wondered
how much more Fischfang could take.

Yet, a mystery. *Hotel Dorado* was luminous. Not in the plot—somewhere in deepest Fischfang-land there was no real belief in plots. Life
wasn't this, and therefore that, and so, of course, the other. It didn't
work that way. Life was this, and then something, and then something
else, and then a kick in the ass from nowhere. In *Hotel Dorado* anyhow, the theory worked. A miracle. How on earth had Fischfang
thought it up? The characters floated about, puzzled ghosts in the cor-
ridors of a dream hotel, a little good, a little bad, the usual tenants of
life. They shared, all of them, a certain gentle despair. Even the
teenager, Hélène, had seen the world for what it was—and love might
help, might not. There were six tables in the dining room, the old waiter
moved among them, you could hear the hum of conversation, the
bump of the door to the kitchen, the clatter of pots and pans as the
proprietor cooked dinner. Thank heaven it wasn't Cocteau! The Game
of Life as a provincial hotel—Madame Avarice, Baron Glutton, and
Death as the old porter. Fischfang's little hotel was a little hotel, life
was a weekend.

Suddenly he realized that they would applaud in the theatres. He almost shivered at the idea, but they would. They'd sit in the darkness and, despite the fact that nobody who'd worked on the film could hear, they would clap at the end, just to celebrate what it made them feel.

It wasn't finished, of course—there were fixes that would have to be made—but it was there. Hugo Altmann called him the morning after he'd sent over a copy, demanded to meet the reclusive screenwriter, discovered his lunch appointment that afternoon had canceled.

"Who would you like to direct?" he asked over coffee.

"I've thought about it."

"And?"

Casson hesitated, chose not to open the bidding.

"Well," Altmann said. "Suppose you could have anybody in the world?"

"Really?"

"Yes. I mean, let's start there, anyhow."

Casson nodded. "René Guillot, perhaps, for this."

"Yes," Altmann said. His ears reddened. "That might work very well."

Altmann was looking at him a certain way: here was Jean Casson, CasFilm, *No Way Out* and *Night Run* and all that sort of thing. Nothing wrong with it. It put people in the seats. Everybody made a little money—if they were careful. He was easy to work with, not a prima donna. On time, pretty much, on budget, pretty much. Not unsuccessful. But now, *Hotel Dorado*. This was different.

20 March, 21 March, 22 March.

Maybe, this morning, the window could be opened. Not too much, just a little. After all, this wasn't exactly a wind, more like a breeze. Somehow, against all odds, spring was coming. One could get used to the rationing, to the Germans, to the way things were, and then one simply did what had to be done. And, if you managed to avoid a trap or two, and kept your wits about you, there were rewards: a draft of *Hotel Dorado* went into Altmann's office, money came out. That allowed

Casson to eat in black-market restaurants twice a week. His apartment felt comfortable—the warming of the season replacing the heating of the baroness. In general, life seemed to be working better. For example his telephone line had been repaired—Madame Fitou told him the crew had been there—even before he realized it was out of order.

At night, he slept alone.

His friends had always claimed that Parisian women knew when a man was in love. Which meant? He wasn't sure, but something had changed. He didn't want the women in the cafés, and, when he decided he did, they didn't want him. He stared at himself in the mirror, but he looked the same as he had for a long time. So, he thought, it must be happening on the subconscious level—mysterious biology. He was, for the moment, the wrong ant on the wrong leaf.

He didn't dream about Citrine—he didn't dream. But he thought about her before he went to sleep. How she looked, certain angles, certain poses, his own private selection. Accidental moments, often—she would as likely be putting on a stocking as taking it off. She ran past a doorway because there was no towel in the bath. Or she made a certain request and there was a tremor in her voice. For him, those nights in early spring, she would do some of the things she'd done when they'd been together, then some things he had always imagined her doing, then some things she'd probably never done and never would. He wondered what she would have felt had she seen the movies he made of her. Of course, she made her own movies, so it wouldn't be a great shock. Would he like to see those? Yes. He would like to.

Thought about her. And talked to her. Shared the tour of daily existence. She actually missed quite a bit here—maybe she would have gotten hot over Casson's images of lovemaking, maybe, but she certainly would have laughed at the comedies he found for her.

At last, in the middle of February, he'd given in and written a love letter. Based on the ones he'd composed in Spain—on the beach and in the railway cars. Wrote it down and put it in an envelope. *Citrine, I love you.* It wasn't very long, but it was very honest. Even then, there was a lot he didn't say—who wants a blue movie in their love letter? Still, the idea came across. He read it over, it was the best he could do. Somewhere between walks-on-the-beach and sixty-nine, a few sentences about life being short, a few more on mystery, mostly just Jean-Claude, wide open, on paper.

Casson went out to Billancourt studios, where René Guillot was directing a pirate film.

> *Seize hommes sur*
> *le coffre d'un mort,*
> *yo ho ho*
> *la bouteille de rhum!*

> *Boisson et diable*
> *ont tués les autres,*
> *yo ho ho*
> *buvons le rhum!*

"Michel?"

"Yes, Monsieur Guillot?"

"Could you move up the mast a little higher?"

"Yes, sir."

"And, everybody, we need it deeper, more baritone, stronger. Yo ho ho! Let's run through it once, like that, and Etienne? Hold the bottle of rum up so we can see it—maybe give it a shake, like this. Yes. All right, *'Seize hommes sur . . .'*"

Casson stood near Guillot's canvas chair—Guillot smiled and beckoned him over.

Casson spoke in an undertone. "Jean Lafitte?"

"Blackbeard."

"Mmm."

Casson recognized the wooden boat, supported beneath the keel by scaffolding. It had been featured in scores of pirate and adventure films; a Spanish galleon, a British frigate, a seventy-four-gun ship-of-the-line in the Napoleonic navy. It was manned, that afternoon, by singing pirates. Some clung to the mast, there were several at the helmsman's wheel, one straddling the bowsprit and a score of others, in eyepatch and cutlass, headscarf and earring and striped jersey. Only luck, Casson felt, had so far saved him from working in the genre. Guillot, he'd been told, was there as a favor, to finish a job left undone by a journeyman director who had disappeared.

Later they sat in the canteen, amid electricians and carpenters, and ate sausage sandwiches washed down with thin beer. "It's a very good screenplay," Guillot said. "What's this nonsense about a recluse in the countryside?"

"It's Louis Fischfang."

"Oh. Of course. He's still here?"

"Yes."

Guillot's expression said *not good*. He smoothed back his fine white hair. He'd been famously handsome when he was young. He remained famously arrogant—egotistical, selfish, brilliant. An *homme de la gauche* consumed with leftist causes, he'd made a passionate speech at the World Congress Against War in Amsterdam in 1933, then denounced Soviet communism after the Hitler-Stalin pact of 1939.

"You think Altmann's a Nazi?" he said quietly.

Casson shrugged.

Guillot thought about it for a moment, then he said, "I should've left."

"Why didn't you?"

"I'm French. Where the hell am I going to go?"

They drank some beer. Guillot spooned mustard onto his sausage. "I wonder about the title," he said. "*Hotel Dorado*. What about something like *Nights of Autumn*? That's not it, but I'm feeling for loss, a little melancholy, something bittersweet. You know me, I like to go right at things. Then also, it struck me, why is the stranger a woman? Better a man, no?"

"We talked about it," Casson said. "We like the idea of a woman. Traveling alone, vulnerable, a small part saint but she doesn't know it. The way the Americans use an angel—always clumsy, or absent-minded. The idea is that *strong* and *good* are two different things."

Guillot stopped chewing—jowls and pouchy eyes immobile—and stared at him for a moment. Then nodded once, *all right—I accept that*, and went back to his food.

"You know," Guillot said, "the last time I heard your name was from Raoul Mies. You'd just signed with Continental, in October I think, and Mies decided that maybe he would too."

"You're serious?"

Guillot spread his hands, meaning *of course*.

"Altmann told me that Mies and, ah, Jean Leveque had signed. So, I decided it would be all right for me."

The electricians at the next table laughed at something. Guillot gave Casson a sour smile. "An old trick," he said.

Casson pushed his food aside and lit a cigarette.

"I don't blame you," Guillot said. "But there's nothing you can do about it now."

"I should've known better."

Guillot sighed. "The war," he said. It explained everything. "It's fucked us," he added. "And the bill isn't even in."

Casson nodded.

"As for this project," Guillot said, "one thing we can do is take it south. It's not heaven, it's Vichy. Instead of Goebbels's people at the Hotel Majestic there's the COIC, the Comité d'Organisation de L'Industrie Cinématographique. It's not all that different—they won't give membership cards to Jews—but there are two reasons to consider it. One is that it's still French, whatever else it is, they don't mean what they say and as long as you stand there they keep talking, and two, you can get out of the country down there a lot easier than you can here." He lowered his voice. "That I do know, because I had somebody *find out*. And maybe that's what, uhh, your writer ought to hear about."

"He will," Casson said.

They sat in silence for a time. Finished the beer. The electricians looked at their watches, stood up and left. "Well," Guillot said—it meant time to go back to work. "You can stay, of course, if you like."

"I have a meeting back in Paris," Casson said.

He met Guillot's eyes, was reassured. They weren't children, they'd spent their lives in the film business, were not strangers to betrayal and back-stabbing. And they were French, which meant they knew how to evade, to improvise, to *reculer pour sauter mieux*—to back up in order to get a better jump. "Tell me one thing," Casson said, "just for curiosity's sake. Why, of all things, Blackbeard?"

"I think it's the godchild of some office that Altmann talks to. I mean, it's just something for the kids on Saturday afternoons, and to play in the countryside, where they'll watch anything that moves. You see, Blackbeard is *English*. A pirate, a brute. In this movie, he walks the plank."

Casson shook his head, in awe at such nonsense. *"Mon Dieu,"* he said sorrowfully.

Guillot smiled, leaned toward Casson, spoke in a conspirator's undertone. "Yo ho ho," he said.

That night when he got home Casson discovered that his letter to Citrine had been returned. He held it in his hands. Somebody had obviously read it, possibly the censors, but, more likely, those bastards at the hotel. He had put the letter in the envelope as he'd been taught in lycée, so that the greeting was the first thing the reader saw when the letter was unfolded. Somebody had put it back in the wrong way. Written across the front of the envelope *Gone Away. Left No Address.*

He didn't read it.

He sat on the couch, still wearing his raincoat, the apartment dark and lifeless. Forty-one-year-old producers. Twenty-nine-year-old actresses with a certain smoky look. What, pray tell, had he thought would happen? He leaned his head back against the cushion. She had left, all right. And one reason was to make certain he was locked out of her life. She knew herself, she knew him, she knew better.

Once again he'd been stupid: had decided that what he wanted to be true, was. And it wasn't. Thus Altmann had deceived him, then Simic, then with Citrine, he'd deceived himself. This couldn't go on. He heard his father saying "Jean-Claude, Jean-Claude."

By force of will, he turned himself back toward commerce. *Survival,* he thought, that's what matters now. It wasn't a time for love affairs—maybe that was what Citrine understood better than he ever could, survival was more important than anything. The city had no difficulty with that, at the end of winter it discovered it was somehow still alive, then went back to business with a vengeance. It wasn't very appealing, some of it, but then it never had been. You work in a whorehouse, Balzac told them. Don't let anybody see how much you enjoy it and get your money up front.

Casson, that first week in April, had a new friend. An admirer. Perhaps, even, an investor. A certain Monsieur Gilles de Groux. Nobility, the real thing, in fact de Groux de Musigny, Casson checked the listing in *Bottin Mondain* and the *Annuaire des Châteaux*. He had a huge, drafty house out in the forest of St.-Germain-en-Laye, just out-

side Paris, where his family had moved in 1688 in order to commis-
erate with the Catholic pretender James II, who'd slipped into France
earlier that year. William of Orange got the English throne, as it happened, but the de Groux family remained, walking on the miles-long
Grande Terrasse that looked out over the city of Paris, breeding
Vendéean basset hounds, reading books in leather covers.

It was Arnaud who had suggested his name to de Groux. Casson
called him after their first meeting. "He wants to make films, he says."

"Yes," Arnaud said. "That's what he told me."

"Where did you say you met?"

"Rennaisance Club."

"How rich is he?"

Arnaud had to take a moment to think about this. All around them,
in the 16th Arrondissement, were the world's great masters of the art
of pretending to be rich. "The money, I believe, is from Limoges.
China. Since the eighteen-hundreds. Does he live well?"

"Big house in St.-Germain. Creaky floors. Gothic maids."

"Sounds right."

"You think he really wants to make films?"

"Perhaps. I can't say. Maybe he wants to meet film stars. He certainly wanted to meet you. Hello? Jean-Claude?"

"Yes, I'm still on."

"You ought to get that repaired."

"Are you going to the Pichards on Friday?"

"I'd planned to."

"See you there."

"Yes. Keep me posted on what happens, will you?"

"I will."

There were film producers who made a living by knowing how to meet
rich people and what to say to them, but for Casson it somehow never
worked out. Some stubborn dignity always asserted itself, they sensed
that, the grand schemes came to nothing. But de Groux was, in Casson's experience, something completely new. A tall, thin, shambling
fellow, no family close by, a shaggy white mustache stained by tobacco,
hair that needed cutting, old wool sweaters that smelled like dogs, and
a yellow corduroy jacket with buttoned pockets, a survival of the

artists-and-models Montparnasse of 1910. No less an aristocrat, of course, for a little eccentricity. A certain drape hung between him and the world; installed at birth, removed with death, never to be shifted in between.

He was, however, very intent on making a film. And it was the apparatus of the business that seemed to fascinate him. He wanted to visit the office on the rue Marbeuf, he insisted they have lunch at the Alsatian brasserie on the corner—assuming that Casson often ate there. He wanted to have a drink at Fouquet—or Rudi's, or Ubu Roi—wanted to go out to Billancourt, wanted to visit the nightclubs around Bastille. In the process they would talk about very nearly everything before returning, rather dutifully it seemed to Casson, to the business at hand.

"I always come back to *The Devil's Bridge,*" he would say. "That same kind of, feeling, the mood of, what would you say?"

"I don't know. Escape?"

"Yes, well, perhaps. But maybe more. We should be ambitious, I think. That's what's wrong with people, these days."

They talked a great deal, and over time it crossed Casson's mind that this man had never actually seen a film.

"Tell me, Gilles," he would say. "What's your favorite?"

"Oh, I can never keep the titles straight."

Vague, perhaps, but very accomodating. Any time or place was good for him, and he never missed an appointment. He traveled in a chauffeured Citroën, seemed to have all the gasoline he needed, had lots of money and ration stamps, and an insatiable curiosity. What did Casson think about the Catholic church? What about Pétain? De Gaulle? The Popular Front? England, Churchill, the French Communist Party.

Good talk, intelligent and cultured. De Groux had spent half a century reading and conversing—born to a rich and idle life, your job was to discover the meaning of existence, then to let your friends know what it was. The discussion of the new film was carried on all over Paris, Casson was even invited to a supper party at de Groux's hunting lodge in the Sologne. *Oh Citrine, I wish you could be here to see this. That's a real oryx head over the fireplace, that's a real duke by the fire, he's carrying a stick with a real ivory horse's head, and he's wearing a real leather slipper with the little toe cut away to ease his gout.*

A cast of characters well beyond Jean Renoir. Adèle, the niece from Amboise. Real nobility—look at those awful teeth. Washed-out blue eyes gazed into his, a tiny pulse beat sparrowlike at the pale temple. Wasn't her uncle the dearest man—insisting that poor old Pierrot be stabled in his horse barns? This proud beast, now retired, who had pounded so faithfully down the paths of the Bois de Fontainebleau after the fleeing hart—would Monsieur care to visit him? *Citrine, I confess I wanted to.* Go to the stable and wrestle in the straw, hoist the silk evening dress and pull down the noble linen. For the son of a *grand-bourgeois* crook from the 16th, a once-in-a-lifetime opportunity. One *never* met such people, they were rumored to exist, mostly they appeared in plays. There really was game for dinner, dark and strong—perhaps the fabled bear paw, Casson couldn't bring himself to ask—with black-blood gravy. And real watery vegetables. "Film!" said a cousin from Burgundy. "No. Not really." Casson assured him it was true. And the man drew back his lips and actually brayed.

There they were, and I among them. Sad it couldn't last—de Groux was a spy, really, what else could he be? It scared Casson because somebody was going to a lot of trouble, and Casson didn't think he was worth it. Or, worse, he was worth it but he just didn't realize why.

Back at the rue Chardin, a visit to the cellar with a flashlight. Ancient stone walls, a child's sled, a forgotten steamer trunk, a bicycle frame with no wheels. On one wall, black metal boxes and telephone lines. What was he looking for? He didn't know. Whatever made that hissing sound. He peered at the wires, seeking a device he could neither name nor describe. But there was nothing there. Or nothing he could see. Or, maybe, nothing at all, it was all in his mind. French phones made noise—why not this noise?

"Tell me," de Groux said, "a man in your position. You must have influence somewhere—a sympathetic politician, perhaps. It's hard to get the permissions, all the *fiches* one must have to do your job. I tell you I'm worried, my friend. All the money we're going to spend. It's not that I don't have it, I have pots of it. It's these musty old lawyers, and the family. They see an old man having a fling, and they worry I'll actually open my fist and a sou will fly out. So you see, I don't want all this to founder on the whim of some little *petit fonctionnaire.* I want to assure myself that when the great battle of the clerks is fought, we are the ones left standing when the smoke clears."

Va te faire foutre, I tell him in my heart, Citrine. Go fuck thyself. But, in the real world: "Well, Gilles, frankly I have stood on the lines myself. I have filled in my share of forms. Sometimes an assistant has been there to help but it's so difficult, you see, crucial, that one must involve oneself. It's that kind of commitment you must have. In the film business."

"No. Really? Well."

A blind reptile, he thought. But it knows there's a nest, and young, and it senses warmth.

And then, it happened again—it seemed everybody wanted to be his friend that spring. This time he was at the office. Four o'clock on a long, wet, gray afternoon, the street outside shiny with rain. His secretary knocked, then opened the door. "A Madame *Duval* to see you," she said, her voice disapproved of the name—who does she think she is, using an alias?

His heart sank. He'd been happily lost in his work, a thousand miles from reality. "Well, send her in," he said.

She sat across from him, wearing a dark suit and a hat with a veil, knees primly together and canted slightly to one side. One of those fortyish Frenchwomen with a sour face and beautiful legs. "I am," she said, "the owner of the Hotel Bretagne. Where your friend, the actress called Citrine, was living." Her voice was tense—this was not an easy visit.

"Yes?"

"Yes. Last Friday, the night clerk happened to tell me that you had written her a letter. By the time it reached the hotel she had left, so he marked it *Gone Away* and returned it." She paused a moment, then said, "He was—was not unpleased at this. A film actress, a producer, star-crossed, an unhappy ending. He was delighted, really, he's a man who takes pleasure in the misfortunes of others, and has reached an age where he's not shy about letting the world know it. It's sad, really."

"I believe he opened the letter and read it," Casson said angrily.

"Shared it with his friends, perhaps, and they all had a good laugh."

The woman thought for a moment. "Opened it? No, not him, he doesn't begin to be that bold, he simply marked the envelope and returned it. And, in the normal course of things, that would be that."

There was more, Casson waited for it.

"However," she said, taking a breath, "I had, *we* had, a certain experience. I knew who she was, although she was using another name—I had seen her in the movies, and nobody else looks like that. Now, I do not live at the hotel, of course, but I happened to be there, late one night, and I went to the second-floor bath to wash out a glass. It was very quiet just then, about two in the morning, and, without thinking, I simply walked in. Well, she was taking a bath. Naturally I excused myself, immediately closed the door. But—"

She hesitated.

"What happened?"

"Nothing actually happened. It took me a minute to realize what I'd seen. There were tears in her eyes, and on her face. And there was a razor blade resting on the soap dish. That's all I saw, monsieur, yet you could not be mistaken, there was no question about what was going to happen in that room. I said through the door, 'Madame, is everything all right?' After a moment she said 'Yes.' That was the end of it, but it's possible that the intrusion saved a life—not for any reason, you understand, reason wasn't involved."

"When was this?"

"Sometime in February. Maybe. Really, I don't remember. About two weeks later we spoke very briefly. I was working on the book-keeping, she'd come in from doing an errand and asked for her key at the desk. We talked for a minute or two, she never referred to what had happened. She told me she would be leaving at the end of the week, had found something to do in Lyons, in the *Zone Non-Occupée,* and she mentioned the name of a hotel."

"Was she unhappy?"

"No. Thoughtful, perhaps. But, mostly, determined."

"She is that."

"Then, after I talked to the clerk, I decided I ought to come and see you, to tell you where she is. For a time I wasn't sure, I didn't know what to do. I argued back and forth with myself. In the end, I'm doing this not because I insinuate myself in the lives of strangers"—the idea was so unappealing she grimaced—"but because I believe, after thinking about it, that she meant for me to do it."

They were quiet for a moment. Casson was conscious of the sound of tires on the rainy street below his window.

"The way she spoke to me," the woman said slowly, "it was as though her emotions, her feelings about life, were uncertain. She didn't know exactly what to do, so she left matters in the hands of fate. It didn't mean all that much to me at the time—I have the hotelkeeper's view of the world, disorder, chaos, stolen towels. I remembered later only because she was who she was, but I did remember. A letter had come, the clerk noticed the return address—he recalled who you were, certainly, and once I was told about it I had to do something. Probably the letter concerns only a forgotten handkerchief."

"No. More than that."

She nodded to herself, confirming what she'd believed. Opened her purse, took out a hotel envelope, reached over and placed it on the corner of his desk. Then stood up. "I hope this is the right thing to do," she said.

Casson stood quickly. "Thank you," he said. "Madame, thank you. I should have offered you something, forgive me, I, perhaps a coffee, or . . ."

A gleam of amusement in her eye. "Another time, perhaps." He was clearly disconcerted—she enjoyed that, particularly in men like Casson. She extended a gloved hand, he took it briefly. Then she was gone.

He tore open the envelope, found the name and telephone number of a hotel in Lyons written on a slip of paper. At the end of the day he met Bernard Langlade for a drink. "Is it hard to find out who owns a hotel?" he said.

"Shouldn't be."

Casson told him the name and location. Langlade called him in the morning. "I take it back," he said. "The Hotel Bretagne, on the Faubourg Saint-Antoine, is owned by a *Société Anonyme,* in Switzerland."

"Is that unusual?"

"No. It's done, sometimes. For tax purposes, or divorce. And, with time and money, you could probably find a name. Of course, even then—"

"No, thank you for looking, Bernard, but probably best just to let it go."

Langlade made a sound that meant *much the wiser choice.* "Especially these days," he said.

Especially these days. There was no calling Citrine from his infected telephone. Every call a new name on somebody's list. He could still see Lady Marensohn across the table in the bar of the Alhambra Hotel. Perhaps it was over, perhaps they believed him, perhaps not.

He'd taken the Métro home from work that night, a man got off behind him. Made the first turn with him, then the second. Casson paused at the window of a boulangerie. The man looked at him curiously and walked by. *Well, how am I supposed to know?* he thought. You're not, came the answering voice, you're not.

Merde alors. After all, it wasn't as though clandestine instincts were unknown in this city. All right, maybe it wasn't the British Secret Intelligence Service one had to elude. But it was husbands or lovers, wives or landlords or lawyers. Casson let it get to be 7:30 in the evening, then left the apartment. By now, when he went out in the street, everyone he saw was an operative—an anonymous little man in an Eric Ambler novel who lived in a rented room and spied on Jean Casson. So, he thought, is it you—in your tuxedo? Or you, a clerk on the way home? Or you, the lovers embracing on the bridge. He hurried along, head down, through the rainy streets, through the fog that pooled at the base of the park railings. He trotted down the Métro stairs, left at the other end of the platform, reversed direction, doubled back, at last sensed he was unobserved and headed toward the river.

Chez Clément—the little sign gold on green, faded pastel and flaked by time and weather. At the end of a tiny street where nobody went, steamed glass window, the hum of conversation and the clatter of dinnerware faintly heard. Inside the door, the smell of potatoes fried in butter every night since 1890. Clément came out of the kitchen, wiping his hands on a towel. Face scarlet, mustache immense, apron tied at one shoulder. "Monsieur Casson." It was like being hugged by a wine-drenched onion. How infernally clever, Clément told him, to stop by this evening, all day long they'd been working, at the stove, in the pots, what luck they'd had, one never saw this any more, perhaps the last—

No, alas, not tonight, he couldn't. Casson inclined his head toward the cloakroom and said delicately, *"Le téléphone?"*

Not *a* telephone, *the* telephone. The one Clément made available to his most cherished customers. Clément smiled, *of course.* The heart had reasons of its own, they had to be honored, sometimes not at home.

He reached the hotel in Lyons. Madame was out.

Was there a message?

No.

12 April. 11:20 A.M. The rain continued, soft cloudy days, nobody minded. Casson walked down the Champs-Elysées, turned right on avenue Marceau, a few minutes later leaned on the parapet of the Pont d'Alma, looking down into the Seine. A blonde woman walked by; lovely, wearing a yellow raincoat. On the banks, rain beaded along the branches of the chestnut trees and dripped onto the cobblestones. The river had risen to spring tide, lead-colored water curling around the piers of the bridges, crosscurrents black on gray, shoals catching the light, rain dappling the surface, going to Normandy, then to sea. *Just a boat,* he thought. How hard would it be? Magic, a child's dream. Carried away to safety on a secret barge.

Casson looked at his watch, lit a cigarette, leaned his weight on the parapet. He could see, at one end of the bridge, a newspaper kiosk— an important day, the headlines thick and black. German planes had set Belgrade on fire, armored columns had entered Zagreb, Skopje had been taken, soon the rest of Macedonia, and the *Panzerkorps* was driving hard on Salonika.

He crossed to the Left Bank, entered the post office on the avenue Bosquet. It was crowded, people in damp coats standing on line, smoking and grinding out their cigarettes on the wet tile floor. He waited for a long time, finally reached the counter, gave the clerk a telephone number, went to the *cabine* and waited for the short ring.

"Hotel du Parc." The voice sounded very far away. "Hello? Are you there?"

Casson gave the name.

"Stay on the line." The sound of the receiver being set down on a wooden countertop.

He waited. In the next *cabine* a woman was shouting at some relative somewhere in France. Where was the money, they were supposed to send it, it should have come days ago, no she didn't want to hear about the problem.

The clerk picked the receiver up. "She's coming now."

Then: "Hello?"

"Hello."

A pause. "It's you."

"Yes."

"I had to leave."

"Yes, I know. How is Lyons?"

"Not so bad. I'm in a play."

"Really?"

"Yes. A small part."

"What sort of play?"

"A little comedy. Nothing much."

"You sound good."

"Do I?"

"Yes."

The line hummed softly.

"Citrine, I wrote you a letter."

"Where is it?"

"It went to the other hotel, but it came back. The woman there told me where you were."

"What does it say?"

"It's a love letter."

"Ah."

"No, really."

"I wonder if I might read it, then."

"Yes, of course. I'll send it along—I just wanted to hear your voice."

"The mail isn't very good, these days."

"No, that's true."

"Perhaps it would be better if you were to bring it."

"Yes. You're right. Citrine?"

"Yes?"

"I love you."

"When can you come here?"

"As soon as I can."

"I'll wait for you."

"I'll let you know when."

"I'll wait."

"I have to say good-bye."

"Yes. Until then."

"Until then."

16 April, 1941.

Now the trees had little leaves and clouds of soft air rolled down the boulevards at dusk and people swore they could smell the fields in the countryside north of the city. Casson bought a train ticket, and made an appointment at the rue des Saussaies to get an *Ausweis* to leave the occupied zone and cross over to the area controlled by Vichy.

A warm day, the girls were out. Nothing better than Frenchwomen, he thought. Even with rationing, they insisted on spring—new scarves, cut from last year's whatever, a little hat, made from a piece of felt somebody had left in a closet, something, at least *something*, to say that love was your reward for agreeing to live another day and walk around in the world.

On the top floor of the old Interior Ministry building, even *SS-Obersturmbannführer* Guske knew it was spring. He came around the desk to shake hands, as tanned and well-oiled as ever, every one of his forty hairs in its proper place, a big leathery smile. Then, with a sigh, he got down to business. Made himself comfortable in his chair and studied the dossier before him, a sort of *now where were we* feeling in the air. "Ah yes," he said. "You went last to Spain to see about locations for a film. So, how did it go for you?"

"Very well. One or two villages were, I can say, perfect. Extremely Spanish. The church and the tile roofs, and the little whitewashed houses."

"Indeed! You're making me want to go."

"It's a change, certainly. Very different from France."

"Yes, here it is, Málaga. My wife and I used to go to Lloret-de-Mar every summer, until they started fighting. Find a *pension* in a little fishing village. What dinners! *Besugo, espadon,* delicious. If you can persuade them to hold back a little on the garlic, excellent!" He laughed, showing big white teeth. Looked back down at the dossier. Read for a moment, then a slight discomfort appeared on his face. "Hmm. Here's a memorandum I'd forgotten all about."

He read carefully, perhaps for three or four minutes. Shook his head in pique at something small and irritating. "I know you are famous for petty bureaucrats in France, but I tell you, Herr Casson, we Germans don't do so badly. Look at this nonsense."

"Sir?"

"I don't have the faintest recollection of anything, you understand, I see people from dawn to dusk, of course, and I only remember the, well, the bad ones, if you know what I mean." He raised his eyebrows to see if Casson had understood.

"What's happened is," he continued, "you told me, or, I thought you told me, that your army service was back in the 1914 war, but here it says that you—well, the people down at the Vincennes military base sent on to us a record that says you were transferred to a unit that was reactivated in May of 1940. Could that be right?"

"Yes. I was."

"Well, I apparently got it wrong the last time we talked because now somebody's gone and written a memorandum in your file saying that you, well, that you didn't actually tell the truth."

"I don't really know what I . . ." Casson felt something flutter in his stomach.

"Ach," Guske said, quite annoyed now. He stood up, walked toward the door. "I'm going to go down the hall and have this put right. I'll be back in a minute." He opened the door and gestured toward a chair in the hall. "Please," he said. "I'll have to ask you to wait in the corridor."

Guske marched off down the hall. Casson wanted to get up and run out of the building, but he knew he'd never make it, and when they caught him he wouldn't be able to explain. He wasn't being threatened, exactly. It was something else—he didn't know what it was, but he could feel it reaching for him.

Hold on, he told himself.

He very nearly couldn't. He closed his eyes, heard typewriters, muted conversations, doors opening and closing, telephones. It was just an office.

Forty minutes later, Guske came back down the hall shaking his head. In a bad humor, he waved Casson into his office. "This is extraordinarily irritating, Herr Casson, but this man at the other end of the hall is acting in a very unreasonable fashion. I mean, here we've had a simple misunderstanding, you gave me some information and it didn't happen to hold with some piece of paper that somebody sent here, and now he's going to be difficult about it."

Casson started to speak, Guske held up his hand for silence.

"Please, there's nothing you can say that will help. I am certainly going to take care of this problem—you can have every confidence in me—but it's going to take a day or two, maybe even a little more. Your trip to Lyons, is it so very urgent?"

"No."

"Good. Then I'm relieved. And you'll appreciate I have to work with this fellow, I can't be getting around him every five minutes. But he's going to have to learn to separate these things—here is something that must concern us, over there is just a nuisance, a little pebble in the shoe. Eh?"

Guske stood and offered his hand. "Why don't you call me back a week from today? Yes? I'm sure I'll be able to give you the answer you want. These telephone numbers in your file, for home and office, they're correct?"

"Yes."

"Very good. Then I'll see you in a week or so. Good day, Herr Casson. Please don't think too badly of us, it will all be made right in the end.

Two days later, a Friday afternoon, a commotion in the *réception* of his office. Casson threw open his door, then stared with astonishment. It was a man called Bouffo—a comic actor, he used only that name. A huge man, gloriously fat, with three chins and merry little eyes—

"France's beloved Bouffo," the publicity people said. Casson's secretary, Mireille, was standing at her desk, vaguely horrified, uncertain what to do. Bouffo, as always in a white, tentlike suit and a gray fedora, was leaning against the wall, fanning himself with a newspaper, his face the color of chalk. "Please, my friends," he said. "I beg you. Something to drink."

"Will you take a glass of water, monsieur?" Mireille asked.

"God no."

"Mireille," Casson said. "Please go down to the brasserie and bring back a carafe of wine, tell them it's an emergency." He handed her some money.

"Now Bouffo," he said, "let's get you sat down." Casson was terrified the man was going to die in his office.

"Forgive me Casson—I've had the most terrible experience."

Casson took his arm—he was trembling—and helped him onto the couch. Up close, the smell of lilac-scented talcum powder and sweat. "Please," Casson said, "try to calm yourself."

"What a horror," Bouffo said.

"What happened?"

"Well. You know Perlemère?"

"Yes. The agent?"

"Yes. Well, some time ago he represented me, and he owed me a little money, and I thought I'd just kind of drop in on him, unannounced, and see if I could collect some of it, you know how things are, lately. So, I went over to his office, which is just the other side of the boulevard. I was in that little lobby there, waiting for the elevator, when there was a commotion on the staircase. It's Perlemère, and there are three men with him, a short one, very well-dressed, and two tough types. Detectives, is what they were."

"You're sure?"

"Yes. One knows."

"German?"

"French."

"And?"

"They're arresting Perlemère."

"*What?*"

"He's telling them he knows this one and that one and there'll be hell to pay once his important friends find out how he's being treated and all this kind of thing. But, clearly, they don't care. Perlemère tries to stop on the staircase and says 'Now see here, this has gone far enough' and they hit him. I mean, they really hit him, it's not like the movies. And he cried out."

Bouffo stopped a moment and caught his breath. "I'll be all right," he said. "Then, one of them called him a Jew this and a Jew that, and they hit him again. It was sickening. The sound of it. There were tears on Perlemère's face. Then, they saw me. And one of them says, 'Hey look, it's Bouffo!' "

"What did you do?"

"Casson, I was terrified. I gave a sort of nervous laugh, and I tipped my hat. Then they brushed by me. Perlemère looked in my eyes, he was pleading with me. There was blood on his mouth. I held the door open a crack after they went out—they threw him in a car, then they drove away. I didn't know what to do. I started to go home, then I remembered your office was over here and I thought I better go someplace where I could sit down for a moment."

Mireille returned, carrying a carafe of wine. Casson poured some in a water glass and gave it to Bouffo. "No good, Casson." He wasn't talking about the wine. Shook his head, tried to take deep breaths. "No good. I mean, who do you go to?"

Sunday night, late—one-thirty in the morning when he looked at his watch. He was reading, wearing an old shirt and slacks. Restless, not ready to sleep. Blackout curtains drawn, light of a single lamp, a very battered Maigret novel, *The Nightclub,* he'd bought at a stall on the Seine. The buzzer by his door startled him. Now what? He laid the book face down on the chair, turned off the lamp, went out onto the terrace. Down below, a dark shape waited at the door. Then a white face turned up toward him, and a stage whisper: "Jean-Claude, let me in." Gabriella, with a small suitcase.

He hurried down the stairs, the marble steps cold on his feet because he was wearing only socks. He unlocked the door and pushed it open. He heard a stirring from the concierge apartment, called out, "It's just a friend, Madame Fitou."

Back in the apartment he poured a glass of red wine and set out some bread and blackcurrant jam. Gabriella was exhausted and pale, a smudge on the elbow of her coat. "It happened on one of the trains," she told him. "Really I can't remember which one it was. I had a first-class compartment, Milan to Turin, then I took the night train to Geneva, eventually the Dijon/Paris express. Then I just barely managed to catch the last Métro from the Gare de Lyon."

"Gabriella, why?"

"I told my husband I was coming up here to see an old girlfriend—as far as anybody knows I arrive tomorrow morning, eight-thirty, on the train from Milan. Do you see what I did?"

"Yes."

"Jean-Claude, could I have a cigarette?"

He lit it for her. She took a deep breath and sat back in the chair. "I had to see you," she said.

This was not the same Gabriella. She'd changed the way she looked—had her hair cut short, then set. She wore three rings: a diamond, a wide gold wedding band with filigree, and an antique, a dull green stone in a worn silver setting, ancient, a family treasure. Clearly she had a new life.

Their eyes met, a look only possible between people who've made love, then she looked away. No, he thought, it isn't that. They'd had one night together, it had been intimate, very intimate. He had wanted her—long legs, pure face—for months, but she turned out not to be someone who lost herself, or maybe just not his to excite. As for her, he'd realized later that she'd been in love with him, the real thing. So, in the end, neither one got what they wanted.

She sighed, met his eyes again, ran a hand through her hair. "I'm married now," she said softly.

"Gabriella, are you in trouble?"

She shook her head. "No," she said, "it's you."

"Me?"

"Yes. One morning last week, after my husband left for work, two men came to the house. One was from the security service, in Rome, and the other was German. Educated, soft-spoken, reasonably good Italian. The German asked the questions—first about my time in Paris, then about you. 'Please, do not worry yourself, signora, this is simply

routine, just a few things we need to know.' He asked about your politics, how did you vote, did you belong to a political party. It was very
thorough, carefully done. They knew a great deal about your business,
about the films you'd made, about Marie-Claire and your friends. He
asked what sorts of foreigners did you know. Did you travel abroad?
Often? Where to?

"I made a great show of trying to be helpful, but I tried to persuade
them that most of my work was typing letters and filing and answering the telephone. I just didn't know much about your personal life.
They seemed to accept that. 'And signora, please, if it's all the same to
you, we'd rather he didn't know we'd been around asking questions.'
That was a threat. The Italian looked at me a certain way. Not brutal, but it could not be misunderstood."

"But you came here anyhow."

She shrugged. "Well, that was the only way. You can't say anything
on the phone, they read your mail. We've had Mussolini and the
fascisti since 1922, so we do what we have to do."

"Not everybody," he said.

"Well, no, there are always—you learn who they are."

They talked for a long time, closer than they'd ever been. Trains and
borders, special permits, passports. It wasn't about resistance, it was
about secret police and day-to-day life. What had it been, he thought,
since the May night they'd spent together—ten months? Back then, this
gossip would have been about books, or vacations. "At the line for the
railroad controls," she said, "they always have somebody watching to
see who decides to turn back."

She yawned, he took her by the hand into the bedroom. She washed
up, changed into silk pajamas, slid under the blankets. "Talk to me a
minute more," she said. He turned the lights off, sat on the floor and
leaned back against the bed. They kept their voices low in the darkness. "It is very strange at home now," she told him. "The Milanese
don't believe they live in Italy. You mention Mussolini and they look
to heaven—yet one more of life's afflictions that has to be tolerated.
If you say 'what if we are bombed?' they become indignant. What, *here*,
in Milan? Are you crazy?"

It felt good to talk to a friend, he thought, never better than when
your enemies are gathering. It felt good to conspire. "It's hard to imagine—" he said, then stopped. Above him, a gentle snore. *Good night,*

Gabriella. Ration coupons—did he have enough to take her for coffee in the morning? Yes, he would have a demitasse, it would just work out.

Really, he thought, who was this Guske to tell him what to do with his life? How did it happen that some German sat in an office and told Jean Casson whether or not he could have a love affair with a woman who lived in Lyons?

THE
NIGHT
VISITOR

24 April, 1941.

4:20 A.M., the wind sighing across the fields, the river white where it shoaled over the gravel islands. Jean Casson lay on his stomach at the top of a low hill, wrapped up in overcoat and muffler, dark hat worn at an angle, a small valise by his side. The damp from the wet earth chilled him to the bone but there was nothing he could do about it. At the foot of the hill, standing at the edge of the river, two border guards, the last of the waning moonlight a pale glow on their helmets, rifles slung over their shoulders. They were sharing a cigarette and talking in low voices, the rough German sounds, the *sch* and *kuh,* drifting up the hillside.

The boy lying next to him, called André, was fifteen, and it was his job to guide Casson across a branch of the river Allier into the *Zone Non-Occupée.* André stared intensely, angrily, at the *sales Boches* below him. These were *his* hills, this was *his* stream, these teenagers below him—nineteen or so—were intruders, and he would, in time, settle with them. By his side, his brown-and-white Tervueren shepherd waited patiently—Tempête he called her, Storm—her breath steaming as she panted in the icy morning air.

These were in fact his hills—or would be. They belonged to his family, the de Malincourts, resident since the fifteenth century in a run-down chateau just outside the village of Lancy. He raised his hand a few inches, a signal to Casson: be patient, I know these two, they chatter like market ladies but they will, eventually, resume their rounds. Casson gritted his teeth as the wet grass crushed beneath him slowly soaked his clothing. Had they left the chateau as planned, at two in the morning, this would not have happened.

But it was the same old story. He was scheduled to go across with another man, a cattle-dealer from Nevers who couldn't or wouldn't get a permit to enter the Vichy zone. The cattle-dealer arrived forty minutes late, carrying a bottle of cognac that he insisted on opening and sharing with various de Malincourts who had chosen to remain awake in honor of the evening crossing—the father, an aunt, a cousin and the local doctor, if Casson remembered correctly. Everybody had some cognac, the fire burned low, then, at 3:20, a telephone call. It was the cattle-dealer's wife, he'd received a message at his house in Nevers and he didn't have to go across the line after all. That left Casson and André to make the crossing later than they should have, almost dawn, and that invited tragedy.

The sentries had themselves a final laugh, then parted, heading east and west along the stream. The dog made a faint sound, deep in her throat—*sentries leaving*. No, Casson told himself, it wasn't possible. But then, he thought, dogs understand war, its memory lived in them, and this one's traditional business was herding stock to safety. A small cold wind, just enough to lift the soft hair on the dog's neck, made Casson shiver. He'd been offered an oilskin, hanging amid shotguns and fishing baskets and rubber boots in the gunroom of the chateau, but he had declined. Well, next time he'd know better.

André, in short pants and sweater, seemed not to notice. "Please, sir," he whispered, "we will go down the hill now. We will stay low to the ground, and we will run. Now I count one, and two, and three."

He rose and scrambled down the hill in the classic infantry crouch, the Tervueren in a fast trot just behind his left heel—dogs were always trained left, thus the right side, the gun side, remained unhampered.

Casson did the best he could, shocked at how stiff he'd gotten just lying on the damp earth for thirty minutes.

At the foot of the hill, André took his shoes off, tied them at the laces, hung them around his neck, then stuffed his socks in his pockets. Casson followed his example, turning up his trouser cuffs as far as the knee. André stepped into the stream, Casson was right behind him. The water was so close to ice that it was barely liquid. "My God," he said. André shushed him. Casson couldn't move, the water washed over his shins. André grabbed his elbow with a bony hand and shoved him forward. The dog turned to make sure of him, soft eyes anxious—did this recalcitrant beast require a nip to get it moving? No, there it went, swearing beneath its breath with every step. Relieved, the Tervueren followed, close by André. For Casson, the sharp gravel of the midstream island was a relief for a few yards, then the water was even deeper and the dog had to swim, her brown ruff floating on the surface. At last, the far bank. The Tervueren shook off a great cloud of icy spray—just in case some part of Casson's clothing had accidentally remained dry. "Ah, Tempête," André said in mock disappointment, and the dog smiled at the compliment.

André sat in the grass to put his shoes and socks back on, Casson did the same. Then they ran up the side of a low hill until they reached a grove of poplar trees on the skyline. André stopped to catch his breath. "Ça va, monsieur?"

"Ça va, André."

He was a wiry kid with black hair that fell over his forehead, the latest in a long line of pages and squires that had been going off on one mission or another since the crusades. This was, after all, not really knight's business, conduction of a fugitive. The knight, red-faced, ham-fisted de Malincourt, was back at the chateau, where he'd settled in to wait for his son with a night-long discussion on the advantages of Charolais over Limousin steers, the price of rye seed, and the national disposition of Americans, who would, he thought, take their time before they got around to deciding they needed to come back over the sea and kill some more Germans.

Casson stayed quiet for a moment, hands on knees. Then a whip cracked the air in the poplar grove. Instinctively, André and Casson flinched. Then two more cracks, close together, this time a spring twig clipped from a branch. The dog—fear had been bred out of her many generations earlier—gave them an inquiring look: *Is this something you'd like me to see about?* André raised the bottom of his sweater, revealing the cross-hatched wooden grip of a huge, ancient revolver, but it was Casson's turn to take somebody by the elbow and before this particular war could get fairly underway they were galloping down the reverse slope of the hillside. They took cover for a moment, then headed south, toward a little road that would, eventually, take Casson to Lyons. At the next hilltop there was a view back to the river, a dull silver in the first light of dawn, and very beautiful.

He had a fantasy about how it would be in Lyons—the lover as night visitor. Long ago, when he'd been sixteen and in his next-to-last year at lycée, he'd had his first real love affair. In a world run by parents and teachers and maids it wasn't easy to find privacy, but the girl, Jeanette—eyes and hair a caramel shade of gold, dusting of pale freckles across the bridge of the nose—was patient and cunning and one day saw an opportunity for them to be alone. It could happen, thanks to a complicated fugue of family arrangements, very early one Sunday morning at the apartment of her grandmère in the 7th Arrondissement. Casson found the door open at dawn, went to a room where a slim shape lay buried beneath heavy comforters. Perhaps asleep, or just pretending—on this point he'd never been certain. He undressed quietly, stealthily, and slid in next to her. Then, just at that moment, she woke up, her smooth body warm and naked next to his, and breathed *"mon amour"* as she took him in her arms.

So he calculated his arrival at the Hotel du Parc for just after midnight. But no sleeping maiden awaited his caress. The hotel, high on the bank of the promontory formed by the Saône and the Rhône, was a Victorian horror of chocolate-colored brick, turrets and gables, off by itself in a small park behind a fence of rusted iron palings, with a view over a dark bridge and a dark church. Brooding, somber, just the place for consumptive poets or retired generals. Just the place for the night visitor.

However.

When Casson climbed the stone stairway that went from the street to the little park, he discovered every light in the hotel ablaze and the evening air heavy with the scent of roasting chickens. A trio—bass, drums, accordion—was pounding away at the Latin rhythm of the dance called the Java. There were shouts of encouragement, and shrieks of laughter—in short, the noisy symphony that can be performed only on the instrument of a hundred drunken wedding guests.

In the middle of it, Sleeping Beauty. She was barefoot, wearing a sash improvised from a tablecloth and shaking a tambourine liberated from the drum kit. She also had—a moment before he could believe his eyes—a rose clenched firmly between her teeth. "Hey!" she cried out. "Hey, hey!" She was leading a long line of dancers, first the groom—in his late thirties with a daring set of muttonchop whiskers, next his bride—some few years older, black hair pinned up, a dark mole on her cheek, bright red mouth, and eyes like burning coals.

The line—little kids and grandparents, friends of the groom, the bride's sisters, assorted hotel guests, at least one waiter—snaked from the dining room through the lobby, around an island of maroon velvet sofas, past the desk and the night manager wearing a wizard hat with a rubber band under his chin, and back to the dining room, hung with yards of pink crepe paper. Casson stood by the door, taking it all in. A fireman performed on the French horn. A man beckoned a woman to sit on his lap and they roared with pleasure as the spindly chair collapsed beneath them. Four feet protruded from the drape of a tablecloth, the people under the table either dead asleep or locked in some static, perhaps oriental, version of coition—it would have been hard to say and nobody cared.

The line reappeared in the lobby, Citrine in the lead, cheeks flushed, long hair flying, a particular expression on her face as she capered—the "savage dancer" of every Gypsy movie MGM had ever made. Then she saw him—"Jean-Claude!"—and ran to hug him. Her small breasts were squashed against his chest, she smelled like wine and chicken and perfume. She pulled back a little, her eyes shone, she was drunk and happy and in love.

Much later, they went up the stairs to her room on the top floor. Very slowly, they went up. On a table in the dining room he had discovered a bowl of red-wine punch, a single lemon slice floating on top, a glass ladle hung on the rim. Therefore, one took this step, then this. Many of these old hotels had been built with a tilting device that operated after midnight, so one had to go upstairs very, very deliberately. It helped to laugh.

The room was small, but very safe—the door secured by what appeared to be a simple lock that took a primitive iron key. But this turned out to be a deeply complicated system, to be used only by cellists or magicians—people with clever fingers. Probably Casson and Citrine could have opened the door themselves, at some future date, but a Good Samaritan happened to walk down the hall in a bathrobe and insisted on coming to their aid.

A small room, dark patterns on the wallpaper and the rug and the bedspread and the chair. Cold; rain a steady patter on the roof, and damp. Casson managed to get his tie off—over his head—threw his shirt and pants at a chair, turned to find Citrine looking sultry, wearing one stocking and an earring. They met somewhere on the bed; stupid, clumsy and hot, bawdy and shameless and prone to laugh. So drunk they weren't very good at anything, hands and mouths working away, too dizzy with getting what they wanted to be graceful or adept. But, maybe better that way: nothing went right, nothing went wrong, and they were too excited to care.

It was like being a kid again, he wanted her too much to be seductive. Her fault, he thought—the way she was, so many shadows and creases, angles and dark alleys; inside, outside, in between. She crawled around, as hot as he was, knees spread or one foot pointing at the ceiling. They didn't stay in one place very long, would find some position that made them breathe hard and fast but then, something else, something even better.

On and on it went. He didn't dare to finish, just fell back now and then to a condition of lazy heat. Not her; from time to time she gasped, shuddered, would stop for a moment and hang on to to him. Just the way, he thought, women were. They could do that. So, she came for both of them. Until, very late at night, she insisted—whispering to him, coaxing—and then he saw stars.

Of course he forgot to give her the letter. Nearly dawn when he remembered; watching her while she slept, in the gray light he could see the color of her hair and her skin, rested a hand on her hip, she woke up and they smoked a cigarette. Out the window, the Lyonnais moon a white quarter-slice from a children's book—it looked like a cat ought to be sitting on it. He rolled off the bed, dug around in his valise, gave her the letter and lit a candle so she could read it. She kissed him, touched his face, and yawned. Well, he thought, when you've been fucking all night it's not really the best time for a love letter.

Five days, they had.

After that there would be too much moonlight for crossing the line back into occupied France. They walked by the gray river, swollen in the spring flood. Late in the afternoon they had a fire in the little fireplace in Citrine's room and drank wine and made love. At night she had to go to the theatre. Casson came along, sat in the wings on a folding chair. He liked backstage life, the dusty flats, paint smells, stagehands intent on their business—plays weren't about life, plays were about curtains going up and down—actresses in their underwear, the director making everybody nervous. Casson enjoyed being the outsider.

It was a romantic comedy, a small sweet French thing. The cousin from the country, the case of mistaken identity, the secret message sent to the wrong person, well, actually the right person but not until the third act. Citrine played the ingenue's best friend. The ingenue wasn't bad, a local girl with carefully done-up hair and a rich father and good diction. But, next to Citrine, very plain. That didn't matter so much—it only made the boyfriend come off a little more of an idiot than the playwright really intended.

The audience was happy enough. Despite rationing they'd eaten fairly well, a version of traditional Lyonnais cooking, rich and heavy, not unlike the audience. They settled comfortably into the seats of the little theatre and dozed like contented angels through the boring parts.

Five days.

Dark, cool, spring days, sometimes it rained—it was always just about to. The skies stayed heavy; big, slow clouds moving south. Casson and Citrine sat on a bench by the river. "I could come to Paris," she said.

"Yes," he said. "But the life I live now is going bad."

She didn't understand.

"My phone's no good. I'm followed, sometimes."

"If the Germans are after you, you better go."

He shrugged. "I know," he said. "But I had to come here."

They stared at the river, a long row of barges moving south, the beat of the tugboat's engine reaching them over the water. Going to places far away.

She recited in terrible English: "The owl and the pussycat, it went to the sea, in the beautiful pea-green boat."

He laughed, rested the tips of two fingers against her lips.

The tugboat sounded its horn, it echoed off the hillsides above the river, a fisherman in a rowboat struggled against the current to get out of the way.

Citrine looked at her watch and sighed. "We better go back," she said.

They walked along the quay, people looked at them—at her. Almond eyes, wide, wide mouth, olive-brown hair with gold tints, worn loose, falling over her shoulders. Long brown leather coat with a belt tied at the waist, cream-colored scarf, brown beret. Casson had his hands shoved deep in the pockets of a black overcoat, no tie, no hat, hair ruffled by the wind. He seemed, as always, a little beat-up by life—knowing eyes, half-smile that said it didn't matter what you knew.

They walked like lovers, shoulders touching, talking only now and then. Sometimes she put her hand in the pocket of his coat. They wore their collars up, looked theatrical, sure of themselves. Some people didn't care for that, glanced at them a certain way as they passed by.

They turned into a narrow street that wound up the hill toward the hotel. Casson put his arm around her waist, she leaned against him as they walked. They stopped to look in the window of a boulangerie. Between the panniers of baguettes were a few red jam tarts in flaky crust. He went in and bought two of them, in squares of stiff bakery paper, and they ate them as they climbed the hill.

"How did you find the *passeur*?" she asked. It meant someone who helped you cross borders.

"Like anything else," he said. "Like looking for a travel agent or a doctor, you ask friends."

"Did it take a long time?"

She had crumbs in her hair, he brushed them out. "Yes," he said. "I was surprised. But then, it turned out my sister-in-law knew somebody. Who knew somebody."

"Perhaps it's dangerous now, to ask friends."

"Yes, it could be," he said. "But you do what you have to."

Their last night together he couldn't sleep.

He lay in the darkness and listened to her breathing. The hotel was quiet, sometimes a cough, now and then footsteps in the hall as somebody walked past their door. Sometimes he could hear a small bird in the park below the window. He smoked a cigarette, went from one part of his life to another, none of it worked, all of it scared him. Careful not to wake her, he got out of bed, went to the window, and stared out into the night. The city was silent and empty, lost in the stars.

He wanted to get dressed and go out, go for a long walk until he got tired. But it wasn't wise to do that any more, the police would demand to see your papers, would ask too many questions. When he got tired of standing, he sat in a big chair. It was three in the morning before he slid back under the covers. Citrine woke up, made a little noise of surprise, then flowed across the bed and pressed tight against him. At last, he thought, the night visitor.

"I don't want you to go away," she said by his ear.

He smoothed her hair. "I have to," he said.

"Because, if you do, I will never see you again."

"No. It isn't true."

"Yes it is. I knew this would happen. Years ago. Like a fortune-teller knows things—in dreams."

After a time he said, "Citrine, please."

"I'm sorry," she said. She took his hand and put it between her legs. "Until we go to sleep," she said.

29 April, 1941.

She insisted on going to the train with him. A small station to the north of Lyons, they took a cab there. He had to ride local trains all day, to Chassieu and Loyettes and Pont-de-Chéruy, old Roman villages along the Rhône. Then, at dusk, he would join the secret route that ran to a village near the river Allier, where one of the de Malincourts would meet him.

The small engine and four coaches waited on the track. "You have your sandwiches?" she said.

"Yes."

She looked at her watch. "It's going to be late."

"I think it's usual," he said.

Passengers waited for the doors to open. Country people—seamed faces, weatherbeaten, closed. The men wore old mufflers stuffed down the fronts of buttoned suit jackets, baggy pants, scuffed boots. The women wore shawls over their heads, carried baskets covered with cloths. Casson stood out—he didn't belong here, and he wasn't the only one. He could pick out three others, two men and a woman. They didn't live in Chassieu either. Taking the little trains was a good idea— until four or five of you tried it at the same time. Well, too bad, he thought, there's nothing to be done about it now.

"What if you came down here," she said quietly.

"To live, you mean."

"Yes."

He paused a moment. "It isn't easy," he said. Clearly he had worked on the idea.

"Maybe you don't want to," she said.

"No. I'm going to try."

She took his arm, there was not much they could say, now. The engine vented steam, a door opened in one of the coaches and a conductor tossed his cigarette away and stationed himself at the bottom of the steps. The people on the platform began to board the train.

"Remember what we talked about last night," he said, leaning close so she could hear him. "If you have to move, a postcard to Langlade's office."

She nodded.

"You're not to call me, Citrine."

The conductor climbed to the bottom step and shouted "All aboard for Chassieu."

He took her in his arms and she held on to him, her head on his chest. "How long?" she said.

"I don't know. As soon as I can manage it."

"I don't want to lose you," she said.

He kissed her hair. The conductor leaned out of the coach and raised a little red flag that the engineer could see. "All aboard," he said.

"I love you," Casson said. "Remember."

He started to work himself free of her arms, then she let him go. He ran for the train, climbed aboard, looked out the cloudy window. He could see she was searching for him. He rapped on the glass. Then she saw him. She wasn't crying, her hands were deep in her pockets. She nodded at him, smiled a certain way—*I meant everything I said, everything I did.* Then she waved. He waved back. A man in a raincoat standing nearby lowered his newspaper to look at her. The train started to pull out, moving very slowly. She couldn't see the man, he was behind her. She waved again, walked a few paces along with the train. Her face was radiant, strong, she wanted him to know he did not have to worry about her, together they would do what had to be done. The man behind Citrine looked toward the end of the station, Casson followed his eyes and saw another man, with slicked-down hair, who took a pipe out of his mouth, then put it back in.

All day long he rode slow trains that rattled through the countryside and stopped at little stations. Sometimes it rained, droplets running sideways across the window, sometimes a shaft of sunlight broke through a cloud and lit up a hillside, sometimes the cloud blew away and he could see the hard blue spring sky. In the fields the April plowing was over, crumbled black earth ran to the trees in the border groves, oaks and elms, with early leaves that trembled in the wind.

Casson stood in the alcove at the end of the car, staring out the open door, hypnotized by the rhythm of the wheels over the rail points. His mind was already back in Paris, holding imaginary conversations with Hugo Altmann, trying to win him over to some version of René Guillot's strategy. The objective: move *Hotel Dorado* to the unoccupied zone, under the auspices of the committee in Vichy rather than the German film board. It would have to be done officially, it would take Guske, or somebody like him, to stamp the papers. But, with Altmann's help, it might be possible.

On the other hand, Altmann liked the film, really liked it, probably he'd want to keep it in Paris. Was there a way to ruin it for him? Not completely—could they just knock off a corner, maybe, so it wasn't quite so appealing? No, they'd never get away with it. Then too, what about Fischfang? As a Jew, nobody was going to give him the papers to do anything. But that, at least, could be overcome—he'd have to enter the *Zone Non-Occupée*, the ZNO, just as Casson had, then slip into a false identity, down in Marseilles perhaps.

No, that wouldn't work. Fischfang couldn't just abandon his assorted women and children to the mercies of the Paris Gestapo, they'd have to come along. But not across the river, it probably couldn't be done that way. *New papers*. That might work—start the false identity on the German side of the line. How to manage that? Not so difficult—Fischfang was a communist, he must be in contact with Comintern operatives, people experienced in clandestine operations—forging identity papers an everyday affair for them.

Or, the hell with *Hotel Dorado*. He'd let Altmann have it, in effect would trade it for Citrine. Of course he'd have to find some way to live, to earn a living in the ZNO, but that wouldn't be impossible. He could, could, do any number of things.

The train slowed, a long curve in the track, then clattered over a road crossing. An old farmer waited on a horse cart, the reins held loosely in his hand, watching the train go past. The tiny road wound off behind him, to nowhere, losing itself in the woods and fields. In some part of Casson's mind the French countryside went on forever, from little village to little village, as long as you stayed on the train.

Back in Paris, he telephoned Altmann.

"Casson! Where the hell have you been? Everybody's been looking for you."

"I just went off to the seashore, to Normandy, for a couple of days."

"Your secretary didn't know where you were."

"That's impossible! I *told* her—if Altmann calls, give him the number of my hotel."

"Well, she didn't."

"Hugo, I'm sorry, you'll have to forgive me. You know what it's like, these days—she does the best she can."

"Well . . ."

"Anyhow, here I am."

"Casson, there are people who want to meet you. Important people."

"Oh?"

"Yes. I have organized a dinner for us. Friday night."

"All right."

"Do you know the Brasserie Heininger?"

"In the Seventh?"

"Yes."

"I know it."

"Eight-thirty, then. Casson?"

"Yes?"

"Important people."

"I understand. That's this Friday, the fourth of May."

"Yes. Any problem, let me know immediately."

"I'll be there," Casson said.

He hung up, wrote down the time and place in his appointment book.

The Brasserie Heininger—of all places! What had gotten into Altmann? He knew better than that. The Heininger was a garish nightmare of gold mirrors and red plush—packed with Americans and nouveaux riches of every description before the war, now much frequented by German officers and their French "friends." Long ago, when he was twelve, his aunt—his father's charmingly demented sister—would take him to the Heininger, confiding in a whisper that one came "only for the crème anglaise, my precious, please remember that." Then, in the late thirties, there'd been some sort of wretched murder there, a Balkan folly that spread itself across the newspapers for a day or two. His one visit in adult life had been a disaster—a dinner for an RKO executive, his wife, her mother, and Marie-Claire. A platter of Heininger's best oysters, the evil Belons, had proved too much for the Americans, and it was downhill from there.

Well, he supposed it didn't matter. Likely it was the "important people" who had chosen the restaurant. Whoever they were. Altmann hadn't been his usual self on the telephone. Upset about Casson's absence—and something else. Casson drummed his fingers on the desk, stared out the window at the rue Marbeuf. What?

Frightened, he thought.

❖

A bad week.

Spring in the river valleys—tumbled skies and painters' clouds—seemed like a dream to him now. In Paris, the *grisaille,* gray light, had descended over the city and it was dusk from morning till night.

He went out to the Montrouge district, beyond the porte de Châtillon and the old cemetery, to the little factory streets around the rue Gabriel, where Bernard Langlade had the workshop that made lightbulbs. The nineteenth century; tiny cobbled streets shadowed by brick factory walls, huge rusted stacks with towers of brown smoke curling slowly into a dead sky.

He trudged past foundries that seemed to go on for miles; the thudding of machines that hammered metal—he could feel each stroke in his heart—the smell, no, he thought, the *taste,* of nitric acid on brass, showers of orange sparks seen through wire mesh, a man with a mask of soot around his eyes, hauling on a long wrench, sensing Casson's stare and giving it back to him. Casson looked away. His films had danced on the edges of this world but it was a real place and nobody made movies about these lives.

He got lost in a maze of smoked brick and burnt iron and asked directions of two workmen who answered in a Slavic language he couldn't understand. He walked for a long time, more than an hour, where oil slicks floated on a canal, then, at last, a narrow opening in a stone wall and a small street sign, raised letters chiseled into the wall in the old Paris style, IMPASSE SAVIER. At the end of the alley, a green metal door—Compagnie Luminex.

Inside it was a beehive, workers sitting at long assembly tables, the line served by a young boy in a cap who, using every ounce of his weight, threw himself against the handle of an industrial cart piled high with metal fittings of various shapes and sizes. In one corner, a milling machine in operation, its motor whining from overuse. It was hot in the workroom—the roar of a kiln on the floor below explained why—and there were huge noisy blowers that vibrated in their mounts.

"Jean-Claude!"

It was Langlade, standing at the door of a factory office and beckoning to him. He wore a gray smock, which made him look like a workshop foreman. In the office, three women clerks, keeping books and typing letters. They were heavily built and dark, wearing old cardigan sweaters against the damp factory air, and had cigarettes burning in ashtrays made from clamshells. Langlade closed the half-glass door to the workshop floor, which reduced the flywheel and grinding noises to whispered versions of themselves. They shook hands, Langlade showed him into a small, private office and closed the door.

"Jean-Claude," he said fondly, opening the bottom drawer of his desk, taking out a bottle of brandy. "I can only imagine what would get you all the way out here." He gave Casson a conspiratorial smile—clearly an affair of the heart was to be discussed. "Business?" he said innocently.

"A little talk, Bernard."

"Ahh, I thought—maybe you just happened to be in the neighborhood." They both laughed at this. Langlade began working on the cork.

"Well, in fact I called your office, three or four times, and they told me, Monsieur is out at Montrouge, so I figured out this is where I'd have to come. But, Bernard, *look* at all this."

Langlade smiled triumphantly, a man who particularly wanted to be admired by his friends. "What did you think?"

"Well, I didn't know. What I imagined—three or four workmen, maybe. To me, a lightbulb. I never would have guessed it took so much to make a thing like that. But, really, Bernard, the sad fact is I'm an idiot."

"No, Jean-Claude. You're just like everybody else—me included. When Yvette's *Papa* died, and she told me we had this odd little business, I hadn't the faintest idea what to do about it. Sell it, I supposed. And we tried, but the country had nothing but labor trouble and inflation that year, and nobody in France would buy any kind of industrial anything. So, we ran it. We made Christmas-tree lights and we had small contracts with Citroën and Renault for the miniature bulbs that light up gas gauges and so forth on automobile dashboards. Actually, Jean-Claude, to make a lightbulb, you have to be able to do all sorts of things. It's like a simple kitchen match, you never think about it but it takes a lot of different processes, all of them technical, to produce some stupid little nothing." He grunted, twisted the cork, managed to get it free of the bottle.

"Bernard," Casson said, gesturing toward the work area, "Christmas-tree lights? *Joyeux Noël!*"

Langlade laughed. He searched the bottom drawer, found two good crystal glasses. He held one up to the light and scowled. "Fussy?"

"No."

"When I'm alone, I clean them with my tie."

"Fine for me, Bernard."

Langlade poured each of them a generous portion, swirled his glass and inhaled the fumes. Casson did the same. "Well, well," he said.

Langlade shrugged, meaning, if you can afford it, why not? "When the Germans got here," he said, "they began to make big orders, for trucks, and those armored whatnots they drive around in. We did that for five months, then they asked, could you buy some more elaborate equipment, possibly in Switzerland? Well, yes, we could. There wasn't much point in saying no, the job would just go across the street to somebody else. So, we bought the new machinery, and began to make optical instruments. Like periscopes for submarines, and for field use also, a type of thing where a soldier in a trench can look out over the battlefield without getting his head blown off. We don't make the really delicate stuff—binoculars, for instance. What we make has to accept hard use, and survive."

"Is there that much of it?"

Langlade leaned over his desk. "Jean-Claude, I was like you. A civilian, what did I know. I went about my business, got into bed with a woman now and then, saw friends, made a little money, had a family. I never could have imagined the extent of anything like this. These people, army and navy, they think in thousands. As in, thousands and thousands." Langlade gave him a certain very eloquent and Gallic look—it meant he was making money, and it meant he must never be asked how much, or anything like that, because he was making so much that to say it out loud would be to curse the enterprise—the jealous gods would overhear and throw down some bad-luck lightning bolts from the top of commercial Olympus. Where the tax people also kept an office.

Casson nodded that he understood, then smiled, honestly happy for a friend's success.

"Now," Langlade said, "what can I do for you?"

"Citrine," Casson said.

A certain smile from Langlade. "The actress."

"Yes."

"All right."

"We have become lovers, Bernard. It's the second time—we had a *petite affaire* ten years ago, but this is different."

Langlade made a sympathetic face; yes, he knew how it was. "She's certainly beautiful, Jean-Claude. For myself, I couldn't stop looking at her long enough to go to bed."

Casson smiled. "We just spent a week together, in Lyons—that's between you and me by the way. Now, I've had some kind of problem in the Gestapo office on the rue des Saussaies. Bernard, it's so stupid—I went up there to get an *Ausweis* to go to Spain, and they asked me about military service and something told me not to mention that I'd been reactivated in May and gone up to the Meuse. You know, there are thousands of French soldiers still in Germany, in prison camps. I decided it would be safer not to admit anything. So, I didn't. Well, time went by, somebody sent a paper to somebody else, and they caught me in a lie."

Langlade shook his head and made a sour face. The Germans were finicky about paper in a way the Latin French found amusing—until the problem settled on their own doorstep.

"The next thing was, they started reading my mail and listening to my phone. So, when I was with Citrine down in Lyons, I told her that if she wanted to get in touch with me she could send a postcard to your office, your law office in the 8th is the address I gave her."

He waited for Langlade to smile and say it was all right, but he didn't. Instead, his expression darkened into a certain kind of discomfort.

"Look, Jean-Claude," he said. "We've known each other for twenty years, I'm not going to beat around the bush with you. If Citrine sends me a postcard, well, I'll see that you get it. On the other hand, next time you have a chance to talk to her, would it be too much to ask for you to find some other way of doing this?"

Casson wasn't going to show what he felt. "No problem at all, Bernard. In fact, I can take care of it right away."

"You can understand, can't you? This work I'm doing matters to them, Jean-Claude. It isn't like they're actually watching me, but, you know, I see these military people all the time, from the procurement offices, and all it would take would be for my secretary over in the other office to decide she wasn't getting enough money, or, or whatever it might be. Look, I have an idea, what about Arnaud? You know, he's always doing this and that and the other, and it's just the sort of thing that would appeal to him."

"You're right," Casson said. "A much better idea."

"So now, here's what we'll do. Let's go back to Paris—I can call a driver and car—and treat ourselves to a hell of a lunch, hey? Jean-Claude, how about it?"

Friday, 4 May. 4:20 P.M.

End of the week, a slow day in the office, Casson kept looking at his watch. Seven hours—and the dinner at Brasserie Heininger would be over. Of course, he lied to himself, he didn't have to go, the world wouldn't come to an end. No, he thought, don't do that. "Mireille?" he called out. "Could you come in for a minute?"

"Monsieur?"

"Why don't you go home early, Mireille—it won't be so crowded on the train."

"Thank you, Monsieur Casson."

"Could you mail this for me, on the way?"

Of course.

A postcard—the people who watched the mail supposedly didn't bother with postcards—telling Citrine to write him care of a café where they knew him. He had to assume Mireille wasn't followed, that she could mail a postcard without somebody retrieving it. It meant he could save an anonymous telephone he'd discovered, in an office at one of the soundstages out at Billancourt, for a call he might want to make later on.

Mireille called out good night and left, Casson returned to the folder on his desk. Best to prepare for an important meeting. The folder held various pencil budgets for *Hotel Dorado,* a list of possible changes to the story line, names of actors and actresses and scenic designers—they were just now reaching the stage where certain individuals were, almost mystically, *exactly right* for the film. Also in the folder, a list of new projects Altmann had mentioned over the last few months; you never knew when one of these "ideas" was going to leap out of its coffin and start dancing around the crypt.

Casson read down the page and sighed out loud. Ah yes, the Boer War. The whole industry was planning movies about the noble Boers that spring, somebody in Berlin—Goebbels?—had decided to make them fashionable. A group of farmers, not exactly German but at least Dutch, thus Nordic and sincere, had carried out guerrilla actions and given the British army fits in South Africa. A war, according to German thinking, that made England look bad: imperialist, power-hungry, and cruel. One German company, Casson had heard, was about to go into production on something called *President Kruger,* a Boer War spectacle employing 40,000 extras.

The phone.

Now what?

Maybe he shouldn't answer. No, it might be Altmann, some change of plans, or even, gift from heaven, dinner canceled. "Hello?"

"Monsieur Casson?"

"Yes?"

"Maître Versol here."

What? Who? Oh Jesus! The lawyer for the LeBeau company!

Versol cleared his throat, then continued. "I thought I would telephone to see if any progress has been made on locating our missing inventory. You will recall, monsieur, some four hundred beards, fashioned from human hair and of a superior quality, provided for your use in the film *Samson and Delilah.*"

"Yes, Maître Versol, I do remember."

"We feel we have been very patient, monsieur."

"Yes," Casson said. "That is true."

He let Versol go on for a time, as he always did, until the lawyer felt honor had been satisfied and he could hang up.

Casson looked at his watch again. Almost five. He lifted the top from a fancy yellow box, unfolded the tissue paper, studied the tie he'd bought on the boulevard earlier that day. Navy blue with a beige stripe, very austere and conservative. Just the thing, he hoped, for the "important people" who had inspired that strange little note in Altmann's voice. Probably it wouldn't matter at all, it would simply mean he had done the best he could.

On the way home, between the La Muette Métro and the rue Chardin, he stopped at the busy café where they saw him every morning. He leaned on the copper-covered bar and drank a coffee. "I may get a postcard here," he confided to the proprietor. "It's from *some-body*—you understand. I'd rather my wife didn't see it."

The proprietor smiled, rubbing a glass with a bar towel. "I understand, monsieur. You may depend on me."

8:40 P.M.

The Brasserie Heininger, throbbing with Parisian life on a Friday night. Once past the blackout curtains: polished wood, golden light, waiters in fancy whiskers and green aprons. Very fin-de-siècle, Casson thought. Fin-de-something, anyhow.

Papa Heininger, the fabled proprietor, greeted him at the door, then passed him along to the mâitre d'. The man said good evening with a certain subtle approval, more to do with what he wasn't than what he was—he wasn't Romanian, wasn't wearing a bright-blue suit, wasn't a coal merchant or a black-market dealer or a pimp.

"Monsieur Altmann's table, please."

A polite nod. *A German, true, but a German executive.* Not so bad, for that spring. Party of four, all men, thus ashes on the tablecloth but at least a vigorous attack on the wine list. "That will be table fourteen, monsieur. This way, please."

Not the best table but certainly the most requested: a small hole in the mirror where an assassin had fired a submachine gun the night the Bulgarian headwaiter was murdered in the ladies' WC. The table where an aristocratic Englishwoman had once recruited Russian spies. The table where, only a few nights earlier, the companion of a German naval officer had been shooting peas at other diners, using a rolled-up *carte des vins* as a blowpipe.

The three men at the table rose, Altmann made the introductions. Clearly they'd been there for a while, most of the way through a bottle of champagne. Herr Schepper—something like that—gestured to the waiter for another to be brought. He had fine white hair and a fine face, a pink shave and shining eyes. One of a class of men, Casson thought, who are given money all their lives because people don't really know what else to do with them. This one was, if Casson understood Altmann correctly, a very senior something at UFA, the Continental Film parent company in Berlin.

The other man waited his turn, then smiled as he was introduced. They shook hands, shared a brief *reniflement*—the term came from the world of dogs, where it meant a mutual sniff on first meeting—then settled back down at the table. *Herr Franz Millau.* Something in the way Altmann articulated the name enabled Casson to hear it perfectly.

He was—nobody exactly said. Perhaps he was "our friend" or "my associate" or one of those. Not a particularly impressive exterior. High domed forehead; sandy hair. An old thirty-five or a young forty-five. Eyeglasses in thin silver frames, lawyer eyeglasses, worn in a way that suggested he only took them off before he went to sleep. And a small, predatory mouth, prominent against a fair complexion that made his lips seem brightly colored. He was not unpleasant in any way Casson could put a name to, so, what was wrong with him? Perhaps, Casson thought, it was a certain gap, between an unremarkable presence, and, just below, a glittering and pungent arrogance that radiated from him like the noonday sun. Herr Millau was powerful, and believed it was in the natural order of things that he should be.

Herr Schepper did not speak French. That kept them busy, with Altmann as translator, discovering that he loved Paris, had attended the opera, was fond of Monet, liked pâté de foie gras. A fresh bottle of Veuve Clicquot arrived, and, a moment later, an astonishing seafood platter. Everyone said ah. A masterpiece on a huge silver tray: every kind of clam and oyster, cockle and mussel, whelk and crayfish—Judgment Day on the ocean floor. *"Bon appétit!"* the waiter cried out.

One small complication.

Altmann and Schepper had to go on to a certain club in a distant arrondissement, where they were to have a late supper with a banker. Schepper said something in German. "He says," Altmann translated, " 'you must take good care of the people with the money.' " Schepper nodded to help make the point.

"That's certainly true," Casson said.

"Well then," Millau said, "you two should be going. Perhaps Monsieur Casson will be kind enough to keep me company while I eat my supper."

Merde. But everybody else seemed to agree that this was the perfect solution, and Casson was effectively trapped. A glass of champagne, a few creatures from the sea, some additional travelogue from Herr Schepper, then everybody stood up to shake hands and begin the complicated business of departure.

At which moment, from the corner of his eye, Casson spotted Bruno. A party of six or seven swept past like ships in the night, Casson had only a blurred impression. Some German uniforms, a cloud of perfume, a woman laughing at something that wasn't funny, and, in the middle of it—Bruno in a silk tie and blinding white shirt, a young woman— blonde, green-eyed—on his arm. Their eyes met, Bruno winked. *Good to see you getting about with the right people, at last—glad you've seen the light.* Then they went around the corner of a wall of banquettes and disappeared.

Altmann and Schepper left.

"Friend of yours?" Millau said.

"Acquaintance."

"Some more champagne?"

"Thank you. How do you come to speak French like that, if you don't mind my asking?"

"No, I don't mind. As a youngster I lived in Alsace—you know, *un, deux, trois, vier, fünf.*"

Casson laughed politely.

"That's the way to learn a language, as a child," Millau said.

"That's what they say."

"What about you, *Sprechen Sie Deutsch?*"

"No, not at all."

"Maybe some English, then?"

"A little. I can get along in a commercial situation if everybody slows down."

Millau took a heavy black cigar from his pocket, stripped off the band and the cellophane. "Perhaps you'd care to join me."

"No, thank you."

Millau took his time lighting up, made the match flame jump up and down, at last blew out a stream of smoke, strong, but not unpleasant. He shook his head. "I like these things too much."

Casson lit a Gauloise.

Millau leaned on the table, spoke in a confidential tone. "Let me begin by telling you that I'm an intelligence officer," he said. "Reasonably senior, here in Paris."

"I see," Casson said.

"Yes. I work for the *Sicherheitsdienst*, the SD, in the counterespionage office up on the avenue Foch. We started out as the SS foreign service, and in a sense we still are that, though success has brought us some broader responsibility."

Millau paused, Casson indicated he understood what had been said.

"We've been getting to know you for a few months, Monsieur Casson, keeping an eye on you, and so forth, to see who we were dealing with."

Casson laughed nervously.

"Ach, the way people are! I assure you, we can't be surprised or offended by all these little sins, the same thing, over and over. We're like priests, or doctors."

He stopped for a moment to inhale on the cigar, making the tip glow red, to see if it was still lit. "We got on to you down in Spain—the British were interested in you, and that was of interest to us. We were . . . nearby, when you met with a woman who calls herself Marie-Noëlle, Lady Marensohn, a representative of the British Secret Intelligence Service who we believe attempted to recruit you for clandestine operations. She is, by the way, residing with us at the moment."

Casson felt the blood leave his face. Millau waited to see if he might want to comment, but he said nothing.

"Our view, Monsieur Casson, is that you did not accept recruitment."

Casson waited a beat but there was nowhere he could hide. "No," he said, "I didn't."

Millau nodded, confirming a position held in some earlier discussion. "And why not?"

There wasn't any time to think. "I don't know."

"No?"

Casson shrugged. "I'm French—not British, not German. I simply want to live my life, and be left in peace."

From Millau's reaction Casson could tell he'd given the right answer. "And who would blame you for that, eh?" Millau said with feeling.

"What got us into this situation in the first place was all these people meddling in politics. All we ever wanted in Germany was to be left alone, to get on with our lives. But, sadly, that was not to be, and you see what happened next. And, more to come."

Casson's expression was sympathetic. He realized that Millau possessed a very dangerous quality: he was likeable.

"We have no business fighting with England, I'll tell you that," Millau said. "Every week—I'm sure I'm not saying something you find surprising—there's some kind of initiative; diplomatic, private, what have you. At the Vatican or in Stockholm. It's just a matter of time and we'll settle things between us. Our real business is in the east, with the Bolsheviks, and so is Britain's business, and we're just sorry that certain individuals in London are doing everything they can to keep us apart."

"Hmm," Casson said.

"So, that's where you come in. My section, that is, *AMT* IV, is particularly concerned with terrorist operations, sabotage, bombing, assassination. We fear that elements within the British government plan to initiate such acts in France, a carefully organized campaign—and if a number of people die it is of no particular concern to them, they tend to be very liberal with French life."

Millau made sure this had sunk in, then he said, "This isn't a fantasy. We know it's going to happen, and we believe they will contact you again. This time, we want you to accept. Do what they ask of you. And let us know about it."

The brasserie was noisy, people talking and laughing, somebody was singing. The air was thick with cigarette smoke and the aroma of grilled beef. Casson took his time, stubbing out the Gauloise in an ashtray. "Well," he said.

"How about it?"

"Well, I don't think they'll actually approach me again," Casson said. If Marie-Noëlle talked to them, he realized, he was finished. Would she? Considering what they did to people, would she? "I made it clear to them it wasn't something I was going to do."

"Yes," Millau said softly, meaning that he understood. "But I'll tell you what." He smiled, conspiratorial and knowing. "I'll bet you anything you care to name that they come back to you."

❖

3:20 A.M.

The music on his radio faded in and out—if he held the aerial he could hear it. *Adagio for Strings,* Samuel Barber. Coming in from far away. Outside it rained on and off, distant thunder muttering up in Normandy somewhere. The worst of the storm had come through earlier— on the way home from the Brasserie Heininger he'd had to take shelter in the Métro to avoid getting soaked, standing next to a woman in a sweater and skirt. "Just made it," he'd said as the rain poured down.

"A little luck anyhow," she'd agreed. "I have to go see somebody about a job tomorrow and this is what I have to wear."

Oh, what kind of job—but he didn't.

They stood quietly, side by side, then the rain stopped and she left, swinging her hips as she climbed the staircase just so he would know what he'd missed. He knew. He lay on top of the covers in the darkness and listened to the violin. It would have been nice to have her with him; big, pale body rising and falling. But Citrine, I didn't.

Good times they'd had in the Hotel du Parc. He'd been leaning against a wall, a cigarette in the corner of his mouth. She told him he looked like a place Pigalle tough guy and he'd given her back the classic line, *"Tiens, montrez-moi ton cul."* Show me your ass. In lycée, they used to wonder if M. Lepic, the Latin teacher, said that to Mme. Lepic on Saturday night.

Casson peered at his watch on the table beside the bed. A few minutes after three. What if he went out somewhere and called the hotel in Lyons—let it ring and ring until an infuriated manager answered. *This is the police. I want to speak with the woman in Room 28. Now!*

Sirens. Air-raid sirens. Now what? Antiaircraft fire—to the north of the city, he thought. Like a drum, in deliberate time. Then he heard airplanes. He swung his legs off the bed, made certain the apartment was dark, went out on the terrace.

Searchlights, north of him, across the river. The AA guns working away, four or five beats to the measure, little yellow lights climbing to heaven. And, then, planes overhead, a lot of them, flying low, the drone hammering off the walls in the narrow rue Chardin. Across the street and down a little way, a couple in nightshirts out on their balcony, the woman with a fur stole thrown around her shoulders, gazing up at the sky. Then he saw others, the whole neighborhood was out.

To the north, bombs, close enough to hear the articulated explosions. Orange light stuttered against the sky—he could see clearly the dark undersides of rain clouds, like frozen smoke, lit by fires. The British are at work, he thought. Among the factories on the outskirts of the city. When the bombing faded to a rumble, fire sirens joined the air-raid sirens. Then the all-clear sounded, and the fire engines were joined by ambulances.

Casson got tired of standing on the terrace, sat against the wall just inside his living room. First edge of false dawn in the spring, the sky not so dark as it was, a few birds singing on the rooftops. The sirens had stopped, now there remained only a certain smell on the morning air. The smell of burning. He was falling asleep. Now that it was dawn, he could sleep, since whatever might come in the night would have to wait another day.

Then, Monday morning, when he got to the office at ten, Mireille had a message for him. "A woman telephoned, a Madame Detweiler."

"Who?"

"The secretary of an officer called Guske. From the rue des Saussaies."

"And?"

"She said to tell you that your *Ausweis* to go to the Vichy zone is under consideration, it doesn't look like there's going to be a problem, and they will have a determination for you by May fifteenth. If you have any questions, you are encouraged to call *Obersturmbannführer* Guske."

"Thank you, Mireille," he said, and went into his office.

Was that good news, he wondered, or bad? After a moment he realized it wasn't good or bad, it wasn't anything. It was simply their way of talking to him. It was simply their way of telling him that they owned him.

THE
SECRET
AGENT

*C*asson stood on the balcony, just after midnight, and stared out over the jagged line of rooftops. The city was ghostly in blue lamplight, and very quiet. He could hear distant footsteps, and night birds singing in the parks. The preparation of an escape, he thought, whatever else it did, showed you your life from an angle of profound reality. Where to go. How to get there. Friends and money must be counted up, but then, *which* friends—who will really help? How much money? And, if you can't get that, how much? And then, most of all, when? Because *these* doors, once you went through them, closed behind you.

There's no question when, he told himself, the time is now. If it isn't already too late.

A few things had to be settled before he left. He started Tuesday morning, getting in touch with Fischfang. This lately was not easy—messages left with shopkeepers, calls returned from public telephones—but by the end of the week they met at a vacant apartment out in the 19th, that looked out on the railyards.

The apartment was for rent, the landlord's agent a plump little gentleman wearing an alpine hat with a brush. "Look around all you like, boys," he said as he opened the door. "And as to the rent, they say I'm a reasonable man." He winked, then trotted off down the staircase.

Fischfang was tense, shadows like bruises beneath his eyes, but very calm. Different. It was, Casson thought, the revolver. No longer kept in a drawer, perhaps worn under the arm, or in the belt—it had a certain logic of its own and changed the person who carried it.

And Fischfang hadn't come alone, he had a friend—a helper or a bodyguard, something like that. Not French, from somewhere east of the Oder, somewhere out in Comintern land. Ivanic, he called himself. In his twenties, he was dark-eyed and pale, with two days' growth of beard, wore a cap tilted down over sleepy eyes. He waited in the kitchen while Casson and Fischfang talked, hands clasped behind his head as he sat against a wall.

Casson gave Fischfang a lot of money, all he could. But, he thought, maybe it didn't matter any more. Now that it was time to meet in vacant apartments, now that Ivanic had showed up, maybe the days of worrying about something as simple as money were over. Fischfang put the packet of francs away, reached inside his jacket, handed Casson a school notebook with a soft cover.

"New draft," Fischfang said. "Though I somehow get the feeling," he added ruefully, "that our little movie is slipping away into its own fog."

Casson paged through the notebook. The scenes had been written in cafés, on park benches, or at kitchen tables late at night—spidery script densely packed on the lined paper, coffee-stained, blotted, and, Casson sensed, finely made. He could feel it as he skimmed the lines. It was autumn, a train pulled into a little station, the guests got off, their Paris clothes out of place in the seaside village. They went to the hotel, to their rooms, did what people did, said what they said—Casson looked up at Fischfang. "Pretty good?"

Fischfang thought a moment. "Maybe it is. I didn't have too much time to think about it."

"Not always the worst thing."

"No, that's true."

Casson paced around the room. The apartment was filthy—it smelled like train soot, the floor was littered with old newspaper. On the wall by the door somebody had written in pencil, *E. We've gone to Montreuil.* In the railyard below the window, the switching engines were hard at work, couplings crashed as boxcars were shunted from track to track, then made up into long trains, Casson peered through the cloudy glass. Fischfang came and stood by his side. One freight train seemed just about ready to go, Casson counted a hundred and twenty cars, with tanks and artillery pieces under canvas, cattle wagons for the horses, and three locomotives. "Looks like somebody's in for it," he said.

"Russia, maybe. That's the local wisdom. But, wherever it's going, they won't like it."

"No." Directly below them, a switching engine vented white steam with a loud hiss. "Who's your friend?" Casson said quietly.

"Ivanic? I think he comes from the NKVD. He's just waiting for the fighting to start, then he can go to work."

"And you?"

"I'm his helper."

Casson stared out at the railyard, clouds of gray smoke, the railwaymen in faded blue jackets and trousers.

"We all thought," Fischfang said slowly, his voice almost a whisper, "that life would go on. But it won't. Tell me, so much money, what does it mean, Jean-Claude?"

"I have to go away."

Fischfang nodded slowly, he understood. "It's best."

"They're after me," Casson said.

Fischfang turned and stared at him for a moment. "After you?"

"Yes."

"Did you do something?"

"Yes," Casson said, after a moment. "Nothing much—and it didn't work."

Fischfang smiled. "Well then, good luck."

They shook hands. "And to you."

There was nothing else to say, Casson left the apartment, Ivanic watched him go.

That afternoon he went up to the Galéries Lafayette, the huge department store just north of Opéra. He found the buyers' offices on the top floor and knocked on Véronique's door. "Jean-Claude!" she said, pleased to see him. A tiny space, costume jewelry everywhere; spread across a desk, crowded on shelves that rose to the ceiling— wooden bracelets painted lustrous gold, shimmering glass diamonds in rings and earrings, ropes of glowing pearls. "The sultan's treasure," she said.

For herself she had great honesty of style—wore a black shirt with a green scarf tied at the neck. Short hair, clear eyes, a great deal of intelligence and a little bit of expensive perfume. "Let's take a walk around the store," she said.

They walked from room to room, past bridal gowns and evening gowns, floral housedresses and pink bathrobes. "Have you heard about Arnaud and his wife?" she said.

"No. What's happened?"

"I had lunch with Marie-Claire yesterday, she told me they weren't living together. He moved out."

"Why is that? They always seemed to have, a good arrangement."

Véronique shrugged. "Who knows," she said gloomily. "I think it's the Occupation. Lately the smallest thing, and everything comes apart."

It was busy in the luggage department—fine leather and brass fittings from the ancient saddlery ateliers of Paris. A crowd of German soldiers, businessmen with their wives, a few Japanese naval officers.

"Véronique," he said. "I need to go south again."

"Right now the moon is full, Jean-Claude."

"So it would be, what, fourteen days?"

"Well, yes, at least. Then there are people who have to be talked to, and, all the various complications."

A woman in traditional Breton costume—black dress, white hat with wings—was demonstrating a waffle iron, pouring yellow batter from a cup into the iron, then heating it over a small gas burner.

"All right," he said. "There's a chance I'll get an *Ausweis*. In a few weeks. Maybe."

"Can you wait?"

"I'm not sure. Things, things are going on."

"What things, Jean-Claude? It's important to tell me."

"I'm under pressure to work for them. I mean, really work for them."

"Can you refuse?"

"Perhaps, I'm not sure. I've been over it and over it, probably the best thing for me is to slip quietly into the ZNO, pick up Citrine, then go out—to Spain or Portugal. Once we're there, we'll find some country that will take us. I can remember May of last year—then it mattered where you went. Now it doesn't."

They stood together at a railing, looking out from the dress department over the center of the store. Two floors below, the crowds shifted slowly through a maze of counters packed with gloves, belts, and handbags. Silk scarves were draped on racks, and womens' hats, with veils and bows and clusters of cherries or grapes, were hung on the branches of wooden trees. "If you leave before the *Ausweis* comes," Véronique said, "and there's some way you can arrange to have it sent over to your office, it would be very important for us to have it. For somebody, it could mean everything."

"I will try," he said.

"About the other, situation, I'll be in touch with you. Soon as I can."

They kissed each other good-bye, one cheek then the other, and Casson walked away. Looking back over his shoulder he saw her smile, then she waved to him and mouthed the little phrase that meant *have courage*.

It rained. Thirty-three Wehrmacht divisions advanced in Yugoslavia. Others crossed the border into Greece. Stuka bombers destroyed the city of Belgrade. An interzonal card from Lyons arrived at a Paris café, addressed to J. Casson. "Waiting, waiting and thinking about you. Please come soon." Signed with the initial X. A dinner party at the house of Philippe and Françoise Pichard. His brother, wounded a year earlier in the fighting in Belgium, had never returned home, but they had word of him, a prisoner of war, doing forced labor in an underground armaments factory in Aachen. Bruno was trying to pull strings in order to get him out.

It cleared. Fine days; windy, cool, sunny. Zagreb taken. The RAF blew up the Berlin opera house. Bulgarian and Italian troops joined the attack on Yugoslavia. Casson had lunch with Hugo Altmann at a black-market restaurant called Chez Nini, in an alley behind a butcher shop out in Auteuil. Fillets of lamb with baby turnips, then a Saint-

Marcellin. Now that he was in contact with SD officers, Altmann was afraid of him—that meant money, replacing what he'd given Fischfang, and a meaningful contribution to the escape fund. Altmann gave his tenth hearty laugh of the afternoon. "My secretary will have a check for you tomorrow, it's no problem, no problem at all. We *believe* in this picture, that's what matters."

It rained. Dripped slowly from the branches of the trees on the boulevards. Casson went to see Marcel Carné's *Le Jour Se Lève* at the Madeleine theatre, script by Jacques Prévert, Jean Gabin playing the lead. The Occupation authority announced the opening of the Institute of Jewish Studies. The inaugural exhibition, to be presented by a well-known curator, would show how Jews dominated the world through control of newspapers, films, and financial markets. Marie-Claire telephoned, Bruno was impossible, she didn't know what to do. "Some afternoon you could come for tea," she said. "It rains like this and I am so sad. I walk around the apartment in my underwear and look at myself in the mirrors." Fighting around Mount Olympus in Greece. Bulgarian troops in Macedonia. On a small errand he went out to the Trinité quarter, a street of fortune-tellers and dusty antique shops. He walked head down through the rain, dodging the puddles, staying under awnings when he could. A black Citroën swung sharply to the curb, Franz Millau climbed out of the passenger side and opened the back door. "Come for a ride," he said with a smile. "It's no good walking today, too wet."

They drove to a small villa in the back streets of one of the drearier suburbs, Vernouillet, squat brick houses with little gardens. The driver was introduced as Albert Singer, a blunt-headed, fair-haired man so heavy in the neck and shoulders his shirt collar was pulled out of shape around the button. At the villa, Millau asked him to make a fire. He tried, using wooden crates broken into kindling, newspapers, and two wet birch logs that were never going to burn anything. Stubborn, he squatted in front of the fireplace, lighting match after match to the corner of a damp section of the *Deutsche Allgemeine Zeitung*. For a time, Millau watched him with disbelief. Finally he said, "Singer, isn't there any dry paper?"

"I'll look," Singer said, struggling to his feet.

"What can you do?" said Millau, resigned. "He does what I tell him, so I have to keep him around."

Casson nodded sympathetically. The room smelled of disuse, of mildew and old rugs; something about it made his heart beat faster. "Do you mind if I smoke?"

"No. In fact I will join you." Millau got out a cigar and went to work on it. With the lights off and shutters closed, the parlor was in shadow. "Did you see the papers this morning?" Millau said.

"Yes."

"Awful, no?"

"What?"

"The bombing. Out at the Citroën plant. Three hundred dead—and to no particular purpose. The assembly line was up and running again by ten in the morning. Casson, no matter your politics, no matter what you think of us, you have a moral obligation to stop such things if it is in your power to do so."

Casson made a gesture—the world did what it did, it didn't ask him first.

"I'll let you in on one secret—we have a special envoy in London now, trying to work out, at least a cease-fire. At least let the horror stop for a moment, so we can think it over, so we can maybe just talk for a time. You can't find *that* wrong, can you?"

"No."

"I mean, we must be honest with each other. We're fellow human beings, maybe even fellow Europeans—certainly it's something we could discuss, but I won't insist on that."

"Europeans, of course."

"Now look, Casson, we need your help or this whole thing is going to blow up in our faces. The people I work for in Berlin have taken it into their heads that you're willing to cooperate with us and they've stuck me with the job of making that cooperation a reality. So, I don't really have a choice."

Singer returned with some newspaper, crumpled up a few pages and wedged them under the grate. He lit the paper, the room immediately smelled like smoke.

"Flue open?"

"*Ja.*"

Millau made a face. Reached into an inside pocket, took out an identity card, handed it over. Casson swallowed. It was his passport photograph. Underneath, the name Georges Bourdon. "Now this gentleman was to be used by the English, and I mean *used,* to assist a terrorist action that is planned to take place in the Paris region. The bombing last night killed three hundred Frenchmen—what these people want to do, and we aren't sure exactly what that is, will no doubt kill a few hundred more. What we need from you is to play the part of this Bourdon person for a single night, then we're quits. You will spend a few hours in a field, is all that is required, then I can report back to Berlin that all went well, that you tried but didn't do much of a job, and in future we're going to work with somebody else.

"I'm an honorable man, Monsieur Casson, I don't care if you want to sit out this war and make movies—after all, I go to the movies—as long as you don't do anything to hurt us. Meanwhile, if things turn out as I believe they will, Europe is going to be a certain way for the foreseeable future, and those people who have helped us out when we asked for their help are going to be able to ask for a favor some day if they need to. We have long memories, and we appreciate civilized behavior. Now, I've said everything I can say—"

There was a wisp of white smoke floating along the ceiling. Singer gazed upward from where he was squatting in front of the fire.

"You stupid ass," Millau said.

"I'm sorry," Singer said, standing and rubbing his hands. "It's too wet to burn, sir."

Millau put a hand against the side of his head as though he were getting a headache. "Now look," he said to Casson. "In a few days we'll be in contact with you, we'll tell you where and when and all the rest of it. Keep the card, you'll need it. Somebody will ask you if you're Georges Bourdon, and you'll say that you are, and show them your identity card. So, now, you know most of what I can tell you. Don't say yes, don't say no, just go home and think it over. What's best for you, what's best for the French people. But I would not be wholly honest if I didn't tell you that we need a French person, somebody approximately of your age and circumstance, to be at a certain place on a certain date in the very near future."

He paused a moment, trying to decide exactly how to say what came next. "You have us in a somewhat difficult position, Monsieur Casson, I hope you understand that."

❖

He took a train back to Paris, got off at the Gare St.-Lazare at twenty minutes after six. For a time he was not clear about what to do next, in fact stood on the platform between tracks as the crowds flowed around him. Finally there was a man's voice—Casson never saw him—saying quietly, "Don't stand here like this, they'll run you in. Understand?"

Casson moved off. To a rank of telephone booths by the entry to the station. Outside, people were hurrying through the rain in the gathering dusk. Casson stepped into a phone booth, put the receiver to his ear and listened to the thin whine of the dial tone. Then he began to thumb through the Paris telephone book on a shelf below the telephone. Turned to the *B* section. *Bois. Bonneval. Bosquet. Botine. Boulanger. Bourdon.*

Albert, André, Bernard, Claudine, Daniel—Médecin, Georges.
18, rue Malher. *42 30 89.*

Seeing it in the little black letters and numbers, Casson felt a chill inside him. As though hypnotized, he put a *jeton* in the slot and dialed the number. It rang. And again. A third time. Once more. Five. Six. Seven. Eight. Casson put the receiver back on its hook. Outside, a woman in a green hat tapped on the door of the booth with a coin. "Monsieur?" she said when he looked at her.

He left. Walked east on the rue de Rome. The street was crowded, people shopping, or going home from work, faces closed and private, eyes on the pavement, trying to get through one more day. Casson came to a decision, turned abruptly, hurried back to the telephones at the Gare St.-Lazare. *Véronique.* He didn't remember exactly where she lived—he'd dropped her off the night of Marie-Claire's dinner party a year ago—but it was in the Fifth somewhere, the student quarter. He remembered Marie-Claire telling him, eyes cast to heaven in gentle despair at the curious life her little sister had chosen to live. *Yes, well,* Casson thought.

It took more than the polite number of rings for Véronique to answer.
"Yes?"
"It's Jean-Claude."
Guarded. "How nice to hear from you."
"I need to talk to you."
"Very well."

"Where should we meet?"

"There's a café at the Maubert market. Le Relais. In a half-hour, say."

"See you then."

"Good-bye."

She wore a trenchcoat and a beret, a tiny gold cross on a chain at the base of her throat. She was cold in the rain, sat hunched over the edge of a table at the rear of the workers' café. Casson told her what had happened, starting with Altmann's dinner at the Heininger. He handed her the Georges Bourdon identity card.

She studied it a moment. "Rue Malher," she said.

"Just another street. He could be rich, poor, in between."

"Yes. And for profession, *salesman*. Also, anything."

Véronique handed the card back.

"What do you think Millau meant when he said I'd put them in a difficult position?"

She thought a moment. "Perhaps—you have to remember these people work for organizations, and these places have a life of their own. Department stores, symphony orchestras, spy services—at heart the same. So, perhaps, this man told a little fib. Claimed he had somebody who could be used a certain way. Thinking, maybe, that such a situation could be developed, in the future, so he'd just take credit for it a little early. On a certain day, perhaps, when he needed a success. Then, suddenly, they're yelling *produce the goods!* Well, now what?"

Casson stubbed out a cigarette. The café smelled like sour wine and wet dogs, a quiet place, people spoke in low voices. "*Merde,*" he said.

"Yes."

"I think, Véronique, I had better talk to somebody. Can you help?"

"Yes. Do you know what you're asking?"

"Yes, I know."

She looked in his eyes, reached out and squeezed his forearm. She was strong, he realized. She got up from the table and went to the bar. A telephone was produced from beneath the counter. She made a call—ten seconds—then hung up. She stood at the bar and talked to the proprietor. Laughed at a joke, kidded with him about something that made him shake his head and tighten his mouth—what could you do, any more, the way things were, a pretty damn sad state of affairs is what it was. The phone on the bar rang, Véronique answered it, said a word or two, hung up, and returned to the table.

"It's tomorrow," she said. "Go to the church of Saint-Étienne-du-Mont, that's just up the hill here. You know it?"

"Across from the school."

"That's it. You go to the five o'clock mass. Take a seat near the crypt of Sainte Geneviève, one seat in from the center aisle. Carry a raincoat over your left arm, a copy of *Le Temps* in your right hand. You will be approached. The man—he uses the name Mathieu—will be holding his hat in his left hand. He will ask you if he might have a look at your newspaper if you're done reading it. You will tell him politely no, your wife hasn't read it yet." She paused a moment. "Do you have it?"

"Yes."

She leaned over the table, coming closer to him. "For the best, Jean-Claude," she said. Then, "Really, it's time. Not just for you. For all of us."

They said good-bye. He left first, walked to the Maubert-Mutualité Métro. There was a Gestapo control after 8:00 P.M. at the La Motte-Picquet *correspondance*, where he normally would have changed trains for his own station, so he got out two stops early and walked to a station on Line Six.

"Excuse me, may I see the paper if you're done with it?"

He was quite ordinary, a plain suit over a green sweater, raincoat, hat—held in left hand, as promised. But there was something about him, the skin of his face rough and weathered a certain way, hair a deep reddish brown, mustache a little ragged—that made it immediately apparent that he was British. Thus something of a shock when he spoke. He opened his mouth and perfect native French came out. Later he would explain: mother from Limoges, father from Edinburgh, he'd grown up in the Dordogne, where his family owned a hotel.

They left the church, walked down the hill, crossed boulevard St.-Michel and entered the Luxembourg Gardens. Handed over a few sous to the old lady in black who guarded the park chairs, and sat on a terrace. It was crowded, couples holding hands, old men with newspapers, just below them boys launching sailboats in the fountain, keeping them on course with long sticks.

They were silent for a moment, Casson got a sense of the man sitting beside him. He was scared, but bolted down tight. He'd done what he'd done, signed up for clandestine service in time of war. Hadn't understood what that meant until he got to Paris, saw the Germans in operation, at last realized how easy it was going to be to make the wrong mistake—only a matter of time. After that, he woke up scared in the morning and went to bed scared at night. But, he wasn't going to let it finish him. Something else would, not that.

"Well," he said. "Perhaps you'll tell me what happened."

Casson had taken the time to think it through and had the answer rehearsed. Simic. The money taken to Spain. The period of surveillance. Finally, the two contacts with Millau. Mathieu listened attentively, did not react until Casson repeated what he'd been told about Marie-Noëlle being in German custody.

"And you didn't tell anybody," Mathieu said.

"No."

For a moment there was nothing to be said, only the sound of the park, the birds in late afternoon, the boys by the fountain shouting to one another.

"I'm sorry," Casson said. "It didn't occur to me to tell someone about it—I really don't know anything about how this works."

"Was that all—they had her in custody?"

"Yes."

"Well, at least we know now."

"You'd met her?"

"No. I suspect she was with the other service, not mine. They're the intelligence people, we're operational. We blow things up. So, what we do isn't exactly secret. Rather the opposite."

"You're in the army, then."

"No, not really. I was a university teacher. Latin drama—Plautus and Terence, mostly. Seneca, sometimes. But I heard they were looking for people who spoke native French, and I was the right age—old enough to know when to run, young enough to run fast when the time came. So, I applied. And then, a stroke of luck, I got the job."

Casson smiled. "When was that?"

"The autumn after the invasion here."

"Eight months."

"Yes, about that."

"Not very long."

Mathieu took off his hat, smoothed his hair back. "Well, they did have training, especially the technical part. But for the rest of it, they taught us the classic procedures but they also let us know, in so many words, that people who have done well at this sort of thing tend to make it up as they go along."

Mathieu stared at something over Casson's shoulder, Casson turned around to see what he was looking at. Down a long allée of lime trees, a pair of French policemen were conducting a snap search—a dark-haired couple handing over various passes and identity cards.

"Let's take a little walk," Mathieu said. They moved off casually, away from the search.

"I'm going to have to ask London what they want to do with you," Mathieu said. "It will take a few days—say, next Thursday. Now, in a minute I'm going to give you a telephone number. Memorize it. It's a bookstore, over in the Marais. You call them up—use a public phone, of course—and ask them some question with an Italian flavor. Such as, do you have two copies of Dante's *Vita Nuova*? Leave a number. If a call doesn't come back in twenty minutes, walk away. You may be contacted at home, or at your office, or en route. If nothing happens, return to that phone at the same time the following day, also for twenty minutes. Then once again, on the third day."

"And then, if there's still no response?"

"Hmm, they say Lisbon is pleasant, this time of year."

28 May, 1941. 4:20 P.M.

"Hello?"

"Good afternoon. Do you have a tourist guide for Naples?"

"I'll take a look. Can I call you back?"

"Yes. I'm at *41 11 56*."

"Very good. We'll be in touch."

"Good-bye."

❖

29 May, 1941. 4:38 P.M.

"Hello?"

"Did you call about a guidebook for Naples?"

"Yes."

"All right, I have an answer for you. I spoke with my managing director, he wants you to go ahead with the project."

"What?"

"Do what they ask."

"Agree to what they want—is that what you mean?"

"Yes."

"Are you sure about this?"

"Yes."

"Can we get together and talk about it?"

"Later, perhaps. What we will want to know is what they ask you to do. That's important. Do you understand?"

"Yes. I'm on their side."

"That's correct—but don't overdo it."

"I won't."

"Are you going to be able to do this?"

A pause. "Yes."

"You will have to be very careful."

"I understand."

"Good-bye."

"Good-bye."

5 June. 2:20 P.M.

"Monsieur Casson?"

"Yes."

"Franz Millau. Have you thought over our discussion?"

"Yes."

"How do you feel about it now?"

"If there's a way I can help—it's best."

"Will you be at your office for an hour or so?"

"Yes."

"An envelope will be delivered. Monsieur Casson?"

"Yes?"

"I will ask you one time only. Did you mention, or allude to, the discussion we had, to anybody, in any way whatsoever? Think for a moment before you answer me."

"The answer is no."

"Can you tell me please, why is that?"

"Why. It might take a long time to explain. Briefly, I was raised in a family that understood that your first allegiance is to yourself."

"Very well. Expect the envelope, and we'll be in touch with you soon. Good-bye."

"Good-bye, Herr Millau."

"And good luck."

"Yes, always that. Good-bye."

"Good-bye."

9 June, 3:20 P.M.

On his way to the Gare de Lyon to catch the 4:33 to Chartres, he stopped at the café where he had his morning coffee. The proprietor went back to his office and returned with a postcard. *Greetings from Lyons—View of the Fountain, place des Terreaux.* "All is well, monsieur?"

"Yes. Thank you, Marcel. For keeping the card for me."

"It's my pleasure. Not easy, these times."

"No."

"It's not only you, monsieur."

Casson met his glance and found honest sympathy: liaisons with lovers or with the underground, for Marcel what mattered were liaisons, and he could be counted on. Casson reached across the copper-covered bar and shook his hand. "Thank you again, my friend," he said.

"De rien." It's nothing.

"I'm off to the train."

"Bon voyage, monsieur."

He read it on the train, sweaty and breathing hard from having jumped on the last coach as it was moving out of the station. A control on the Métro, a long line, French police inspectors peering at everyone's identity cards as the minutes marched past and Casson clenched his teeth in rage.

The writing on the card was careful, like a student in lycée. It touched his heart to look at it.

> My love, it's 3:40 in the morning, and it feels and sounds the way it does late at night in these places. My chaos of a life is right here by my side—it likes to stay up late when I do, and it won't go to bed. You would say not to care, so, maybe, I don't. I write to say that spring is going by, that nothing changes in this city, and I wonder where you are. I am very alone without you—please try to come. I know you are trying, but please try. I do love you. X

He looked up to find green countryside, late afternoon in spring among the meadows and little aimless roads. *Citrine*. For just a moment he was nineteen again—to go to Lyons you took the Lyons train. Or you went to a town along the ZNO line and found somebody to take you across. Then you found your lover and together you ran to a place where they would never find you. *No*. That didn't work. Life wasn't like that. And it didn't matter how much you wanted it to be.

The sun low in the sky, long shadows in a village street, a young woman in a scarf helping an old woman down the steps of a church, Café de la Poste, an ancient cemetery—stone walls and cypress trees, then the town ended and the fields began again.

As it turned out, he could have let the express to Chartres leave without him. A long delay, waiting for the 6:28 local that would eventually find its way to Alençon. He used the time to buy paper and an envelope at a stationer's shop across from the terminal, then wrote, sitting on a bench on the platform as the sun went down behind the spires of the cathedral.

He loved her, he was coming, life in Paris was complicated, he had to extricate himself.

He stopped there, thought for a time, then wrote that if there had to be a line drawn it would be a month from then, no more. Say, July 1. A voice inside him told him not to write that but he didn't listen to it. He couldn't just go on and on about *soon*. She needed more than that, he did the best he could.

❖

The train was two hours late, only three passengers got off at Alençon; a mother and her little boy, and Casson, feeling very much the dark-haired Parisian, lighting a cigarette as he descended to the platform, cupping his hands to shield the match flare from the evening wind.

"You must be Bourdon." He'd been leaning against a baggage cart, watching to see who got off the train. He was barely thirty, Casson thought. Leather coat, longish—artfully combed hair, the expectantly handsome face of an office lothario.

"That's right."

"I'm Eddie Juin."

They walked into a maze of little lanes, three feet wide, wash hanging out above their heads. Turned left, right, right, left, down a stairway, through a tunnel, then up a long street of stairs to a garage. It was dark inside, fumes of gasoline and oil heavy in the air, cut by the sharp smell of scorched metal. "I wonder if you could let me have a look at your identity card," Juin said.

"Not a problem."

Casson handed over the Bourdon card, Juin clicked on a flashlight and had a look. "A salesman?"

"Yes."

"What is it you sell, if I can ask?"

"Scientific equipment—to laboratories. Test tubes, flasks, Bunsen burners, all that sort of thing."

"How do you do, with that?"

"Not too badly. It's up, it's down—you know how it is."

Juin handed the card back, went to a stained and battered desk with a telephone on it, dialed a number. "Seems all right," he said. "We're leaving now."

He hung up, opened a drawer, took out several flashlights, put them in a canvas sack and handed it to Casson.

"Is this your place?" Casson asked.

"Mine? No. Belongs to a friend's father—he lets us use it." He ran the beam of the flashlight over the steel tracks above the pit used to work under cars, then a stack of old tires, then showed Casson what he meant him to see. "Better button up your jacket," he said, voice very proud.

It *was* beautiful. A big motorcycle, front and rear fenders stripped, the paint worn away to a color that was no color at all. "What year?" Casson said.

"1925. It's English—a Norton 'Indian.' "

Juin climbed on, jiggled the fuel feed on the right handlebar, then rose in the air and drove his weight down hard on the kick starter. The engine grumbled once and died. Juin rose again. Nothing on the second try, or the third. It went on, Juin undaunted. At last, a sputtering roar, a volley of small-arms fire and a cloud of smoke from the trembling exhaust pipe. Casson hauled up the metal shutter, then closed it again after Juin was out, and climbed on the flat seat meant for the passenger. "Don't try to lean on the curves," Juin shouted over the engine noise.

They flew through the streets, bouncing over the cobbles, bumping down a stairway, the explosive engine thundering off the ancient walls, announcing to every Frenchman and German in the lower Normandy region that that idiot Eddie Juin was out for a ride.

They sped over a bridge that spanned the Sarthe, then they were out in the countryside, Casson imagining that he could actually smell the fragrant night air through the reek of burned oil that traveled with the machine. They left the Route Nationale for a *route departmentale,* then turned onto a packed dirt road that didn't have a number but probably had a local name, then to a cowpath, five miles an hour over rocks and roots, across a long hillside on a strip of beaten-down weed and scrub, over the hill to a valley spread out in the moonlight. Juin cut the engine and they rolled silently for a long time, coming to a stop at last on the edge of a flat grassy field.

It seemed very quiet, just a few crickets, once the engine was off. Casson climbed off the motorcycle, half frozen, blowing on his hands. "Where are we?" he asked.

Eddie Juin smiled. "Nowhere," he said triumphantly. "Absolutely nowhere."

1:30 A.M. Three-quarter moon. They sat by the motorcycle, smoking, waiting, watching the edge of the woods at the other end of the field.

"Alençon doesn't seem so bad," Casson said.

"No, not too bad, and I'm an expert. I grew up in at least six different places, one of those families that never stopped moving. Saves money, my dad said—some bills would never quite catch up with us—and, he'd say, it's an education for life!" Juin laughed as he remembered. "It's Lebec who's from Alençon, and his uncle, who's called Tonton Jules. Then there's Angier, and that's it. Tonton Jules farms over in Mortagne, the rest of us met up in Paris."

"At the office."

"Yes, that's it. We all worked for the Merchant Marine Ministry, first in Paris, then over on the coast, in Lorient. We didn't have it too bad—snuck out early on Friday afternoons, chased the girls, caught our share. But when the Germans came they tossed us out, of course, because they put their submarine pens in over there, for the blockade on the English. So that left us, Athos, Porthos, and Aramis from the fourth floor, with time on our hands. Well, what better than to find a way to fuck life up for the *schleuh*? Return the favor, right? And as for Tonton Jules, they captured him on the Marne in 1915, sent him to Germany in a cattle car. Apparently he didn't care for it."

He paused for a moment and they both listened for engines but it was very quiet. "So," he said, "how is it in Paris these days?"

"You miss it?"

"Who wouldn't."

"People are fed up," Casson said. "Hungry, tired, can't get tobacco, there's no coffee. In the beginning they thought they could live with it. Then they thought they could ignore it. Now they want it to go away."

"Wait a minute." Juin stood up. Casson heard the faint throb of a machine in the distance. Juin reached inside his coat and took out a snub-nosed automatic.

A farm tractor towing a haywagon materialized at the end of the field, Casson and Eddie Juin went to meet it. Tonton Jules swayed in the driver's seat. He was a fat man with one arm, and he was drunk. His nephew Lebec was dark and clever, could have been Eddie Juin's brother. Angier had an appealing rat face, Casson guessed he would go anywhere, do anything. Easy to imagine him as a kid jumping off railway trestles on a dare. "*Salut*, Eddie," he said. "Are we on time?"

Juin just laughed.

❖

They heard the plane at 3:12 A.M., headed south of east. They each took a flashlight and stood in a line with Juin to one side to make the letter *L*. This showed wind direction when, as the plane came closer, they turned on the lights. Juin then blinked the Morse letter *J*—a recognition signal for that night only, which meant *we're not a bunch of Germans trying to get you to land in this field*. The plane did not respond, flew straight ahead, vanished. Then, a minute later, they heard him coming back. Juin tried again, and this time the pilot confirmed the signal, using the airplane's landing lights to flash back a Morse countersign.

The plane touched down at the other end of the field, then taxied toward them, bouncing over the uneven ground. No savoir-faire now, they ran to meet it, Tonton Jules wheezing as he tried to keep up. It wasn't much to look at, a single propeller, fixed landing wheels in over-sized hubs, biplane wings above and below the pilot's compartment. On the fuselage, next to a freshly painted RAF roundel, was a black flash mark and a peppering of tiny holes. With difficulty the pilot forced back the Perspex window panel, then tore the leather flying cap from his head. He allowed himself a single deep breath, then called out over the noise of the engine. "Can somebody help? Ahh, *peut-être,* can you—*aidez-mah?*"

"You are hurted?" Lebec said.

"No. Not me."

He was very young, Casson thought, not much more than nineteen. And he certainly didn't look the hero—tall and gangly, unruly hair, big ears, freckles. The man sitting behind him grabbed the edge of the cockpit with his left hand and clumsily struggled to his feet. Clearly his right arm had been damaged. He appeared to be cursing under his breath. Angier used the tail fin to scramble up on the back of the plane, then slid himself forward to a point where he could help the man get down to the ground.

The pilot looked at his watch. "We should move along," he said to Casson. "I'm to leave here in three minutes."

"All right."

"You'll have to help me get the tail swung round. And, don't forget, *n'oublah* thing, the two, uh—*deux caisses, deux valises.*" The last burst forth with the fluency of the determinedly memorized.

Lebec climbed onto the wing, then helped the pilot work two suit-cases and two small wooden crates free of the cockpit. "Damned amazing, what you can get in here," the pilot said. Lebec smiled—no idea what the pilot was saying but an ally was an ally.

They handed down the cargo—carried off to Tonton Jules's wagon—then Lebec jumped to the ground and saluted the pilot, who returned the salute with a smile, then tossed his flying cap back on and tried a parting wave, devil-may-care, as he revved the engine. "Best of luck, then," he shouted. *"Bonne shan!"*

He reached up, pulled the housing shut. Eddie Juin took hold of the tail assembly and started to turn the plane into the wind, everybody else ran to help him. The plane accelerated suddenly, there was a blast of hot exhaust as it pulled away, then a roar of fuel fed to the engine as it struggled into the air. It flopped back down, bounced off the field, touched one wheel a second time, then caught the wind and climbed into the darkness. The people on the ground listened for a time, peering into the dark sky, then lost the whine of the receding engine among the night sounds of the countryside.

Verneuil, Brézolles, Laons—Casson drove east toward Paris in the spring dawn.

The end of the operation had been complicated. *Système D,* Casson thought, always *Système D,* make do, use your ingenuity, improvise—it was simply the way life was lived. They'd left the field headed for a small village nearby, where a man who drove a milk truck to Paris twice a week was supposed to pick up the supplies delivered from England, leaving Casson and the operative free to take the train into the city. But the truck never appeared, so Eddie Juin had to come up with an alternative. Off they went to another village, where a barn on the outskirts hid a Renault—a four-year-old Juvequatre model, slow, steady, inexpensive, a family car.

Casson drove through first light, staying on the 839. The two crates and two valises were in the trunk. Next to him, the man he had come to think of as the sergeant—though he used the name Jerome—bled slowly into the pale-gray upholstery.

"It's not so bad," he said. "You could hardly call it shrapnel. More like, specks. But, iron specks, so I'll have to see a doctor, sooner or later. Still, not bad enough for me to go back to England—no point at all to that."

"What happened?"

"Well, at first everything went perfectly. We came in at eight thousand feet over the coast at St.-Malo—no problem. Picked up the rail line to Alençon a minute later—we spotted the firebox on a locomotive going east and we just flew along with him. Next we had yellow signal lights, for ten miles or so, coming out of the big freight junction in Fougères. After that, the track was between us and the moon and we just followed the glow on the rails. But somebody heard us, because ten minutes later a searchlight came on and they started shooting. Nothing very serious, a few ack-ack rounds, and Charley thought maybe a machine gun. Then it was over, but my arm had gone numb and I realized we'd been hit."

Casson slowed down for a hairpin turn at the center of a sleeping village, then they were back among the fields.

He saw now how they worked it. First came Mathieu, the university man, getting the system organized. Next came the sergeant—almost certainly a technician. Why else bring him in? Short and muscular, working-class face, speaking French in a way that would fool nobody. Not his fault, Casson thought. Likely something he'd taken up years ago in hopes it would advance him in the military. So he'd put in his time in classrooms, dutifully rolled his *r*'s and nasalized his *n*'s, but finally to very little purpose—he might as well have worn a derby with a Union Jack stuck in the band and whistled "God Save the King" for all the good it was going to do him.

Casson slowed for a one-lane bridge, the stream below running full in spring flood, water dark blue in the early light. The sergeant had winced when he tapped the brake. "Sorry," Casson said.

"Oh, it's nothing. Twenty minutes with a doctor and I'll be fine."

"It won't be a problem," Casson said.

Well, he didn't think it would be. What doctor? He only knew one doctor, his doctor. Old Dr. Genoux. What were his politics? Casson had no idea. He was brusque, forever vaguely irritated by something or other, and smelled eternally of eucalyptus. He'd been Casson's doctor for twenty years, since university. One day Casson had noticed his hair was white. Good heavens! He couldn't be a Vichyite or a Fascist, could he? Well, if not him, who else? The dentist? The professor at the Sorbonne faculty of medicine who lived across the street? Arnaud had once had a girlfriend who was a nurse. No, that wasn't going to work, old Genoux would just have to do the job.

He worked his way through the medieval town of Dreux, intending to pick up the 932 that wound aimlessly into the Chevreuse valley. But then he somehow made a mistake and, a little way beyond the town, found himself instead on the N 12, with a sprinkling of early traffic headed for Paris. Well, all the roads went to the capital, the N 12 was as good as any other.

Going over a rail crossing, the springs plunged and the cargo gave a loud thump as it shifted in the trunk. The sergeant opened his eyes and laughed. "Don't worry about *that*," he said confidently.

An explosion, is what he meant. The shipment from England included radio crystals, which would allow clandestine wireless-telegraph sets to change frequencies, 200,000 francs, 20,000 dollars, four Sten carbines with 4,000 rounds of ammunition, time pencil detonators, and eighty pounds of the explosive cyclonite, chemically enhanced to make it malleable—*plastique*.

"The trick," he added, "is actually getting it to go off."

The town of Houdan. A place Casson had always liked, he'd come here with Marie-Claire for picnics in the forest—*long ago and far away*. They'd owned a set of chairs and a table that could be folded up and carried in the trunk of the car. She always brought a cloth for the table, he would pick up a pair of langoustes with green mayonnaise from Fauchon, and they'd sit by a field for hours and watch the day.

The road turned north, the sun was up now, light glistening on the wet fields, the last of the ground mist gathered over the streams. The sky had turned a delicate, morning blue, with a rose blush on the horizon. Something world-weary about these dawns in the country around Paris, he'd always felt that—*well, all right, one more day if you think it's going to do you any good*. The next village on the road seemed closed up tight, the shutters still pulled down over the front of the café. Casson spotted a road marker and decided to take the 839. The town

ended, there was a bridge, then a sharp left-hand curve through a
wood, which straightened out to reveal some cars and trucks and
guards with machine pistols.

Control.

They had a moment, no more. Casson hit the brake, rolled past five
or six policemen who waved him on, down a lane formed by portable
barriers—crossbraced x's of sawn logs strung with barbed wire. Coming up on the control, Casson and the sergeant had turned to each
other, exchanged a look: *well, too bad.* That was all. Then Casson said,
"Close your eyes. You're injured, unconscious, almost gone."

A young officer—*Leutnant*—in Wehrmacht gray appeared at the
window. *"Raus mit uns."* He was impatient, holster unsnapped, hand
resting on his sidearm.

Casson got out and stood by the half-open door, nodded toward the
passenger side of the car. "There's a man hurt," he said.

The *Leutnant* walked around to have a look, bent over and peered
into the car. The sergeant's eyes were closed, mouth open, head back.
A bloody rag around his arm, a dark stain on the upholstery. The *Leutnant* hesitated, looked in Casson's direction. Casson saw a possibility.
"I don't really know exactly how he got himself in this condition but
it's important that he see a doctor as soon as he can." He said it
quickly.

The *Leutnant* froze, then squared his shoulders and walked away.

The road lay in shadow—six in the morning, shafts of sunlight in
the pine forest. Five cars had been stopped, as well as two rickety old
trucks taking pigs to market. Amid the smell and the squealing, a German officer was trying to make sense of the drivers' papers while they
stood to one side looking sinister and apprehensive. By the car ahead
of Casson, four men, dark, unshaven, possibly Gypsies, were trying
to communicate with a man in a raincoat, perhaps a German security officer. Suddenly angry he yanked the door open, and a very pregnant, very frightened woman struggled out with hands held high in
the air.

The young *Leutnant* came striding back to Casson's car, a policeman in tow—an officer of the *Gendarmerie Nationale,* French mili-

tary police with a reputation for brutality. The gendarme was angry at being asked to intervene. "All right," he said to Casson, "what's going on?"

"This man is injured."

"How did it happen?"

"I'm taking him to a doctor."

The gendarme gave him a very cold look. "I asked how."

"An accident."

"Where?"

"Working, I believe. In a garage. I wasn't there."

The gendarme's eyes were like steel. *Salaud*—you bastard—trying to play games with me? In front of a German? I'll take you behind a tree and break your fucking head. "Open the trunk," he said.

Casson fumbled with the latch, then got it open. The intense odor of almonds, characteristic of plastic explosive, came rolling out at them. The *Leutnant* said "Ach," and stepped back. "What is it?" the gendarme said.

"Almonds."

The two valises were in plain sight, packed with francs, dollars, radio crystals, and explosive. Tonton Jules, just before they left, had tossed an old blanket over the two crates holding the sten guns and ammunition. Casson, at that moment, had thought it a particularly pointless gesture.

"Almonds," the gendarme said. He didn't know it meant explosive. He did know that Casson had been caught in the middle of something. Parisians of a certain class had no business on country roads at dawn, and people didn't injure their upper arms in garage accidents. This was resistance of some kind, that much he did know, thus his patriotism, his honor, had been called into question and now he, a man with wife and family, had to compromise himself. He stared at Casson with pure hatred.

"You had better be going," he said. "Your friend ought to see a doctor." For the benefit of the *Leutnant* he made a Gallic gesture—eyes shut, shoulders up, hands in the air: *Who knows what these people are doing, but it's clearly nothing that would interest men of our stature.*

He waved Casson on, down the road toward Paris.

Salaud. Don't come back here.

❖

10 June, 1941.

"Hello?"

"Good morning. I was wondering if you might have a life of Verdi, something nice, for a gift."

"The composer?"

"Yes."

"I'm not sure, we may very well have something. Can we call you back?"

"Yes. I'm at 63 26 08."

"All right. We'll be in touch."

"Good-bye."

"Good-bye."

This time they met in the church of Nôtre-Dame de Secours, then walked in the Père-Lachaise cemetery. At the gate, Mathieu bought a bouquet of anemones from an old woman.

They walked up the hill to the older districts, past the crumbling tombs of vanished nobility, past the Polish exiles, past the artists. They left the path at the Twenty-fourth Division and stood before the grave of Corot.

"Are you sure of the doctor?" Mathieu asked.

"No. Not really."

"But the patient, can return to work?"

"Yes."

"We'll want him to work on the twenty-third."

"It won't be a problem."

"His arrangements?"

"He's up in Belleville, in the Arab district. Above a Moroccan restaurant—Star of the East on rue Pelleport. If he can stand the couscous, from dawn to midnight, he'll be fine. I suggested to the owner that the wound was received in an affair of *family honor,* in the *south,* somewhere below *Marseilles.*"

"Corsica."

"Yes."

Mathieu gave a brief, dry laugh. "Corsica, yes. That's very good. The owner is someone you know?"

"No. A newspaper advertisement, *room for rent*. I put on a pair of dark glasses, paid three months in advance."

Mathieu laughed again. "And for the rest?"

"Hidden. Deep and dark, where it will never be found."

"I'll take your word for it. When are you going to make contact?"

"Today."

"That sounds right. Difficult things—the sooner the better."

"Difficult—" Casson said. It was a lot worse than *difficult*.

Mathieu smiled a certain way, he meant it was no easier for him, that he was just as scared as Casson was.

Making sure that nobody was looking at them, Mathieu took a folded square of paper from his pocket and slipped it among the stems of the anemones. Then he leaned over, placed the flowers on the tomb.

"Corot," Casson said.

"Yes," Mathieu said. "He's off by himself, over here."

They walked back down the hill together, then shook hands at the boulevard corner and said good-bye. "They'll make you go over it, you know. Again and again. From a number of angles," Mathieu said.

Casson nodded that he knew that, then turned and walked to the Métro.

It was Singer who picked him up in a black Traction Avant Citroën on the evening of 15 June and drove him out to the brick villa in Vernouillet. The parlor, even as the weather warmed up, still felt dark and damp and unused. Millau had a technician with him, a man who wore earphones and operated a wire recorder to take down what Casson said.

Millau had just shaved—a tiny nick freshly made on the line of the jaw. He worked in shirtsleeves, his jacket hung in a closet, but despite the suggestion of informality the shirt was freshly pressed and laundered a sparkling white. He was, evidently, going to meet someone important later that evening. Only after they'd greeted each other and made small talk did Casson realize he'd been wrong about that. *Jean Casson* was the someone important—the shave and the white shirt were for, well, not so much him as an important moment in Millau's life.

Mathieu had been right. He was made to go over the story again and again. He was comfortable with plots and characters, had spent much of his professional life in meetings where people said things like *what if Duval doesn't return until the following evening?* That gave him a slight advantage but not all that much, and the mistakes were always there, waiting for him. Perhaps they wouldn't be noticed. He'd changed the Alençon names to code names—fish. *Merlan* drove the car, *Rouget* the truck, *Angouille* sat beside him, the shotgun on his lap.

It ran, he hoped, seamlessly into the truth: the single-engine Lysander a single-engine Lysander, the pilot young and gangling and rather awkward, and the navigation guides were as they'd been: signal lights along the track, locomotive fireboxes, and the glow of moonlight on the steel rails. They had come in at 8,000 feet over St.-Malo, were later hit by an antiaircraft burst—Millau nodded at that. The copilot was slightly wounded. The shipment included radio crystals and money, Sten guns and *plastique*.

"And where is it now?" Millau asked.

"In the store room of an empty shop, down among the old furniture workshops in the faubourg St.-Antoine. I bought the *droit de bail*— the lease—from an old couple who retired to Canada just at the beginning of the war. It was for a long time a *crémerie*—you can still smell the cheese. The address is eighty-eight, rue des Citeaux, just off the avenue St.-Antoine, about a minute's walk from the hospital. In the back of the shop is a storage locker, lead lined, no doubt for cold storage using blocks of ice. The shipment is in there, I've padlocked the door, here are the keys."

"You bought it direct? From Canada?"

"From a broker in Paris. LaMontaine."

"Who is expected to come there?"

"They haven't told me that. Only that it must be kept safe and secure."

"Who said that, exactly?"

"Merlan."

"Beard and spectacles."

"No, the tall one who drove the car."

"When did he say it?"

"The last thing, before I left. I would be contacted, he said."

"How?"

"At home."

"The Bourdon address?"

"Yes."

"Good. That simplifies things for us. It will be of great interest, of course, to see who collects the explosive and spends the money, who uses the radio crystals—to send what information. It's like a complicated web, that reaches here and there, and grows constantly. It may be a long time before we do anything. In these operations you must be thorough, you have to get it all. You'll see—before it's done it will involve husbands and wives, lovers and childhood friends, brothers and sisters, and the local florist. Love finds a way, you see. And we find out."

"Clearly, you are experienced."

Millau permitted himself a brief, tight smile of pleasure in his achievement. "Practice makes perfect," he said. "We've been taking these networks apart since 1933, in Germany. Now in France, we've had one or two—we'll have more. No offense meant, my friend, but the French, compared to the German communist cells, well, what can one say."

He would remember the evening as a certain moment, almost a freeze-frame; three men looking up at him from a table on the crowded *terrasse* of a restaurant, Fouquet as it happened, on a warm evening. All around them, a sea of faces, the world at night—desire and cunning, love and greed, the usual. A Brueghel of Paris in the second spring of the war.

Casson had been driven back to the city by Singer, asked by Millau to join him "and some friends" for a drink. As he approached, the men at the table—Millau with his fine eyeglasses and cigar, and two pale bulky northern men, Herr X and Herr Y, looked up and smiled. *Ah, here he is!* Superbly faked smiles—*how much we admire you.*

They chatted for a time, nothing all that important, a conversation among men of the world, no fools, long past idealism. Poor Europe, decadent and weak, very nearly gobbled up by the Bolshevik monster. *But for them.* Not said, but clearly understood.

The champagne arrived, brought by a waiter who had served him many times in the past. "Good evening, Monsieur Casson." Three menus in German, one in French.

Herr X wore a small pin, a black-and-gold swastika, in his lapel. "One thing we wonder," he said, leaning forward, speaking confidentially. "We were talking to Millau here before you arrived and you told him that there was a copilot on the flight. We hear it a little differently, that the Lysander brought in an agent. Can you see any reason why somebody would say that?"

"No," Casson said. "That's not what happened."

Millau raised his glass. "Enough work!" he said.

For a time it was true. Herr Y was from East Prussia, the Masurian lakes, where stag was still hunted from horseback every autumn. "And then, what a feast!" Herr X worked over in Strasbourg. "Some problems," he said reflectively, "but it is at heart a reasonable part of the world." Then, a fine idea: "I'll tell you what, I'll get in touch with you through Millau and you'll come over there for a day or two. Be a change of pace from Paris, right?"

It was after midnight when Casson got home. He tore his jacket off and threw it on the bed. He'd sweated through his shirt, it was wringing wet. He took it off, then went into the bathroom and looked at himself in the mirror. God. It was black under his eyes. A dark, clever, exhausted man.

THE
ESCAPE

H 18 June, 1941.

e met Mathieu at dusk, in the waiting room of the Gare d'Austerlitz. They walked in the Jardin des Plantes.

"They know what happened," Casson said. "That an agent was brought in."

Mathieu walked in silence for a moment. "Who is it?" he said at last. *Eddie Juin? Lebec? Angier?* "I don't know."

"It will have to be shut down." Mathieu was very angry.

"Yes. Perhaps it's only—you know, the French talk too much. Somebody told somebody, they told somebody else. Each time, 'now, don't tell anybody.' Or, just maybe, it could have happened in London. People in offices, people who work at airfields."

"Yes, it could have," Mathieu admitted. Too many people, too many possibilities. "At least we found out. They would have taken over the network and run it."

The gravel path was bordered by spring beds, tulip and daffodil, poet's narcissus, the air heavy with manure and perfume.

"They want me to go to Strasbourg," Casson said.

"Did they say why?"

"No."

"Will you go?"

"I have to think about it, probably I will."

They walked in silence for a minute or two, then Casson said, "Mathieu, how long does this go on?"

"I can't say."

"There's a record being built—a wire recording they made in Vernouillet, I've been seen with them. What if the war ends?"

"We'll vouch for you."

They reached the end of the path, a wire fence. Beyond were rakes and shovels and wheelbarrows. Mathieu took his hat off, ran a thumb around the lining to secure it, then put it back on, pulling the brim down with thumb and forefinger. "Don't do anything until the twenty-third, then we'll talk again. That's the night—all hell's going to break loose and we're using that to get our job done. Meanwhile, you should go on as usual."

They came to the gate, shook hands. "Be careful," Mathieu said.

Casson couldn't sleep the night of the twenty-third. He went to an after-curfew bar and drank wine. The bar was in a cellar off an alley, it had a packed-earth floor and stone walls. A long time ago, some madman had managed to coax an upright piano down the narrow staircase—perhaps he'd taken it apart. Clearly it was never going anywhere again, and that gave somebody the idea for a nightclub. The piano's sounding board was muffled with a blanket, and an old woman in a gown played love songs and sang in a whispery voice. The cigarette smoke was thick, the only light from a single candle. Casson paused at the bottom of the stairs, then a woman took him in her arms and danced with him.

She smelled of cleaning bleach and brilliantine, had stiff hair that scratched against his cheek. They never spoke. She didn't press herself into him as they danced, just brushed against him, touched him enough so he could feel everything about her. When the sirens started up, she froze. A man nearby called out in a hushed voice, "No, please. One must continue," as though that were a rule of the house.

The rumbling went on for a long time, sharply felt in the cellar because stone foundations built in the Middle Ages carried the vibrations of the bombs and the gunnery beneath the city. A plane went down that night on the rue St.-Honoré, a Lancaster bomber made a fiery cartwheel along the street, sliced through a jeweler's and a millinery shop, then came to rest in the workroom of a dress designer.

Walking home after curfew, Casson stayed alert for patrols, kept to the walls of the buildings. The streets rang with sirens and ambulance bells, searchlights swept the sky, there was a second wave of bombers, then a third. The southern horizon flickered orange just as he slipped into the rue Chardin, and he felt the concussions in the marble stairs as he climbed to his apartment.

Later the telephone rang. He'd fallen asleep on top of the covers, still dressed. "Yes?" he said, looking at his watch. It was twenty minutes past five.

"Jean-Claude?"

"Yes?"

"It's me." It was Marie-Claire, she was crying. He waited, finally she was able to speak. "Bernard Langlade is dead, Jean-Claude."

He went to the Langlades' apartment at seven, the smell of burning was heavy in the air. At the newspaper stands, thick headlines: VILMA AND KAUNAS TAKEN, WEHRMACHT ADVANCES IN RUSSIA. Then, just below, PARIS BOMBED, REPAIRS TO FACTORIES ALREADY BEGUN.

He was the last to arrive. Arnaud opened the door, Casson could see the Pichards, Véronique, a few friends and relatives talking in quiet voices. The Langlades' two grown children were said to be en route to Paris but the bombing had caused havoc on the railroads and they weren't expected until nightfall. When Casson entered the living room, Marie-Claire hugged him tight. Bruno was in the kitchen, he shook his head in sorrow. "This is a rotten thing, Jean-Claude," he said. "Believe me, there will be something important done in his memory, a subscription. I'll be calling you."

Yvette Langlade sat on the end of the couch. She was white, a handkerchief gripped tight in her fist, but very self-possessed. Casson pulled a chair up next to her and took her hand, "Jean-Claude," she said.

"I'm sorry."

"I'm glad you could be here, Jean-Claude."

"What happened?"

"He went out to Montrouge, to the factory."

"In the middle of the night?"

"Something went wrong earlier in the evening—a door left open, or maybe an alarm went off. I'm not sure. A detective called, demanded that Bernard come out to Montrouge and make sure everything was secure. Because of the defense work, the police are very sensitive about things like that. So, he went—"

She stopped for a moment, looked away. The friends who'd arrived first were busy, had claimed the small jobs for themselves: Marie-Claire and her sister making coffee, Françoise Pichard straightening up the living room, her husband answering the telephone.

"He had to do what they told him," Yvette said. "So he changed his clothes and went back out to Montrouge. Then, then they called. This morning. And they told me, that he was gone." She waited a moment, looked away. "They asked a lot of questions." She shook her head, unable to believe what had happened. "Did Bernard store explosives in the factory, they wanted to know. I didn't know what to say." She took a deep breath, pressed her lips together, squeezed Casson's hand. "It's *madness,*" she said. "A man like Bernard. To die in a war."

Véronique brought him a cup of coffee—real coffee, courtesy of Bruno—and they exchanged a private look. He didn't know exactly what part she played in the British operation, but she could have known that sabotage was planned under cover of an air raid. Now, he thought, her look suggested that she did know. He read sympathy in her eyes, and sorrow. But, also, determination. "Careful with this," she said, handing him a cup and saucer. "It's very hot." She turned to Yvette. "Now," she said, "I'm going to bring you some."

"No, dear. Please, I can't."

"Yes, you can. I'm going to go and get it. And Charles Arnaud has just gone out for fresh bread."

After a moment of resistance, Yvette nodded, accepting, giving in to the inevitable. Véronique went off to get the coffee.

My fault, Casson thought. His heart ached for a lost friend. Not that he would survive him very long. They would meet in heaven, Langlade would explain what was what, the best way to deal with it all. Casson wiped his eyes. *Merde,* he thought. They'll kill us all, with their stupid fucking wars.

24 June, 9:10 A.M.

"Good morning."

"Good morning. I'm looking for a copy of the *Decameron,* by Boccaccio."

"Any particular edition?"

"No. Whatever you have."

"I'll take a look, I'm sure we have something."

"I'm at *43 09 19.*"

He was in a café on the boulevard St.-Germain, noisy and crowded and anonymous. The phone rang a moment later.

"Yes?" It was Mathieu on the line.

"I've decided to go to Strasbourg. Right away, because I need to be in Lyons on the first of July."

"Please understand, about Strasbourg, that we really don't know what's going on there."

"Perhaps I can find out."

"It will help us, if you can."

"I'll call Millau this morning, let him know I'm ready to go."

"All right." There was a pause, a moment's hesitation. "You have to walk very lightly, just now. Do you understand?"

"Yes. I know."

All day he felt numb and lifeless. He went to the office, though it seemed to him now a dead place, abandoned, without purpose. He looked in the bottom drawer of his desk, found the notebook with the last version of *Hotel Dorado* and began to read around in it. A few days earlier he'd tried to locate Fischfang, but now he really had disappeared. Perhaps gone underground, or fled to Portugal. Maybe arrested, or dead. Perhaps, Casson thought, he would never know what happened.

He began to clean up his files—this actually made him feel better, so he made some meaningless telephone calls to settle meaningless problems. Soon it was time for lunch; he went to the bank for cash, then returned and took Mireille to the Alsatian brasserie on the corner, slipping black-market ration stamps to the waiter, ordering the grandest *choucroute* on the menu. *Bernard,* he thought, *you used to eat this with me even though you hated it.* Warm sauerkraut, garlic sausage, it made him feel better, and he silently apologized to Langlade because it did.

He flirted with Mireille all through lunch. How it used to be when they were young. Going out dancing in the open pavilions in the early days of spring, falling in love, secret affairs, stolen hours. The bones in the backs of her hands sharply evident, Mireille worked vigorously with knife and fork, delicately removing the rind from a thick slice of bacon as she talked about growing up in a provincial city. "Of course in those days," she said, "men didn't leave their wives."

It was still light when he got home. Trudged up the stairs, put the key in the lock, and opened the door. Standing at the threshold, he smelled cigarette smoke and froze. *It is now,* he thought. Inside, a board creaked, somebody moving toward the door.

"Well, come in." Citrine.

He put his hand on his heart. "My God, you scared me." He closed the door, put his arms around her, and hung on tight, inhaling her deeply, like a dog making sure of somebody from a long time ago. Gauloises and a long train ride on her breath, along with the licorice drop she'd eaten to hide it, very good soap, her skin that always smelled as though she'd been in the sun, some kind of clove and vanilla perfume she'd discovered—the cheaper the better, the way Citrine saw it.

"It's all right I came?" she said. She could feel his head nod yes. "I thought, oh, he's alone long enough. I'll just go up there and throw the schoolgirls out—probably he's tired of them by now."

He walked her down the hall and back into the living room. They sat close together on the couch. "How did you get in?"

"Your concierge. She will not stand in the way of true love. Especially when it's movie actresses. Also, she knew me from before. Also, I bribed her."

"That's all it took?"

She laughed. "Yes."

He kissed her, just a little. She was wearing a tight brown sweater, chocolate, with her yellow scarf tied to one side. A pair of very expensive nylon stockings caught the early evening light.

"I don't care if you're mad," she said.

"I'm not mad."

She studied him a moment. "Tired," she said. "What is it?"

He shrugged. "I don't even look in the mirror."

"A long time by the sea, I think."

"Yes."

"Under the palm trees."

"Yes. With you."

She lay on her side on the couch and he did the same—there was just room. "Do you want to make love right away?" she said.

"No. I want to lie here. Later, we can."

The evening came, birds sang on the roof across the street, the sky darkening to the deep Parisian blue. She took the stockings off and put them carefully aside. He could just see her in the living-room dusk as she put one foot at a time on a chair and rolled each stocking down.

She headed back to the couch, he held up his hand.

"Yes?"

"Why stop?"

"What?"

He smiled.

"You can't mean—" Her "puzzled" look was very good; heavy lips apart, head canted a little to one side. "Well," she said. She understood now, but was it the right thing? She reached around behind her for the button on the waistband of her skirt. "This?"

"Yes."

The telephone rang. It startled him—nobody called at night. It rang again.

"They'll go away," she said.

"Yes," he said, but he sat upright on the couch. *Answer the phone.* On the third ring he stood up.

She didn't like it.

"I have to," he said.

He walked into his bedroom and picked up the receiver. *"Casson!"*

Mathieu screamed. *"Get out! Get out!"* The connection was broken.

"Citrine."

She ran into the bedroom.

"We have to leave."

She disappeared into the living room, swept up coat, valise, hand-bag. Stockings in hand, she forced her feet into her shoes. Casson went to the balcony, opened the doors, looked out. Two black Citroëns were just turning into the rue Chardin. He slammed the doors, ran back into the living room. "Right now," he said.

They ran out the door, then down the stairs, sliding on the marble steps. Citrine slipped, cried out, almost fell as they flew around the mid-floor landing, but Casson managed to pull her upright. *What were they doing?* They had no chance, none at all, of beating the Citroëns to the street door. They reached the fourth floor, he pulled Citrine after him, down to the end of the hallway, a pair of massive doors. There was a buzzer in a little brass plate, but Casson swung his arm back and pounded his fist against the wood. Eight, nine, ten times. The door was thrown open, the baroness stood there, wide-eyed with fright, hand pressed between her breasts. "Monsieur!" she said.

Casson was out of breath. "Please," he said. "Will you hide her?"

The baroness stared at him, then at Citrine. Slowly, the surprise and shock on her face turned to indignation. "Yes," she said, her elegant voice cold with anger. "Yes, of course. How could you think I would not?" She took Citrine by the hand and gently drew her into the apartment.

As the door swung closed, Citrine stepped toward him, their eyes met. She had time to say "Jean-Claude?" That was all.

Casson did try, tried as hard as he could. Raced down four flights of stairs, footsteps echoing off the walls. When he reached the street, the men in raincoats were just climbing out of their cars. They shouted as he started to run, were on him almost immediately. The first one grabbed the back of his shirt, which ripped as he fought to pull free. He punched the man in the forehead and hurt his hand. Then some-body leaped on top of him and, with a yell of triumph, barred a thick forearm across his throat. Casson started to choke. Then, a caution-ary bark in harsh German, and the arm relaxed. The man who seemed to be in charge was apparently irritated by public brawling. A word from him, they let Casson go. He stood there, rubbing his throat, trying to swallow. The man in charge never took his hands out of the pockets of his belted raincoat. A sudden kick swept Casson's feet from under him and he fell on his back in the street. From there, he could see people looking out their windows.

24 June, midnight.

Midnight, more or less—they'd taken his watch. But from the cell in the basement of the rue des Saussaies he could hear the trains in the Métro, and he knew the last one ran around one in the morning.

He was in the basement of the old Interior Ministry—he'd had no idea they had cells down here, but this one had been in use for a long time. It was hard to read the graffiti on the walls, the only light came from a bulb in a wire cage on the ceiling of the corridor, but much of it was carved or scratched into the plaster, and by tracing with his finger he could read it—the earliest entry *16 October, 1902, Tassot*. And who was Tassot, and what had he done, in the autumn of 1902? Well, who was Casson, and what had he done, in the spring of 1941?

The wall was covered with it. Phrases in cyrillic Russian, in Polish, what might have been Armenian. There was Annamese, and Arabic. Faces front and profile. Crosses. Hearts—with initials and arrows. Cocks and cunts, with curly hairs. Somebody loved Marguerite—in 1921, somebody else Martine. This one wrote *Au revoir, Maman*. And that one—a tall one, Casson had to stand on his toes—was going to die in the morning for freedom.

When he heard a deep rumbling sound, he thought for a moment that the RAF was attacking the factory districts at the edge of the city. *And under cover of the bombing, said Wing Commander Smith-Wilson, our commando team will attack the Gestapo office on the rue des Saussaies and rescue our valiant agent from his basement prison.* But it wasn't bombing, it was thunder. Rain pattering down in a courtyard above him somewhere. A spring rainstorm, nothing more.

"One thing I will tell you." A deep voice, from a cell some way up the corridor. Good, educated French, the melancholy tone of the in-

tellectual. Not exactly a whisper, but the voice low and private, confidential. "Can you hear me?"

"Yes."

"Are you injured?"

"No."

"Then I will tell you one thing: sooner or later, everyone talks. And
it's easier on you if it's sooner."

He waited, heart pounding, but that was all.

There was no bed, he sat on the stone floor, back against the damp
wall. The last Métro train faded away, the hours passed. Perhaps he
could have hidden with the baroness, but then, not finding him, they
would have searched the building. They had, no doubt, searched his
apartment, but there was nothing for them to find there. Now, what
remained was a final scene, he'd manage it as well as he could. The
post in the courtyard, the blindfold. Farewell, my love.

What worried him came before that—"sooner or later everyone
talks." *I don't want to tell them,* he thought. But he had no choice,
and he knew it.

They came for him an hour later.

A functionary, and his helper, an SS corporal in a black uniform. The
functionary was a small man in his twenties, wearing a mole-colored
suit with broad lapels. Hair parted in the middle; weak, sulky mouth.
He said to the corporal, "Unlock this door." Disdainful, chin in the
air—*you see, I run things around here.* Casson stood, they walked on
either side of him, down the corridor, then up long flights of stairs.

Somebody's son, Casson thought. A high official in the Nazi party—
what shall we do with poor X? Well, this is what they'd done with him.
They reached the top floor, Casson had been here before, for his meetings with Guske. All around him, office life: people talking and laughing and rushing about with papers in their hands. Typewriters
racketing, telephones ringing. Of course, he thought, the Gestapo
worked a night shift just like the police. A clock on the wall said 3:20.
They took him to Guske's office, made him stand against a wall at attention. "Could I have some water?" he said. He had a terrible, burning thirst—was that something they were doing to him on purpose?

"Nothing for you," said the functionary. He picked up the phone, dialed two digits. A moment later: "We have him ready for you now, Herr *Obersturmbannführer*."

Guske arrived a few minutes later, all business and very angry. He gave Casson a savage glare—very much the honest fellow betrayed by his own good nature. Well, they'd see about *that*. He was dressed for an important evening; dark suit and tie, cologne, sparse hair carefully arranged for maximum effect. On his pocket, a decoration—swastika and ribbon. To Casson's guards he said "Get out," in a voice only just under control. Then paced the office until a heavy woman in SS uniform rushed in with a file. Guske took it from her and slammed it on his desk, and she ran out of the office.

Guske walked slowly over to him and stood there. Casson looked away. Guske drew his hand back and slapped him in the face as hard as he could, the sound was a crack like a pistol shot. Casson's face was hot, and tears stood in the corners of his eyes.

"It's nothing," Guske said. "Just so we understand each other." He went back to his desk and settled in, still breathing hard. He thumbed through the file for a moment but he really didn't have his concentration back. He looked up at Casson. *"I'm* the stupid one. I gave you my hand in friendship, and you turned around and gave me the *Dolch-stoss*—the stab in the back. So, good, now it's clear between us and we'll go on from there. And, when I'm finished with you, Millau gets what's left." He sniffed, turned one page, then another. "The trouble is, we have not come to a true understanding of this country. The Mediterranean type is unfamiliar to us—it does not hesitate to lie, because, the way it sees the world, honor means nothing. But then, when it thinks nobody is looking, it runs out of its burrow, where it hides, and gives somebody a vicious little bite."

Guske read a note pinned to the inside cover of the dossier. "What is HERON? Code for what?"

"I don't know."

Guske's face was mottled with anger. "And who is Laurent?"

Casson shook his head.

Guske stared at him. Casson heard the typewriters and the telephones, voices and footsteps. The rain outside the window. It seemed very normal. "I need," Casson said, "to use the bathroom."

Guske thought about it for a moment, then opened the door and called out, "Werner, come and take him down the hall."

The functionary came on the run. Took him past offices, a long way it seemed. Around a corner. Then to an unmarked door, which he opened, saying "Be quick about it." He closed the door. Casson stood in front of a urinal.

On the wall above the sink, a window. Gray, frosted glass. Probably barred, but not so Casson could see. But then, he thought, why would they have bars? This is the Interior Ministry. The top floor. For the French, the most important people would be housed on the second floor. In former times, the top floor would have served the Ministry's minor bureaucrats—what would they want with bars in a bathroom? Casson walked to the sink and turned it on, drank some water, put his hand on the glass of the window. Top floor, he thought, six stories down to a courtyard.

You'll die.

But then, what did that matter? Better now, he thought, before they go to work on me.

"Just a minute."

He put his index fingers under the two handles and very gently pushed up. Nothing. Locked. He could back up to the door, take a run, and jump through it, smashing the glass, tumbling six stories to the courtyard below. He pushed harder, the window moved. Opened an inch. The night air rushed in, it was black outside, and pouring rain.

Lower the window. Go back to Guske's office. Explain everything to him. Try to talk your way out of it—crawl, do whatever you have to do.

He listened, held his breath. Against the background hum of office business he could just make out Werner's voice. It spoke German, but Casson could easily understand the tone of it. He was explaining something—he was being important. Casson raised the window, perhaps a foot. A damp, sweet wind blew in on him and he could hear distant thunder, a storm up the Seine somewhere, the sound rolling down across the wheatfields into Paris.

He put one knee on the edge of the sink, pulled himself through the window, then froze, terrified, unable to move. The night swirled around him, the courtyard a thousand feet below, the wet cobblestone gleaming in the faint spill of light from blacked-out windows. He forced himself to look around: the window was set out a little from the slanted plane of the roof, slate tile angled sharply up to the peak—

copper sheathing turned green with age. To the left: a cascade of white, foamy water. He followed it, found an ancient lead gutter, eaten through by time and corrosion, water pouring through the hole, spilling off the edge of the roof and splashing into the courtyard below.

If he stood on the window ledge . . .

He had to force his body to move—he was trembling with fear. He got himself turned around, feet dangling into space, pulled himself to his knees by using the inside handles of the window, then stood up, back to the courtyard. The rain was cold on his face, he took a deep breath. The gutter ran to a perpendicular roof. He could inch over—feet on the gutter, body pressed flat against the slate—and climb the angle. He would then be—he would then be somewhere else.

He heard the bathroom door open, heard Werner cry out. He let go of the window handles, lifted his right foot from the ledge and placed it on the gutter. Werner ran toward the window, Casson left the ledge and let his weight shift to the gutter. It rolled over, dumping its water, then dropped three inches. Casson bit down against a scream and clawed at the wet slate for traction.

Werner's head appeared through the window. He was pale with terror, his carefully combed hair hanging lank from its center parting. Suddenly he leaned out, took a swipe at Casson's ankle. Casson crabbed sideways along the gutter.

From Werner, a taut little laugh—just kidding. "Tell me, what on earth do you think you're doing out there?"

Casson didn't answer.

"Mm?"

Silence.

"Perhaps you will end it all, eh?" His voice was low, and edged with panic. It was, at the same time, hopeful. To allow an escape was unthinkable, but suicide—maybe they wouldn't be quite so angry with him.

Casson couldn't speak. He closed his eyes, felt the rain on his hair and skin, heard the storm in the distance. From the darkness, from the very root of his soul, he said slowly, "Leave me alone."

A minute passed, frozen time. Then Werner gave an order, his voice a shrill whisper. "You come back in here!" Casson could hear a life in the words—all the failures, all the excuses.

Casson moved another step, the gutter sagged. He stretched his arms as high as they would go, discovered a mossy crack between the slate tiles. He tried it—it was possible, just barely and not for long.

Now Werner saw everything he'd worked for about to fall apart. "One more step," he said, "and I call the guards."

Casson counted to twenty. "All right," he said. "I'm coming back." But he didn't move. He could imagine Guske in his office, looking at his watch.

"Well?"

"I can't."

"You must try!"

"My feet won't move."

"Ach."

Teeth clenched with fury, Werner wriggled through the window then stood on the ledge. "Just stay still," he said. "I'll help you."

Casson drove the tips of his fingers through the moss, into the shallow crack. Werner stepped daintily off the ledge, made sure of his balance, then, leaning his weight on the roof, began to move slowly sideways. Casson shifted his weight to his hands, lifted his right leg as high as it would go and rammed it back down against the gutter.

Nothing happened.

Until Werner's next step—then he mewed with fear as the gutter came away. Then he vanished. For part of a second he thought it over, at last allowed himself a loud whine of indignation that ended, briefly, in a scream. The lead gutter hit the cobbles with a dull clatter.

Thirty seconds, Casson thought, no more. The crack between the tiles deepened, and he moved along it quickly. Reached the corner where the two wings of the building met, shinned up the angle to the peak, lay flat on the copper sheathing and tried to catch his breath. As he looked over the other side he saw a row of windows—the same type he'd just crawled out of. The only difference was a narrow spillway, wedged between the slanted roof and a stone parapet.

Now they discovered Werner.

He heard shouts from the courtyard, somebody blew a police whistle, flashlight beams swept everywhere, across the façades of the building and the roof. He rolled off the peak and let himself slide down to the spillway. There he stayed on his knees, looked over the parapet, saw a sheer drop to a narrow street. He had no idea what it might be, the city was a maze—secret courtyards, blind alleyways, sense of direction meant nothing.

He ran along the the spillway, looked in the first window. Blackout curtain. At the next, the curtain was slightly askew. He could see an office in low light, a cleaner in a gray smock was polishing the waxed parquet with a square of sheepskin tied to a broom. Casson tapped on the window.

The man looked up. Casson tapped again. The man walked slowly to the window and tried to see out. *The Lost King,* Casson thought. An old man with snow-white hair and thin lips and rosy skin. He moved the blackout curtain aside and cranked the casement window open a few inches. "What are you doing out there?" he asked.

"I escaped. Over the roof."

"Escaped? From the Gestapo?"

"Yes."

"Bon Dieu." He ran a hand through his hair, smoothing it back, thinking. "Well, over here we're the National Meteorological office, but, we have our Germans too, of course." He stopped, the shouts from the courtyard on the other side of the building could just be heard. "Well, then, monsieur, I expect you may want to climb in here, and permit us to hide you."

25 June, 1941.

"Good morning."

"Good morning. I was wondering if you have, a certain book."

"Yes? What would that be?"

"An atlas."

"Yes? Of what country?"

"France."

"Perhaps, we could call you back?"

"No. I'll be in later."

"But sir . . ."

He hung up.

Not the same person, and, he thought, not French.

German.

❖

25 June, 1941.

The baroness answered the phone in a cool, distant voice. "Hello?"

"Hello. This is your neighbor, from upstairs."

"Oh. Yes, I see. Are things going well? For you?"

"Not too badly. My friend?"

"Your friend. Has returned to Lyons. I believe, without difficulties."

"I'm glad to hear it."

"You are, you know, very fortunate to have such a friendship."

"Yes, I do know that."

"In that case, I hope you are careful."

"I am. In fact, I ought to be going."

"Good-bye, then. Perhaps we'll meet again, some day."

"Perhaps we will. And, madame, thank you."

"You're welcome, monsieur."

25 June, 1941.

"Galéries Lafayette."

"Good morning. I'm calling for Véronique, in the buyers' office."

"One moment, please."

"Hello?"

"Hello, may I speak with Véronique, please."

"I'm sorry, she hasn't come in today, perhaps she'll be in tomorrow. Would you care to leave a message?"

"No, no message. I'll call back tomorrow."

"Very well. Good-bye,"

"Good-bye."

A café in the Tenth, busy and crowded. Casson went back to his table. Took a sip of his chicory-laced coffee. The Lost King and his colleagues had been very generous, had given him a shirt, a cap, an old jacket, and a few francs. They had even hit upon a scheme to persuade the Gestapo that their intensive search of the building was likely to prove fruitless— one of the men who took care of the furnace had snuck upstairs to the street floor of the Interior Ministry and, simply enough, left a door open.

Still, kind as they'd been, Casson was in some difficulty. Everything was gone: apartment, office, business, friends, bank accounts, passport. He was down to fourteen francs and Citrine—who would be safe, he thought, as long as she stayed in Lyons and didn't call attention to herself.

So then, he asked himself, *what next?* He imagined Fischfang, sitting across the table, ordering the most expensive drink on the menu. Now that the hero has given his pursuers the slip, what becomes of him? *His uncle dies, he inherits.* Casson looked at his watch, but there was nothing on his wrist.

He drank up his coffee, left a tip, and went out to the street. A clock in the window of a jewelry store said 10:10, Casson started walking. A long walk, from the 10th Arrondissement all the way across the river to the Fifth. He had no identity papers, so the Métro, with its snap searches, was dangerous. Besides, he thought, he really couldn't afford the five sous it cost for a ticket.

A warm day, the city out in its streets. Casson hadn't shaved, he pulled the worker's cap down over one eye, walked with hands in pockets. Good camouflage, he thought. Women going off to the shops gave him the once-over—a little worn, this one, could he be refurbished? He took the rue Pavée in the Jewish district, past a chicken store with feathers floating in the air. He saw a tailor at work through an open shop door, the man felt his eyes, looked up from a jacket turned back over its lining, and returned Casson's wry smile.

He crossed the Seine on the Pont d'Austerlitz, stopped for a time, as he always did, to stare down at the river. Still swollen and mud-colored from the spring rains, it rubbed against the stone piers of the bridge, mysterious in the rolls and swirls of its currents, opaque and dirty and lovely—the soul of its city and everybody who lived there knew it.

He worked his way around the rough edges of the Fifth, avoiding the eyes of Wehrmacht tourists, taking the side streets. The place Maubert was hard on him—the smell of roasting chicken and sour wine was heavy on the air, and Casson was hungry.

The café where he'd met Véronique earlier that spring was deserted, the proprietor rubbing a dry glass with a towel and staring hypnotized into the street. Casson stood at the bar and ordered a coffee. The owner jiggled the handle on the nickel-plated machine, produced a loud hiss and a column of steam, the smell of burnt chicory, and a trickle of dark liquid.

"Seen Véronique today?" Casson asked.

In return, an eyebrow lifted in the who-wants-to-know look. "Not today."

"Think she might be in later?"

"She might."

"Mind if I wait?"

"Fine with me."

He waited all day. He took his coffee to the last table in the back, kept the cup in front of him, pored over yesterday's newspaper, and, at last, broke down and spent three francs in a *tabac* for a packet of Bulgarian cigarettes.

A workers' café, Véronique had called it. Yellow walls dyed amber with smoke, slow, steady stream of customers—a red wine, a beer, a coffee, a *marc*, a *fine*, elbows on the bar. At six, some students came down the hill and stood in a crowd by the door, imitating one of their professors and having a good loud laugh. Casson looked a second time, and there was Véronique, in the middle of it, getting an envelope from the owner.

She was startled when he appeared next to her. Then she nodded her head toward the square. "Let's go for a walk, Jean-Claude."

They walked from cart to cart in the Maubert market, pretending to shop, staring at baskets of eels and mounds of leeks. Casson told her what had happened to him, Véronique said he'd been lucky. As for her, she'd been warned in person, at the office. "I'm leaving tonight, Jean-Claude. I just stopped at the café for a final message."

"Leaving for where?"

"South. Over the mountains."

They were standing in front of a mound of spring potatoes, red ones, the smell of wet earth still on them.

"Jean-Claude," she said. "I want you to go to number seven, in the rue Taine. Immediately. The man there will take care of you. You know where it is?"

"No."

"Bercy. Near the wine warehouses."

"All right."

An old man in an ancient, chalk-striped suit strolled over to the potato cart and stood near them, just close enough to overhear what they might be saying. Casson wanted to bark at him, Véronique took his arm and walked him away. "Oh this city," she said in a low voice.

They stood in front of a barrow filled with dusty beets, the little girl minding the store was no more than eleven. "Ten sous, 'sieur et 'dame,'" she said hopefully.

Véronique took a breath and let it out slowly. Casson could tell she sensed danger. "So now," she said quietly, "we've done this shopping, and, old friends that we are, it's time to part. We'll kiss each other farewell, and then we'll go."

Casson turned to her and they kissed left and right. He saw that her eyes were shining. "Good-bye, my friend," she said.

"Au revoir, Véronique."

The last he saw of her, she was walking quickly through the crowd in a narrow lane between market stalls. Just as she turned the corner, she gave him a sudden smile and a little wave, then she vanished.

It was the sharp edge of the war on the rue Taine—an apartment of little rooms, all the blinds drawn, above a dark courtyard. There was a .45 automatic on the kitchen table, and a Sten gun in the parlor, candlelight a dull sheen on its oiled barrel. The operative was British, but nothing like Mathieu—this man was born to the vocation, and 1941 was the year of his life.

"You're going to England," he said. "We're closing down the network, saving what we can, but you can't stay here."

It was the right, probably the only, thing to do, but Casson felt something tear inside him.

"You'll like England," the operative said. "We'll see you don't starve, and you'll be alive. Not everybody is, tonight."

Casson nodded. "A telephone call?"

"Impossible. Sorry."

"Perhaps a letter. There's somebody, in Lyons."

It was the wrong thing to say. "Help us win the war," the operative said. "Then you'll go home. Everything will be wonderful."

An hour later they brought in a wounded British airman, face the color of chalk. Casson sat with him on a battered sofa and the man showed him a photograph of his dog.

At midnight, two French railwaymen came for the airman.

At 1:30, Casson was escorted to another apartment in the building.

His photograph was taken, then, at 2:10, he was handed a new identity—passport with photo, *Ausweis,* work permit—a thousand francs
and a book of ration stamps.

Back at the first apartment, he dozed for a time. The operative never
slept, worked over coded transmissions—there was a clandestine radio
in another building in the neighborhood, Casson guessed—and listened
to the BBC at low volume. Sometimes he made a note of the time—
the *Messages Personnels* were long over for the night, but Casson
thought he was being signaled by what songs were played, and the
order they were played in.

Casson left at dawn. The woman who took him out was in her fifties,
with dark red hair and the hard accents of northeast France. A Pole,
perhaps, but she didn't say. He sat silent in the passenger seat as she
drove. The car was a battered old Fiat 1500, but it was fast, and the
woman made good time on the empty roads. She swung due east from
Bercy, and was out of Paris in under a minute. They stopped for a German control at the porte de Charenton, and a French police roadblock
in Montreuil. Both times the driver was addressed—as the passports
were handed back by the officers—as "Doctor."

After that, they virtually disappeared, curved slowly north and west
around the city on the back streets of small towns and secondary
roads. By eight in the morning they were winding their way toward
Rouen on the east—much less traveled—bank of the Seine. Outside a
small village the driver worked her way down a hillside of packed dirt
streets to the edge of the river, just across from the town of Mantes.
The car rolled to a stop at the edge of a clearing, two black-and-white
spaniels ran barking up to the driver and she rumpled their ears and
called them sweethearts.

Beyond a marsh of tall reeds, Casson could see a houseboat—
bleached gray wood with a crooked piece of pipe for the stove—tied
up to a pole dock. A young man appeared a moment later, asked the
driver if she wanted coffee. "No," she sighed. "I can't stop." She had
to be somewhere in an hour, was already going to be late. To Casson
she said, "You'll remain here for thirty hours, then we'll move you
north to Honfleur. These people are responsible for you—please do
what they ask."

"Thank you," Casson said.

"Good luck," the driver said. "It won't be long now."

A family lived on the houseboat, a young man and his wife and their three little girls. Casson was taken to a bedroom with heavy drapes on the windows. The woman brought him a bowl of lentils with mustard and a piece of bread. "It's better if you stay inside when it's daylight," she said. He spent the day dozing and thumbing through a stack of old magazines. At dusk, they said he could take the air for a half-hour. He was happy for that, sat on the sagging dock and watched birds flying over the river. There was a mackerel sky just before dark, the last red of the sun lighting the clouds, then a dark, starless evening, and a breeze that rustled in the leaves of the willow trees that grew on the river bank.

His heart ached—he could only unwind the past, looking for another road that might have led to a better place, but he could not find it. He tried to tell himself that Citrine would understand, would sense somehow that he'd escaped from the Germans and would come back to her in time.

He really did try.

He went back out again at dawn. Cruel of this countryside, he thought, to be so beautiful when it was being taken from him. The Vexin—above Paris along the river—was fighting country, rather bloodsoaked if you knew the history. But then, people fought over beautiful things, a side of human nature that didn't quite have a name. The oldest of the little girls, seven perhaps, came out to the dock and said "*Maman* says the sun is coming up now, and will the monsieur please take coffee with us."

As good a moment as any to say good-bye, he thought, the little girl standing close to him on the dock. Just a bend in a river, and dawn was always good to a place like this, gray light afloat on the water, a bird calling in the marsh.

Later that day they took him up to the port of Honfleur in a truck. The driver was in charge of the final stage of the escape line and briefed

Casson as they drove. "You'll go out on a fishing boat. We leave at dawn, sail to the mouth of the river with the rest of the fleet and stand to for German inspection. You will be hidden below decks—your chances of passing through the inspection are good, the Germans search one boat in four, and use dogs only now and then. After the inspection the fleet will be fishing—for conger eel—in a group. A German plane flies over periodically, and we are permitted only enough fuel for thirty-five miles of cruising. Sometime during the afternoon, you will be transferred to a trawler allowed to work farther out at sea, a trawler with an overnight permit. These boats are sometimes searched by German minesweepers. At the midpoint of the Channel, between French and British waters, you'll be taken on a British navy motor launch, and put ashore at Bournemouth."

He stayed that night in another bedroom with heavy curtains—this time in a house on the outskirts of a coastal village. Then, at 4:30 A.M. on the morning of 28 June, he was taken to a small fishing boat in the port of Honfleur, and led to a secret compartment built behind the belowdecks cabin—entered by removing a section of wall from the back of a storage locker.

He was joined first by a young woman, exhausted but calm, clearly at the end of a long and difficult assignment. They were never to speak, but did exchange a smile—bittersweet, a little hopeless—that said virtually everything there was to say. What sort of world was it, where they, where people like them, did the things they had done?

Moments later, the arrival of an important personage; a tall, distinguished man, his wife, his teenaged sons, and three suitcases. Casson guessed this was a diplomat or senior civil servant, being brought to London at de Gaulle's request. The man looked around the tiny space with a certain muted displeasure—he'd clearly not been informed that he was going to have to *share* a hiding place, and it was not at all to his taste.

The compartment was sealed up and they got under way almost immediately, the throb of the engine loud in the small space. Casson, his back resting against the curved wood of the hull, could feel the water sliding past. There was no light, it was very hot, he could hear the others breathing. The boat slowed, then stopped for inspection, and as the engine idled the smell of gasoline grew stronger and stronger in the compartment. Above them, boots stamping on the deck. The Germans were talking, laughing with each other—they felt really good today, they'd had a triumph of some kind. Time crawled, the boat rising and falling on the heavy swell in the harbor. Casson felt sweat gather at his hairline and run down his face.

Then it ended. The German patrol boat started up with a roar, their own engine accelerated, and the boat moved forward; somebody on the other side of the wall said, "All right, that's over. We'll let you out as soon as we clear the harbor."

On deck, Casson breathed the salt air, gripped the railing, and watched the land fall away as the boat moved out to sea. It was the end of the night, hills dark against the sky, faded moon, white combers rolling in to shore.

Good-bye.

Forever—he knew that. This was what life cost you, you lost what you loved. He closed his eyes and saw her, felt her breath on his face, felt her skin against him. Then he was in the sea.

Cold. The shock of it made him gasp, then swim for his life. Behind him, great volleys of angry threats and curses. Ahead of him, now he could see it, the beach.

Citrine.

THE WORLD
AT NIGHT

ALAN FURST

A Reader's Guide

The Research of Alan Furst's Novels

Alan Furst describes the area of his interest as "near history." His novels are set between 1933—the date of Adolf Hitler's ascent, with the first Stalinist purges in Moscow coming a year later—and 1945, which saw the end of the war in Europe. The history of this period is well documented. Furst uses books by journalists of the time, personal memoirs—some privately published—autobiographies (many of the prominent individuals of the period wrote them), war and political histories, and characteristic novels written during those years.

"But," he says, "there is a lot more"—for example, period newsreels, magazines, and newspapers, as well as films and music, especially swing and jazz. "I buy old books," Furst says, "and old maps, and I once bought, while living in Paris, the photo archive of a French stock house that served the newspapers of Paris during the Occupation, all the prints marked as cleared by the German censorship." In addition, Furst uses intelligence histories of the time, many of them by British writers.

Alan Furst has lived for long periods in Paris and in the south of France. "In Europe," he says, "the past is still available. I remember a blue neon sign, in the Eleventh Arrondissement in Paris, that had possibly been there since the 1930s." He recalls that on the French holiday *le jour des morts* (All Saints' Day, November 1) it is customary for Parisians to go to the Père Lachaise Cemetery. "Before the collapse of Polish communism, the Polish émigrés used to gather at the tomb of Maria Walewska. They would burn rows of votive candles and play Chopin on a portable stereo. It was always raining on that day, and a dozen or so Poles would stand there, under black umbrellas, with the music playing, as a kind of silent protest against the communist regime. The spirit of this action was history alive—as though the entire past of that country, conquered again and again, was being brought back to life."

The heroes of Alan Furst's novels include a Bulgarian defector from the Soviet intelligence service, a foreign correspondent for *Pravda*, a Polish cartographer who works for the army general staff, a French producer of gangster films, and a Hungarian émigré who works with a diplomat at the Hungarian legation in Paris. "These are characters in novels," Furst says, "but people like them existed; people like them were courageous people with ordinary lives and, when the moment came, they acted with bravery and determination. I simply make it possible for them to tell their stories."

Questions for Discussion

1. If you asked Jean Casson to define the word *honor,* what would he say? Which, if any, of the following would be included: Loyalty to friends? Loyalty to country? Loyalty in love? Loyalty to self?

2. After his meeting with Simic, in which he is first offered the chance to work for British intelligence, Casson thinks to himself, *"You think you know how the world works, but you really don't. These people are the ones who know how it works."* How would you say Casson's understanding of the world has changed by the novel's conclusion? Has he become one of the people who know how the world "really works"?

3. To what extent is Casson culpable for the death of his friend Langlade?

4. During the early years of the German Occupation of France, a common question, which Langlade poses to Casson, was this: "If your barber cuts hair under the Occupation, does that make him a collaborator?" How would you respond? What would you have done in similar circumstances?

5. Alan Furst has said that his books are written from the point of view of the nation where the story takes place. Describe the French point of view as it appears in *The World at Night.*

6. Critics praise Furst's ability to re-create the atmosphere of World War II–era Europe. What elements of description make the setting come alive? How can you account for the fact that the settings *seem* authentic even though you probably have no firsthand knowledge of the times and places he writes about?

7. Furst's novels have been described as "historical novels," and as "spy novels." He calls them "historical spy novels." Some critics have insisted

that they are, simply, novels. How does his work compare with other spy novels you've read? What does he do that is the same? Different? If you owned a bookstore, in what section would you display his books?

8. Furst is often praised for his minor characters, which have been described as "sketched out in a few strokes." Do you have a favorite in this book? Characters in his books often take part in the action for a few pages and then disappear. What do you think becomes of them? How do you know?

9. At the end of an Alan Furst novel, the hero is always still alive. What becomes of Furst's heroes? Will they survive the war? Does Furst know what becomes of them? Would it be better if they were somewhere safe and sound, to live out the war in comfort? If not, why not?

10. How do the notions of good and evil work in *The World at Night*? Would you prefer a confrontation between villain and hero? Describe Furst's use of realism in this regard.

Suggested Reading

There is an enormous body of literature, fiction and nonfiction, written about the period 1933–1945, so Alan Furst's recommendations for reading in that era are very specific. He often uses characters who are idealistic intellectuals, particularly French and Russian, who become disillusioned with the Soviet Union but still find themselves caught up in the political warfare of the period. "Among the historical figures who wrote about that time," Furst says, "Arthur Koestler may well be 'first among equals.' " Furst suggests Koestler's *Darkness at Noon* as a classic story of the European intellectual at midcentury.

Furst, as a novelist of historical espionage, is most often compared with the British authors Graham Greene and Eric Ambler. Asked about Ambler's books, Furst replies that "the best one I know is *A Coffin for Dimitrios.*" Published in 1939, a month before the invasion of Poland, Ambler's novel concentrates on clandestine operations in the Balkans and includes murder for money, political assassination, espionage, and drug smuggling. The plot, like that of an Alan Furst novel, weaves intrigue and conspiracy into the real politics of 1930s Europe.

For the reality of daily life in eastern Europe, Furst suggests the novelist Gregor von Rezzori, of Italian/Austro-Hungarian background, who grew up in a remote corner of southeastern Europe, between the wars, and writes about it brilliantly in *Memoirs of an Anti-Semite,* which takes place in the villages of Romania and the city of Bucharest in the years before the war.

To see life in that period from the German perspective, Furst says that Christopher Isherwood's novels *The Last of Mr. Norris* and *Goodbye to Berlin* are among the best possible choices. The sources for the stage plays *I Am a Camera* and *Cabaret,* these are novelized autobiographies of Isherwood's time in Berlin; they are now published as *The Berlin Stories*. Furst calls them "perceptive and wonderfully written chronicles of bohemian life during the rise to power of Adolf Hitler and the Nazi party."

For a historical overview of the period, Alan Furst recommends Martin Gilbert's *A History of the Twentieth Century, Volume Two: 1933–1951*. All the major political events that rule the lives of the characters in Alan Furst's novels are described, in chronological sequence, in this history.

ABOUT THE TYPE

This book was set in Sabon, a typeface designed by the well-known German typographer Jan Tschichold (1902–74). Sabon's design is based upon the original letter forms of Claude Garamond and was created specifically to be used for three sources: foundry type for hand composition, Linotype, and Monotype. Tschichold named his typeface for the famous Frankfurt typefounder Jacques Sabon, who died in 1580.

SOMETHING
MIGHT HAPPEN

Julie Myerson was born in Nottingham in 1960. She is
the author of four previous novels: *Sleepwalking*, *The
Touch*, *Me and the Fat Man* and *Laura Blundy*. Her
work has been translated into many languages.

Julie Myerson

SOMETHING MIGHT HAPPEN

V

VINTAGE

First published in Great Britain in 2003 by
Jonathan Cape

Vintage
Random House, 20 Vauxhall Bridge Road,
London SW1V 2SA

Random House Australia (Pty) Limited
20 Alfred Street, Milsons Point, Sydney
New South Wales 2061, Australia

Random House New Zealand Limited
18 Poland Road, Glenfield,
Auckland 10, New Zealand

Random House (Pty) Limited
Endulini, 5A Jubilee Road, Parktown 2193,
South Africa

The Random House Group Limited Reg. No. 954009
www.randomhouse.co.uk

A CIP catalogue record for this book
is available from the British Library

ISBN 0 099 45352 5

Papers used by Random House are natural, recyclable
products made from wood grown in sustainable forests.
The manufacturing processes conform to the environ-
mental regulations of the country of origin

Printed and bound in Great Britain by
Bookmarque Ltd, Croydon, Surrey

For Esther Freud –
who understands about the place

I

People think when someone is stabbed they just fall down on the ground and die. Well they don't. When Lennie is found on that morning in the car park on Pier Avenue, they can tell from the mess that she dragged herself around for some time before she gave up.

Quite some time, in fact. Maybe even as much as a quarter of an hour. Crawling like a baby on her hands and knees, grabbing and swiping at door handles and bumpers, fingers tacky with her own blood. Then at some point slipping down and losing consciousness there in the nettles by the Pay & Display machine. They say they can't be certain about when it was, the precise moment that her heart stopped – but they can assure us that it was immaterial. She wouldn't have seen, wouldn't have known.

The one good thing, Mawhinney says, is that her brain would've shut down as her lungs filled up.

But I don't want the details. One moment or several? A curdled sigh, a spattered red breath, brown saliva clotting in her mouth? All I care about is that they're right, that it was quick. All I need to know is that her heart was not still beating when her attacker moved back in and cut it out.

Early October and four in the morning and no wind at all, just the blackest darkness, so dead and dark and black that if you stopped to think about it, you might find you couldn't breathe. All the lights out. And then all of them on, one by one – pop, pop, pop – the world reviving, turning large and transparent.

Something's happened.

He rings me at the deadest time, sleep holding me down. Since the baby that's how I've been, a dead person, trying to surface. Still I grab the phone the second its ringing hits my dreams.

Tess, he goes, Tess – and straightway I can tell his voice is all wrong.

What? I say, struggling to sit up and focus. What is it? What's going on?

I'm –

The silence crackles.

I'm sorry, he says.

What do you mean, sorry? Why?

Oh Tess, he says and he sounds like he's going to cry.

Al, I go, for fuck's sake – what?

She's not here.

What?

You were right. She hasn't come home.

She hasn't?

She's just — I don't know where she is — she's not here.

Outside, a dark whoosh of wind in the poplars. If it was light you would see them bending. You get that by the sea — sudden changes, things getting crushed and flattened. I used to like it. It used not to scare me at all.

Next to me in the bed meanwhile Livvy is lying on her back in her white babygro, poppers done up to the chin, mouth softly open and arms flung back. A swirl of blackish hair on her head. Mick funnily enough is lying in a similar babyish way but on his front — black matted hair pushed up, hands bunched into two hot fists. Dreaming of a fight is what it looks like.

Tess, he says, what am I going to do?

Call the police.

I've done that.

You want me to come?

He says nothing. Liv snorts. When did I feed her? I slide my fingers under to feel her nappy. Damply heavy with pee. I must have fed her in the night, in my sleep.

I'll come, I tell him. Wait for me.

I get out of bed, change the baby, get dressed.

In one way it is not a surprise. In the beach hut that night, the feeling is cold and hard, painful and unsettling. I shouldn't have let him come. It shouldn't have to be complicated.

I take the tumbler of wine from his hands. Take a sip.

Put it down on the wooden floor which is slippy with the years of sand falling off our bare feet.

You should get back, I say. But he doesn't move. He just looks at me.

She'll be in bed. She'll have gone to sleep.

No, I say. It's not that.

What, then?

He reaches forward, half grinning, tries to take his drink back. I stop him.

The truth is, he's lazy. Whatever he gets from me, he imagines he can't get from anyone else.

It's not that, I say again. Batting him away.

He settles back in the old deckchair and looks at me. His old jeans, his big feet in their salt-stained boots. A bleached tidemark where he has walked in the edge of the sea. He looks at the joint in his hands – his rough, furniture maker's hands – tips off the ash.

For God's sake, Tess, he says at last, I wish you'd calm down.

I sigh.

You're even making me jumpy, he says. What the fuck is it? Why're you in such a state?

I say nothing.

He shrugs, smiles. He likes to think I'm this uptight person. He thinks he's won.

I'm scared, I tell him and he leans forward.

What are you scared of, Tess?

I don't know.

It's not true though. I think I do know, even then.

★   ★   ★

4

The thing is, she is not the type to have something happen. She has everything going for her. Beauty, talent, kindness. She even sometimes goes to church.

It's the one thing she and Alex argue about, the only thing. It's not God, she says, just something bigger, greater then her. She needs to feel there is a larger Good out there.

You might think she's this good and pliable person but actually she's not, she's dogged and fixed. She's the strong one. She does exactly as she pleases. When we first came here, she was the one who said it would all be fine, who believed most certainly in the dream we had.

The only thing I have more of than her is kids. Double the amount. People ask me how I do it, as if there's some kind of trick to having four. But it's easy. I do it for myself. I can't help it. There's nothing to beat walking down the street on a sunny day with them all clean and happy and no one crying or fighting behind you and knowing just how it all looks. A perfect mother with her perfect life.

These are the facts. That she dies on a Monday night in October, some time between eleven and midnight, following a PTA meeting at the school on Marlborough Road. That she gets to that meeting around seven and it ends around twenty to eleven — later than usual, but then it is Lucy Dorry's first time as Chair and most people who can, stay on for a drink after.

That they reckon, anyway, that she reaches her car

around 10.45, but that she never manages to get into it. She never even makes it around to the driver's side. Her keys are found lying on the ground just beneath the passenger door. All the paintwork around the lock is scratched furiously and the nails on her right hand are ripped and bloody and broken.

Both of us, with our perfect lives. She can't believe it when I tell her I'm expecting Liv. At thirty-eight!

You're saying I'm past it?

No, she replies and I notice the flicker of a frown in her eyes. Just the thought — and she shudders — of going through it all again.

I can't wait, I tell her as boisterously as I can. And it's the truth, I can't.

And work?

I can do that too, I say. Because I've already decided that I'll have to.

She turns and looks at me with eyes full of something, but what exactly I can't tell.

I wish I had your guts, she says. And your energy.

Which makes me laugh because, in my book, it takes guts and energy to deny yourself these things. And Mick and I have never been good at limiting ourselves, at sitting down and planning. In fact, none of our kids were planned exactly — or that's what we always tell people, laughing at ourselves. Just one big happy haphazard family. That's the story we tell ourselves.

And I am over the moon about Liv — from that first mysterious morning when the simple act of stirring the hot milk into Rosa's instant oat cereal makes me turn and hold myself, perspiring, over the sink.

When I tell Mick, he does nothing. He doesn't move. He is sitting there at the table and I bend and whisper it in his ear and maybe I expect that he will pull me to him, but he doesn't move a single muscle.

You're not pleased?

He looks at me.

I don't know. I'm not 'not' pleased.

Oh great.

I fold my arms and feel the buzz of my blood, my heart.

It's a shock, that's all.

We haven't been using anything.

I know, he says, I know, but I thought –

You thought what?

That we were being careful.

I laugh.

I suppose I thought it was very unlikely, he says.

His voice is small and tight. He sounds like a little boy who's been jumping again and again out of the highest tree and then the very last time has forgotten to bend his knees when he lands and has got himself hurt. Cross with the tree, cross with himself.

I've just chucked in my job, he reminds me, as if I didn't know.

Well, I tell him, this is good. You can be the nanny. You can do some writing.

He doesn't laugh.

With a new baby? I hope that's a joke.

But when he sees me looking at him and half laughing and half about to cry, he does get up and come and put his arms around me, bends his head to mine. I smell the blackness of his hair, the familiar day-old smell of beard, of husband.

So, he says.

So – what?

So we'd better get on with it then.

And that's it, that's all. That's the beginning of our daughter Olivia.

The last person to see Lennie alive is John Empson, PTA Treasurer and Chairman of the Christmas Lights. I know John well. His bookshop is next door to the clinic and he gives me discounts. In return I gave him ultrasound for nothing when he tore the ligaments in his knee. It's how we live in this place. You give what you can and you get back what you need.

On that night, John walks with Lennie as far as the junction of Marlborough Road and North Parade. It is bitterly cold by then, the kind of rough, sea cold that goes right through your clothes and hits your bones. A light rain has started up and Lennie is hurrying, they both are, and since she only has on a thin cardigan and no umbrella, she holds her papers up over her head.

Like this, John says later, using his big, grey hands to show the police. As if they could protect her, he says, terror and disbelief cracking his voice.

John and Lennie chat briefly about this and that – about how glad they are to have Lucy on board, about what should be done about the frustrating delay to plans for bike racks outside the caretaker's office (despite the money having officially been raised) – and so on. Then, because John is heading back to the High Street on his bike, he zips his big green waterproof and they separate, each making a dash for it.

In any other town perhaps, he might have seen her to her car, but not in this one. No one expects that here. This town really is a safe place, everyone knows that. Even in winter, even after dark, it's a place where, once kids know how to cross a road sensibly, they can pretty much go around alone.

What happens next is Alex says sorry to Gemma Dawson, who popped over from Trinity Street to keep an eye on the kids when he went out. She's only supposed to have been there for ten minutes or so, until Lennie came back. Gemma says that's OK. She imagined the meeting had gone on longer or that they'd all gone to the pub or something. She wasn't bothered. And she was watching TV and she lost track of the time anyway. Monday's a good telly night and it makes no difference to her where she watches it.

When Gemma's gone, Alex stands for a moment in the front room. Turns off the gas fire. Picks up Gemma's empty Coke glass and the TV guide. Then, after checking the boys are safely asleep in their beds, he opens the front door and, leaving it ajar, goes a little way down the lane with a torch.

He's not that worried, not yet. Alex is practical. He

doesn't worry until he needs to. But it's not like Lennie
— she isn't the type to take off and go somewhere
without telling him. That's him — he's the one who
does that.

In October the night dew gets so heavy it feels like
rain. You can smell woodsmoke and, yes, if you breathe
in hard enough, the larger smell of sea. Alex looks but
he doesn't know what he's looking for. He shines the
light into the black tangled hedgerows, lets it move across
the pale grit of the road — not perhaps wanting to think
of why he is doing it, but doing it all the same.

Well, I couldn't just sit there, he tells me later. I had
to get up and do something and I didn't know what else
to do.

He sees nothing, hears nothing.

He thinks of leaving the boys asleep and setting off
on foot up to the school but knows Lennie will think
that's irresponsible. What if a fire starts? What if Connor
has one of his dreams and wakes in a panic to find the
house empty?

In the end he goes back in and calls the Farrs. Geoff
answers — no, it's fine, they're not in bed yet. He gets
Maggie. Who sounds surprised. And then worried. She
can only confirm what Alex realises he already knows.
That Lennie left the meeting an hour ago — at least an
hour in fact, since she wasn't even the last to go.

Alex feels his stomach start to slide. He holds off calling
for as long as he can bear it. Then he rings the police.
And me.

★ ★ ★

10

He is standing outside in the drive when I get there. Next to him, a police car — sour stripes in the fuzzy dark. The dirty moon of the porch light shining, not yet dawn, not even close — the lane still grey, the hawthorn hedge a smudge of black at the bottom of the lawn.

I heave Livvy's seat up over one arm. She's getting heavy, the plastic digs into my arm, rubs against my hip. For a second her eyes flick open, unseeing, then back shut again.

You should have called, I tell him.

I did.

No, I mean sooner — straightaway.

He looks blank.

What could you have done?

I can't bear his face.

Been here with you —

He rubs his eyes.

I feel bad enough getting you up now —

Oh Al — don't be stupid, I tell him, shivering.

And Mick — ?

Mick's asleep.

He looks at me.

Tess — I mean, how could you have known — ?

I didn't, I tell him again, I don't —

But — what you said?

I shake my head.

You know what you said.

I've no idea why I said it, I tell him.

Tess —

OK, I say, I felt afraid.

What d'you mean afraid? Of what?

I don't know, I tell him, I mean it, Al. I don't know what of.

We stand in silence for a moment. I hear the crunch of footsteps by the back door. Police.

Do you think she has left me? he says.

I try to laugh.

No, I say. No Al, I don't.

A policeman comes out of the house and nods at us. I watch him cross the gravel to the car and lean in to speak into the radio.

Lennie would never leave, I tell him, though it's only as I say it that I know it's true. She never would. Not just go.

The policeman comes over.

All right? he says.

Alex takes a quick breath.

We're going to the school.

You'll call me?

I pick up Liv's seat. He nods.

They're going to search the creek and the marshes, he says. If they get nowhere at the school.

Pure terror on his face.

She wouldn't go anywhere, I tell him again. Not willingly. I just know she wouldn't.

Sometimes there are things that I know.

Sometimes at the clinic, treating a patient, I feel my fingers slip in between the usual rhythms and catch something else, something I wasn't looking for. It might be something I don't want to know – superfluous to the treatment. It's possible in my work to have too much information – to have it all come flying so hard at you that you lose focus.

What bollocks, says Mick as he sorts the washing on the kitchen floor. What sort of things, anyway?

I don't know, I say, just things.

You mean if someone's going to move house or get divorced or win the lottery?

No, I'll say. For fuck's sake, Mick. You know I don't mean that.

Well what then? If they'll live or die?

I'll flush.

I don't know.

And he laughs. Not because he doesn't understand, but because of the opposite: he thinks he understands too well. I can't surprise him any more. All these years together and what is there left to discover?

So I keep quiet. When I pick up on Ali Ledworth's pregnancy long before the doctors do (two tests in a row come back negative), I say nothing about it at home. And when poor Janey Urbach is knocked down in Bury on a one-way street by a car going the wrong way and suffers appalling spinal damage, I know better than to mention to Mick that the last time I treated her I felt something – a heavy weight hanging over her – as unmissable as a cloud blotting out the sun on a hot day.

And when I tell Alex I feel that Lennie will be OK, it's a lie. I don't. Not at all. Ever since that moment in The Polecat her presence – normally solid and resilient

13

and unremarkable – has been unfurling and undoing itself, snagging, tearing, falling apart.

Anne Addison types out the minutes from that night's meeting. She tells me it feels almost wrong, putting down on paper what amount to Lennie's last words, her last recorded comments – made only an hour or so before she died. She types them up and copies them, but does not circulate them yet, out of respect for the family, she says.

There is a report on the Quiz Night – Lennie recorded as saying she's disappointed by how little was raised and querying the amount spent on food. Maybe we should just get people to bring stuff next time? she suggests. Nothing fancy, just maybe quiches and baguettes and cheese and maybe a dip or two?

One or two people disagree. They feel that, for the price of the ticket, a hot meal is expected. Lennie's shrug is not minuted of course, but I can see it, clear as anything – her sitting back, blonde head bent, picking intently at her nails, deciding not to push her comments any further.

Lennie is good – better than me – at knowing when to shut up. Which is a good thing because there's always a bit of trouble at these meetings. There's always someone disgruntled, someone who resents the way someone else says something, someone who refuses to cast a vote.

There's a brief discussion about the Carnival Parade, which is going to be the last week of June along the sea front. Last year I took this on, but this time Lennie's agreed to do it. Someone suggests a competition at the school to design a Carnival poster – Maggie says great, she has a book-illustrator friend who would judge it. Maybe his publisher would even donate prizes? I know there would have been a murmur of pleasure at that. But Barbara Anscombe, who likes to get her oar in, ignores Maggie and says the post office should also be approached – see if they'd be willing to provide balloons and maybe smaller prizes for runners-up.

Then there's the usual argument about who the proceeds should go to. Barbara says Marie Curie.

What? Again? says Sally Abrahams, whose son is on his gap year in Nepal. Shouldn't we be raising awareness of something beyond the town – Christian Aid, Action Aid, something a little more multicultural?

Cancer affects people in all cultures, says Barbara firmly and Polly Dawson points out that many people in the town know someone who has died of cancer, though no one dares look at John who lost his wife so recently.

But Lennie agrees with Sally, that it might be nice to have a change. She knows, for instance, that the WI in Westleton are raising money for African farmers (a snort here from Barbara) – and what's to stop them going back to Marie Curie at Christmas?

All of this, except Barbara's brief snort of derision, is minuted by Anne Addison.

Later, shocked, baffled, interviewed by police, everyone who attended the meeting agrees that Lennie behaved quite normally, that there was nothing strange or different about her behaviour at all. A bit tired, perhaps, they all

15

concede, but then who isn't tired on a Monday night after a day's work followed by feeding the kids before rushing out again?

At a quarter to ten, the meeting is declared closed and Lucy, Lennie, Polly, Sue Peach, her daughter Sophie and Maggie lay out a selection of crudités, tortilla chips and dips. Bottles are opened, paper cups pulled from their cellophane.

Sue lets drop that she's thinking of doing an Open University degree, now that her youngest has started full-time school. And Lucy says something along the lines of how terrific and that if she had her time all over again she just knows she'd study with a whole lot more passion.

And Lennie laughs and says, Ah but isn't that what being a student is all about? Taking life for granted? Living in the moment and for the moment and with no sense of what the future holds?

Everyone – Sue, Maggie, Polly, Sophie, Charlotte, Sally, Lucy, Barbara, John, Anne – remembers this comment of hers. They all mention it in the police interviews. No one can bear to think that, less than an hour later, the person who made it is dead.

2

When you live right bang up close to someone, it can be hard to get far enough back to see them clearly. Or maybe your eyes do look, but your brain can't take it in. Like you never notice your own kids growing, or your own baby getting proper hair.

When Alex tries to give the police a physical description of Lennie, he gets confused. He goes almost crazy trying to think what she had on — earlier for instance when she screamed at Max about the state of his room, or kicked the washing-machine door shut and swore because it hurt her foot, or made the boys' tea in a hurry and upset Connor by slightly burning the frilled edges of his second fried egg. He knows she did these things, but he can't see her doing them.

This shocks him.

Like she'd already gone from our lives, he tells me later.

You were in a panic, I say. It's not your fault. You couldn't think.

I say it but I know it's meaningless. And he just looks at me – just screws up his eyes and rips the skin from the ragged side of his thumbnail and I know what he's thinking: he's trying to imagine the last time he saw her, trying to retrieve it from the deadest, most faraway part of his mind.

He tells the police he thinks she may have had on a red shirt, a shiny one.

Satin? they say.

He nods.

Something with a sheen anyway. Satin or silk, he says. Is there a difference?

Al shuts his eyes.

And jeans, he says. Jeans and slip-on trainers, blueish-grey ones, the type with the knobbly sole –

After clothes, they ask him about other things. The state of his marriage. He tells them it's fine, it's normal – no, no rows recently, not that he can think of. Nothing major anyway. And does Mrs Daniels have any history of depression or other illness such as seizures or fits?

No, Alex tells them, relieved that this part at least is completely true. Never, no. Lennie's a fit and healthy person, never ill, never down, nothing like that.

He explains that she's a potter, a ceramicist – that she's just had her stuff included in a show in London. That a couple of big stores have bought her stuff – that she's doing well. They ask him what he does and he tells them he makes furniture. And maybe he smiles because he knows how it must sound. The potter and the furniture maker in their cottage by the sea. They ask him how his business is doing and he says, Good – thinking it a strange question – good enough, he says. Trying to stop his stupid hands from shaking so hard.

She would never go off without telling me, he adds then, hating the small whine of helplessness in his voice. But they seem to accept this and he relaxes. It's only when the officers step outside for a moment that he finds himself overwhelmed by the lingering tang of their aftershave and rushes to the downstairs toilet to be sick. A quick, odourless and painless throwing up, like a dog or a baby.

Almost six. I crouch on the edge of the musty sofa and feed Liv by Alex and Lennie's gas fire in the half-dark. She's not hungry – just gums my nipple in a kind of half-dutiful way, then relaxes her lips and lets it slip away off her tongue. You think that babies are these fragile little creatures, at everyone's mercy, but they're not. I know that and Liv knows it too. She knows what she wants from life and she's learning the knack of how to get it.

I pull my bra back up and replace the pad and at that moment hear the upstairs toilet flush and then Max's voice saying something cross. Then the creak of the stairs.

Not just Max, both of them.

Where's Mum and Dad? Why're you here? Is it a school day? Connor wants to know, one hand in his mouth, the other down his pyjama bottoms.

Mum broke down somewhere, I tell them, and Daddy's had to go and pick her up and sort out the car –

He can't fix cars, says Max straightaway.

No, I say, I mean, get it to a garage or whatever.

But Max looks suspicious.

So – you mean she broke down and stayed in the car all night?

No. I think she stayed at Maggie's, I tell him.

That's weird, he says, frowning.

Is it?

You know it is. Why wouldn't she just walk back here?

I search for an answer but it's not necessary, I've lost him. He's already switched on the TV and is holding the remote and staring intently at the screen.

Are you allowed TV in the mornings? I ask him. He shrugs and turns it off, chucks the remote on the sofa. He's a good boy really.

He won't be long, I say.

How long? Connor asks. How long will he be?

He pours himself a bowl of Coco Pops. Some have spilled on the table and he leans over and thumbs them straight into his mouth.

I ask Max to get some milk and he does.

Not semi-skimmed, says Connor quickly.

Yeah, yeah, says Max, ignoring him.

Just normal milk, says Connor, looking anxious. No lumps.

I love these boys. I love them just about as much as my own — my Nat, my Jordan, my Rosa, my Liv. When they were born, I was the third person in the world to hold them — after Lennie, after Al.

Connor pulls up his T-shirt with a basketball player on and looks at me.

Look, he says.

What? Look at what?

At this.

He stretches backwards. So skinny I can see right through him — through to the blood that threads between his little snappy bones. Nipples so tiny, like an afterthought that you can't believe in. A network of pale blue and mauve. Goose pimples.

You're cold, I tell him. Haven't you got anything to put on? Where's your pyjama top?

I don't like it, he says. And I'm not cold.

He stares at me and shivers, still holding up the T-shirt. He has got it, all of Lennie's whiteness — her creamy skin and hair, a real, milky blondeness you think you can taste on your tongue.

Connor, I say, what am I supposed to be looking at?

This, he says, indicating a small, scrubby mauve tattoo on his breastbone. Already coming off.

And this — pulling his elbow round he shows me the snake tattoo curled there.

It's not real, he says. It soaks off.

He rubs at it, frowning.

Wow, I say. Great.

It's from a comic.

The Beano, supplies Max, mouth spilling cereal.

Has Jordan got one? Connor asks me.

Um, I don't think so.

Jordan's too old for *The Beano*, Max informs him.

Shut up!

Mum's getting a real tattoo, Max tells me, keeping his eyes on my face. On her bum.

Connor whips around, to see if he means it.

She is! Max insists, laughing now. Connor relaxes and his eyes rest on Liv.

Why's she here?

Because she's too little to leave behind.

He gazes at her thoughtfully. Like Lennie too he has no eyebrows – just a ridge of white-blond hair. And where are the others? he says. Where's Jordan?

At home asleep, I tell him. Why aren't you asleep? It's dreadfully early.

Something made me wake up, he says. I don't know what.

Liv makes an upset noise and I pull her out of the seat and lay her on a blanket on the floor. It's not the cleanest – stained with old Ribena and covered in dog hairs. Liv lies there, almost happy for a second, then suddenly and inexplicably not so happy – kicking, fast and angry and breathless. Building to a wail.

I pick her back up and she pants furiously, rescued from herself.

I want Mum, says Connor.

Shut up, says Max in a vicious monotone.

Shush, Max, I say, be nice.

I'm not nice, Max says.

I do, says Connor, I want her. Where is she?

Sweetie, I say and touch his head.

I joggle Liv up and down to keep her quiet. Every time I stop she takes a breath, ready to cry, so I joggle her again and the breath subsides unhappily.

Max gets up and windmills the air with an extended right arm, practising his bowling technique. After that, he hops around the room on one leg, hugging himself, the sleeves of his pyjamas stretched right down beyond his wrists.

OK, I say, do you want to see what's on TV?

No, says Max.

Can't you go now? asks Connor with a little wail in his voice. Can't Mummy get up?

Didn't you listen? She's not here you stupid fat moron, Max tells him, lungeing suddenly and shooting a hand from a flopping sleeve just long enough to pinch him hard on the thigh.

Quickly, Connor slams his hand into Max's face. The TV remote control falls to the floor and the casing splits off.

Now look what you've done you little bastard, says Max.

He's not allowed to say that, says Connor.

He looks at me to see what I'll do and then when I do nothing he begins to cry and so does Liv.

OK, I tell them, I'm going to sit down and see if I can feed Liv. Who wants a chocolate biscuit?

They're for Saturday, Connor says helplessly.

Never mind. I'm in charge. Have one now.

What, in the morning? says Max, eyes fixed on my chilly, half-bared breast. But he gets the packet and helps himself to one anyway.

Outside, the sky is losing its thickness and blackness. Soon, if you were to go upstairs and stand in Lennie and Alex's wide, bare bedroom you'd be able to make out the two rigid funnels of smoke rising from the Harriman's Brewery.

Mick rings. Behind his voice are all the ordinary sounds of our house: Rosa shrieking, Fletcher barking, Nat shouting at him to shut up.

Mick shouting at them to be quiet.

What's going on? he says. I tell him I don't know.

Where's Alex?

You mean you haven't heard anything?

No.

I take a breath. It's hard to know what to say with the boys listening. Mick knows what I'm thinking.

Don't, Tess, he says, it'll be OK.

Silence. Max is screwing the Yoyo wrappers into a hard, green foil ball.

Shall I come and get the boys, then? Take them all to school?

I don't know – I begin.

I've got to take this lot.

I don't know, I say. I mean, should they go to school?

Come on, he says, of course they should go. What else are they going to do today?

24

I catch Max's face watching me, then turning to see if he can flick Connor on the back of his head with the ball. Livvy begins to cry: a slow, spiralling wail.

In his heart, or so he tells people later, Alex already knows. It can happen. That the usual rules melt away and you just find you know things. Facts queue up and slide, unasked, into your head, ears, heart.

Or, maybe it's true. Maybe Lennie's pain and dying does somehow get to him across the car park, over the tangly dark of Bartholomew's Green and down into Spinner's Lane. Or, more likely, is it just that when the worst things happen, time isn't the same any more? It twangs and collides and you can't any longer tell the hot and dirty moment when you knew from the clean, sweet, cold one when you didn't.

Alex's father killed himself when he was twelve and Alex was the one who found him there on the landing with the inside of his head pouring black stuff on the carpet. He always holds this fact up as a blanket – a protection against anything else happening. You can see why. Shouldn't he be safe now? Hasn't he had the worst? Hasn't he?

Alex is in the police station for a very long time. The longest hour of his life, he tells people later. Finally two police officers come to find him. One is called Mawhinney. He's not from here – that's how he knows it's serious. He's a black-haired, slightly European-looking man with big thick wrists and straight dark hair poking up beneath the collar of his shirt. A funny name, he'll

25

remember it. It's about to be dawn but the air still holds the cloaked-off smell of night. Dim and quiet. Despite that, in the black conifer between the police station and Flook's newsagent's next door, a single blackbird is singing its heart out. Alex keeps hearing it, poor fucker, coping with the whole dawn chorus alone.

Slowly, through the tiny square of window, the light grows less dirty, shrubs and telegraph wires get more distinct. Alex remembers this. He tells me later that he remembers every detail of that room, that place, every sound, every smell. As if his body is on high alert: unable to stop itself from taking everything in.

And he is sitting at a table and smoking. And he hasn't touched his tea which tastes horrible, of the machine, but he has a pack of freshly opened cigarettes in front of him.

I keep trying to give up, he tells the duty officer behind the desk. And then something happens and I start up all over again.

The officer thinks what a nice fellow Alex is. Just an ordinary chap, friendly and approachable. A good guy – the type you'd lend money to, or trust with your wife and kids. He'll remember this fact later, when friends ask him about this terrible night, this terrible case. How can there be a God, for Christ's sake, he'll say, when the worst things always happen to the most decent people?

If Alex could think at this moment, he might be thinking the same. Instead, Oh God, oh God, he goes when he sees them coming in, Mawhinney and the other one. Oh, he goes, oh God, oh Jesus Christ.

Mawhinney holds out his hand – a forthright hand, used to facts and upset and awful things. Alex quickly stubs out his cigarette. Holds himself very still.

He wishes they didn't have to tell him what he already knows.

No, he says. Touching the suddenly foreign-feeling skin of his cheeks, face, eyes, with his hands (the hands that already feel cut off from him, like the hands of another person), No, please God no –

The words make little sense though he understands every one of them. Your wife. Has suffered. Some sort of violent attack. Has not survived.

Has not. Suffered. Violent. In a different order, the words might not spell the end. No, says Al. Please God no – he says it again several times.

One of them puts a hand on his arm and Alex lets him, even though he doesn't like being touched by strangers and especially not by men.

He asks if they could light him another cigarette. The younger one grabs the pack while the older one – Mawhinney – keeps his hand on him. And though he can barely take the cigarette when it is held out to him, so badly are his hands shaking, still he somehow manages to smoke it in long, trembling gasps.

Mick comes by with the dog and the kids. Everyone shouting, leaves lifting, trees bent over by the wind. The sky is white. Jordan has no coat on, just his frayed school jumper.

I ask him where his zip-up fleece is and he shrugs in

a shivery way. Mick thinks I fuss too much but I hate the idea of my kids being cold. Jordan is nine, a year older than Connor, but just as thin. All our boys, Lennie's and mine, are thin. Rosa and Liv, on the other hand, are padded and rounded – big girls with a layer between them and the world.

Look at him, I say to Mick. He's freezing.

Mick stares at me and doesn't seem to take in what I say.

He is, I say. He's shivering.

Yesterday was warm for October, but not last night and not today. Here at Lennie's, even with the gas fire on it's not enough. I've just turned the heating right up.

Fletcher is pulling and jumping and trying to get the lead in his mouth. It's what he does. Mick loops the lead over the gatepost and yells at him to sit and stay. Louder than usual. The dog looks upset and sits and then straight-away gets up again, happy, expectant.

There was no bread! Rosa bursts out. For the packed lunches!

That's enough, Rosa, Mick tells her.

I was only saying –

Shut up, he says.

Rosa scowls.

I mean it, he says. Do I have to say it again?

I tell Rosa to shush. The sun shoots out and sends a wet, piercing light up over the brownish lawn, the path, the bins.

Mick – I say, but he doesn't look at me.

I'm taking Max and Con to their gran's, he says.

OK.

Suddenly Max is there at Mick's elbow. What? Aren't we going to school then?

That's right, boy, says Mick. He touches Max gently on the arm, but looks down at his keys.

Why? says Max. What's going on? Where's Dad?

Why is he missing school? Are we all missing it? Jordan asks quickly.

No, says Mick, Not you. Look, you lot –

Why not? asks Nat immediately.

What? Oh great, snaps Rosa. So they get to miss school and we don't?

She folds her arms and looks horrid.

Mick turns and fixes her with a terrible stare and her eyes turn furious.

Just give me a reason why that's fair, she demands.

You shut up right now or I'll give you more than that, says Mick.

Watched by all of us, Rosa bursts out crying. Mick looks like he's about to hit her but he doesn't. He does nothing. Lets his hands drop to his sides. Rosa thinks she's won.

Happy now? she asks him through her tears.

Mick and I look at each other.

What's going on? I ask him.

He says nothing.

You better tell me, Mick, I say.

He touches his face.

Come on, let's go inside, he says.

★　★　★

The bin men find her. The dawn refuse collection. Pitch dark at first, then grey sea, bleached early morning sky. Seagulls wheeling and squealing and hanging, steadying themselves in the air over the same piece of ground.

She is lying on her front, one arm under her, the other thrown out, concealing the worst of her injuries. That's what we are told. That she is still wearing her red satin shirt and cardigan but her jeans and pants have been pulled right off one leg and caught around her right ankle. That though there is no sign of her having been assaulted, her sanitary pad, with its modest brown smear of blood, is lying there on the concrete next to her.

My knees feel weak as water. All the muscles that normally hold me up have lost their zip, their strength. Mick tells the children to wait in the garden. He knows they won't venture out of the little wooden gate. Somehow we walk together over the hall mat, him ahead, him taking me. Our feet slip a little, moving over paper – letters that have come for Alex and Lennie. We don't pick them up.

What? I ask him. Mick, please tell me, what?

I can smell his body, the worry on him, the heat. His face is dark with whatever it is.

He pushes me into the sitting room and shuts the door.

I think I say please. Or tell me. That's what I say: Tell me, Mick. As if it was that easy.

And my teeth are shivering in my head, like I'm so cold I can't hold my jaw still, which is silly really. And even the ends of my fingers have gone hot and fizzy. I'm afraid.

He takes my hand. His own fingers are cool.

At first they think (or hope) she might be drunk or asleep – though, even at the height of the season, drunks, and especially ones with their underpants ripped off, are unheard of in this place. Then they see that the visible arm is too long and all splayed out at the wrong angle. And in the same moment they realise that the dark puddle in which she lies half submerged isn't mud as they thought, but blood.

One of the men dials 999 on his mobile.

There's normally a very small, half-hearted police presence in the town, but it doesn't wait around for murders to happen. Several more cars and an ambulance are summoned at once from Wrentham and Halesworth. Within twenty minutes there are sirens, winking lights, crackling radios, as police park diagonally to block the road and then proceed to tape off the car park and the adjoining areas. The electric milk van is stopped and told to go back round the other way, along North Road. The tide turns. A series of black groynes point up like fingers at the sky.

After perhaps half an hour, a small yellow and white tent is erected. It flaps about in the early morning wind that comes off the sea. Yellow tape is strung between the bollards of the car park. No one is allowed to cross it – only one or two police are let through and even they have to be cleared by the grey-haired man in a white jacket who arrived ten minutes earlier, looking tired-out and carrying a small nylon bag.

Paramedics stand around. Grim faces. Confusion. What are they waiting for? Is someone just injured or are they dead? At last a police officer walks briskly forward, head down, talking into his radio. They immediately let him through the tape. His breath is a cold cloud and he looks at no one.

He pulls a coat on over his neon jacket, which glints oddly in the bright sea light. He is followed by two WPCs, one of them frowning hard and carrying something small and heavy. The wind blows the clouds apart and everything is lit up and sparkly-yellow in that split second. Far out to sea is a perfect little boat with a brown sail. You can tell the wind is strong because of how the boat scuds along. Eager and fast. It looks like it's going to be a lovely day. That's what it's like the morning they find Lennie – everyone says that, everyone remembers it. An especially lovely day for the time of year.

Someone has died. The whisper goes around. A woman's body has been found – attacked and left for – yes, a female, someone from here – no one knows who. No, they haven't said. Yes, dead.

No one says murdered, not yet, not then.

A good soul from one of the B. & B.s on North Parade appears with several mugs of tea – by which time a crowd of dog walkers and delivery people and shop-workers has gathered. A couple of chambermaids from The Angel, shivering in their black. People speak quietly to one another. Someone's mobile phone starting up and the culprit walking away, guilty, to answer it.

Meanwhile, three or four hefty gulls alight on the concrete wall by the bins — in case such an improbably sudden crowd means food.

Oh Tess, he says.

Have they found her? Even as I speak the words, something in my throat settles and hardens and the answer bubbles up.

Yes, he says, they have.

I wait and then whisper, And — ?

I'm afraid they have, he says again.

It's — bad?

He takes a breath. There's sweat on his face, and on mine.

I think she's dead, he says. He takes a breath, corrects himself, No. I mean — she is — oh Tess — she is dead.

Dead. Lennie is dead. The air around my head blooms into a massive, soft silence. Everything stops and my ears are velvety with it.

Tess?

I am about to answer him but instead the floor comes zooming up to meet my face.

It's OK, I can hear him saying, it's OK.

With my head between my knees and him holding me, I breathe. Big, hurting breaths, in and out. Down there in that other world, I notice things — the bare patches on Lennie's blue carpet, the crumbs and dust bunnies beneath the edge of the sofa. Two rubber bands.

33

A piece of Lego and next to it something sticky, dulled with fluff, a spat-out fruit gum perhaps.

Deep breaths, Mick says and him saying it reminds me of us in labour, having our babies. The most together we have ever been. Except that right now this moment I have no memory whatever of having Liv.

How? I ask him, and he tells me. He tells me what has been done to Lennie. After a few moments, he asks me if I am OK. He asks even though he knows the answer. It's not his fault. It's only because he loves me.

And outside the wind has dropped and the kids are all standing just as we left them. Such good children – so quiet, all of them, no one touching or nudging anyone else, not a cry or complaint or a yowl of anger from anyone. You would not know there were five children huddled out there on the damp porch step.

3

Mick drops our kids at school and then drives Max and Con on to Alex's mother Patsy in Halesworth. Alex has already told Patsy. She knows. She says she'll have the boys as long as necessary. No one knows how long Alex'll have to spend with the police.

Mick asks Patsy if she's sure she'll be OK? She tells him she's fine. She's taken 4 mg of valium on her GP's advice and a neighbour has come in to be with her.

Have a drink, Mick says to me, have a stiff drink.

I stare at him.

I'm OK.

Go on, he says. I mean it – you'll feel better.

Have you? I ask him.

I'm driving.

I'm OK, I tell him again.

What are you going to do?

I don't know. Tidy up here then come home.

You'll walk?

Yes.

I watch the children pile into the car, oblivious and ordinary, hands and feet scuffing, shoving their rucksacks in the back, getting Fletcher to jump in afterwards.

We've told them nothing, Alex will do it, he should be the one. For a moment or two all I see is their small white faces in the back window. And Connor especially – smiling, tilting his head back in a naughty-happy way, looking just like Lennie.

The air around Liv's head smells of milk. Her mouth is open, one small fist pushed up hard against her cheek. I know that if I were to prise it open I'd find sweat, fluff and grit from where she lay on the blanket on the floor. I stay for a moment, just looking. Checking. I always do that with my kids. Check them. I even still do it to Nat, yes even now, even though I can tell from the strange, large, folded-up shape of him that these days it's a pretty redundant thing to do.

After I've looked at her, I put away the cereal packets and rinse the bowls in the sink – then put on Lennie's rubber gloves and rinse the sink as well, swishing it around with my fingers. Next to the sink is Lennie's hand cream, the pump-head clogged with greasy pinkness where she's used it. A sparkly hair clip that she wore

36

recently – when? why don't I remember? – with two of the sparkly bits come off.

The phone rings. I jump. It's only Mick.

Tess, he says, you're to get out of there. They're going to seal it off. You're not to put your fingerprints on anything else – a forensics guy is coming over any minute now.

Tears come to the back of my throat.

But – if I'm not here – how'll he get in?

He has a key. Tess, I mean it – just leave. Now. That's what they said. They don't want fingerprints everywhere. Just get out. Just pull the door behind you and come home.

You've already dropped the kids?

Yes. I thought you'd be back. Shall I come over and get you?

I try to understand how much time has gone since Mick left. More than I think. Shock pulls everything tight around you.

No, I tell him, I'm coming. I'm coming now.

We live about a four-minute walk from Lennie and Al. Down Spinner's Lane, across the Green and up Victoria Street to the row of little cobble-fronted cottages by the church. To get there you pass the doctor's surgery, Pratt's newsagent's and an Antiques & Curios shop that belongs to Margie Pinnerman but is hardly ever open. The rest is residential – silent, pebble-dashed semis and then the older, more desirable cottages with names like Sailor's Stash and Ebb Tide. More like a bunch of racehorses, Mick remarked when he first saw the names painted on their proud little plinky-planky china plaques.

Our street is quite different from Lennie and Al's. The cottages in Spinner's Lane have larger gardens and uglier fronts and look out over the marshes. But ours have white-painted walls with ragged hollyhocks bursting out over the tops and through the cracks. Our gardens are more like yards – just enough room for a bike perhaps and a row of washing – but inside our houses are bigger than they look, and from our tiny bathroom windows you can see the sea.

It ought to be easy. To go and get my coat, my little, sleeping baby, creep out, close the door behind me. But the cats – Lennie's two angry tabbies – circle me, mewing loudly. I don't like cats, something Lennie will never understand. She can't understand that a person could be afraid of a small furry thing.

But I know where she keeps the food so I get it from the shelf by the back door and pour some onto a plate, make a kissing noise with my lips like she does.

And they come, slowly, tails stuck up in the air. The one with the white patch on its face looks at the food, then back at me, disgust on his dreamy cat face. Then they both sit back and start washing.

The moments fall away and whole seconds go by before I notice that a man is in the room. A stranger, a man, about thirty years old with lots of darkish hair and an odd, quiet face. Standing there and looking at me.

My heart clenches and then dips.

Oh!

Sorry, he says quickly, I really am so sorry.

He says it but he's almost smiling. I am grabbing at the edge of the counter, hot and trembling.

I didn't mean to make you jump. I should have knocked. It's just –

I say nothing.

The door was open, he says, looking more helpless now. And I was told the house was empty.

I'm – it is. I'm going, I tell him.

Oh look, don't feel you have to – he says, but he's looking all around him at the room. Which already isn't Lennie's room.

Are you police? I ask him, because he doesn't look like it.

That's right. Sorry.

He nods.

You're the forensics guy?

I'm Ted Lacey, he says, I'm – I'm called family liaison. I'm here to –

I fold my arms tight against me in case he tries to shake my hand.

I'm with the police, he begins again, but I deal with –

The family.

Right, he says quietly, keeping his eyes on me. Yes.

Tess, I say, I'm Tess. A friend of –

He blinks.

Yes, he says. Yes. I know that.

★ ★ ★

And he just stands there.

Are you OK? he says at last.

I'm fine, thanks.

He looks at me.

Is that your job? I ask him. To ask if I'm OK?

No, he says and shrugs, looks away.

I smile. I don't know why.

Look – he begins, then stops.

I daren't look at him. He's so young. Something about him makes the room tilt.

Maybe I look dizzy.

Why don't you sit down? he says.

No, I tell him, I'm fine. I just need a cigarette.

He watches as I pull open Lennie's kitchen drawer. She has a secret supply, I tell him without knowing why, of cigarettes.

He says nothing.

I find them quickly, hidden between the clingfilm and the roll of sandwich bags. Also, a pink plastic lighter with the Virgin Mary on. A present from Barcelona, it says.

We did give up, I tell him. At New Year.

Oh, he says.

But we keep them here. Just in case.

He looks at me and the way he does it makes me feel funny.

I'm going home, I tell him. Now. In a minute.

OK.

It's just, I tell him, my husband wouldn't want me smoking.

He looks down at the floor. I see how shiny his shoes are. Definitely not from around here. I offer him the pack. He shakes his head. He hasn't moved.

I flick the lighter and the flame whooshes up too high over the Virgin's head and then goes off.

Shit.

I drop it. The cigarette too.

Fuck.

He reaches forward, bends down, picks them up for me. I look into his hair, which is black as anything and dense and shiny.

He watches me fumble all over again with the lighter.

Shall I do it? he says at last.

OK then.

I put the cigarette between my lips and pull back my hair which is falling everywhere and he lights it for me. I suck it quickly in and let it hit me hard all over before I weep.

And at home, there's Mick, standing lost in the middle of something in the room where he can't settle or do anything, which is how I feel too. And he's been crying.

I ask if he's heard anything from Alex and he says no, he hasn't. He's still with the police as far as anyone knows.

My head feels hot.

I can't believe it, I say.

Tess, he says.

Who? Who would do it? Who would do such a thing to someone here in this place?

This is a safe place – that's what I want to say.

Mick sits down heavily on the sofa, putting his hands in his eyes, trying to stamp out the tears with his fists.

I don't know, he says.

Poor Al, I say. Poor kids.

Go and lie down, he tells me. I mean it. Take Liv and just go and sleep.

I can't.

But you've been up half the night.

So have you.

Not as long as you.

I'm afraid, I tell him. I'm afraid of lying there and not being able to sleep and then I'm afraid of going to sleep and having to wake up and – go through it all again.

I begin to sob. He comes over and puts his arms around me, rests his chin on my hair.

We've got to tell the children, I say.

Of course.

Well how, for fuck's sake?

We'll just tell them.

What, tonight?

It'll have to be tonight. Otherwise they'll hear it from someone else.

He takes his arms off me and away and steps back. The front of his shirt is now wet from my face.

I love you, I tell him.

He says nothing. I ask him if he thinks Patsy will have told the boys by now.

I don't know, he says.

42

He stands there, arms hanging down by his sides. He has on a very creased shirt with a huge greasy mark on the front. It must be the first thing he picked up off the floor in the other world that was this morning.

He looks at me.

I don't know, he says again.

You'd think it might be impossible to sleep but once I get in there onto those chilly, milk-stained sheets with the baby in beside me, I fall into an easy, dreamless place. I wake to find the sky white and the pillow and the corner of my mouth wet, a ball of tissue clenched in my hand.

You'd think there would be wailings of sirens outside, or at least the sound of something going on, but there's nothing, same as usual, just the comforting purr of the wind in the pines.

Liv has woken already and stayed silent and kicking, small huffing breaths – careful wide eyes watching the ceiling. Fairies, Rosa always says in that authoritative voice of hers. She's watching fairies.

I pull her over to me and I kiss her. Not for any reason, just because I always do. For a single quick second the kissing makes me forget what has been happening. I breathe her in, she smells of new piss. The earthy sweetness of it makes my throat fill up.

Downstairs, Mick is sitting blankly on the kitchen sofa with the phone book open on his lap and a bottle of whisky on the table at his side. Also, some slices of cheese in a plastic wrapper and no plate. I am amazed Fletcher hasn't had them, but he's asleep against the door jamb, paws together, dead-dog style.

Has he rung?

No.

I look at Mick carefully. He looks about eight years old, skinny and tired.

You managed to sleep?

A little.

Good.

I go and sit softly by him, Liv on my lap.

What're you doing? Who're you ringing?

He stares ahead of him as if he has to listen a long time to take in the words. Then he puts his hand on my knee.

We have to do something about the roof, he says, as if it's obvious.

What? I say. You mean now?

Since Mick left the paper and has been at home, he's made a special effort to keep up with DIY. Getting all those jobs done that nag at you. It's his way of being more than just a house-husband. And last week some time, Jordan's ceiling developed a long brown zigzag and started oozing water. But it's been dry since then and I've forgotten it.

He jabs his finger on the page to mark a place and looks up.

Don't you realise, Tess, he says, Jordan's ceiling is bust. It's about to cave in.

Oh, I say, trying to think back to the other life, the sweet life of yesterday when we had this as a problem.

It won't go away just because of –

No, I agree.

And there's more wet weather on the way.

Oh darling, I say and I try to look at him but suddenly he's not there, or at least I can't see him properly.

4

The thing about this place is, it isn't on the way to anywhere. It's the end of the road, a dead end – creek, sea and river on three sides, the road going up to the A12 on the other. Apart from in the height of summer when the holidaymakers descend, a stranger would be noticed right away.

Certainly, no one here lives in fear of crime. Pat, the local copper, is too busy untangling the kids' kites that get stuck in the dog rose and gorse that slopes down from the prom to go chasing criminals. And the last time a panda car came flashing up the High Street was when poor Ellie Penniston fell off her bike.

Even our vandals are considerate. When the donations box was stolen from the Sailors' Reading Room, the culprit went out of his way to return the box. And when the Conservative Club, the United Reformed Church and a couple of small lock-up businesses on the harbour were all broken into in the space of a single night, it was assumed it must be someone from the new council houses down beyond the pier which look out over Might's Creek.

All sorts are housed there, Barbara Anscombe complained at a heated local residents' meeting. Travellers, even.

One of the happiest and most picturesque seaside towns in all England, that's how our town is referred to in the booklets *Best of Suffolk* and *Coastal Rambles* that you can pick up at the Tourist Information Centre on the High Street.

The town's most pressing concerns are quaint and small. Such as what to do about the graffiti on the public toilets off North Parade. Or, should a second Thai take-away be allowed to open in place of Caroline's Orthopaedic Shoes in the High Street? And how to make people take notice of the Clean Up After Your Dog campaign? (Free doggy bags are provided by the local Society but still there are individuals who do not use them.)

And then, that night in autumn – the coldest October night for ninety years according to the *Bugle*. He binds her wrists with nylon twine. He hits her twelve or maybe fifteen times on the chest, neck and head with something blunt and heavy – possibly one of the larger lumps of shingle from under the pier – before he uses the blade on her.

The day of Lennie's death ends with a dozen officers in white gloves crawling on hands and knees to search the whole car park – now emptied of all but a handful of cars – including Pier Avenue and the area beyond the beach huts where the dunes roll down to the sea. They have to get it done before high tide, so they move methodically yet quickly, aware always of the creeping water and the fading light. The area is still taped off and no one is allowed in. At one point a Labrador slinks under the tape and comes bounding up to them joyously licking and pouncing. The owner calls it off quickly, mortified.

Nothing whatsoever is found.

Straight after school we tell the children. We sit them down and tell them that last night a bad man came along and hurt Lennie so badly that she's never coming back.

Is she OK? Nat wants to know.

Mick looks at me.

I'm afraid she died, Nat, he says softly.

Rosa takes a breath. She's been killed?

That's right.

She and Jordan both burst into loud, immediate, shocked tears. But Nat just bends his head and gazes at the floor. I watch him and I know that the odd half-smile, half-grimace on his face is from fear and shock. He can't look at anyone, he won't join in.

It's easy to comfort Rosa and Jordan – I throw my arms around them and I cry too. Meanwhile Mick sits beside Nat and rubs a point between his shoulder blades and Nat lets him for a while and then shakes him off.

Was it a gun? Jordan wants to know. Mick looks quickly at me and then says in a small, tight voice, Yes, boy, yes, it was.

Nat looks up despite himself.

What was anyone doing with a gun? he says, shocked. I mean, around here? Isn't that illegal?

Well, says Mick, yes. Of course. But there are lots of questions they can't – I mean, they don't know every-thing yet.

Did she die in hospital? Rosa asks. Did she know she was going to die?

I squeeze her hand.

We hope not, I tell her. We really hope not.

Jordan cries again and I hold Rosa's hand in one of mine and his little, cold and slightly sticky one in the other and he soon stops. I listen to his breathing. No one says anything for a moment or two.

We love you all very much, I tell them, and this is the hardest thing that's ever happened to us. Now what you've got to do is try and help Max and Con.

How? demands Rosa, her voice cracking with grief and fury. How can we help them if they don't even have a mum any more?

They've got a dad, Nat points out with unnecessary vigour.

Mick ignores him.

You've got to be very, very kind, he says. I mean it, guys. They're going to be sad and upset for a very long time.

And shocked, I add.

Yes, he says, Mummy's right. Shock takes a very long time to get over.

Will they still come round here? asks Jordan anxiously.

Of course, boy, says Mick, cupping his fingers around Jordan's bony knee. Jordan gives a little sob of relief.

Of course they will, I say. They're going to need us, they all are, Alex too.

I don't want to be horrid, but I'm just so glad it wasn't you, says Rosa suddenly and she puts her forehead on my arm and weeps into my sleeve.

Oh darling, I say.

Well, begins Mick, but he doesn't finish.

We sit in silence for a long time after that, just the five of us and Liv on her blanket on the floor. After a while Fletcher hears the strange sound of silence and comes padding over, slapping his tail from side to side, shoving the fish-fur of his nose into everyone's hands.

He doesn't know, Rosa observes.

No, I say.

Is there anything you want to ask us, guys? Mick says after a moment or two.

Jordan gives him a quick look.

Have we missed *The Simpsons*? he says.

Mick and I go in the kitchen and listen to the sound of them all laughing at the TV in the next room. Three lots of laughter, then silence, then more bubbling laughter again.

They're laughing.

Mick shrugs.

I stare into the fridge and then the cupboards one after another and try to think what to make for their tea. He meanwhile sits in the big chair and holds Livvy on his lap, looking at her as if he's never seen her before, as if she's someone else's child, or something that is supposed to be a child but doesn't look quite right. Eventually Livvy gives a little gasp of dissatisfaction at being held so still.

Of course they are, he says, picking up the phone with his free hand and using his thumb to press redial – trying Alex again. Of course they're laughing. What do you expect?

I rub my eyes, pull out a pack of quick macaroni.

I wonder what I do expect. The thought hangs there fuzzily.

They're just kids, Mick says, a tiny crack showing in his voice. Kids compartmentalise. It's not real to them yet. But it will be – it'll sink in.

Mick knows about kids. Or at least, I know about them as a mother, but he understands how their heads work. Before he went into journalism, back in London, he was a teacher and he worked in a rough school and dealt with the toughest kids – eleven- and twelve-year-olds who'd had no breakfast and had to be frisked for flick-knives and razor blades before they even started lessons. One time a kid set fire to the toilets during PE and Mick had to put it out and in doing so suffered burns all over his hands. He still has the scars – great shiny streaks where the hair never grows. Monster hands, Rosa calls them.

When he first started on the paper, everyone warned him to watch out for the editor who was a difficult, moody and unpredictable sort of man. But Mick just laughed. He never had any trouble from the guy. Not after dealing with all those kids.

At teatime, the children eat their macaroni cheese without complaint. Nat drinks his cup of milk without investigating it for lumps. Rosa even asks for seconds. She squeezes ketchup all over what's left on her plate and mixes it in till the sauce turns a glossy pink.

She's playing with her food, Nat points out, tipping back on his chair.

Nat darling, I say, let it go.

Yes, but –

Nat, says Mick. And Nat sighs and kicks at the table leg.

We decide to leave them thinking Lennie was killed with a gun because it's somehow cleaner. Guns leave small neat holes in people – or that's the impression kids get off the TV. People with guns do it from a safe distance. They don't come after you as you lie in a car park bleeding to death. They don't rip your heart out.

Later I hear Jordan kicking a beat-up tennis ball around the empty dining room with Fletcher. It's the dog's favourite game and one which makes him go absolutely, religiously still. The way they do it is, Jordan kicks the ball across the room till it hits the skirting board and bounces off – and that's the dog's cue to move, to dart for it and grab it before Jordan can.

Jordan and the dog have a collection of these tennis balls – balding and dirty and bit right open some of them, by Fletcher's sharp teeth. We are always finding them – stuck behind radiators, in the clean-laundry basket, in the tangle of wires behind the TV.

Which would you rather, Jordan mutters to the dog as he drops the ball, be shot by a gun or chased by a shark until you wet your pants with fear?

At ten the kids are finally in bed. We are still sitting there in the room that's gone cold and dark and quiet. And at last there it is, the sound of him at our back door.

Al!

I jump up from my chair.

We never bother locking our door, not until we go to bed, and even then just with the one turn of the key. He knows this and comes straight in. Behind him, the man I met at his house, the family liaison man.

Well? Someone says, but it's not Mick and I don't think it's Al either because he just stands there and says nothing.

I put my hands to my face. I'm shaking all over and I feel sick. Seeing him makes it real, brings home to me what has really happened. And her absence. Normally if something had happened, Lennie would be here by now. We'd all be here together.

But Mick knows what to do. He goes right over and clasps him around the shoulders, pulling him in – at the same time nodding to the other guy who hangs back in the shadows. Maybe he introduces himself to Mick, but I'm not sure.

Alex looks worn out. When Mick lets go and steps back, he moves across the room to me and puts out his arms and holds my head tight against him.

Don't, he says. Don't speak.

His fingers are on my face. And I don't know what to do, though I smell him – his exhaustion and confusion and grief and the breath that hasn't eaten anything in a long time.

The boys? Mick says then. Where are the boys?

Still at Patsy's, Al says. I took them back there. It's OK. They're – I mean, I've – been with them.

You told them?

Al shuts his eyes for a quick second.

Mick pulls out a bottle of whisky.

OK, he says, a drink.

Lacey refuses but Alex sits down and has a glass just like it's any other day. At our kitchen table. Keeping his coat on – the coat that sits on him like a husk.

He looks at his drink but doesn't drink it.

Con was sick, he says. Everywhere. All over Patsy's fucking sofa.

I take a breath.

I suppose that's to be expected, Mick says.

Yes, says Lacey in a low, quick voice. It's the first time he's spoken and we all look at him. He looks down, as if he'd prefer not to have the attention on him.

I mean, he says, all kinds of reactions are normal, especially with young kids and —

He doesn't finish.

This is Ted, by the way, Al says, as if he's suddenly remembered his manners. He's been so great — you wouldn't believe it, how he's looked after me today.

Lacey gives a weak smile.

He's done all this before, Al says in a harder voice.

Lacey shakes his head, rests his elbows on his knees and clasps his hands together.

You know, Alex tells him, this is my home from home. These two lovely people are our best friends, our oldest mates, everything —

He breaks off.

I look over at Lacey. Blotting my eyes with the sleeve of my jumper.

Ted's sticking by me, Alex says, been with me all day. He's even going to stay over. Are you sure about that, Ted — that you want to stay over?

Lacey says, I think it's best —

You see? Al says, looking at us as if it's all a bit of a joke — probably because he's in shock.

Where will he sleep? I ask Al, and he looks at me.

In the studio, he says. He means Lennie's studio.

Great, Lacey says.

Good, says Mick.

Alex says that what Lacey needs right now is a photo.

Of her, he says, taking a mouthful of whisky, a nice little snap.

55

He spreads his hands on the table and studies his knuckles.

You don't mind? he says, only I can't face –

I squeeze his shoulder.

Hey, I tell him, I'll get it now.

Lacey stands up and looks at me.

It's for the press, he says.

Oh.

I'm really sorry, he adds, to have to ask for it now.

I tell him it isn't a problem, I'll get it. In my hurry to move towards the stairs I kick the chair and disturb Fletcher who comes wobbling up out of sleep. Stretching, yawning, shaking himself, claws clicking on the stone floor.

Give me two minutes, I say.

In our house, in our family, I am the archivist. I am the one who can produce evidence to show that we were all here and happy together. But it can be lopsided, this evidence. So, there are loads of photos of Nat as a baby, and plenty of Rosa too, in all situations, all moments of life. Fewer of Jordan and then, as poor Liv was born, they tail off altogether.

I think I have one hazy faraway one from the day she came into this world – and then nothing at all until the one where Lennie is holding her up in the garden of the pub at Blackshore and she is wearing the faded paisley hand-me-down sunhat that all of our kids have worn at one time or other. Also, because Mick took most of the pictures, he is more absent than he should be, too. But not Lennie and Al – they're in nearly all the pictures. A

56

measure of how much they've always been here with us in our lives.

Fletcher is loudly lapping water as I open the little door and start upstairs.

I'm halfway up before I realise Lacey is right behind me.

Sorry, he says softly. Just – wait a moment.

I stop and turn.

It's just – I didn't want to say it in there. This photo, it's going to be all over everywhere, in the papers and on TV and so on – what I mean is, he and the children will be seeing a lot of it –

Oh, I say, thinking how helpless he looks.

It needs to be current, obviously, he says, and it needs to be – well –

How they'd want to remember her?

Lacey takes his eyes away from mine.

Yes, he says, that's right. Thanks.

That night, the first night of our knowing that Lennie is dead, I sleep a strange sleep of amazement. Amazed that I can sleep at all. Again and again in the blue darkness, the fact of what has happened slips over me. Icy, amazed, over and over again.

That's what I was most afraid of – of waking up and having to think about it. I can't. I can't think about her. I can't think about the car park.

Livvy sleeps right through. Only the second time ever. I ought to be pleased but it scares me to death. At 5 a.m. I poke her to check she's still breathing. She is.

Mick brings me coffee. I mention to him about Liv.

He says, For God's sake, Tess, she's shattered. Leave her. Let's enjoy it while it lasts.

Enjoy. The word wedges itself in the air between us.

The school is closed while the police make enquiries, but the kids know better than to say they're glad. They watch TV downstairs while we drink coffee and wait for the phone to ring. If I can just get through the morning without crying, I think.

The man called Mawhinney comes round to have a word with us. They're making house-to-house enquiries throughout the town, he explains. Though obviously, he adds, he would have wanted to talk to us anyway, because of our relationship with the family.

He says he's sorry to have to do this when we're still feeling so raw and having it sink in, but he needs to ask us both exactly where we were on the night it happened – between eleven and, say, eight in the morning.

I blush hot to my hair, but Mick doesn't hesitate. He takes my hand and squeezes it. He tells Mawhinney that he and I were both in bed.

We were exhausted, he tells him, really shattered. That's why Tess didn't go to the meeting. She's on the PTA and she should have been there but she just couldn't face it. I wouldn't have let her go. I think we went to bed at – well at a guess – ten, ten thirty.

Mawhinney listens.

Would that be earlier than usual then?

Mick pinches at his nose with his thumb and finger as he thinks about it.

Pretty early for us, yes.

Something unsaid floats past me. In my hand the balled-up tissue is coming apart with dampness. Bits of it sticking to the sides of my fingers like skin.

Mawhinney turns to me. I can see he is trying to be kind, to make it easy. I wonder if he has a wife and kids at home and if he goes home and takes a beer from the fridge and tells them all about his day.

Is that right? he says and you can see by his eyes what he expects me to say.

Yes, I tell him, yes, that's right.

Then I remember a sudden, true thing: that I had to stay awake to feed the baby. I tell Mawhinney this, though my heart bangs crazily as I say it.

He listens without much interest.

Oh yes, says Mick just like it's not important at all, so you did, I'd forgotten that.

I glance down at Mawhinney's little notebook. He hasn't written anything down.

We're bringing her feeds forward, I explain, or trying to anyway.

My voice sounds reasonable. I hate myself.

Why did you say that? I ask Mick once Mawhinney has gone.

He looks up from the floor where he's kneeling on newspaper and cleaning Rosa's brown school shoes.

Why did I say what?

About us being in bed at ten thirty?

He goes on dabbing polish in with the cloth,

59

working it carefully into all the cracks and creases. He breathes through his mouth as he does it, his tongue touching the inside of his top lip. That's what he does when he concentrates. Mick's good at concentrating. He says that's how you make the smallest jobs satisfying.

Because we were, he says carefully.

I swallow, taste polish in the back of my mouth.

You were, I tell him. I wasn't.

He sits back on his heels in an unsurprised yet exasperated way.

Oh for fuck's sake, Tess —

I wasn't.

You wanted me to tell him that?

I gaze at him. Sometimes his confidence amazes me. I thought you'd tell the truth, I say.

Well I was in bed, he says. And as far as I know you were too. As far as I'm concerned I was telling the truth.

He says that but his eyes narrow. He's angry.

But I got up, I tell him. You know I did. You know I got up.

He says nothing, picks up the shoe.

Don't you want to know where I went?

He hesitates and I don't like the look on his face.

You're saying I should stop you?

No. I don't know.

You can't have it both ways, Tess.

He laughs then. He laughs because he knows my position is ludicrous. You can't make someone want to know things. Just like you can't force someone to be

60

jealous or upset or aroused. They either are or they aren't and that's it. There are no halfways.

But I love him, I tell myself. I do. I would never, never want to be married to Alex – thank God I didn't stay with him, we'd have been hopeless together, fatal, lethal, always knowing what each other wanted and getting there quicker, wanting it first.

Now, every clock in the house is ticking, but each one says a different time. Mick's job is to wind them up. He's the one who likes antique clocks, the noise and the work of them, not me. If it were up to me, I'd have something modern: fierce red digits glinting in the dark.

The thing about Mick is, he thinks it's clever not to rise to things.

I'm not trying to hide anything from you –

That's what I tell him, but he shrugs.

I know, Tess. I don't think you are. It still doesn't mean I need to know.

It's your life, he says when I don't reply to this. Your life, your time.

No, I say as carefully as I can. Don't you see how maddening it is when you say that? It's not. It's our time.

He laughs.

What? What's funny?

He doesn't answer, just laughs again. Then turns away and begins the thing of buffing the shoe. He does it hard. Rosa's feet will shine. Not that she'll notice.

I went to The Polecat, I tell him. That's all.

He gives me a quick look.

Fine.

Fine?

Lucky you're still alive, he says and his voice is small and dull and tight.

He places Rosa's shoes perfectly straight on the mat by the back door and folds the newspaper and stuffs it in the recycling. He recycles every piece of paper in the house, Mick does. Sometimes he recycles things before I've had a chance to read them.

I think he's going to leave the room then, but he doesn't. He comes over. Holds me for a quick moment.

Let's not do this, he says. Please, Tess. Not now.

I kiss the bristles on his cheek.

I don't want to do anything, I tell him.

He sighs.

I thought this was what you wanted anyway, he says. I thought it was the whole point?

What? I say. The whole point of what?

Of everything. Of what you say you want in life?

I don't know what I do want any more, I tell him.

He pauses and looks at me.

It's not relevant to any of − this − where you were.

Is that why you lied?

I didn't lie. I just told them what I knew for certain.

But don't they have to − look at everything?

He touches my face, my cheek, my jaw. I shiver.

You tell them then.

What?

Tell them where you were.

You think I should?

No. I don't. Where would it get you? What's the point of confusing things further. For God's sake, Tess, I was only trying to help you, keep you clean.

Clean?

Out of it. Uninvolved.

You think I should be grateful?

Don't put words into my mouth.

5

It turns out the coroner needs two people to identify the body – another person, an independent witness who knew Lennie, as well as her next of kin. Bob, her dad, is struggling to get his doctors' permission to fly over from Philadelphia. But he is eighty-one and frail with a poorly heart and the journey itself will be hard enough.

Mick says he'll do it – go to the morgue with Alex. At first I try to persuade him out of it. It should be me. He's never seen a dead person and I have. I cut up plenty when I was training.

Those were strangers, he says. This is completely different.

Is it?

Tess. For fuck's sake. You know it is.

Anyway, he tells me, he wants to go – he wants to do this for Alex. And for Lennie. He means it, but I am tempted to remind him of how little more than a year ago just the sight of Livvy's reptilian shadow on the ultrasound almost made him pass out.

When I hear that Lacey is going with them, I feel better. In all these hours, Lacey's barely left Alex's side. Mick says that's the whole point of what he does – to offer continual support, twenty-four hours a day.

When Alex comes and sits in our kitchen – hunched at our plate-strewn, crumb-covered kitchen table still wearing his rough and musty-smelling coat and rolling cigarettes with shaky hands, now Lacey comes too. They make a strange pair – Alex with his pale face and fair unwashed hair and visible grief, Lacey smaller, darker, younger, mostly silent and watching.

Mick says that's how he's trained to be – to make himself invisible, so that he doesn't inhibit any of us, so that he doesn't intrude. He accepts my offer of a cup of coffee and then just sits there in his smooth, dark London clothes, elbows on his knees, watching us all. Maybe he's looking for clues. Maybe he's thinking that by finding out how we all live, he can somehow work out how Lennie died.

He's not a detective, Mick says.

I say I think he seems far too young to have such a terrible job and Mick agrees.

I couldn't do it, he says, but I think he's good. He's a good guy. I like him.

★ ★ ★

Alex tells us that new details have emerged from the post-mortem. He says they suspect the killer used a lino-cutter. He says that Lennie's sternum was cracked open, her ribs forced apart like the bars of a cage. The vessels that pumped blood from her heart were severed in a surprisingly methodical way, the organ lifted out intact. Though the initial attack was frenzied, uncoordinated, the subsequent surgery on her torso was carried out with chilling accuracy and cool.

The fucker knew what he was doing, in other words, he says.

I take a breath and catch Lacey's eye. He holds my gaze then looks away.

Mick lowers himself into a chair, his face bloodless.

But how can they possibly be so specific? he wants to know.

The angle and depth of the cut, says Alex simply. He looks at us and shrugs and his voice doesn't wobble or falter. It just stays exactly the same.

Meanwhile other things have come to light. We know now that her underclothes were partially pulled off. That she wasn't sexually assaulted. That the bludgeoning to her head was so frenzied that large fragments of her skull lodged in her brain causing extensive haemorrhaging. Which means her assailant would have been covered in blood. It would be impossible, the police say, to inflict those kinds of injuries and on that scale and remain unbloodied.

He probably left in a car. Police say they want to trace

the owner of a silver Fiat Uno that was seen on the junction of Hotson Road and North Parade around the time of Lennie's death. Anyone who knows anything at all should come forward. They appeal again and again for help from anyone who was in the pier end of town on that night.

You wanted my mummy to die, Connor tells Rosa as they sit together on the low, flinty wall at the end of Spinner's Lane.

Rosa is shocked. She calls him a liar. He calls her a bitch and throws a handful of gravel at her. She throws a handful back and then runs sobbing all the way home, leaving her anorak behind on the wall.

You know he didn't mean it, I tell her.

He did! Rosa sobs. He did, he did! He called me a bitch!

I know better than to try to hug Rosa, but I touch the biscuity top of her head.

Poor Connor, I say.

He called me a bitch! Don't you even care?

Rosa —

She pushes me off.

Leave me alone, she says. Get your hands off me. If you're going to side with him. You only care about him.

I never know what to do with Rosa — she has all of Mick's surly cleverness combined with the pouchy beginnings of breasts already (and she's only eleven) plus a frighteningly clear idea of what she expects from the world. Mostly it lets her down.

Sometimes I think we would be closer now if I'd never had Liv. Having another baby made me go down in her estimation. It's true – she despises me for it.

It's an alien, she told me when she saw how the baby's fast-growing body turned my navel inside out. You've been taken over.

It's just all a bit much when you're her age, Lennie suggested. She's too young and too old for it. She can't see what's in it for her.

I laughed. There were times back then when I couldn't see what was in it for me either. But Lennie was right. She was better at working Rosa out than anyone else. Poor Rosa. Just as she was learning to do cartwheels and hand-stands and to make her own body bright and ruthless and elastic, there I was, slow and large and weighed down.

When Liv was born, Lennie gave Rosa a kitten. She named it Maria. She said it was the best present anyone had ever given her.

All I have left of Lennie, Rosa says now as Maria's warm white weight spills through her fingers.

I tell her that Connor must be very mixed up right now.

Just think of how he must be feeling, I say.

Well, he should think of my feelings, she replies.

You don't really think that, Rose.

I didn't want Lennie to die, she says.

Baby, no one thinks you did.

He does. He thinks so –

No, listen darling, that's what I'm saying. Connor's eight years old and he's lost his mum.

Almost nine, says Rosa.

What?

He's almost nine. And I've lost my – friend.

OK. Nine, I say, but that's a terrible thing to have happen to you. Think of how awful you're feeling. Then multiply it by a thousand.

Rosa stops crying then and grows still and silent. After some minutes she takes my hand and feels my fingers, my two rings, the soft, fleshy pads under my nails. She asks me where Lennie is right now.

The question takes me by surprise.

You mean where's her body?

Yes.

Well, it's in a morgue, I tell her carefully. That's the place near the hospital in Ipswich where they look at her to see how she died.

But they know how she died –

More or less, yes.

Rosa frowns.

So – what – aren't they going to bury her then?

Eventually, yes of course they are. Or cremate her.

Rosa slips one of the rings off my finger and puts it on her own. This is a favourite thing of hers to do. The ring sits lopsidedly on her thin little finger. She spins it absently round.

Who'll decide? she says.

It'll be up to Alex.

Rosa shudders.

I wouldn't want to be underground, she says. But I wouldn't want to be burnt either.

You mustn't think of it like that, I tell her, taking back the ring and easing it onto my own finger. You're not you when it happens.

No, but – what? Just a body?

That's right.

Oh, well, I wouldn't want my body to be burnt or underground then. It's the same.

It won't be your body. Because you won't be you.

But I will be me! Rosa insists. My body is still me –

Not in that sense, not in the feeling sense.

It will be for me, she says firmly.

You can't possibly know that.

But I do!

No you don't, I tell her as gently as I can.

Rosa says nothing. Then, Yes I do, she whispers.

I take her in my arms and hold her tight enough to feel the fizz of her heart. She doesn't fight me this time.

Now Nat knows things. He knows about Lennie's heart, and he knows she wasn't shot. He's heard stuff. At school, in the street. Kids of twelve read the papers. Details are going round. Mick calls him downstairs and shuts the door.

We're talking about a very, very disturbed person, he says, looking him all the while unflinchingly in the eye as he always does when he's telling something serious to the kids. A sick person. Someone badly in need of help.

A psycho? Nat asks a little too eagerly.

Well, psycho's a silly word they use in the movies, Nat. Real life is mostly a lot more boring and nasty and banal.

70

But if by psycho you mean someone who is so inade-
quate that they get some kind of kick out of killing
someone in this terrible way, then yes I suppose so, a
psycho.

Will he get life? Nat asks. Swallowing.

If they catch him, Mick says, yes, I'm pretty sure he will.

I bet Alex wishes there was the death penalty, Nat says,
and his eyes bunch up in sympathy. I bet he wishes this
was in America.

Mick looks at him patiently.

Not for a sick person, Nat, he says. It's not right to
kill a sick person.

It's never OK to kill, right? says Nat and this time he
looks at me.

Never, I agree.

Nat pauses and fiddles with a rubber band he's picked
up off the table.

But what if they don't catch him? he asks, stretching
the band between his fingers.

This time Mick looks at me.

They're going to try very hard to catch him, I say.

Do you think he's upset? I ask Mick, once we hear his
feet thudding back up the stairs.

No, he says, getting himself a drink out of the fridge.

What? Not at all?

Not especially, I don't think so, no.

He roots around for a beer. They're all at the back.
When he has it, he grabs the bottle opener, rubs it on
his jeans, looks at me.

I think he's just put it away.

Oh.

Don't worry, he adds. It's perfectly healthy.

Is it?

Not everything has to be talked about, Tess.

He tilts his head back and sips as if nothing was wrong. I look at him.

Really? I say, I'm surprised. You never used to think that.

Didn't I?

No.

Are you sure you know what I used to think? I mean, you always assume you know what I'm thinking, he says more gently.

Do I?

I bite my lip.

I don't mean to – assume things, I begin, then I backtrack. Anyway, don't you assume you know things?

I don't think so.

You don't? Of course you do.

Mick shrugs, puts the beer down on the table.

I don't know. I don't give it much thought. I mean, I don't think like that. I get on with life instead.

He says it like that, as if it's perfectly normal and true, but there is a kind of pain and tension in his face as he says it and it occurs to me that, for perhaps the first time ever, there is pain between us, too. Why? I don't think it's about Lennie, not really, I don't think you can blame that. No. I actually think it's about us – him and me and how we are together.

Later, when I let it back into my head, the idea shocks me. I decide it cannot be true. It must just be that all the grief and shock has got mixed up and seeped into our feelings about each other. If someone you care about dies violently, it infects everything. Anyone would agree with that.

I know what Lennie would say about this. Don't be stupid, she'd say. You're going through a difficult time, that's all. Don't generalise or say or do things you'll regret. Just hang on in there and wait for it to pass. Because it will. It'll pass.

A man rings from the coroner's office. For a chat, he says. He apologises for disturbing us, but explains that he is supposed to take Mick through what will happen that afternoon at the morgue – how much he'll see, what it will be like, etc.

Mick takes the phone and walks slowly into his study and shuts the door. He's in there for a few minutes. When he reappears, he looks tired. He tells me that the man said that only Lennie's face will be visible, that the rest will be covered by a sheet.

There aren't any marks on her face, he says. Nothing visible apparently, not even any bruising.

He stands there and looks at me and scratches at his arms.

Was it supposed to make me feel better, do you think? he says.

I don't know, I say.

I mean, couldn't Lacey have told me all that?

Would you have asked him?

He sighs.

I don't know. I mean, maybe not.

Later, when he's gone, I take the chance to cut Rosa's toenails. She makes such a fuss that I am forced to bribe her with a bag of Doritos.

What do you want to do, Rosa yowls as I grab her slim, white foot and prop it on my knee, torture me?

Yes, I say to shut her up.

Even though it's only five – way too early to drink – I pour myself a glass of wine, a big one.

You never cut the boys' nails, Rosa complains as she crams her mouth with Doritos.

How do they get shorter then? Tell me that.

Rosa giggles.

What d'you think happens? You think they just drop off?

It's discrimination, she says happily. You just want to get me.

I smile and drink my wine in big, quick gulps, feel my edges soften. Rosa wipes bright orange Dorito dust from her mouth and onto her jeans. She sneaks a glance at me as she does it. Normally I would shriek at her, but I don't, I barely notice. I feel strangely untouchable, as if I've slid sideways into someone else's life. It's a good feeling. After some moments, I leave the room and walk upstairs.

I put Liv down and curl up on the sagging, Marmite-stained kids' sofa with Jordan. We watch *Tomorrow Never*

Dies and I let him zap forward to the action bits, even though this is something he's not normally allowed to do. You either watch the whole of something, Mick always tells the kids, and watch it properly, or you do something else useful instead.

This, apparently, is how Mick got somewhere in life and it's a position that, on the whole, I agree with. So Jordan can't believe this waiving of the rules.

Are we being slobs? he asks me hopefully.

You bet.

Do you like Bond?

I love it.

No. I mean him – James Bond? Do you actually like him?

He's great, I say, and, exhilarated by my attention and approval, Jordan turns and pats my face tenderly. His fingers smell of heat and cheese.

I love you, Mummy, he says.

Yeah, yeah.

You're so beautiful – I mean, you look so young.

I laugh.

I mean it – you only look about thirty-five, he says and I kiss the soft skin next to his eyes where the freckles spill over so enthusiastically you can't believe he will one day be a man and shave and have serious, grown-up thoughts.

Mummy needs another drink, I tell him and he pauses the video so I can go to the fridge to replenish my glass. But he rewinds a little before he pauses it. He doesn't want me to miss anything.

In the kitchen the windows are black and battered

with rain. The fridge is white, the wine bottle yellow and cold. I put my hands on it, feel the chill. It goes straight to my heart.

When I return, Jordan is kneeling up on the sofa, waiting.

What would you do if a baddie came in now? he asks me urgently as I set the wine down on the carpet and he unpauses the film. He watches me, watches my face, waiting to see what I'll say. On the screen, a Chinese girl is swimming underwater (again), black hair waving in the gloom.

I'd call the police, I tell him.

Yes OK, he says impatiently. But what if they didn't come?

They would, I say – surprised that Lacey's serious face slips into my mind – they would come.

But, he insists, I mean, what if something happened to them on the way?

Oh Jordan –

Or if they didn't hear the phone?

There are people whose special job it is to answer the phone, I tell him. So if you dial 999, of course they answer and they come.

Hmm, he says, more or less satisfied.

But he's missed one of the fights – they shot at the Chinese girl when she came out of the water – so we have to wind back. As he holds the remote up and concentrates on the screen, I slip my arms under his and feel the snap of his little chest, the warmth of his neck, his baby hair.

You smell like a rabbit, I tell him.

But he's not listening, and before I can stop it happening, the room blurs and tears come.

By the time Mick gets back I've got Jordan into the bath. Then climbed the stairs to watch the sun go down over the creek from Nat's shambles of a room at the top of the house.

It's a violent, chemical sunset – smouldering as if something poisonous has been chucked across it. The colours are sharp and exhausting – or is that three glasses of wine on an empty stomach? Just watching it takes the breath out of me. I watch for a long time. It feels like the first time I've looked properly at anything since Lennie's death.

After that I sit down and try to feed Liv, but she's in a wriggly, fed-up mood. Maybe I shouldn't have had the wine. And soon after, there's the sound of the front door, keys dropped on the shelf. My heart sinks.

He comes in bringing with him the smell of outside, plumps heavily down in a chair with his jacket still on.

Well, he says.

I wait and he looks at me.

Well?

He was wrong.

Who was?

Him. The guy who phoned.

Oh.

Yeah. I mean her face was clean, but –

I feel the blood creep down my body.

But what – ?

Yeah.

He takes a breath, pauses, blinks hard.

Oh darling, I say.

He is not exactly crying. He takes a breath, a gulp, covers his eyes.

What he omitted to tell me, he says in a strangled voice, is that the top of her head is fucking well gone.

No –

He doesn't look at me.

There's nothing there, Tess.

You could see?

Mick shuts his eyes and the blood rushes to my head.

There was a sheet over it, he says, but yes, you could see.

Liv begins to cry. I try to put her back on the nipple, teasing her mouth open with my fingers. But a curdled lump of milk slides out of her mouth and down into my bra, making everything wet and cheesy.

I grab the cloth.

I'm sorry, I tell him.

What do you mean? It's not your fault.

Look, I begin.

He pushes both fists into his eyes.

Don't always try to make things better, he says, I mean it, Tess. Leave it, OK?

OK.

We sit in silence for a moment. The room swerves. My bra is cold and damp against my skin. I feel a little sick.

Have a drink, I tell him. I did.

I did, I think, and it worked.

Clearly, he says.

We watched a whole Bond film, I tell him, Jordan and me, all the way through.

You're drunk, he points out.

Yes, I agree — and I hold my baby tight and close my eyes and the room whistles brightly and then just fades away.

6

Our town is surrounded on three sides by marshes – Bulcamp Marshes, Angel Marshes, Tinker's and Woodsend and Buss Creek. Now they're beauty spots where bird-watchers go, but a long time ago, people drowned there. There are all sorts of stories.

Ellen Bloom aged 20 months, beloved daughter of Chad and Susannah, stumbling down the mud flats after dark. Rosa once found Ellen's little stone, strangled by ivy and splattered with lichen, in the graveyard at St Margaret's.

Or, the young man who forced himself on a local girl and then tied a brick around his foot and drowned out of shame. Or the girl who, rushing to see her secret lover, took a fatal wrong turn and was sucked down like a leaf.

Two seconds of bad luck and your life closes over your head.

The most recent is poor Anne Edmondson's son Brian. Many in the town still remember him. A clever lad and keen sailor, all set to read engineering at Leeds University. The plaque's inside the church. Brian John Edmondson aged 17 years and a good swimmer. Departed this life August 10th, 1958. No one knows why he just went out there one still summer night and drowned.

People say that if you drive down the old Dunwich Road at night and dare to stop the car and turn off the engine, you'll hear things.

Oh yeah? Alex and Mick say when Lennie and I come home and tell them this. You mean the fucking owls and wind in the trees.

I used to laugh too. Until Roger Farmiloe who pumps the petrol at Wade's garage told me he'd heard crying out there. So had his dad. And his uncle Peter too – fifteen years in the Merchant Navy and would laugh in your face if you said you believed in ghosts, Roger said. And yet.

In fact many brewery workers and darts players, farmhands and van drivers, people who you'd think might scoff or know better, have wound down their windows on dark nights and been so scared that they've driven back into town in a blazing hurry and refused to go back, not even if you paid them, or so they've all said.

Yes, says Mick, but after how many pints at The Anchor?

None, I reply. Roger said his uncle Peter was stone-cold sober.

This cracks him up.

That's harder to believe than all the fucking ghost stories put together, he says, laughing.

Lennie's death is good for trade, with both police and reporters in town. Both hotels are immediately full and the coffee shops, delis and snack bars have queues forming outside at lunchtime. Linny's The Outfitters even considers opening up the room at the back and laying on some kind of cold, takeaway food, something it has not thought of doing since back during the summer of the Queen's Silver Jubilee in seventy-seven.

Even Somerfield runs out of bread and meat halfway through the week and has to be restocked. And The Griddle stays open till seven each evening serving its famous cream teas and exotic ice creams, instead of closing as it normally does at half past five, though Ann Slaughter is heard to complain that Mei Yuen's next door starts frying at five and the smell puts people off their tea.

The photo that I gave to Lacey appears on TV as well as on the front page of the papers. I think Mick took it on holiday in France a couple of years ago when we all went away together and liked it so much we thought we'd always do it except we didn't, we never did it again.

In it she is wearing a striped pinkish T-shirt and she's smiling and screwing her eyes up against the bright sunshine and her hair is that little bit longer, strands of it caught in the wind across her face. She's not tanned – Lennie was too fair to tan – but she looks well and happy, standing there next to her boys. Of course the papers cut Max and Con off – they wanted just Lennie. So there she is, oblivious, alone and smiling.

And suddenly, there she is, all around us, even in Curdell's newsagent's on the High Street. It's too much for some people, to see her beaming out at them like that from the racks. Too close up and personal. One or two get all shaky or have a little cry when they go in to buy cigarettes or their lottery ticket. Some mums won't even take their kids in the shop but leave them outside instead, by the fishing nets and buckets and spades and windmills, next to the Wall's Ice Cream sign that flaps in the wind in the place where people usually tie their dogs.

On the Friday I go back in to work. Though everyone understands why I've been postponing appointments, I can't leave the clinic shut for long. I have a number of older patients who rely on me.

It smells cold in there – we have a constant problem, with the damp. I turn on the heating and water the plants, stuff some towels in the washing machine and turn on the computer to look up the appointments. As it crackles into life, I realise that Lennie's e-mails from just a few days ago will still be on it. Not wanting to see them, I go straight into the diary.

I've been there about twenty minutes when there's a

knock on the door at the front. It's not the door we use. Patients come in through a side door in the alleyway they call Dene Walk. I lift the front blinds and see that it's Lacey. Surprised, I indicate to him to go round to the side.

Sorry, he says when I open the door in my white coat, jeans and clogs with my woolly jacket still on top, I should have phoned –

No, no, I say. It's OK.

Have you got a moment?

He looks past me into the room. I step aside to let him in.

As I apologise for the cold and explain that the heating system's old and takes a while to get going, I feel myself blushing. If he notices, he doesn't show it.

You work alone here?

I've done less since the baby. There used to be a partner. But he left and went back to London. Making tons more money there.

You're busy?

I shrug.

There's enough to keep me going.

No, he says, I meant – today.

Oh, I say, colouring furiously again. No one's in till this afternoon – I mean, I cancelled all the earlier appointments this week. It's the first time I've been in – since –

He nods.

I just came in to get things – organised.

I offer him a chair and he sits, looks around him.

84

What's the smell? he asks me.

I frown and sniff.

Oh. I don't know. Lavender? I use a lot of oils.

He looks at me.

Do you? What for?

Massage, I tell him. Soft-tissue work.

He seems to think about this. And then, I'm sorry, he says. About the other day. The morgue.

Oh, I say, it wasn't your fault.

Was he OK?

Just upset, I tell him. What about Al? I haven't seen him.

Lacey looks at me.

Eucalyptus, he says.

I feel myself smile.

The smell –

Yes. Quite probably.

Just then Liv gives a gasp from under the desk. I normally put her down on a small mattress on the floor behind the filing cabinets.

Lacey laughs in surprise.

You've got the baby down there?

I laugh back and squat down to pull her up against me. She smells hot and fusty, of sleep.

She gazes at Lacey and then she smiles. So does he.

You're honoured, I tell him. Mostly she cries when she sees strangers.

Am I a stranger?

Well –

She's seen me before, he points out.

OK. But not very much.

He stands up then and I'm thinking several things – how hard he is to talk to, how awkward and how this awkwardness makes me shy. And also that he seems to be about to go and I don't even know why he came, what he came to say.

Look, he says abruptly, do you want some coffee or something?

Coffee?

Yes.

He coughs a little cough of embarrassment and my heart races. I glance down at Liv and flush again.

We have coffee here, I say.

No, he says. No – I mean out somewhere.

I laugh.

I haven't got long.

Come on.

All right, I tell him, OK, fine.

Outside it has turned into an OK day. Warmish and lightish, almost not like autumn at all, but late, lingering summer, the last dregs of brightness.

I put Liv in the buggy, tuck the blanket in around her and clip her in. Her small white fingers flutter a moment on my wrist and I feel almost happy.

So, he says as we wheel up the High Street. Where to?

No idea, I say.

Come on, he says, you know this place.

OK, I go. Follow me.

We head for the front, the prom. Up past Curdell's and the grocer's and The King's Head and John Empson's and Somerfield. Across the marketplace, wheels joggling on the cobbles. He doesn't speak. I glance at his reflection in the dark windows of Pam's Florist's. I feel him beside me but I don't look.

The Whole Loaf Deli has its shades down as if it's lunch. Hard to tell if they're open or not. Outside there are two people with large woven shopping baskets.

Do you know, I ask him since he has already brought it up, how soon they'll release her – the body, I mean?

You mean for a funeral? he says and I nod.

He hesitates, pushing his hands through his hair.

No, he says, not really. It could take a while.

We've reached the Sailors' Reading Room. He glances uncertainly down the steep and narrow steps to the prom. The metal handrail is splashed in places with birdshit. One or two pink poppies still bloom in the gorse.

Can you help me lift it? I ask him.

What, all the way down there? That's where we're going?

It's worth it, you'll see.

He takes the other side of the buggy and helps me down, me in front and him behind.

You know, he says once we reach the concrete esplanade at the bottom and put the buggy down, how Alex feels? About her heart?

I flush with surprise.

What? What about it?

Getting it back, I mean.

I stop the buggy and turn to stare at him properly. The wind drops and my head feels suddenly warm and light.

No, I say, I don't. What do you mean?

That he doesn't want to bury her without it?

Oh, I say. He hasn't said that to me.

Oh, well I'm sorry. I thought he might have.

No.

Lacey seems flustered. Again he pushes his hair back from his head – a pointless thing to do since it springs straight back.

I think, he says slowly, hesitating, I mean, I don't know how to put this, but I think Alex may have unrealistic ideas about what I can do –

You?

With regard to bringing it back I mean. Finding it.

I take a breath.

Well, you can't can you? I say.

He looks at me again.

Look, he says. Do you mind me talking to you like this?

No, I say without even thinking.

Despite this, he seems to hesitate.

It's just – I can understand it – he doesn't want to bury her without it.

But he'll have to?

He looks away from me, at the beach, the sea.

I think so. Yes.

I press my fingers on my mouth, stopping a rush of tears from coming.

Have you said that to him? I ask Lacey.

What?

That he'll have to.

No, he says and I turn my face away into the wind. I don't want to cry in front of him.

I'm sorry, I tell him as we continue on along the prom, it's just that I can't really think about it for very long, any of it –

I know, he says. It's OK. You don't have to.

I'm sorry, I tell him.

Don't be silly, he says.

I look away from him and try to think. The tide is out – a distant frill of brown – and the shingle shines all over with smallish creeks. I love the beach best like this.

Some little kids are running and shouting and building something in the sand exposed between the bumps of shingle. They have swimming costumes on even though it's October, but they dash around in the jagged, goose-pimpled way of kids by the sea, waving their spades and shrieking.

You're used to this, though, aren't you? I tell him.

We stand for a moment and watch the kids – their small, curvy backs and tense, startled little legs. A dog is barking and barking at the far-out waves the way Fletcher used to when he was young and crazy, and a woman is hanging wet towels on the railing of one of the beach huts.

Used to what?

I mean this stuff – dealing with it, the really terrible stuff.

I know he's looking at me.

He says, It's my job. To support people – the victims and their families. But I don't think anyone gets used to it.

Do you stay in touch with people? – I mean, afterwards?

Not always. Mostly not. Sometimes they just want you out of their lives.

Oh?

They want to start again and not be reminded. That's fine. It makes sense.

But, I say, what about you? Don't you ever get – attached?

He smiles. Doesn't answer.

Or them, I insist. Sometimes they must get attached to you?

If they do, he says, it's fake. That's what you have to remember. It's only because you're with them for twelve or fourteen hours a day. You have to withdraw – carefully.

How? I ask him. How do you do that?

It's called an exit strategy.

He smiles again and looks at me.

It's not as bad as it sounds, he says. It's just a job.

You must be very strong, then, to do it.

Not especially, he says. Just a good listener.

Al doesn't talk much, I point out suddenly though I don't know why.

No, Lacey agrees, he doesn't. Where's this coffee, then?

In the buggy Livvy gurgles and bats at her toy.

Estelle's is the next one along, I tell him.

What's Estelle's?

The Tea Hut. Look, down there.

OK.

The best place.

If you say so.

I do.

The day after Lennie died, they had Estelle on the local TV news. They showed her putting hot water in the big metal teapot, looking sad, looking out to sea.

She said, This is a very rural community and everyone knows everyone else and we are all so very shocked that such a terrible crime could happen here in our midst.

At Estelle's you can buy just about anything. Windmills and lilos and pocket kites and buckets and spades, the lot. When they were younger, the kids would nag us for the little packs of paper sandcastle flags, the ones you can get for 35p. They'd swear to us that they couldn't build a sandcastle without them – and then we'd find them later, discarded and crushed and sandy at the bottom of the nappy changing bag.

I park the buggy and Lacey goes over and buys two mugs of coffee filled the way Estelle always fills them, to the brim. He brings them over carefully, picking his way between the big white plastic chairs.

We came here all the time, I tell him, pulling my coat up around me, Lennie and me, you know. Even in winter.

Jesus, he says, looking around him, I can't say I really see the point of this place in winter.

Oh, winter's the best, I say, vaguely disappointed that he should say such a thing.

I try not to think of Lennie and me, huddling on the shingle in our jumpers with a mug of weak Earl Grey from Estelle's, taking it in turns to watch the kids. When the beach is empty, you can let them run and run till they're no more than tiny black specks heading for Blackshore. As long as you can still see them, they're safe, you can relax. And then if the sun slides out from under a cloud, a moment of pure yellow heavenly warmth, before the grey returns.

Lacey is looking at me.

Can I ask you something? he says.

What sort of thing?

Well – ah, OK, it's this. I need to know what sort of a relationship Lennie and Alex had.

You can tell he finds this a difficult question to ask because he looks me straight in the eye as he asks it. His gaze doesn't wobble. I feel the blood hit my face.

Goodness, I say. You mean their marriage – were they happy together?

Lacey nods. That sort of thing, yes.

But – I hesitate – I mean, shouldn't you ask Alex that?

Oh, well, I have.

And?

He shrugs, looks down at his knees.

As you yourself said, he doesn't talk much.

But – why ask me?

Come on, he says. She was your friend, wasn't she? Women tell other women things.

I think hard. I think about what to say.

I'm sorry, he says. I've embarrassed you.

No, I tell him quickly, no, of course you haven't. I understand — that you have to ask these things.

Lacey puts down his coffee mug and scrapes his chair back a little on the concrete. Shoves his hands in his pockets, waiting.

It's just, I say, it's difficult. So soon after.

He says nothing, waits, looks at me.

Do you think you were a good friend to her, Tess? he asks me then. And I notice two things: that it's the first time he's used my name and also that the question bothers me more than I thought it would.

I take a breath.

Not always, no, I tell him.

He looks surprised.

Do you mind telling me why?

It's personal, I tell him. And I don't think it's relevant.

Relevant to what?

To — this.

It could well be, he says.

I don't think so, I tell him.

Isn't that for me to decide?

I look at him then. He's leaning forward, wrists on his knees, the way he did when he was listening to us all in our kitchen at home. I look in his eyes and try to discover what he's expecting to hear.

Is it part of your job, I ask him, to question me like this?

Yeah, he says, you know it is.

93

I make an exasperated noise and he laughs. Not seeming to mind that I haven't answered him.

OK, he says at last. OK, forget that. Tell me something else instead.

What?

I don't know. Anything. Whatever you like.

Afterwards, we walk a little way together along Pier Road – claustrophobic with its leylandii and dwarf conifers, porches crammed with dead geraniums. I always think that and I think it now. But if I cut across the playground and the churchyard, it's the quickest way back to the clinic.

By the phone box on the corner I stop.

I'm going through there, I tell him, indicating the grassy field with its swings and slides and big old tyre which hangs above a bark-chip-strewn expanse.

The church clock is striking. Eleven already.

Oh, he says. Right.

I'll see you, I tell him. Thanks for coffee.

Take care, he says and he looks at me.

You OK? he asks me.

I'm fine.

Thanks for your time, he says. Maybe we can do it again?

Maybe, I say uncertainly. Then a thought occurs to me. It was random, wasn't it? I ask him suddenly, my heart racing. Just a random, horrible, vicious thing? She was just in the wrong place at the wrong time –

He stares at me.

Hey, he says, why'd you suddenly say that?

I don't know. It's just – been in my head.

There's no such thing as random, he says slowly, not really. Not in that sense.

I shiver.

Meaning – ?

Tess, there'll be a reason, a kind of logic to it –

You think he's local? Someone we might all know – someone living right here in this town?

Is that what you think? he asks me quickly.

You're the expert, I say and he gives me a sober look.

No, he says, I told you. Not in that way. I'm not much of an expert, not really.

I leave him then. In the playground a couple of mothers – I don't know them – are sitting at the picnic benches near the climbing frame, chatting and watching over their toddlers who are picking up handfuls of the bark chips and chucking them at each other. As the gate swings shut behind me, I hear squeals of laughter, then the sound of someone crying and then – very faint and only in blotted snatches – the sound of someone practising the organ deep inside the walls of the church.

7

For days and days, people have been laying flowers in the car park. Even strangers from Reydon and Wangford – people who didn't even know her – have brought bouquets and laid them there. The pile is growing. It feels like it will never stop. If you go near the pier, it hits you. The decayed sweetness of freesias and roses wrapped in cellophane and blown on the wind.

Alex isn't comfortable with it. He says it's not what Lennie would have wanted and anyone who knew her agrees. On Sunday morning, Canon Graham Cleve lets it be known that Lennie's family would far rather people made a donation to one of her favourite charities instead. But no one takes any notice. The flowers keep on piling up and Winton's, the bigger florist's in the High Street, stays open till 7 p.m. four days in a row to cope with the demand.

Two national papers run obituaries of Lennie – proper longish obituaries that talk about her with a serious kind of respect, as if she was someone you'd have heard of. In the world of ceramics she was on the way up, though, as Alex likes to point out, they still wouldn't give her a show of her own in London.

The photo they use is the one taken about three years ago by one of the local papers. In it she is bent over a glossy wet pot, strands of hair falling in her face, fingers and apron squidgy with clay. Because she's concentrating, the expression on her face is unsettling – savage, almost. It's a different Lennie from the one we knew. Certainly I never saw her look like that.

Someone from the Crafts Council is quoted as saying, Leonora Daniels was a welcome breath of fresh air in ceramics, relying as she did on her instincts rather than following the whims and vagaries of fashion. Bollocks, Alex says. He's sure this person never even met Lennie, let alone had anything good to say about her when she was alive.

Meanwhile everyone in the town has their own small thing to add.

She was so normal, Peggy at the dry-cleaner's tells me when I go to pick up the curtains. There was no side to her, no side at all.

She was ever such a nice person, one of the dinner ladies at the school tells the *Gazette*. I hardly knew her but she always went out of her way to say hello.

★　★　★

Almost a week has passed and the whole town knows that no killer has yet been caught. Daphne Ellison, who works on the till at Somerfield, tells me that everyone she meets is talking about security. People who never thought twice about leaving their doors on the latch now double-lock them, even during the day. More than once, she's seen the locksmith's van parked in Cumberland Road or Skilman's Hill or next to the cottages at Woodley's Yard.

It's sad really. You don't want to give into it, she says, the fear I mean. But it's all right for me, I've got a husband. What can I say to my poor old mother who lives alone?

Now everyone supervises their kids closely. Mick won't let Nat go out alone to the playground and he's not allowed to hang around on the Green with the other kids like he used to. In fact, plenty of people I know won't venture out across the Common or do the marsh walks alone now, not even to watch the sun go down or exercise their dogs. And certainly no one would dream of going near the pier, or hanging around anywhere in the town after dark.

I bump into Alex at the school gates. He looks terrible – pale, unshaven, used-up, glittery-eyed. Some days he lets us call for Con and some days he doesn't. He'll only accept so much help, even from us. He says he's still trying to be a normal father, and I can sympathise with that.

Naughty girl, he says, once I've shouted at Jordan to come back for his PE kit and waved him goodbye.

What?

I hear you've been hanging out with Ted Lacey.

I blush straightaway and hate myself for it. I should know better. I should know Alex better.

I try to look him in the eye.

We talked, I say, yes. Why?

And, he says in a mock-accusing voice, you had coffee and went for a walk.

I look at him. I can hear the dryness in his mouth. I wonder vaguely, helplessly, if he might be ill.

Are you all right? I ask him.

He smiles.

Perfectly fine. Why? Don't I look it?

No, you don't actually. You look – terrible.

We start walking, away from the school, and he rubs his face. I see that his hands are shaking.

Have you eaten today?

Yes, Mummy.

Al –

Well for Christ's sake. What the fuck do you expect me to say?

I touch his sleeve and he pulls away.

I never see you any more, he says.

I look at him.

What? I say. But you see me all the time –

No. I mean alone. I don't see you alone any more.

I stop.

You don't need to see me alone.

Don't I?

What's this all about? I ask him. Seriously – what's the matter?

99

You know what the matter is. Seriously.

No, I say. I don't. I mean today – this – what's it about?

He shrugs.

I glance down at my watch.

Got an appointment? he says.

No.

What, then?

Moments later.

I was thinking, I say.

What? He gazes at me greedily. What were you thinking, Tess?

You really want to know?

He rubs his eyes, yawns, looks at me. Waiting.

I don't understand why you never told the police – about coming to the hut. On the – on that night.

He looks exasperated. But says nothing.

Mawhinney has no idea, does he? I say. That you were there?

I look at him hesitating.

How do you know that? he says quickly.

Well it was obvious, I say. From – by the way he spoke to us.

He touches his face, glances at me.

And you said nothing?

No, but – I don't understand why you haven't told him, I say.

Don't you?

No, I say again, I don't.

A thought seems to occur to him.

Mick still doesn't know — that I was there with you?

No, but —

He relaxes. Licks his lips.

It's fine, Tess, it's OK.

But —

Just leave it, OK?

No, I tell him. It's not OK actually and I can't just leave it. No one's telling the truth here, not even Mick.

He laughs and makes a face.

You don't say? Not even Mick.

You know what I mean, I tell him.

It's not a question of the truth, he says. It's just that we don't need to confuse things.

It's lying, I insist. You're all lying. So am I.

I haven't lied, he says and his voice is suddenly pinched and hard.

By omission you have. By not telling the police everything.

Oh for God's sake, grow up, Tess, Alex says and he snaps off a branch of elder as we turn the corner into Woodley's Yard.

I'm silent for a moment and then I turn and face him.

Well — I may tell them, I say.

He brushes my cheek with the elder twig. It's scratchy.

Ow, I say.

What you do is your business.

Exactly, I agree. Yes.

Except that Mick will have to know I was there with you on that night.

I think about this.

It's fine, I say. He isn't really very interested. Plus we were just talking. There's nothing to hide.

Isn't there?

I look at him and feel a sudden surge of anger.

No, Al. There isn't.

He stops and takes me by the shoulders. Puts his face near mine. The grip of his fingers is too hard. His nails dig in a little.

How about this then? he says.

He kisses me, hard, on the mouth. He's trying to do it properly but it doesn't work. There's something crazy and awful about how hard he's trying. Like he's trying to cram it in. I taste the tip of his tongue, feel the chin bristles, the sourness, the sad unwashedness of him.

I push him off. My cheeks are burning.

For God's sake, Al – what're you doing?

He smiles stupidly. But his eyes are burning.

Giving you something to hide, he says, smiling as if it's all a big joke.

I look at him and I'm trembling.

You're sick, Alex. You're ill. I mean it. You need some help.

He throws his head back and looks at the sky. Says nothing.

I mean it, I say again. I'm not just saying it, Al. I think you are.

He spreads his arms out like a bird, fingers splayed.

I'm fine, he says. Never better. Don't give me hassle, Tess. Don't be so touchy.

He begins to walk off, away down the lumpy, lush

grassy path that gives into Spinner's Lane.

It's just a kiss, Tess, he sings back after me. Just a little harmless kiss. What's a kiss, for Christ's sake, between old friends?

I stand there, watching him. In the hedge there are blackberries, clusters of them covered in cobwebs. The sky crackles above me.

It's not real, I hear him say, from far away now, none of it's real. It's not happening. It's just another thing on the TV –

I smell the wind from the sea.

A murder mystery, he calls. A suspense thingy –

I taste salt in my mouth like blood.

I love you, Tess! he shouts. You know I do. I always have and I always will. Lennie knew it too.

That's the last thing he says before he disappears from view behind the hedge.

Lennie knew it too.

It's not true.

I start walking the other way. I am sick with shame.

At home, I look around for Mick and can't find him anywhere. The kitchen smells of washing powder, coffee, dog. A pile of tomatoes has rolled off the table onto the floor but fortunately Fletcher hasn't touched them. He doesn't like tomatoes. Nat says they're poisonous to dogs. He read it in a book of dog facts. The trouble with Nat is, he'll read all about dogs but he won't take Fletcher out for a walk.

I shout for Mick.

Liv is asleep in her rocker on the floor, fat-cheeked and peaceful, lips wet with spit.

The back door is open onto the yard. I can smell cigarettes.

Mick?

He's out there, standing looking at the bare fence and holding a cigarette carefully between thumb and finger. He sees me and doesn't move, just smiles.

You're smoking, I say.

That's right, he says. Ten out of ten for observation.

I look at him.

You've smoked, he says.

Yes, but –

Well, then.

I stand there for a moment, say nothing.

What's the matter? he says.

I'm extremely worried about Alex, I tell him at last.

Oh?

Yes – I take a breath – he tried to kiss me just now.

Mick holds the cigarette away from him and tilts his chin and laughs loudly.

Why? When did you see him?

At school. Just now. Coming back.

Ah. Sweet.

No, I say, staring at him. Mick, I mean really kiss. Snog.

Mick laughs again, more coldly.

Was it good?

Mick –

Did you kiss him back?

He flicks his ash onto the scrubby flowerbed where

Nat and Rosa like to set fire to blades of grass with a magnifying glass and where Jordan once grew a sunflower.

Mick, I say, what's the matter with you? Al's really weird. He's in a state. I was shocked. I mean, I don't know why he's doing this –

Oh, come on, says Mick, look at the poor man. Give him a break.

And you – all you want to know is if I kissed him back?

A joke.

Mick screws up his eyes and takes a last drag of his cigarette.

Well it's not funny. I think he's cracking up. Seriously, Mick, I'm worried about him.

Well – Mick looks pretty unmoved – I'd leave it. He'll get over it. He's very stressed just now.

I stare at him.

You don't mind?

He shrugs.

I'd mind if it meant anything, of course I would. But it doesn't. It's absolutely nothing. Insignificant.

Thanks, I say.

You know what I mean. Poor old Al.

But he was talking in the strangest way, saying odd things.

What sort of things?

Just – I don't know – stuff. It didn't make sense.

So, he says, stubbing his cigarette out on the peeling metal garden table, what is it exactly that you want me to do about this?

Mick, I say, I'm just telling you.

I know.

So − be a bit nicer −

Sorry. I didn't mean not to be nice.

Couldn't you talk to him?

And say what?

I don't know.

We fall into silence. Mick sits on the edge of the table. Fletcher comes padding out, sniffs at the concrete paving.

Maybe you should talk to Lacey about it, Mick says, if you're really worried.

I couldn't do that, I say straightaway.

Of course you could. He knows Alex, he's with him, he knows about this stuff.

No, I say. I just couldn't. You talk to him.

I think it's better coming from you −

Well, I can't, I say, I just can't. I don't want to, OK?

OK, says Mick. Well, leave it then.

At dusk, the High Street changes. It's taken over by kids in nylon clothes, kids whose parents we don't know, who live in the rows of pebble-dashed semis down beyond the marshes, with their scrubby, barren back gardens and kitchens that smell of frying.

They clutch their cans and hang around the video shop or the Chinese takeaway − or else sit smoking on the swings in the playground, leaving their empty cigarette packets at the foot of the infants' slide or kicking up the bark chips with their trainers.

But mostly they just stand at the bus shelter where

the odour of cleaning fluid only just masks the smell of piss. The timetables behind the glass are yellowed and old. There are two buses a day, three on market days. But the kids never get on these buses. They don't go anywhere. They just stand and wait.

Popping out to get milk before Somerfield closes, I catch sight of Lacey standing at the bus shelter, talking to a bunch of them. He is talking and they are listening, awkward, one or two of them kicking with their feet at the wire litter-bin outside Curdell's.

Lacey doesn't see me. I hurry past and down Bank Alley before he has a chance to turn.

Lennie's dad sits in the big pine chair in our kitchen and tells me how he's always been planning to come over to visit Lennie and his grandsons but has never been given a clean enough bill of health to fly.

This time, he says, I thought it might be different. I was hoping they'd just give me a bunch of pills and say, Get yourself on the first plane, Bob — just look after yourself is all.

While he talks, Bob doesn't look at me, but plucks away at the sleeve of his jersey. With Al and the boys, he didn't break down, not once. Then he came over and stood in the middle of our kitchen and just wept. Because he doesn't know us, Mick said. He doesn't feel he has to be strong.

Bob used to be a lawyer.

In Manhattan. But I've been retired for twenty-two years now, you know — twenty-two years!

Twenty-two years is a long time, I tell him.

He explains that he retired young, so he'd have time to do all the good things – the stuff you dream of doing.

He gives a bitter laugh.

What a joke, he says. My wife, Maya, she died a year later. A year almost to the day.

I tell him how sorry I am to hear that.

Anyway, he says, Lennie did make it – she did come over with the boys – what? – six years ago now, maybe seven. Certainly it was when Connor was still in diapers –

Max remembers it, I tell him, he definitely does, he still talks about America.

Bob brightens. Does he?

Then his face falls.

But the damn doctors, he says. My heart, my blood pressure, all that crap. So I never got to come and see where she lived. Not till now –

He pauses and his eyes fill up again.

And, you know? It's such a beautiful place!

It is, I tell him, I know, that's why we all came here, it is.

For a moment, Bob puts his head in his hands and is silent. The clock on the dresser ticks.

Oh Christ, he whispers. Oh Jesus, oh Christ.

I touch his shoulder.

I wish, I tell him softly, I wish there was something I could do or say.

He takes a breath.

There's nothing, he says. Just letting me be – just letting

me sit here in your lovely home, you know? That's enough.

I turn around and put the kettle back on.

You're a lovely person, he says, you know that? A lovely girl.

Not that lovely —

Oh yes, I mean it. If I was a few years younger —

I try to laugh.

You were a good friend to her, he says, I know you were. I could tell, you know, I could — from the things she wrote, the things she said —

I loved her, I tell him.

She should have gone into the legal profession, he says. Would have made a superb lawyer, she would.

Well, I say, she was a great potter —

She was?

Yes. Always selling her stuff, you know —

Really? Bob says doubtfully. But you make great money in the law, you know.

Yes, I tell him, but it's a big thing, what she did. You should be proud. It's not at all easy — to make a living from art.

You're an artist? he says.

No, I smile, I'm an osteopath. You know — I fix backs and necks and knees, that sort of thing.

Bob looks forlorn.

I don't have any trouble with mine, he says.

Well, that's good.

It's about the only thing, he says, that doesn't give me trouble.

You should eat something, you know? I tell him. A piece of fruit? Some cheese?

He shakes his head.

I wish you would.

Bob says nothing. Then he asks me if I realise how fat Lennie was as a baby? So fat that they worried at first, him and Maya, that something might be wrong with her. But the doctors reassured them that she was healthy and she was.

A sweet, fat baby. Never any trouble to her mother or me, he says. A placid little thing she was, always smiling, always happy. She was enough for us. We never even thought of having more kids, never even got the idea into our heads. Maybe we should've – or maybe we even did, I forget now – but anyhow the time just went and, well, Len was enough for us. She filled up our time.

Later, when Bob has gone back to Alex's, Lacey rings.

I have this small problem, he says. Just that Lennie's dad needs to stay in the studio and I can't get a hotel room till tomorrow night.

You can stay here, I say at once before I've even thought about it. Hating how my voice sounds twittery. Hating as well the feeling of not being able to breathe.

He pauses. He sounds nervous.

Look, he says, you're not just saying it? You've really got room?

It's fine. The boys can shuffle up.

Thank you, he says. You really are sure?

Of course I'm sure. I wouldn't offer otherwise.

Well, thanks very much. It's just for the one night, OK?

Don't worry about it, it's fine.

We ought to make Nat move out and put Lacey in there, but frankly Nat's room is too much of a mess.

Nat's room's stinky, says Rosa without looking up from her drawing. I mean it. It really smells.

Yeah, says Jordan, of farting. It smells of all the farting he does.

Shut up, says Nat.

That's enough, I tell him.

Make him clear it up, says Mick. He ought to anyway.

No, I say. It's too much hassle. It's a week's work, anyway. Lacey can go in with Jordan.

In the bunk bed? asks Rosa. Really?

With me! shrieks Jordan immediately. I'm not having police in my bed.

But as he says it he thinks about it and his face changes.

Actually, he says, cool. I'll do it.

You're doing it anyway, I tell him, whether you think it's cool or not.

He can go on the bottom. He can't touch anything though, Jordan says, thinking of his Warhammer stuff.

Nat sniggers. What's he going to want to touch of yours, poo-head?

Nat, says Mick, shut up. That's enough.

I think he's nice, says Rosa, still concentrating on her sketch pad. I do. I really like him. Connor says he's going to live with them.

Mick laughs.

Of course he's not, I tell her gently, poor man. He has a home and family of his own in London.

Rosa looks up, interested.

Does he? Has he got kids?

I look at her and realise I have no idea. I know nothing about Lacey except that he comes from London and is on transfer or whatever they call it.

He can't have, Nat says, or he couldn't be away from them this long.

He could, says Rosa. Some dads go away to work. Don't they, Dad?

Yes, says Mick and I know what he's thinking. He's thinking: yes and some dads even work.

He looks too young to have kids, I tell them, but he might do. We should ask him maybe.

At the clinic, I tear a hole in the rough blue paper on the bed so that June Sedgely can put her face in the gap.

Are you cold? I ask June, who says she's sixty but I guess is closer to seventy-five.

Not really, says June in her thin, polite voice. I pull the string to turn on the electric wall heater. My fingers are freezing.

I'm sorry, I tell June, my hands are awfully cold.

June laughs agreement as I touch her.

I work my fingers up and down June's spine.

There's a little inflammation, I tell her. The connective tissue doesn't feel right –

You can tell all that, June says, just by feeling?

I smile.

Not always, I tell her. I can't always feel it. But I can today.

How's that baby of yours? June asks me. She has kids of her own but none of them have produced a grandchild for her. It's a sore point. We've discussed it.

Big and heavy, I tell her. She's growing fat.

She's a good feeder?

I'll say.

June tries to nod her head and I feel the movement up and down her spine. A spring, a tremor.

And that poor man, June says. How's he coping?

Alex? He's doing OK.

Not what I've heard, June says, her voice muffled by the blue paper. I've heard he's gone a bit crazy. Insisting on making her coffin all by himself.

My fingers stop.

Really?

It's what I've heard. Jan Curdell told me. She heard it from the woman at the farm shop. I don't know how she knows —

I'm sure it's not true, I tell her.

You haven't heard it?

No, I say firmly.

Oh well, says June, and you'd know.

She sighs.

Those poor kids, she says. It's unthinkable.

Yes, I tell her, it is.

★ ★ ★

Lacey's already there when I get home, sitting in the kitchen with Mick while he peels potatoes for supper. Each of them has a glass of red wine and on the table is an open bag of crisps. Mick has on his thickest jersey with the zip front and no socks. Lacey has loosened his tie and taken his jacket off – the first time I've seen him without it. His hair sticks up as if he's been running his hands through it. I don't know what they're talking about but when I come in they stop. From upstairs you can hear the kids – pounding of feet, the frequent shrieks of complaint.

Livvy's lying on her mat on the floor, gazing at the back of the sofa. I kick off my shoes, pull her onto my lap. Kiss her four times on the soft, wide moon of her forehead – four fast kisses to make her laugh.

She does. She squeaks.

In the quick pocket of silence that follows, I can feel Lacey watching her, the way people watch babies when they're embarrassed or tired or don't know what to say. I don't look at him. I hold her away from me, hold her up under her sweet, fat arms, and then zoom her back for another four kisses. Up and in, up and back. She does her cartoon giggle. He watches her, watches me.

Mick grabs a handful of crisps.

So, he goes, how was work?

Oh, I reply, OK.

You sound fed up.

No, I say, I don't think so. Not fed up. Just tired.

I look at Lacey and he smiles at me. I think what a

nice smile he has – expectant, careful, kind. And then the kids come down.

What's for tea? asks Jordan, sniffing the air.

Rosa eyes the crisps while holding her kitten nuzzled against her shoulder.

Maria peed on the beanbag, she says. It wasn't her fault.

Get everyone to wash their hands, Mick says.

Can I have a crisp? says Rosa.

No, says Mick. Wash your hands.

From now on, Nat says, the little ones are banned from PlayStation. I mean it.

I wish he wouldn't say that! We're not little! screams Rosa.

The kitten wriggles away and jumps to the floor. The cat flap bangs and before anyone can grab his collar, Fletcher rushes at it with a great long skid across the floor, barking loudly.

Why can't I? says Rosa, back on the crisps. Can't I even have one?

Crisps are for grown-ups, I tell her.

Oh great! she says. I get it – and kids are just minor beings, right?

Rosa slams out of the room. Mick yells at her to come right back. Nat hits Jordan and he bursts into tears.

Mick throws a tea towel onto the table.

Still glad you came? he says to Lacey.

After supper, the kids go to bed and we sit and watch the news. Lennie isn't on it any more. Now it's just about the government and war and tax. Mick seems to have run out of talking. He half does the crossword, half throws a tennis ball for Fletch. Each time he chucks it, the dog bounces off to fetch it, drops it at his feet, then sinks down, chin on paws, eyes on Mick's face. If Mick doesn't throw it again within five seconds, he barks.

That dog doesn't give up, does he? Lacey remarks at one point and I think Mick laughs.

When Lacey yawns and excuses himself, I go upstairs with him to show him where to go and give him towels and stuff. The landing is dark and messy, with Mick's papers strewn on the floor and washing hanging on the airer. The sound of breathing comes from Jordan's room.

He doesn't exactly snore, I tell Lacey, but he's a bit of a heavy breather. I hope he doesn't keep you awake.

Lacey smiles.

I can sleep through anything, he says.

Lucky you.

I know. It's a skill I was born with.

I laugh and so does he.

We stand on the landing together in the half-darkness and I hand him a big towel and a small one, both fat and crunchy from the outside washing line.

There's hot water, I tell him, if you want a bath.

Thanks, he says, but I'm OK. All I want to do is sleep.

He looks at me. We stand there a moment, with only the mess and the darkness between us.

It's very good of you, he says.

Don't be silly, I say.

Well, it is.

He hesitates.

What? I say.

Mick told me, he says. About Al – what he did.

I feel the heat rush to my face.

He did?

You shouldn't worry about it, you know.

I'm not – I mean, I'm not worried about that. It's just, I'm worried about him.

He doesn't know what he's doing, Lacey says, not just now.

I say nothing.

He's barely able to think straight.

OK, I say. You're right, I know.

I smile.

What?

Mick wasn't supposed to tell you –

Oh? I'm sorry.

It's OK.

We stand there a moment on the landing and then we say goodnight.

Rosa asked me something, I say suddenly.

Oh?

Yes. She asked me if you had kids.

He looks at me.

And I didn't know the answer. We hardly know anything about you.

He looks at me and my heart thumps.

Or – your life, I say.

My life?

Yes, I say in a whisper.

There's nothing to know, he says.

Oh?

I mean, I don't. No kids, no wife —

Nobody?

Just a girlfriend.

I blink.

Natasha, he says.

Ah, I say. In London?

In London, yes.

Oh, I say.

Tess, he says softly, look —

Yes?

I'd like to talk to you — about all of this — about Alex.
Are you around? Maybe tomorrow? Or the day after?

I almost laugh.

I'm around, I say, all the time. You know I am.

He smiles.

I'll find you then?

Yes, I tell him. Find me.

8

But it's not just Lacey who wants to talk. Mawhinney wants to interview me again. Alone, he says, without Mick.

An incident room has been set up in the back of the Dolphin Diner on the pier, in the storerooms, where catering boxes of ketchup and salad cream, and bumper-sized tins of peeled plum tomatoes and baked beans are piled to the ceiling. Orange plastic stacking chairs and formica tables have been borrowed from the school and the murder squad have brought in filing cabinets and phones and a couple of computers. Each window contains a smooth grey square of sea. When the weather's bad, the walls moan and shudder and waves heave and smash against the windows.

Mick's already been in there. He says that even with the big doors shut, you can still smell the frying and hear the clatter of cups and hiss of steam from the Ramirez brothers in the Dolphin Diner. Normally the brothers would be thinking of shutting down now for the winter, but not this year. It's their busiest October ever. They've never taken so much out of season.

Taped to the wall of the incident room is a map of the town blown up big, with yellow post-it notes all over it and the car park and pier area outlined in pink day-glo marker. Other significant spots such as Alex and Lennie's cottage and the area around the school are also marked in colours.

Looking at this map, I can't believe how the distance between all those familiar places is skewed and unlikely. The detailed hugeness of it turns our neat and cosy town into this great big alarming place full of alleyways and twisty streets and endless nooks and crannies. Places where a murder could happen. Places where a murderer could quite easily slink away and hide.

Mawhinney asks me to go in and see him at two, but at five past he's still not there.

It's lunch, says a man sitting at a desk eating a burger. He said he had some stuff to do.

When I tell him Mawhinney was expecting me, he shrugs.

I can call him on his mobile if you like?

He picks up a biro and uses it to stir his coffee.

No, I say, it's OK. I'll go for a walk, shall I?

Ten minutes, says the man. Give him at least ten.

★   ★   ★

I have Liv in her sling, so I decide to go down on the beach, something I can't easily do with the buggy. The wide concrete steps are gritty with sand, the public toilets are shut for the winter. So is the coastguard's red and yellow hut, padlocked up.

The tide is right in and brown water crashes against the groynes and against the pairs of legs of the pier which stretch a long way out to sea. Rosa always says it looks like a big long creature, crawling slowly away from the shore.

I shut my eyes for a second, feel sun squeezing through the clouds and onto my face. The wind blows my hair and ruffles Livvy's too, but she's deep asleep, head wedged against the strap of the sling. A seagull swoops down over us and for a second its shadow wobbles on the sand. Then away. When the sun goes in, all the shingle turns dark blue.

Far off there's a young man with fair hair walking along the beach with a carrier bag. If I look the other way, I can just see the car park, but I won't look, not today. Sometimes, in a bad winter, that part of the prom is sand-bagged up and the beach huts beyond the pier are dragged into the car park and stood there on bricks, since on a rough night the sea can come crashing over the low wall. If that had been the case this year, then Lennie couldn't have parked there.

I walk a little bit further along, away from the pier, but the sling is killing my shoulders and anyway when I turn around I see someone I think is Mawhinney going in, so I go back.

★   ★   ★

He says he's sorry, that he got waylaid. He seems more tired than when I last saw him. His clothes smell of smoke, his jacket's creased, his tie's pulled undone.

How's that baby of yours, then? he asks me, peering at Liv's dark head in the sling. Got the feeding sorted yet?

Not really, I say.

Our first was the worst, he says. The second was a dream after that.

Better that way round, I tell him.

But we stopped there, he says. And you've got four? I don't know how you do it, how you manage.

We don't always, I tell him, though I know it's not true, not really. And also that Mick would never tell anyone that. Mick would never even feel it. He may not have wanted Livvy, not really, but once the deed is done, he's loyal. That's Mick for you.

OK, Mawhinney says and he pulls out a bunch of files from behind him then puts them down again. What I wanted to ask you is, do you know a boy named Darren Sims?

Yes, I tell him, surprised. Of course. Everyone knows Darren. Why?

Mawhinney looks at me and hesitates.

Works at the farm shop in Blythford?

That's right, I say. Now and then he does, anyway. I think he just helps out. Why?

He's been in already, of course, to talk to us – all those young blokes have – funny lad is he?

He has a few problems, I tell Mawhinney carefully. Educationally, I mean. But he's OK. He means well.

Yes, Mawhinney says slowly. That's about what I thought.

Why do you want to know about him? I ask.

Mawhinney hesitates.

Despite the dumpy warmth of Livvy against me, I shiver. Outside you can hear the sea slamming at the creeping legs of the pier. I wait for him to answer. Instead he goes off on another tack.

You and Mrs Daniels – Lennie – were good friends? he says. Close friends, you know, intimate?

Yes, I tell him, slightly impatient. Yes, you know we were.

Mawhinney spreads his fingers out on the table. He takes a breath and looks at them as if they were something interesting and new.

The thing is, he says, and this is very difficult, you must forgive me, I know how this must sound – would she have told you if she was involved with Darren in any way?

I stare at him.

What? Lennie?

He nods.

With Darren? What do you mean involved?

He looks me in the eye this time. Well – I mean sexually.

I can't help it – I laugh.

I'm sorry, I tell him, shaking my head. I mean, no way.

Mawhinney gives me a cool look.

You're surprised by the idea?

Yes of course. Totally. Well, it's not true – she wasn't.

You can't believe that would have been the case?

No, I say again. No way.

123

I run my fingers over the top of Liv's head and Mawhinney folds his big arms and tilts his chair back. He waits a second or two before saying, Well, Darren has implied to us that it was.

I laugh again. Liv stirs against me, makes a snaffly sound with her lips.

Implied?

He's said as much.

Well then, I say, he's having you on. He's making it up.

Pretty sick thing to do, Mawhinney comments.

I shrug.

He has problems. I mean, I'm not standing up for him or anything. I'm just saying he has.

Mawhinney seems to think about this.

You think he'd say such a thing to get attention?

Quite possibly, I say.

Even though it made him – possibly – a murder suspect?

I shrug.

I thought people confessed all the time to things they'd never done – disturbed people, I mean – I thought the police were used to that?

You think he's disturbed? Mawhinney says quickly.

No, I begin, and then another thought creeps in.

You're not thinking Darren did it, I say. You don't think he killed her?

Mawhinney smiles.

I'll be honest with you, he says. It's really impossible to know anything at this stage. Time is passing.

Darren wouldn't hurt anyone, I tell him, I just know he wouldn't.

Mawhinney says nothing. He has the face of someone who's heard it all before.

As we go through the next room I try to glance again at the map, but Mawhinney seems eager to move me on. The post-it notes have what look like phone numbers on them. I wonder if these are leads the police are chasing – or whether that's just the way it is on TV.

I'd be most grateful, he says, if you'd keep this conversation just between ourselves.

What about Lacey? I say and feel my colour rise as I say it.

What about him?

Does he know, about Darren?

Mawhinney holds the door open and I catch a whiff of deodorant as his arm goes up.

Oh, he says, Lacey knows.

He reaches in his trouser pocket and tears the foil down on a packet of Trebor Mints and offers me one. I shake my head.

Darren didn't even know Lennie, I say. Or she didn't know him. Not any more than I do anyway. They may well have spoken at the farm shop but that's it.

Mawhinney considers this.

Trouble is, he says, you think you know someone – you could swear you knew what they were capable of – and then they go and surprise you. Human nature.

He smiles at me.

Happens all the time in this business.

★　★　★

Darren is one of a small gang of lads – Dave Munro, Roger Farmiloe and Brian Whittle, too – who spend a lot of the day in The Red Lion doing nothing much except watch TV.

The day after Lennie dies, Darren very nearly makes the six o'clock local TV news. But in the end they plump for his mate Brian, who's employed by Waveney District Council to sweep the area between North Parade and the pier and therefore has a closer connection to the scene of the crime.

Meanwhile reporters have spoken to just about everyone in town: hotel people, shopkeepers, chamber-maids, the staff at the brewery, the woman who cleans the toilets at The Anchor.

Ellen Hasborough, who runs the Whole Loaf Organic Deli on the corner of East Street and Pinkney's Lane, tells the local radio station that, Our rustic idyll is shattered. People used to come from miles around for a peaceful day here, for our famous coastal-path walks. I can't see it happening any more.

And a local councillor is reported as saying, They are lovely people here and it's a shocking business. The whole community is taking it very badly.

With no funeral in sight, the town creates its own small marks of respect. The flag which normally flies from the mast in the middle of St James's Green is lowered for a week and the bakers and the fish shop draw down their shades even though business goes on as usual behind them. Even the Ramirez brothers go so far as to place an old-fashioned black-edged notice in

the window of the Dolphin Diner next to the dusty
fisherman's netting and dried starfishes, expressing their
Deepest Sympathy for the family of Lennie Daniels who
was so close to our hearts. Which, as Mick notes, is rich,
considering that for two years running Lennie begged
them to donate a fish and chip supper for the school
summer raffle, only to be met both times with a flat
and charmless refusal.

Next day, Saturday, Lacey finds me on the promenade.

A thunderstorm during the night has left the air soft
and silky, the crackle washed out of it. The tide's far out,
the groynes exposed, the brown beach laced with
hundreds of glistening creeks.

The drama class Rosa and Jordan go to on Saturday
mornings has been cancelled, so we're on the beach
instead, chucking a frisbee on the driest band of
shingle. Fletcher is straining on his lead, desperate to
go down and join them, but he's not allowed. There
are places where dogs have to be on a lead, even out
of season.

It's chilly but there's no wind. One or two brave, elderly
people have opened up their beach huts and put kettles
on and started edging down to the sea, towels wrapped
around their waists.

Suddenly he's behind me.

They're not really going in are they?

Oh, I say, blushing furiously.

Sorry, he says, I could see you were in a dream.

Well, I say. Hi.

It's freezing, he says. Do they really swim in this?

I shrug.

It's warm enough, once you get in.

Lacey shivers.

I was looking for you, he says as Fletcher wags and wiggles.

I try to turn Liv's buggy round so it doesn't face into the wind.

Oh? I say. Really?

It sounds ruder than I meant it to. I glance towards the kiosk. Estelle is watching us intently, cloth in hand.

Lacey looks at me.

Want some coffee? he says.

OK. Please.

I watch him get it – his tall straight back as he stands there talking to Estelle. How Estelle smiles and leans her elbows on the counter, then touches her hair.

So, he says, when he returns with two mugs.

So, I ask him, you got yourself a room?

He smiles at me.

Yes, he says, I got one. Thank you.

He's laughing.

What? What's funny?

You are. He rips open a sachet of brown sugar and crumbs spill on the white table. You make me laugh. The way you talk, all your funny questions.

It's you, I say. Then I blush again.

And you're always blushing, he says.

I ignore this.

I only asked you if you got a room —

I know, he says, and he sits back in his chair, relaxed. I didn't mean that.

What, then?

He thinks for a moment.

Only that it's possible to talk to you for ages and find out nothing.

I laugh.

What exactly would you want to find out?

I don't know, he says. You tell me.

You see! I cry. That's what you do all the time — turn everything back into a question.

Lacey smiles. At my feet, Fletcher wimpers, strains at the lead and then pants.

Poor dog, says Lacey. Can't he join them?

No, I say, we'd never get him back.

I watch as Lacey rubs Fletcher's head, pulls at the silky scrags behind his ears.

Does he want a drink?

I shrug.

Lacey picks up Jordan's Mickey Mouse bucket.

I'll get him one, shall I?

If you want, I say. The tap's over there.

He goes over to the low concrete wall and fills the bucket and carries it back. He carries it the way Jordan would — concentrating, taking care not to spill any.

He sets it down in front of Fletcher and the dog laps enthusiastically.

There, you see, Lacey says, he was. Poor dog was thirsty.

★ ★ ★

The wind blows and Estelle's tub containing beach bats and fishing nets falls over and rolls clattering over the prom. Estelle comes out and gathers it up and takes it back. The old people are coming out of the sea now, tiptoeing up over the shingle, towels over their shoulders.

The frisbee flies up and clatters across the concrete near us. Lacey straightaway picks it up and tries to throw it back. But he can't do it because the wind is against him and it lands back on the prom. Both kids shriek at him.

Like this! Jordan shouts, showing Lacey the flick of the wrist. Fletcher is now vigorously chewing the side of Jordan's bucket. I take it from him.

You said you wanted to talk about Alex, I remind him.

He looks surprised.

Yes, he says, yes. If you don't mind. There's something I need to ask you, actually.

You mean to do with the investigation?

I can't really claim that it is, he says. Or at least, it might be, but, well, I'm not sure.

Well, I say, go ahead.

You'll blush if I ask it.

Really?

I laugh and my heart races.

Yes, he says, I think you will.

I wait and he looks at me.

You and Alex, he says, you used to be involved?

Well, yes, I say steadily. We went out. Years ago. Before Lennie and before Mick. It's not a secret — everyone knows that.

Lacey thinks about this.

I've known him since I was a teenager, I say. I'm very fond of him. Mick's known him almost as long.

Lacey's silent. I wait.

OK, he says, OK, but — I'm sorry to ask but — is there still an excitement between you and Alex?

I put my hand to my face.

What? You mean now?

Yes. Now.

Lacey's eyes are on my face.

No, I say quickly as the blood rushes to my cheeks. Well, no, I don't think so.

I make myself busy by stuffing the bucket into the buggy's rain hood.

You're not sure? Lacey says.

I mean, as I said, there used to be. A long time ago. We — liked each other. But it's over, from my point of view.

And from his?

I try to look Lacey in the eye.

Why on earth are you asking me this? I mean, has he said something?

Not a word, Lacey says in a strange, solemn voice. I promise you. Nothing.

Well then, I say, it's a bit personal, isn't it?

I'd still like an answer, he says gently.

Well, I — excitement's a funny word for it, I tell him at last.

What word would you use, then?

I feel suddenly drained, exhausted.

Look – is this really relevant to anything? I ask him.

I don't know, he says. Is it?

Minutes pass and we both do nothing. Just sit in silence and watch the kids and the sea.

Sorry, he says. I shouldn't have asked you that.

I keep a blank face.

I don't care, I say. Ask me anything you want. I'll tell you anything. I don't care about anything much just now.

He pauses a moment.

This must be a nightmare – for you, he says at last.

In a nightmare, you wake up.

I'm sorry, he says again.

Is that it? I ask him.

What?

Is that all you're trained to say? Sorry? Because really I'd have thought they'd have given you something better.

Better for what?

For – I don't know – for fobbing people off with.

He says nothing.

Sorry, I say after another moment, I didn't mean that. I'm just so fucking sick of it all.

Yes, he says.

I hate how it's become the way we live. Every day we wake up and it starts over – all of this.

You're still in shock, he tells me.

I think about this.

I don't know, I say. Am I? I'm surprised at how OK I feel, really. Like I'm in a dream and most of me is somewhere else.

Lacey's looking at me.

Everyone responds differently, he says.

But, I insist to him, it can't last – you have to come out of it eventually, don't you?

I don't know, he says quietly. I've never experienced what you're going through.

Also, I tell him, I feel different –

Different in what way?

I don't know – bad, irresponsible –

Really?

Yes. Like I could fuck things up and not care at all.

What sort of things?

I don't know. Just things. It's as if I genuinely don't care at all – or there's nothing at stake. Not even the kids sometimes. It scares me.

Why?

Because it's not normal. It's not how I usually am.

You're too hard on yourself, he says. None of you are to blame for what happened.

I know that, I say.

Well then, I say after a pause. Maybe I'm just very angry.

Tess, he says gently, you have every right to be.

Why would anyone do it? I ask him.

He looks at me carefully.

Why would anyone want to take her heart?

Do you know what a trophy-taker is? he asks me.

No, I say. And then it dawns.

A body part, he says. Any part. It's usually something smaller, something sexual maybe. A heart is rare.

133

Why?

He takes a breath.

Well – it's very hard to take out.

I look quickly away at the sea where the horizon dissolves and water and sky blur.

Sorry, he says, but you did ask.

Tears spring to my eyes.

She's dead, I tell him, I know that. I know she's not coming back. But you see, to me – this place is still so full of her.

Lacey says nothing.

You think I'm silly, I tell him and I pick up a paper napkin and hold it to my eyes, or mad. Crazy.

No, he says. No I don't.

He passes me another napkin. His fingers close to mine.

I don't think you're any of those things, he says.

Then what?

He doesn't answer.

I fold the damp napkin, over and over, smaller and smaller.

In the end, I tell him, it's this. Your life – anyone's life – it just doesn't belong to you, does it?

He is silent for a very long time and then he says, No. It doesn't. But you still have to act as if it does.

Alex says that all he wants is for people to leave him alone now.

He says he's sick of all the offers of help – sick and tired of people cooking him food and leaving toys and notes and stuff in the porch. He doesn't want any babysitting, or a free takeaway from Mei Yuen's, or a bag of plums or a bacon quiche or an unripe marrow. He doesn't want his windows cleaned for nothing, or extra fish thrown in when he orders from the fish shop. He especially doesn't want the king-sized crocheted blanket, a monstrous acrylic thing in cheap scarlets and blues and pinks, made by the ladies of the Reydon Society.

He says his GP's given him some Prozac. And that's it, that's nice, that's all he really wants for now. Just that and maybe the chance to bury Lennie. Ideally with her heart – but if that's not possible, then what's left of her, laid to rest, without it.

But none of it may be possible, not for a while anyway. Lennie's body is still being looked at and Alex has been warned that a second, independent autopsy may be required. It could be some time before the coroner will release the body to the family for a funeral.

Meanwhile, Bob's worrying about how long this is all taking. It's impossible, apparently, for anyone to say. He's frail, he ought not to travel unnecessarily, but it could be weeks and he's wondering if he should fly back and then return when Alex has more information. And Bob has dogs at home. He's concerned about his dogs. Two chocolate Labs, one of whom is elderly and needs regular injections. A neighbour is taking care of them right now.

But I can't rely on their kindness forever, he says.

He tells me how Lennie phoned him just about every week and how he was thinking of getting e-mail so they could stay in touch that way as well. Keeping up with the times. Except maybe not, maybe he could never have done it, because these days his hands don't work so well.

Look at them – he spreads his ropy, mottled fingers in front of him. See? I have the shakes nearly all the time now.

He frowns at them.

I don't think they look too bad, I tell him.

He ignores me.

She was very popular with the boys, you know, he says. As a teenager. A good-looking girl, like her mother. Though she could be wicked, you know, really wicked – oh my goodness – playing them off against each other –

He laughs. So do I.

I can just see it, I say.

Can you? he says, narrowing his eyes. I pitied some of those poor guys, oh my God, oh dear, I really did –

He stops and recovers himself.

And what about you? he says. Bet you had a lot of guys after you? You're a good-looking girl as well. Now don't mess with me, I bet you did.

Some, I tell him, but not a lot.

He tries to look astonished.

But – a girl like you?

You're exhausted, I tell him.

You know, he says, I can't see you well. You do look very far away to me.

You're just exhausted, Bob.

Yes but I can't rest though, he says quietly. I'd like to sleep, I really would. But I won't. Not now. That's the tragedy.

I push a fresh cup of coffee towards him and his fingers close around it, eager as baby's fingers. He does this, even though we both know he'll leave it to go cold like the last one.

I shouldn't really have coffee, he confesses.

How about a brandy then? I say.

He begins to weep.

OK, he says and I pour him a generous one and he downs it in two swift gulps. Then he tells me he's not allowed that either.

But what the hell, he says. You know, the way I figure it, who's left to mind?

9

Two o'clock in the afternoon, a dark day. The kids at school for at least another hour and Liv down for her nap, arms flung up beneath her blue bunny blanket.

Mick wraps his arms around me.

What? he says. What is it?

I try to wriggle out.

What's what?

You seem far away.

I don't think so.

Something's getting to you.

I look at him.

I mean, something else, he says.

I'm fine, I tell him. Hearing the coldness creep into my voice.

He releases me, drops his arms down to his side.

You want me to leave you alone?

I turn and look at him.

I didn't say that, no.

Then – what, Tess? Tell me –

I sigh.

Oh Mick, I say, I don't know. I don't mind – I don't care what you do. What do you mean, leave me alone? I'm not asking for anything. What you're doing is fine.

He smiles, but I can read the smile. Unreasonable, it says.

What you do is always fine, I tell him.

I love you, he says. Do you know that?

Thank you.

What do you mean, thank you?

Just – I'm glad.

It's not something you say thank you for.

What, then?

He kisses my hands, both at once, then separately, finger by finger.

You're in another world these days, he says.

Well, I say, we all are. Aren't we?

He stops the kissing.

Maybe, he says. But I'm trying not to be. And the difference is, I feel you want to be.

I remember a time when sex was a glue, a healer – it would smooth, ease, mend, bring us closer together. As well as for pleasure – we could rely on it for that, nearly always anyway. Not any more. Now it's a thing that comes between us, pushing us further away.

Upstairs, the bed is still unmade, still covered in child clutter. Livvy's bright-coloured teething monkey and a pile of Rosa's navy school socks. On the carpet, Jordan's forgotten homework sheet – signed by us but never delivered to school – a pack of Disprin, a pair of my knickers.

Mick sweeps the stuff off and pulls the duvet back and I lie on the sheet which is cool as water. I start to undo my jeans.

No, he says, let me –

He does it slowly and carefully, laying each bit of clothing aside like someone who knows they'll have to pick it up later.

I laugh.

What?

You don't have to fold them, I say.

He smiles grimly, determined to be amused, yet obviously bothered that the mood's disturbed. He senses it's going to be tough, that I won't play.

But, I think, I want to do this.

He kisses my face, my neck, my hair. Then he takes his own clothes off more quickly. I put my face close to his body, dutifully take in the familiar chill of his skin, the folds, the curves, the hair.

Come on, he says and pulls the duvet over us, pulls me onto him, gathers my hair so it doesn't dangle in his face.

It ought to be possible, I tell myself as his fingers move over my bottom, my thighs. I try to get them into my head – those weird and dirty thoughts, hot and shameful,

140

to get me going. It usually works for me. But it's impossible and my mind is pulled up and away and I float free. Instead I see Lennie, biting her lip as she tries to back her car into a tight space on an afternoon after school a long time ago. I see the pier, battered by wind and storms, and all those ketchup cans piled up behind Mawhinney. And the slice of grey, choppy sea through the window behind.

And then, suddenly, I see Darren Sims. I remember his denim jacket lying on a clay-spattered stool in Lennie's studio. I check the memory – it feels real – and I tense up at this surprising thought.

Mick wets his fingers and puts them inside me.

He kisses my nipples, touches me, delves around. I try to feel it. I try to push the thoughts away, but they come creeping back, unstoppable as smoke.

My conversation with Mawhinney comes into my head.

Mick pushes me over onto my back.

Hey, he says as, lazy-eyed, he licks his fingers and strokes between my legs again. What are you thinking?

Nothing, I tell him. I'm trying to concentrate.

On what?

On this. The sex.

He sits up. He's giving up.

I push him over. His penis is standing right up. I bend my head and grasp its stem like a flower and kiss the end of it. It smells of spit and cheese and the hotness of men before sex. He makes a little noise of encouragement.

141

Before he can start asking to come inside me, I make my fingers into a circle and then hold him there.

He lies back and closes his eyes. He has a lovely face when his eyes are closed – young and smoothed-out and trusting.

Oh, he says, oh, o-oh.

Moving my hand up and down, I feel like a sober person watching a drunk one.

You like this? I ask him in the low, barely-there voice I use to make him come. It pleases you?

He moans.

I stroke the length of him and then bring my hand tight around him again and move it up and down.

He groans.

I think of how many times we must have done this – and then I realise that I can't remember any of them. I can't remember how love felt in the days before Lennie died.

Each time I tighten my hand, he moans. I try kissing the tip of him again, slipping it in my mouth, and it's clear from the sounds that he likes it but eventually it hurts my neck so I lift my head up again.

Through the window is the silvery, waving eucalyptus tree that could do with a trim, and beyond it, sky. Afternoon sun is squeezing itself out from between grey clouds. Later it will rain.

Hey. Not too hard, Mick whispers, eyes still closed but reaching out with his hand to mine. Get some oil.

Under the bed is a small brown glass bottle of oil. I reach down and unscrew the cap and tip some into my hand and slide my fingers over him. He sighs. I slip my hand up and down, up and down, until he begins to pant and lift his pelvis up off the bed and then I know it's about to be over, and then it is.

When he comes, there is such a big, arcing spray of gunk that some of it goes on his face.

I should make you lick it off, he says and I try to look as if, on another day, I might've.

I wait till Mick has gone to fetch the kids from school and I'm alone in the house. And then I dial the number of The Angel where Lacey's staying.

OK, I tell him when they put me through. Maybe it's this. I don't want to lie to you about Al. He's my friend – he's always been my friend – but it's more complicated than that as well –

Yes, says Lacey. He waits. I can hear his attention, his concentration. I go on.

He loves me, I say. And – well – I love him too. I told you. But he's let it get – bigger –

Yes, Lacey says again. I've no idea what he's thinking.

Look, I tell him, I'm trying to be honest here.

He waits.

And, I say, it's not just that. He's sometimes told me things. Stuff I wished he wouldn't – about him and Lennie.

What sort of things? Lacey says.

Just stuff.

What stuff?

About their relationship. I mean, I asked him not to, but he still did –

Did what?

Go on about it – how they weren't always happy together.

Really? Lacey says, though he doesn't sound especially surprised.

Lennie never said that, I tell him, never. Only Al.

And you didn't think he should have told you?

No, I say. But –

But what?

Well, I still spent time with him, didn't I?

Lacey's quiet.

You think you let him? Lacey asks.

My heart thumps.

I wasn't a good friend to Lennie, I tell him then.

But Tess, he says slowly, you mean, you and Alex – you've –

No! I tell him, horrified. No, never. I would never do that. Not to Lennie, not to Mick. But I've sometimes been lonely. And he's been there for me. He knows me. And I find his attention and his company –

Lacey waits.

Tempting, I say. Flattering. Satisfying.

I can understand that, Lacey says.

Can you?

Everyone gets lonely, he says.

I glance at my watch. Mick will be back soon.

I'm not sure I should have told you any of this, I say.

I'm glad you did.

Well – it's not all –

Oh?

No, there's something else. It's to do with that night – when she died. I was there, you see.

Now Lacey's voice changes.

What? he says. What do you mean?

I have a place I go to, I tell him, a beach hut – one of the huts on the front, the other end, towards Gun Hill. It's mine. I go there at night sometimes. I was there that night, the night it happened –

Really? he says, and it sounds like I have finally surprised him. On your own? So late at night?

Yes. No.

I feel tears coming and take a breath to stop them.

Not on my own. Not this time. Usually I do – go there alone. It's always felt so safe. I get up in the night and I just go there – the whole point is to be alone. Otherwise, in the life I have, I never get to be in peace or in silence, not ever. You can't understand that, can you?

Lacey is silent.

But that night?

Alex came. He insisted. He knows I go there and he came. Mick doesn't know.

He doesn't?

No. Al's done it before. Come there. To talk about her – about their problems. Anyway we drank some wine. They'd had a terrible fight that evening, a really big one, and he was thinking of moving out.

Lacey says, You didn't tell Mawhinney any of this?

No, I say.

Why not?

145

I didn't think —

Didn't think what?

I suppose I just didn't think.

And that's all?

Well, I tell him, only that we were talking about all of this and suddenly I had this feeling — such a strong feeling — that he should go home to her. I was very frightened. I knew something was going to happen —

What do you mean, something? Lacey asks me quickly. How could you know?

Sometimes I just — feel things.

There's a silence at the other end of the phone.

You could never have known, Lacey says finally. Don't punish yourself, Tess.

But —

You're rationalising after the event. It's a common enough thing to do.

I decide to let this go.

I told him, I say. I told him to go straight home and be with Lennie —

And he did?

He did, I tell Lacey. He waited all night. And then he called me.

After school Jordan and I walk Fletcher across the Common towards Blackshore. On our left, the golf course, on the right, dull-faced cattle chomping lippily on gorse.

You know what it means when the cows lie down? Jordan asks me. That it's going to rain!

Certainly, the air is damp and clotted, the sky tight with swollen clouds moving too fast across it.

Once we've passed the golf course we let Fletcher off. He's a dog of habit and he knows exactly what to do. He sits and waits to be unclipped and then he soars.

Good dog! Jordan shouts and Fletcher darts away, ears flat, belly low to the ground. He isn't allowed into the cow field but we let him scoot and dodge over the long-grassed Common which stretches as far as the coastal path on one side and to the fishing shacks and chandlers of Blackshore on the other.

It's wonderful to see Fletcher run – same as I think it might be to fly a kestrel or hawk. It makes me feel smaller, safer, a speck on the ground.

We continue on up the lane, towards the water tower. In the distance, a tractor putters and stops, then putters again. Jordan is asking me whether, if a child stole some money from his parents when he was a child, and then the parents found out, they could sue him.

But they wouldn't want to, I tell him. Mums and dads never want to take their kids to court –

Yes, he says, dancing backwards impatiently along the asphalt road in front of me. But that's not what I mean – I mean if the parents found out when the child was a grown-up – would they punish him then?

I laugh.

But sweetheart, he'd still be their child. When your child grows up you go on loving them just the same, however old or grown up they are –

But Jordan isn't satisfied.

147

Wouldn't they at least be cross? he wants to know.

Well, maybe, I say. But when a child does something bad like take money, usually his mum or dad just want to find out what's wrong and why he did it. That's more important than punishing him, you see.

Jordan thinks about this.

The cows are following us along the line of the hedge. Fletcher's nowhere in sight.

But has it ever happened, he insists, that a mum or dad takes their child to court when they're grown up?

He snaps off a long stalk of cow parsley and waves it like a sword. Oh look, Mummy! he says, because Fletcher has found another dog. Back on the road, next to the damp verge, he is sniffing the rear end of a lean, shabby, black and tan animal. Both dogs very still, alert, erect, concentrating.

I know whose dog that is, I tell Jordan – and I look around for Darren Sims. Except I can't see him. Seconds later, he climbs out of the ditch.

Hiya, he says.

Hi, I say, hoping we can move on quickly. I don't really want to get stuck with Darren.

You didn't see me there, did you?

No, I tell him.

Did you come out of the ditch? Jordan asks, staring at him in frank and open amazement.

Yeah, he says. You see down there? – he indicates down behind the hawthorn tree that grows on a steep slope beyond the ditch. Jordan nods and stares.

Well, I found something.

What? says Jordan. What?

Want to come and have a look?

Yes, says Jordan immediately, but I pull him to me.

Not today, Darren, I say. We have to get back.

Oh, Mummy, says Jordan.

Another time maybe, I say. Or you could just tell us what you found?

Darren grins at me. His neck is spotty and his Adam's apple sticks out too much.

I'm keeping it to myself, he says, still smiling. No one else will find it, that's for sure.

Jordan starts to move towards the ditch, but I grab his sweatshirt. The sky is darkening.

Another day, OK? I say and take a step back towards home. Darren's dog comes swaying and sauntering up, looking depressed. Fletcher has already disappeared, back into the furthest smells of the Common.

Darren doesn't move.

That dog of yours, he says. Coming along nicely isn't he? How old is he now, then?

Two and a half, says Jordan proudly.

Two and a half? says Darren. Really? I'd have had him down as younger. Runs around a lot, doesn't he?

When he was a puppy, Jordan says, he fitted in my mum's handbag.

Inexplicably Darren's face falls.

He doesn't bite, does he? he says.

No-o, says Jordan, kicking grit on the road, losing interest.

Darren looks at me.

Them dogs the police had, he says. Did you get a look at them? They weren't German Sheppers, I don't know what they were, even me nan didn't know – did you see the teeth on them?

Which dogs, I say, when?

All last week, Darren says. Days and days. Dogs and dogs, sniffin' all around the pier and whatnot.

Maybe they were bloodhounds, Jordan offers.

Something occurs to me and I bite my lip.

Darren, I say carefully, you do know, don't you? About Lennie? Mrs Daniels – what happened?

He looks hurt.

Of course, he says slowly. Of course I do. It's all my mum and my nan want to talk about. All that business.

Well then, I say, police often bring in dogs. They're just going over that area in detail I would imagine, it's what they have to do.

Doing their job, says Darren.

Exactly.

She was going to give me a job you know, he says then.

I look at him.

Who was?

Her. Mrs Daniels.

Really?

Darren looks pleased with himself.

Yeah, she was. Sweeping and that. And learning to make them things of hers.

She said that?

Yeah. She promised. Had me round and gave me a Coke. She promised. Won't happen now, though.

No, I tell him, it won't.

A shame, isn't it? he says. It would have been good.

It would, I agree.

And he says goodbye and we watch his long body and the skulkier one of the dog move slowly up the hill towards the golf course.

Jordan skips along beside me in silence.

I wonder what Darren found, he says.

Yes. I wonder.

Shall we go back and have a look?

No. Not now.

Mummy, what sort of dog is Darren's dog?

Mongrel, I suppose, I say.

No! says Jordan. Mixed breed. You don't say mongrel.

Oh, I agree. Right.

Yeah, says Jordan, it's like Mixed Race. And Special Needs.

He turns to look at me.

Is Darren Special Needs?

Alex stops by the clinic just as I'm locking up and putting the rubbish out in Dene Walk. Suddenly he's there in front of me, next to the scrubby buddleia that springs out from the cracked cement of the wall.

What is it? I say. What's happening? Are you OK?

They're having a fire practice, he says. At The Angel. Loads of old people lined up in the car park.

Oh, I say.

Laugh, then, he says.

Why?

Because it's funny. You should have seen them.

What is it? I ask him.

What do you mean what is it?

Why're you in such a weird mood?

I'm not, he says, I'm great. Why? Do I always have to be down and suicidal?

No, I say, but I don't like the look in his eyes, a glitteriness that means trouble.

I mean it, he says when he sees me looking at him, I thought I'd just drop by and say hello.

I say nothing, squash the garbage bag down into the dustbin and try to get the lid to shut. A smell of decay mixes with the whiff of setting lotion and cigarette smoke from the hairdresser's across the alleyway. Suzanne Hair Fashions is open late on Wednesdays. Their new beautician smokes all the time. She's probably out in the yard right now, puffing away.

I shiver because I've taken off my whites but not put my cardigan back on.

I've got to lock up, I tell him. Fine, he says and follows me in. He sits down on the edge of the reception desk, on a bunch of papers – a whole load of cheques and order forms that Nicky who comes in on Tuesdays has left for me to sign. I pull the papers out from underneath him. He doesn't help me. Then I go and get my cardigan off the hanger.

What is it, Al? I say again. Please tell me.

He laughs. I told you, nothing's wrong, I'm great. I just had this hankering to see you alone, that's all. Anything wrong with that?

I sigh. I'm tired and I want to get home.

I can't play games, I say, switching the answerphone on and starting to shut down the computer. I'm tired.

I don't know what you mean, he says. What games?

How are the boys anyway? I ask, ignoring him. Are they OK?

I believe so, he says. They're round at your place actually.

Oh?

Mick said he'd feed them.

And does he know where you are right now?

Alex laughs.

No, he doesn't actually.

As I go into the next room to get my bag, he says, I loved her, you know.

What? I call out. Even though I heard him perfectly. I pick my bag up off the floor and stand there, waiting.

I loved her, he says. It may not always have looked that way, but I did.

I know you did, I tell him more gently as I come back in. I move the appointment book out of the way, stack sets of notes on top of the cabinet for filing. I put a hand on his wrist.

You don't have to tell me that, Al, I say.

But he's not listening.

They think I killed her, he says.

I stare at him.

No they don't. Don't be so ridiculous –

Oh yes, he says, very softly this time. Oh Tess, I mean it, they do.

No —

I mean it. Would I lie about something like that?

They? Who's they?

Lacey. Lacey does.

But, I say, suddenly slow and stupid, I thought you liked Lacey?

He thinks I did it. He thinks I cut up my wife. He thinks I took her heart out and went and hid it somewhere just for fun.

I sit down. He looks at me.

You've got it wrong, I tell him. There's no way Lacey would think that.

Whatever, Alex says, suddenly sour. You should know.

What do you mean?

He doesn't reply.

What's that supposed to mean? I say again.

He says nothing.

I just — don't — believe, I tell him, that he would think that.

I can see it all over his face, says Alex. All the time, whenever he talks to me.

Oh, I say, relaxing a little. So he's never actually said anything?

Alex folds his arms and closes his eyes.

He doesn't have to.

Oh for God's sake, you're being ridiculous, I tell him. I'm sorry but you are.

Don't you think you look ridiculous, he says, going round with him all the time?

I pull my cardigan on.

Everyone knows it, he says. You've been seen.

Oh don't be so stupid, I tell him.

I said you've been seen.

So, yes, I say, OK. I know him. We all do – he's been here in our lives for days. It's his job – to look after you and the boys.

Ah, says Alex, but the word is, he only sticks around because of you.

My heart jumps.

Well, I say, the word's wrong. In fact all he wants to do is talk to me about you.

That's what he says?

Alex smiles. I ignore him.

Who the hell's saying this anyway? I ask him. Who's this everyone?

Who do you think? he says. The whole fucking town.

I suddenly feel sorry for him – for his tired face, his red eyes. I go over and touch his arm.

Al, I say, don't do this. Please. You don't mean it. I know you don't. Please, Alex.

He shrinks from my touch, flexes his hands and stares at them.

You look terrible, I say. What is it? Aren't you sleeping?

I love you, he says then.

No, I say steadily. You don't.

I can't stop thinking about you. All the time, when I should be thinking about this.

Oh Al, you know that's not true.

It is. I do. I love you. If she hadn't – if she wasn't gone – I'd still feel it and I might still tell you.

155

No you wouldn't. It's just all of this. You're confused. You said you loved her just now.

Not in this way.

He puts out his hand but I pull away from him.

Don't tell me. Please. I don't want to hear about it.

He makes a funny sound then, half of pain, half of excitement, and he pushes up the sleeve of my cardigan and lays his fingers on my bare arm.

I never wanted to hurt you, he whispers.

But you haven't, I reply. I don't know what you mean, Al. You haven't hurt anyone.

IO

Everyone's behaviour has altered for the worse.

At school, Jordan has been lashing out at other kids, even the bigger ones. He punched and kicked Debbie Suffling who, though tall and strong-looking, actually has a blood condition that means she must not be hit.

Julie Edmunds, his teacher, sent Jordan straight to the head's office where he sat stony-eyed and sullen and refusing to say sorry. That's what Julie tells us when we go in to see her – that it's not the incident itself but his total lack of remorse about it that she takes most seriously.

I'm sure he's sorry, Mick tells her. He's just too proud to say it.

We don't encourage that sort of pride in this school,

Julie says. We try to encourage children to respect others and put the truth first.

And she eyes Liv's buggy and I know what she's thinking: what's she doing with another baby at her age when she can't even control the ones she's already got?

But it's not just Jordan. Rosa, who's loud and difficult at home but normally an angel at school – so good and conscientious that she will literally sweat if she doesn't get her homework done on time – has lost her pen, her PE kit and half of her books, and been in trouble more than once for talking in assembly.

Our Rosa? Mick says. Talking in assembly?

Not only that, but her shoelaces are fraying, her shirt's perpetually splattered with ink, her fingers are grubby and her arms covered in strange itchy spots which she picks till they bleed.

Who's throwing ink at you, Rose? I ask her. Someone's flicking it at you, aren't they?

It's my cartridge, she says flatly. It leaks.

All over your back?

She makes an ugly face at me.

And the spots – I wonder if they're flea bites. We must get Maria a flea collar, I say.

It's not Maria, Rosa almost shouts. Maria's fine. You leave my kitten out of this!

Well, what's biting you, Rosa?

I don't know, she says. Mosquitoes, maybe?

In November?

Leave me alone, she says. I'm fine, OK?

What is it? I ask her when she bursts into sudden tears. What's the matter, darling?

But she won't talk to me, just stomps upstairs. Half an hour later I find her asleep on her bed with the kitten purring on her chest.

And then there's Nat. I'll ask him to do a simple thing like empty the dishwasher or tidy his room or eat an egg on toast or remove his school blazer from where he just lets it drop in the hall and he'll immediately attack me.

Why do you insist on making my life hell? he screams.

I'm surprised at how much I want to hit him – I, who've never laid a finger on my kids. How can Nat – once the sunniest, easiest boy (far easier in many ways than the other two) – have turned into this monster? He sits in his room with the curtains shut and something electronic in his hand. He slouches around the house complaining. And then there's the food thing.

OK, I say as he pushes his plate away, why aren't you eating? It had better be good.

You – know – I – hate – scrambled – eggs.

I don't know that at all.

I told you. Last time. I hate the skin on them.

What skin? There isn't a skin –

There is, look. And he pokes with the edge of his fork.

Eat them, boy, Mick advises softly from behind his paper.

Oh God! Nat wails, letting his head sink into his hands. I'll throw up, I'll be sick.

Don't you dare be sick! I warn him.

All this organic crap, he mutters.

It's not organic, I shriek at him. These eggs are not organic!

Whatever they bloody well are, Nat says, I don't like them.

Swear again, says Mick, and you'll get no pocket money this weekend.

But, I say, my anger mounting, you don't like anything. You don't like porridge, or baked beans, or toast, or fried, poached or boiled eggs or anything except fucking processed cereal with sugar on it.

She's swearing, Nat tells his father. You don't say anything to her.

Mick ignores him.

I push Nat roughly out the way so I can wipe the table.

Ow, he says.

What? I say.

That hurt.

I didn't touch you.

That's a lie. You did.

I look at him. My heart pounds. I would like to hurt him.

I can't eat, he says flatly.

Why not? I ask him in a calmer voice. Why can't you eat?

I have a full feeling.

And you didn't have this full feeling when you ate a whole pack of citrus Polos yesterday?

Nope, he grins. That's because Polos are nice.

And eggs aren't?

No.

He is smiling at me.

It's not funny, I say.

I'm not laughing, he says. And laughs.

Leave him, Mick says. He'll eat later. Won't you, Nat?

Nat says nothing. He doesn't say yes.

No, I say, I won't leave him and he won't eat later, he'll eat now and he'll eat what I've cooked for him even if I have to feed him like a baby.

Nat shoves the plate away again, defiant, waiting. I feel a tear, a ripping inside me. I step forward and slap him hard on the face. Hard as I can. A flat noise — a satisfying gasp from him.

He stares at me for a dazed moment then begins to cry.

Good.

Trembling, I chuck the whole plate of eggs in the sink. Then, not wanting to waste it, I scoop up what I can and put it in Fletcher's bowl. The dog, alert to the sound of food, rushes up and eats it in two swift gollops.

I wish I was dead, Nat says.

Don't you ever say that.

I do. I want to be dead. It would be a relief. I really really hate you.

Go to your room, says Mick quietly.

He gets up but I don't let him go. I grab him by the shoulders.

Never say that, I yell, shaking him hard, do you hear

me? Never, ever fucking well say you want to be dead!

With each word I shake him harder. He is sobbing but he does not resist. The whole thing takes only a few seconds but it feels like much longer. There is time for me to understand that he no longer feels like my child, my flesh. There's time to understand what I could do.

He's crying but he's far too shocked to hit back. If he was not so shocked, he might, he would. He's getting so big he could hurt me, I know that.

Go, I tell him. And when he doesn't move, I scream the word again.

Two pale strings of snot hang and wobble from his nose. He runs from the room. He is humiliated. So am I. I sit and I shake. I won't look at Mick. I don't have to look at him to know he isn't on my side.

Lennie's Pay & Display machine, the one where it happened, has been removed by the police. But there's another, closer to the pier itself, which is where they've put all the bouquets. Except that now most of these are dead and brown and battered by the wind – each bloom reduced to a colourless mush, each stem and frond black and dead.

Someone should remove them, I say to Mick as we stand there and look at them.

He says nothing. I glance at him, his profile, stern and tight and shut off from me in the wind. Unguessable.

How will we go on living here? I ask him.

He takes my hand. His jacket is zipped to his chin, against the wind. There's a strong breeze today. Everything that can move is moving. The sign with the boating-lake opening times on it, the grey tarpaulins pulled over the big boats, the conifers next to the phone box on Pier Avenue.

Bad things have happened nearly everywhere, he says. All the time – think about it, they must have. It's just that you don't know about them.

I say nothing.

He squeezes my hand, then puts an arm around me, pulls me to him.

Other things will happen, he says.

Will they? What things?

All sorts of things, he says. You'll see. Good things.

In her buggy, Liv is concentrating so hard on her transparent teether that her toes are curling and uncurling with the effort of it.

Don't get like this, Tess, Mick says suddenly.

I look at him, surprised by his tone of voice.

What do you mean? Like what?

He sighs.

Like this. Don't go all helpless on me –

Christ, I say, I was only being honest.

That's what you call it?

Yes. It is what I call it.

Do you think I don't feel as you do? How do you think I'm coping? We have to move on from this. We all have to. Think about the kids.

I do, I tell him as the tears creep up on me, I do think of the kids.

So, OK, he says, be serious. What are you saying? That

we should leave this place? Just pack up and leave, just like that?

Not just like that –

Well, then.

I don't know, I tell him, but it's a possibility. Isn't it?

He looks away from me, his face grim.

Not for me, he says, no, it isn't.

But why not? You haven't even got a job – you've got least of all to lose, I point out.

Thanks, he says. Thanks for rubbing that one in.

I didn't mean that. I meant you're free.

Yeah? No freer than you.

I don't feel free, I say.

Livvy flings her arms up in the air and makes a noise of total happiness.

She's lost a sock, Mick says.

I glance back along the way we've come but I can't see it anywhere. It must have dropped off somewhere along North Parade.

OK, so you don't feel free. But you feel free enough to leave? Mick says.

I think about this.

If it's the right thing, then yes, I do.

Vic Munro, Dave Munro's father, comes out of the Dolphin Diner. He walks over, lighting a cigarette, hands cupped against the wind.

Terrible things happen everywhere, Mick says before he reaches us. Running from here won't solve anything. It's not the place, Tess –

What is it, then?

All right? says Vic. Mick says something back. Vic's nails are thick and yellow-grey. I look past him, past his stained puffa jacket and long oily hair, out at the grey and swollen chop of water that stretches beyond Covehithe. A small boat bobs out there, some way off.

They got anything yet? Vic asks us.

People still talk about Lennie's death as if it's the only subject.

Mick shrugs.

You know as much as I do.

They did house to house, or door to door, whatever, on the first day, says Vic. Everyone I know has been seen.

Mick nods.

But they won't get him now, Vic says. Not if he's gone this long they won't.

He gives a mirthless little laugh and sucks so hard on his cigarette that his cheeks cave in. His skin is a mass of tiny wrinkles, the sort of skin that would make Rosa stare in amazement. Vic was a fisherman once long ago – he even worked on the lifeboats. But then he had some kind of nervous breakdown and now he doesn't do much of anything at all except bet on the dogs or the horses and sit all day in the Dolphin Diner and drink tea with the Ramirez brothers.

He once tried to set himself up as a painter and decorator, but did such a terrible job of Barbara Anscombe's hallway that the two of them are still locked in a legal dispute over it.

Where you off to then? Vic asks, turning to me this time.

School, I say. To see our son's teacher.

Again, says Mick.

Vic grins, He's been a bad boy then?

He stubs his cigarette out on the white metal railing.

Dave was always being hauled up, you know, he says. Whole of his time in that place. I was in and out of there like a bloody jack-in-the-box. I expect they were glad to see the back of him, the bugger. Him and Darren Sims, the pair of them.

Oh I'm sure they weren't that bad, says Mick.

Oh, they were, Vic says cheerily.

Just then I catch sight of a figure on the beach – tall and straight and walking ever so slowly along the wet part of the sand where the tide licks it.

Lacey.

Quickly I look the other way, out to sea. The brown sailing dinghy has moved a long way, almost out of view towards Covehithe.

We should go, I tell Mick as I glance once more at the figure on the beach.

We say goodbye to Vic and move off up Hotson Road towards the school. I hold Mick's arm as he pushes the buggy.

You think Lennie would want us to run away? Mick says.

I don't know, I reply. I've no idea what Lennie would want.

We've been happy here.

Yes, I agree. We have.

★ ★ ★

Bob is picking at the sandwich I've made him and telling me about Alex.

He says he wants to make it himself. The coffin. That's what he's saying now.

Oh, I say. Someone else told me that as well. A patient of mine.

Well, says Bob, how the hell would a patient know?

I shrug.

It's a small place. Things get around.

Bob sighs.

Anyway, he says, I'm surprised he hasn't told you anything about it.

He doesn't tell me everything.

Bob sighs again.

Well you know, I tell him, maybe it's a good idea. I mean if he wants to. It's what he does for a living after all – he knows about wood. It does make a kind of sense.

You think so? Bob says.

Yes, I think, I do.

In fact, if I shut my eyes I can almost see him doing it. Choosing the wood and bringing it back to his barn, handling it, touching it. Sawing and mitring and glueing and machining.

Bob sighs again and looks at his sandwich. He hasn't eaten a mouthful.

He has all the necessary tools, I guess. He said something about wanting to use American red oak. I don't know that wood – do you?

He looks at me and his mouth turns down and his eyes fill up.

Oh Bob, I say, you're not keen on this idea are you?

He doesn't answer, only feels around in his jacket pocket for his pills and then, when he finds them, takes them out and stares at them.

Did I take one of these things already this morning?

You took one at eleven.

He continues to stare at the pills. His lips are shut in a tight straight line.

It's just, I was going to go along and look into it myself, you know. I never paid much towards the wedding – she had to go ahead and do it all so quickly and Maya was really so ill by then and –

I reach out and put my hand on his wrist.

I ought not to feel this way, he says.

Don't be silly, I tell him.

She's still my child, he says.

When Bob's gone off to have a rest, Rosa – who is supposed to be off school poorly – bounces in.

Hey, you look better, I tell her.

She seems to think about this.

I'm not better, she says slowly and carefully, I'm just trying to be nice that's all.

But your tummy's OK?

Kind of. It's gone into my head now.

I look hard at her, wish I could understand the ups and downs of her. She turns away from me.

What's the matter with Bob? she says.

Things are very hard for him right now, I tell her and she frowns.

If my child had been killed by a bad man, I'd hunt him down and shoot him or something. I'd want revenge.

Well, I pick Livvy's rattle up off the floor where she has flung it, life isn't like that, Rosa. Not real life. You can't just go round killing people.

I know, I know.

Rosa sighs and blows out a puff of air so her fringe goes up. She watches the effect in the big mirror on the other side of the room and, seeming to like it, does it again. Fletcher is lying on the floor. He likes the cool of the lino, even in winter.

Rosa places one bare foot on him.

Hey, I say. Careful.

Rosa ignores me.

Don't put your weight on him –

He likes it, she insists, still watching herself in the mirror. He's my own personal fur rug.

She stands for a moment and sings to herself.

So, she says, is he unhappy about the coffin?

I look up, surprised.

What do you know about that?

Well, Con told me. How Alex is being really mean about it and all that.

He said that?

Mmm, Rosa sits down next to Fletcher who opens his eyes and lifts his head towards her.

Why? What did he say? In what way mean?

Well – Rosa rubs Fletcher's tummy with small brisk hands – he says they're each allowed to do a design, Con and Max, right?

I come over and sit by Rosa.

What? I say. What do you mean, a design?

You know! she says impatiently. They can each design a picture or some writing or something – it doesn't have to be a picture – to be carved on the side of it –

You mean actually on it? On the coffin?

Yeah. Only Con doesn't want to do either, not a drawing or some writing – he doesn't like drawing because he's no good at it, so he wants to stick some stickers and pictures on. Or something that he's got anyway. And he won't let him.

What, Alex won't let him?

No and I think it's really unfair.

I think it's unfair too. In fact, I think everything's unfair. I don't know what's wrong with me. I'm not the person I used to be. I can't focus on anything. Mick finds me standing at night in the garden in a black cold wind without a jumper on.

What are you doing? he calls from the porch. You'll freeze to death. Aren't you cold?

No, I say, enjoying the feel of my skin turning itself inside out, I'm not. I'm not anything.

What I am is numb, deliciously cut off and numb and unsettled. Mick would never understand – it's beyond anything he believes in. All the things that used to please me, that were a part of my good, blameless, ordinary life, are gone. I'm so impatient. Each normal thing – each school run, each family meal – has lost its sweetness and its shine and is just something to be got through. Until I can get away and be alone with these feelings.

And this isn't about Lennie, it wouldn't be right to claim that. This isn't shock or delayed grief or anything with a reasonable name. It's just, I feel I have the power to predict which way things might go. And the knowledge that just now only one thing keeps me going. The possibility, always there, that I might see him.

But I am rushing down Bank Alley having cut through Tibby's Green, late for my first appointment, my mind so filled up with him that when he materialises right bang there in front of me, I am for a second or two stunned.

Oh, he says. Hello, Tess.

I'm hot and tired and I haven't put on make-up or brushed my hair.

Oh, I say. Hello.

Hello, he says again.

You're still here then?

Yes.

His hands are in his pockets and he tilts his head back a little as he looks at me.

No baby?

It takes me a moment to realise what he's talking about.

At home, I tell him. She's with Mick. I left her. I'm – going to work.

He stands there absolutely still, frowning slightly.

So what's going on? he says. Where've you been?

Where have I been? I say, surprised.

Yes. After you phoned me, you disappeared. I've been looking all over for you.

But I've been – here, I tell him, flushing.

Where?

Here. At home, at the clinic – everywhere.

He smiles.

Outside the butcher's, there is sawdust on the pavement. In the window fake grass, brightest green – a foil for the pink and red of the meat.

Are you OK? he asks me.

Yes, I tell him. I push my hair out of my face and my heart swerves. No, not really, I'm late.

And I turn and do something I didn't think I could do. I run up the High Street, past Butlers', past Parsons' Tea Rooms and Sheila Fashions. Past Mei Yuen's and the dry-cleaner's and up to the spot where I can see the safe wooden sign for Empson's Books rocking gently in the wind.

By the time I reach the clinic, I'm already missing him. But I had no choice. I suddenly knew that if I let myself stand there on that pavement with him a moment longer, things might not remain the same. Your whole life can be changed in a single moment if you let it.

I park the car on North Road just next to the boating lake, about fifty or maybe a hundred metres from the place where Lennie died. The lake is closed for the winter, a large heavy chain and padlock draped across its wrought-iron gates. Some paddle boats are pulled up on the side of the grey, wind-rippled square of water, under the tarpaulins – the rest have probably gone to be spruced up and repaired for next year.

In front of me is the cream concrete face of the Dolphin Diner and, beyond, the long wind-lashed expanse of the pier. It has a fitness centre on it now, except that no one goes to it as far as I can tell. And next to that, the arcade with its money machines.

I sit in the car and look at the pier and think of Mawhinney and all those others slaving away to catch someone who Vic Munro thinks will never be caught.

I look at the pier for a long time, till my hands no longer know where they are or whether they're still on the steering wheel or on my lap, till I no longer remember where I am or what I'm doing or why.

I wonder if I'll see Mawhinney come out, but I don't. I see no one. I wait for a long time, till the windscreen is specked with rain, and still no one emerges from that pale concrete building.

After that, I leave the car where it is and walk along the front as far as my hut. The Polecat. It is almost dark, the sky greenish with dark, but I know the walk so well I don't need light.

It's spotting harder now with rain and because I haven't been here since that night – haven't been able to bring myself to come – I can feel the nervy pulse of my blood in my tongue, my throat, in the hotness of the hair behind my ears.

The sea is crashing down. You can tell by the sound of it that the waves are pretty huge.

At the end of the concrete ramp, a couple of kids are forlornly skateboarding, but otherwise no one's around, just the waves making a tearing sound as they hit the groynes. Soon their darkness will join up and melt into the dark of the sky. I love that moment when you can't see what's what any more and sea and sky are one.

The key to The Polecat is in my pocket. It's a normal key, small and steel, the type that would open a shed or cupboard. I put my foot on the second wooden step of the hut and shove the key into the lock and at first it won't turn but then I push a little harder and it does, it gives.

The door falls open. I stand there in my hut and breathe in hard, enjoy its familiar smell of slightly damp curtains, wood preservative and the faintest, blueish whiff of gas.

Later, back home, I climb the stairs and I look at Livvy, asleep in her cot. I stand there and wonder what I'm doing. Panic builds in me. I don't recognise the person I've become. I stand there and I hold my fingers up to my eyes, ready to wipe the tears before they even come.

The hanging of the Annual Art Circle Exhibition at the old school gym is something that Lennie usually organises. It's not really about the art — tepid purplish watercolours of the area, the ferry, the fat silhouette of Blythburgh church, the creek at dawn — but about the spirit of community. There are some dedicated amateur painters in our town. All the paintings and drawings are for sale, with a percentage of the proceeds going to charity. Harriman's always donate the wine for the private view.

Everyone has agreed that this year the exhibition will be dedicated to her memory. Some people considered that it should actually be cancelled, but Polly and Maggie insisted that Lennie would have wanted them to go ahead. They say they intend to make it the best yet. They're roping in everyone they can find to help with the hanging.

I call Mick and tell him I'm dropping Liv back after work so I can go and help.

At the gym? he says. But I thought you were going to get out of it?

I was, I tell him, but I've thought about it and it wouldn't be right.

I put down the phone and breathe in the silence.

I don't go there. I hurry instead down Stradbroke Road, where a man is smoking a cigarette with one hand and sweeping crab apples into the gutter with the other. Further on, by the lighthouse, some oldish women are standing on the corner with their PVC shoppers. One of them, Mrs McGowan, is a patient. She waves and I wave back.

I turn quickly onto St James's Green. It's dusk and a brisk wind ruffles the surface of the sea. Alan the greengrocer is just closing, pulling in his awning, dragging in the crates and buckets, folding the cloth that looks like bright green grass. A brightly coloured poster in his window announces that he stocks fireworks. It will probably stay there till Christmas – everything does in this town. As I pass, Alan looks up and raises a hand to me. I do the same and hurry on.

I I

In the hotel reception, a girl with fiercely pulled-back hair is chatting on the phone, pretending she hasn't seen me waiting there. I ask her if Lacey is in. She shrugs.

No idea, she says. I haven't seen him go out.

So he's in?

Unless I wasn't looking at the time.

I ask her if she'd mind calling him. She asks rudely for my name and I tell her.

He says to go on up, says the girl, with no expression at all on her face. Straightaway picking up the other phone to carry on talking. I start up the wide, hushed staircase then have to come back because I don't know his room number.

Four, the girl snaps.

Up on the first floor, a chambermaid is hoovering the

landing. I think I recognise her. She may have babysat for one of us. She moves the hoover out of the way as I knock on his door.

He doesn't have a jacket on. Just a kind of dark shirt with a blueish T-shirt under. He hasn't shaved either.

Hello, he says.

Hello.

I can't look at him. I hold on to my handbag and touch the buttons on my coat and look at the room.

What a surprise, he says.

He offers me the only chair, pulling it out from the girlish, glass-topped dressing table. I sit. Next to me are small careful piles of his loose change.

This is awful of me, I say.

He looks at me with relaxed interest.

Why?

I mean, just barging in like this.

Barge in any time, he says with a bit of a smile.

Yes, I say, but unannounced.

They rang me, he says, from reception.

Oh look, I tell him, you know what I mean.

He has nothing to say to that. He asks me if I want a drink.

I look at my watch. Though I know what time it is.

OK, I say.

He opens the minibar.

Gin, whisky or vodka?

Vodka.

He pours it carefully, hands me a glass.

178

I take a sip. The taste is blue, metallic.

Do you want something in it?

He passes me a tonic.

Thanks. I pull back the tab and tip it in, watching the quick fizz.

I can smell cooking and bar smells from downstairs. He holds up his drink and looks at me. Far away a phone rings. He keeps looking as if he's about to laugh.

Well – cheers, he says.

I smile. And dare to look around. The place is very neat. You wouldn't think a person was even staying in it. As well as the change piled on the table, there's a wodge of folded notes. A large notebook, a couple of pens. A laptop computer. A jacket, his one, flung on a chair. And a towel. A pair of boots pushed carefully under the TV. And a faint, enticing smell in the air – a smell of him.

He moves a newspaper and sits there on the neat, oatmeal corner of the bed and looks at me. He doesn't seem to feel any need to speak. The silence spills over between us and terrifies me.

You like your room? I ask him.

It's OK, he says. Apart from the noise of the bloody barrels.

What?

First thing in the morning. They start trundling them around, or unloading them or something. You should hear it. Before six it starts, the noise is incredible –

It's the brewery, I point out.

Yes, he says, looking at me.

I sip my drink, feel it pounce into my heart.

Tell me about Natasha, I say then, surprising myself.

He looks up quickly.

Natasha?

Yes, I say. Tell me what she's like.

I feel my cheeks get hot.

You're blushing, Tess, he says.

I laugh. For once I don't care.

I always blush, I tell him, with you. You know that. You should be used to it by now.

He bites his lip.

I can't get used to anything about you, he says quietly.

No? I hold my breath.

No.

Well, I say softly, I don't know. Is that good?

I don't know either, he says to me. It might be. It might not.

For a moment we're both silent. He puts down his drink.

There's not much to say about Natasha, he says. I mean, I don't know what you want to know. We go right back, I've known her years.

What does she do?

He looks at me.

She's a solicitor.

In London?

In London, yes. She does other things as well. She works with children, as a volunteer. Counselling and stuff.

She does a lot, I say.

Yes, he agrees. She does.

She sounds nice.

She is, yes.

He looks at me, waiting. We both wait and say nothing. I wonder what she looks like. How old she is. Whether he's spoken to her today. What he said.

So, I ask him, do you like it here?

This town?

I nod.

Not much, he says.

Really? Why not?

He shrugs.

It puts me on edge, he says. Too much water, too much sky.

But I love that! I tell him straightaway before I can stop myself.

Well, I know you do, he says, obviously. That's why you moved here. But I'm a city boy. I like buildings, people, mess, dirt.

I used to like that, too, I tell him.

But not any more?

No. I don't think so, no.

He smiles at me.

And Natasha? I say.

What about Natasha?

Does she like that, too?

His face when he looks at me is unchanged.

She does, I suppose, yes.

I look down at my drink.

I don't live with Natasha, he says.

Oh, I say. You don't?

No.

★ ★ ★

The windowpane has turned black and outside in the street there are noises now – evening noises that I suppose I must be used to because I hear them all the time. Except not normally from up here.

I hear the heavy, clanking sound of the security grille of the Amber Shop. A lorry backing up. A child's shrill complaint, wanting something. A lone bicycle bell. Ding ding.

I don't think of my own children. I've never been so far from them. For now, they're little specks, they're nothing, they don't exist. If I ever wanted to shock myself, this would be the moment and this would be the way.

Tell me something, he says as he leans over to pour me the rest of the vodka. Why did you run away from me?

I make an effort to sit up on the chair, cross my legs the other way.

What? I say.

The other day. In the street. You ran away.

Did I?

Yes. You know you did.

I put down my glass and knit my fingers together and sigh.

I did, I agree, yes, I'm sorry.

No need to be sorry.

Well, I am.

Why?

Because it was rude –

No. Why did you do it?

I think about this.

Oh, well, I was scared, I tell him at last.

He looks at me closely, as if it can't be true.

Really?

Yes. I think so.

What, scared of me?

No, I say, struggling to get it right, not of you, just — well — I didn't know what was going to happen.

In what way happen?

I glance up and my heart bumps. I can't say it.

I can't say it, I whisper.

He is sitting on the edge of the bed and he reaches out and touches my hand, the one that is on the table, the one without the glass. Just touches it. The touch — warm, terrifying — makes me breathless. I don't look at him. My heart flips over.

And do you know now? he says.

Know what?

Do you know — what's going to happen?

No, I say. Leaving my hand there, looking at it.

No? You don't know?

I take a breath and look at the window again. Shut my eyes. I daren't even think about it, I say.

The moments pass. Nothing happens. I take my hand back and put it in my lap. Safe.

Why did you do that? I ask him.

Oh Tess, he says, don't ask me that —

He leans forward from where he sits on the bed, but he doesn't touch me.

Tess, he says.

Yes?

You came to see me, he says.

I shouldn't have. I'm sorry. I didn't think, I just did it without even thinking –

But I love that! he says. The way you just do things – so frank. I mean it. That's what I liked about you from the start.

I'm not frank, I tell him, looking at him now. I'm not being frank with Mick. I'm only frank when it suits me to be.

You're lovely, Lacey says quietly.

I close my eyes.

I shouldn't be sitting here, I tell him.

It's easy to say that.

Is it?

You're lovely, he says again.

Well, I tell him, it's easy to say that too –

Not for me.

It's wonderful that you think it – I mean, it's exactly what I want you to think – but I also think I'm misleading you.

Oh? he says.

I mean, I don't really want anything to – happen.

You don't?

He is looking at my face all the time.

I'm sorry, I tell him, I really shouldn't have come. You see, it's – I'm waiting.

Waiting?

To get used to you. For this to wear off.

For what to wear off?

This thing – this –

He smiles, waits.

This pull, I say.

He sits back and gives me a long look.

Do you feel it, too? I ask him.

Yes, he says, I feel it.

I just want to be your friend, I tell him and he smiles
again even more.

Me too, he says.

This feeling. It will pass. I know it will. In the end
you'll just seem ordinary to me.

Oh, he says, sounding disappointed. Will I?

Yes, eventually.

He seems to consider this.

But, hey, look, what if I don't?

No, I tell him firmly, that's why I'm here, if you want
to know. To make it happen –

It?

Make me used to you –

But, he says, not laughing now, how do you know,
Tess, that it works like that?

I just know.

You know a lot of things.

Yes, I agree, I do. I told you I did. But please don't
touch me.

He lies back on the bed with his drink. He does exactly
as I ask, I'll give him that. He doesn't touch me or come
near. But he might as well not bother to do this distance-
keeping. Because the truth is he has found a place in

185

me that no one else has ever discovered – not Alex, not Mick – and he's there right now and it makes me go absolutely still and calm, hypnotised.

I don't tell him this.

Talk to me, he says. He is a little drunk. So am I. The room has become both larger and smaller, our place in it more tilted and strange. Amazing how drink stops you minding about things.

I ask him if he likes his work. He hesitates.

I keep on telling myself I'll stop, he says, that this will be the last one. Then something else comes up – and I worry about why I'm doing it.

What do you mean worry?

Well, each new case, the details of it, the people, it takes a piece of you. You get sucked into people's lives –

Is that bad?

Not bad exactly, but taxing. Difficult.

He looks at me and smiles, such a warm smile.

I told you before – you get too involved. It can be sort of – hard to resist.

Because you're good at it?

No, he says, because it's too interesting, too exciting. Whether you want it to or not it gives you a buzz.

He looks at me.

Yes, even something like this, he says. Does that shock you?

No, I reply, wondering whether I mean it.

It should, you know – it's not a good thing. You get habituated. That's not healthy.

I shrug and the room tips a little.

Lots of things aren't healthy, I tell him.

Your job is, he says. The job you do is healthy.

I try to think about my job, but in my head it dwindles and slips away from me.

It's all I can do. I've never thought about it like that.

Yes, but do you like it? Does it give you a buzz?

I laugh.

I can cure babies of colic and make them sleep all night. I can make old people walk more comfortably. I can take pain away.

He stares at me.

That's wonderful. It's just what I would expect you to be able to do.

Would you? I ask him.

Yes, he says. You're an angel. I thought that from the start. There's something boundlessly good and true about you.

I laugh.

Boundlessly good and true? I like that!

No, he says and his face is suddenly serious, there is. I mean it. I wouldn't say it otherwise.

In the end I begin to cry.

What? he says. What is it?

Nothing, I tell him. Just — I may be drunk.

He gets up and moves over to me. It only seems to take a second, too little time to stop him.

It's your fault, I tell him.

What is?

All of it.

His hands are on me, on my shoulders, but I pull back.

Tell me, he says. What's made you cry?

I ought to go, I tell him and I put down my glass and reach for my coat. He looks at me.

You know something? he says.

What?

No. Forget it. I was going to say a bad thing.

Don't, I tell him, suddenly wanting more than anything for him to say it.

OK, I won't. But look, tell me something. Is it working?

Is what working?

This thing of ours — is it wearing off?

I glance at his face.

I don't know, I say as I pull on my coat. It may take a little while.

He says nothing. He just lies back on the bed and smiles.

Will I see you again? he says, and when I don't answer he doesn't look at all surprised, just goes on smiling.

I can't lie to Mick. I tell him half of the truth. A version anyway. That I ran into Lacey and had a drink with him. That's where I've been. Yes, really. All of this time.

A drink?

Well, two.

He stares at me blankly from the sofa where Livvy is lying, cranky and fidgety, across his lap.

But what about the exhibition?

Oh, I say as casually as I can, they had enough people. More than enough. They were fine.

He stays looking at me and saying nothing.

What? I say.

More than two drinks, he says.

No, I chuck my coat at the chair but I miss and it slithers off onto the floor. I pick it up again. It's just – I'm not used to it.

It's true. I haven't drunk properly since Liv was born.

He says nothing. He looks at the TV, then back at me.

This baby's very hungry, he says at last.

I know, I tell him because my breasts are bursting.

You think you should feed her when you've been drinking?

I shut my eyes.

I have to – now. But OK maybe we should start trying her on formula.

He makes a face of surprise.

I thought you wanted to carry on as long as possible?

I do.

Well, then.

He stands up, hands her to me. Livvy's eyes gleam at the sight of my face.

My head aches. As she gasps and closes her mouth over my nipple, fixing me with her hot black eyes, Mick goes to the kitchen and returns with a glass of water. Passes it to me. In silence.

Thanks.

I put my finger into Livvy's small, proffered fist. She releases the nipple a second to register pleasure, takes a quick breath, latches on again. How could I be late for this child?

Mick sits down in the armchair, watches the TV, then watches me. Eventually he flicks the TV off.

So. What did you talk about? he says. I feel a rush of sympathy for him.

What? With Lacey?

Of course with Lacey.

Not a lot.

Come on, Tess —

Oh, you know, all sorts of things, I tell him vaguely.

It's nearly the truth. When I think back, there are no words I can grasp.

Stuff about his work, I tell Mick.

Fair enough, he says, and what are you doing now?

I'll feed Liv and maybe watch the telly a bit, I say. And then go to bed.

Fine, he says and gets up.

Where are you going?

Bed. I'm skipping the TV part. I've done that. Turn off the kitchen light before you come upstairs, he says.

I change Liv and put a clean sleepsuit on her and lay her gently in her cot. I wind up her mobile, the one that takes a full seven minutes to run down.

Normally this would send her off, but tonight she barely needs it, she's ready to sleep. Maybe it's because she had a chance to get properly hungry, because I wasn't on tap for once.

Anyway her eyes flutter open briefly and then shut again. Her thumb is jammed in her mouth, the cuff of her sleepsuit pulled up over it, her fat cheek moving furiously as she sucks. If we're lucky, she might not wake now for a whole six hours.

In the bedroom, Mick looks asleep, the duvet pulled up right over his head and only the top of his black hair poking out.

I take off all my clothes then go to the drawer on the landing and pull out the boned and buttoned and strappy thing in violet lace that Mick bought for me before I got pregnant with Liv, in the days when I still had a body and knew what to do with it. A piece of underwear, I don't remember what you call them – half alive it seems now as I turn it over and around in the thick, drunk half-light and try to remember how it goes on.

Hooks and eyes, maybe twenty pairs of them. You do them up in front of you and then when they're done, you twist the whole thing round. I hold my breath, feel the lace rub on my skin. Then push my two breasts, tired and empty of milk now, into the funny, strapless cups.

I try not to look in the mirror. Instead I go back in the bedroom and sit on Mick. He makes a small sleeping noise and then he half wakes up.

What? he says. Tess, for fuck's sake, what're you doing?

I turn off the light, kiss him as if I mean it.

Sex.

What?

I thought we could do it.

I think at first that he's going to resist but then I feel it – him moving under me – and I think how I'd forgotten how easy it all is. So easy if you just don't think about it first. He touches the tops of my breasts, the place where the flesh is crammed in and jiggly. Then he slows and hesitates.

No, he says.

What?

You're drunk.

I'm not.

I know you are.

Not any more.

OK. Then come here, come and kiss me first.

I tell him I don't want that, I just want to do it.

He lets his hands fall back on the bed.

I want you to be aroused, he says.

I am – I am aroused.

He sighs and puts a hand between my legs.

Wet me, I tell him. Go on – do it. Spit on your fingers.

But he doesn't. Instead he kisses me – a small, snappy kiss on the inside of my arm. It's not enough.

I bend my mouth to his ear, smell the warm sleep and skin smell of it.

Hit me, I suggest in a whisper. Hit me if you want.

He touches my mouth.

No, he says, in a voice thick with the beginnings of desire, I don't want.

I want you to do things, I tell him.

Come here, he says. Let me get you wet properly.

No.

I want you to enjoy it too, he says again, moving his fingers over my thighs, trying to put his tongue on any part of me he can reach.

Fed up of trying, I sit and put my hands on his bare chest and I wriggle on him and try to stuff him into me. But it won't go, it just bends, only half stiff. He pulls me off at last and sits up.

Ow. Stop it. What are you doing?

I don't know, I tell him truthfully. I notice in a distant kind of way that my eyes are closed.

I don't know either.

He sounds hurt. As he speaks I feel his hardness sliding away. He gives a long sigh and reaches for his watch and tips the face to read it.

I don't know what's the matter with you, he says. I can't begin to work out what the matter is. Don't you want me any more? Is there something else you want?

I lie down in silence, arms folded on my chest like a stone person on a tomb.

Is there?

I close my eyes. The world tilts. I'm spilling out of it.

Is there something or someone else? he asks me again, and as he says the words, I try to listen, try to ask myself the same question, Is there?

Speak to me, Tess, he says as sleep comes up and punches me in the face.

In the morning, the garment is somehow off me, down by the side of the bed. Downstairs I can hear the sound of the TV and, above it, the children shouting. My head hurts and my throat is sore. Mick brings me coffee.

Last night, he says, a weird thing happened.

I know, I say.

He doesn't seem angry any more. He sits there on the edge of the bed in his old saggy jeans.

No, he says, not that. I mean while you were out.

I'm sorry, I tell him.

He ignores me.

Well, at about six or six thirty, the dog went crazy – barking furiously as if there was someone there – and when I went down, there was no one. But the back door was open –

I sit up.

My God, Mick, I say, but who'd have opened it? Were the kids downstairs?

Well, he says, it could have been anything – the wind, or maybe it wasn't properly shut in the first place –

It shouldn't open on its own like that.

No, he agrees, but listen. That's not all. Fletcher was really going berserk, you know, running in and out and growling and growling –

Someone was there?

No. But I could hear the sound of talking. Just a very low, quiet voice, barely audible – and then I realised Jordan was in the room and he looked like he'd been crying and I asked him what was the matter and who had opened the door and he wouldn't tell me.

My heart goes cold.

It wasn't Bob? You're sure Bob hadn't just popped round and forgotten to close it or something?

No. It wasn't Bob. In fact Jordan said it was Rosa who'd opened it. So I called her down and I could tell by her face that she knew what was going on, so I assumed he was telling the truth. And then I got quite cross – and guess what she told me?

I stare at him and shake my head.

She said that Lennie had done it.

I take a sharp breath.

What?

She said that she and Jordan keep on seeing her.

Panic squeezes my heart.

I don't –

Mick looks calmly at me, watching my face.

Just that. That's what she said.

But – I put my coffee cup down – seeing Lennie? What do they mean, seeing? Mick – ?

She said they keep on seeing Lennie and she keeps on telling them things.

Oh God no, I say. What sort of things?

He laughs suddenly.

Tess, he says, look at you. You look petrified. You don't believe it, do you?

But –

Come on, he says, it's one of Rosa's funny stories. Except it's not funny – she's scaring Jordan. I told her so. I'm not having it. It took a while to calm him down.

Jordan's seen her too?

Mick sighs.

He says he has. Christ, please don't get in a state about it, Tess. Or I wouldn't have told you. It's a game, clearly.

I say nothing.

It's perfectly natural. It's a child's game, a way of dealing with a terrible situation. The only slightly worrying thing is the door.

But – I thought it was Rosa?

No, I told you, Jordan said it was her, but she denied it. She swore she'd been nowhere near it. And for some reason I believe her.

But someone opened it.

He frowns.

The wind? There's no other explanation.

But – you're just going to leave it? Aren't you worried?

He thinks about this.

I don't know, he says. Are you?

Suddenly his face collapses and he looks a little tired. He looks at me.

At least I was sober, he says. Christ, at least I was bloody well here.

12

Alex has nearly finished the coffin. It lies on the work-bench in the draughty outhouse where he works – a huge, sleek thing, carved out of the reddest wood I've ever seen.

He watches me look at it.

Well?

I shiver.

It's beautiful, I say, it's very – big.

Yes, he says softly. Yes, I wanted it big.

He waits, clearly expecting more.

I like how the sides are curved, I say. It looks like it's been blown from inside –

That's the wood. It's the best stuff to work with – you can do just about anything with it.

I run my fingers over it. It feels warm.

Expensive, he adds, and hard to get hold of.

It's lovely, I say.

He tells me that both boys helped him polish it.

They wanted to, he adds quickly as if I might have doubted it.

Rosa comes in. Stops when she sees it.

Is that – ?

For her, I say quickly, yes.

She frowns.

It looks more like a bath.

Alex smiles.

Oh well, he says, fine. That's OK. I think that's cool.

Rosa gives him one of her looks.

Rosa – I take her firmly by the shoulders – shush. Go out. Find Jordan – go on, I mean it. Out.

Alex pays no attention.

And look, he says, touching my arm, have you seen?

He shows me where he's sanded a small area on the side and the boys have drawn pictures. Even Connor. A pirate with strange bobbly feet, waving a flag saying Mum. Max has carved his name and a long and steady row of kisses.

He wouldn't do a picture, Alex says. I left him alone and that's what he did – one kiss is for every year he knew her, that's what he said.

We stand there for a few moments. He wipes his hands on his jeans. So, he says, how's things?

All right.

Still seeing Lacey?

I flush.

What do you mean?

He smiles.

Al, I say, for God's sake.

I'm sorry, he says, keeping his eyes on me. But look here, don't you ever think of Mick?

He slides a cigarette from a pack on the bench and lights it.

What do you mean, think of Mick?

He says you got drunk. You and him.

I sit down on the bench.

He told you that?

Yes. It's funny because he said nothing to me about it.

Who? Who said nothing?

Lacey.

Why would he?

No, he says in a colder voice, I suppose you're right. Why would he?

I look at him, standing by the empty coffin, smoking and waiting.

So is it true?

I look at his cigarette.

Give me some of that, I say.

He passes it.

Is it true? he asks me again louder.

Yes, OK, we had a drink. So?

He smiles and says nothing.

We both look at the coffin.

All we need now, he says, is to get her back –

I stare at him.

Her body, he says, to go in it.

Ah.

You know, the undertakers recommended I put some kind of upholstery in it.

Really? I say, enjoying the dirt-taste of smoke in my mouth.

Oh you know – they're so conservative these people, wanting to do things in a certain way. I'll have that back now, he says about the cigarette. You shouldn't smoke you know.

Neither should you, I say. Handing it back.

He takes it. His fingers are filthy, the nails yellow.

No, he says, but you really shouldn't. I'm expendable.

What a ridiculous thing to say. Your boys need you.

He looks at me.

They needed their mother, too.

You know what I mean.

He sighs a long sigh and stubs out the cigarette.

There, he says, OK?

Ignore them, I tell him, the undertakers – you don't have to do as they say.

Oh I did. I am. I told them – it's only going to be bunged in the ground for fuck's sake –

Quite.

He smiles.

But then I went one better, he says. I told them I'd make my own lining anyway. And do you know what I'm using?

I shake my head.

Con's old baby sheet. The flannel one he used to drag round when he was little –

I swallow.

The one he had to take with him everywhere, remember?

You've still got that?

Upstairs in a chest. Lennie must have put it away for, well, I don't know for what.

It's not something you'd throw away, I tell him quietly.

Women, he says. Typical Lennie. I mean, I wouldn't have kept it.

I shake my head.

But it's come in useful now, he says.

But is it big enough? I ask him. It's not very big, surely?

He laughs.

Do you think she'll mind what the fuck size it is?

No.

He passes me a roll of kitchen towel and I wipe my eyes, blow my nose.

I don't understand you, he says at last.

What? What don't you understand?

You were always there for me, my best friend, I could say anything to you.

Al, I say.

And then –

No. Don't do this.

Lennie dies and –

Al –

You stop loving me. Just like that.

I say nothing.

I'm serious. I really don't understand it, he says.

It's not like that –

Well what is it like? Tell me, Tess, I really need to know. What happened?

What happened to what?

To us.

Nothing, I say, nothing happened.

I'm squatting by the freezer, trying to pull out two frozen pizzas without spilling ice and peas everywhere, when the phone rings. Fletcher nudges at me and I push him away.

I hear Mick talking for a moment, then he comes in and hands the phone to me.

For you.

I take it and feel him watching my face. Fletcher tries to poke his nose in the freezer.

Oi, says Mick and grabs his collar.

Good news, Lacey says, I just told Mick. They reckon they'll release the body within maybe ten days –

Oh – I turn my face to the cold blank square of the window – that's good.

I mean, they haven't named a day, but they reckon it's safe for Alex to make arrangements.

Arrangements?

For the funeral.

I take a quick breath.

Oh God, I say, I can't believe it.

I know.

I'm silent for a moment.

It'll be tough, Lacey says, especially for the kids. I mean now, after all this, to see her buried.

He wants that? Not cremation?

Yeah. I just don't think he wants anything further done
– to her –

He pauses and I hear his breath.

And you, he says more quietly, are you OK?

Oh yes, I say as brightly as I can. Fine, we're all fine.

I meant you.

Yes.

You knew I meant that?

Yes, I say again.

Mick looks at me.

Yes, thanks, I say again.

Mick gets the airline to extend Bob's ticket, for reasons
of compassion, though a small supplement has to be paid.
Which Mick says is totally out of order – he'll probably
write and complain when all of this is over. He says this,
but we both know he won't. He doesn't let Bob know
about the supplement of course. Bob phones his neighbour who says he is only too happy to take care of the
dogs.

The boys won't recognise me when I go back, Bob
says sadly. I'll be a stranger to them.

He shows Jordan a photo – two hefty, elderly chocolate Labs gazing at the camera from a driveway strewn
with golden leaves and pine cones.

Give them lots of treats, Jordan advises. Spoil them.
Mum and Dad always bring us something if they go away.

What do you mean if we go away? says Mick. We
never go anywhere.

You did once, Jordan says. You went to London.

Oh, says Mick, yeah. For one night.

Get them some treats, says Jordan again and he goes over to Bob and puts a hand on his knee. Bob acts like it's perfectly normal to be touched this way but you can see he likes it. He picks up the small, grubby hand and holds it in his own. Jordan leans against him.

Aha, he says, but I have to be careful of their teeth. And their weight, you see. Too many treats and the goddamn doctors would be onto them just as they are onto me –

You should never give a dog chocolate, Jordan says. Not human chocolate –

Is that so? Bob says. Well, I must say I didn't know that. Where did you hear that, boy?

On the internet, Jordan says. You can find out all sorts of stuff on the internet, like do you know what the word for a girl dog is?

That's enough, Jordan, says Mick, but it's OK, Bob is already laughing.

Normally plots at St Margaret's are expensive and extremely hard to come by, but Canon Cleve has somehow managed to get Lennie a place. She's going to be buried on the west side, not far from the ancient yew whose dense black branches spread into the playground on Tibby's Green.

Rosa seems exceptionally pleased. That yew is her favourite tree.

I once left something extremely precious in it, she says, and when I came back it was still there. After a whole week!

204

Really?

Yes – she looks triumphant – it's the tree. It has these powers –

Powers?

She smiles.

You wouldn't understand. But basically it looked after the thing for me.

Great, I say. So what was it? What did you leave?

My lucky stone, she says, the one with a hole in it. I left it in the hidey-hole. Lennie knows which one.

She talks about her in the present tense, I tell Mick later, as if she's not gone at all.

I know, he says. I've heard.

But – isn't it weird? Why's she doing it? Do you think it's OK?

It's a habit she's got into. Once the funeral's over, maybe that will change things.

Maybe, I say.

Everything's weird at the moment, he says. This is such a weird time – a time of nothing happening. Nothing and everything.

I look at him in surprise.

What? he says.

Nothing. Just – you're right. I know what you mean.

The best thing, I overhear Rosa telling Jordan in the bathroom that evening as he cleans his teeth, is she can see the playground from there. There'll be stuff to watch, she won't be lonely.

Out on the landing, I stop and listen.

Jordan says something I can't hear because his mouth is full of toothpaste.

And the tree will shelter her, Rosa adds with some authority. It's always good, you see, to be under a tree.

I go into the bathroom. Rosa is standing naked except for her knickers, school clothes strewn around her on the floor.

She won't actually be buried under the tree, darling, I tell her. Not right beneath it anyway.

Rosa's face falls. Jordan looks at me carefully and then at her.

Oh? But why not?

You can't dig under an old tree. Think about it. There are all these big roots and they spread a long way.

Rosa shoves her hand in her knickers and glances in an agitated way at Jordan. Jordan spits in the bowl and glances back at her. For a moment they don't look like my kids at all.

What? I ask them. What's the matter with you two? What is it?

Rosa is already shutting off from me, staring away out the window. But Jordan wipes his mouth on a towel and turns to me.

She says under it.

What? Who? Who says under it?

Rosa turns from the window and takes off her knickers, then flings them in the laundry basket as if she's scoring a goal.

Shut up, she says to Jordan. He's just being stupid, she

explains. The thing is, we just want her to be buried in a happy place, that's all.

She smiles at me in a cheery way. As if I'm stupid.

She will be, I tell her. I swear to you, she will be.

Rosa shrugs. But Jordan gazes at me and I hate how tired and grey his face is.

You're a tired boy, I tell him and I hold out my arms and he comes.

Do I have to have a bath? Rosa asks. She bounces a couple of times in front of the mirror, watches the budding pouches of fat on her nipples jiggle up and down, watching us, too.

Not if you think you're clean. I nestle Jordan on my lap even though he is too big.

I am clean.

Then don't have one.

You don't mind?

Not really. Not today.

Rosa looks pleased with herself.

But will we go to the funeral? Jordan asks me.

I look at his face.

Do you want to?

Yes, says Rosa quickly. Of course! Yes!

And you, I ask Jordan, do you?

Yes, he says.

Then of course you will, I tell them. If you want to.

Mawhinney clears a space for me to sit down. He looks pleased to see me.

Just the person, he says.

He takes an armful of papers and moves them out of the way – and then the files and dirty coffee mugs. The room is more chaotic and untidy than when I last came here.

Sorry, he says, indicating the mess. We're getting sick of this makeshift office.

I don't blame you, I tell him.

Through the window, it's a bright day, the sea rough and striped with sun.

I say no to his offer of coffee.

Look, I tell him, there's something I left out, when you first came and talked to us. A small thing, or I thought it was. But I realise I should have told you – even though I shouldn't think it will change anything –

Oh? Mawhinney looks at me pleasantly.

I'm really sorry, I tell him. In fact I'm embarrassed.

He smiles.

It's this, I say. I have a beach hut on the front. I've had it for years –

Oh lucky you, he says quickly. They're great, those beach huts.

I look at him, try to smile.

And hard to come by, he adds.

Well, yes.

I stop a moment. He picks a paper clip up off the desk, smiles cryptically. Why do I feel he's playing with me?

Suddenly, he tips his head back and laughs. Then he leans forward and touches my arm.

It's OK, he says. It's just – I'm sorry, I've just spoken to Alex.

What?

I think I know what you're going to say.

Really?

He just told me –

I stare at him.

Alex? Told you what?

I'm glad you've come in. I was about to come and talk to you myself.

I don't understand, I say. What's he told you?

That you were there in the hut that night. You and Alex. That you saw Darren –

Darren? Sorry – what – Darren?

Isn't that what you were going to tell me?

Yes, I say. Well, no. I mean yes about the hut. But no, we never saw Darren.

You can see this foxes him. He puts down the paper clip he's been fiddling with and looks at me, perplexed.

Darren Sims?

No. Definitely not.

He says you did.

Alex said that?

Well, yes.

Well, I didn't.

You're sure of that?

Absolutely. I never saw Darren, I tell him, definitely not. I don't know when Alex could have seen him either. I mean we were together all that time.

Now Mawhinney looks displeased.

He told me he saw him outside, he says. That he was outside the hut hanging around as he left.

Well, I say, shaking my head, he never told me —

I have to say, Mawhinney points out stiffly, that this is quite important. I can't go into details but we have stuff on Darren. One or two possibly crucial things.

I try to laugh.

But Darren didn't have anything to do with all this.

Mawhinney looks at me sharply.

I can't discuss it with you I'm afraid, he says, but I do need to know whether you saw him —

Well, I didn't.

He folds his arms and looks at the clock.

Would you sign a statement to that effect?

Yes, I tell him. Yes, of course I would.

Lennie's funeral is finally fixed for next Friday at two. Before then the church has got to be swept and waxed and polished. Rosa and I go along after school to help, taking Livvy with us.

Polly's in charge of the flowers. She's getting them in specially from Yoxford. Which has annoyed Lyn Hewitt, the florist from Winton's. White lilies and Michaelmas daisies. The lilies have got to be cut as late as possible on the Wednesday in the hope that they'll stay fresh till the Friday.

They won't, Lyn tells Barbara Anscombe, who relays the information back to Polly. They'll be brown around the edges by the start of Friday, you'll see.

Liv is cutting a tooth and very scratchy, needing to be held all the time, but Rosa's very good and helpful. She goes around with a soft yellow duster and does the back of every pew with Pledge and then collects up the kneelers to give them a good dust-bashing out in the porch.

Everyone notices how helpful she is.

I wish she could be like that always, I tell Polly. Or at least more of the time. I'd settle for that.

Oh, she's a good girl, Ellie Penniston says. Reminds me of my niece at the same age, such a lovely girl. She died too, you know, asthma attack.

I'm not dead! Rosa shouts from the porch.

She carries five kneelers at a time back into the church, struggling under the weight. Then she trails a duster over the walnut chest by the altar.

Not you, darling, I tell her. She means Lennie.

Livvy starts to cry. I scoop her up.

Does everyone know someone who is dead, do you think? Rosa asks me as we stand and pile up the hymn books and prayer books and watch the pale band of sun slip through the plain glass of the altar window.

Not everyone, I tell her, but many people, I suppose, yes.

Maggie sees us and comes over and gives me a hug. She says she's glad the funeral's happening at long last.

It's like everything's been on hold for so long, she says. I feel we just need to let go and say goodbye.

Rosa stares at her but no one notices.

I don't know, says Polly who's sitting in the choir stalls, going through the rota. I just don't know if I can face it all again. Just when life was finally getting back to normal. It sounds selfish, but I feel I've had enough grief to last me a lifetime.

If only they'd caught him, Sally says. You know they've been talking to Darren Sims again?

No, I say, I didn't know that.

Why are they talking to Darren Sims? Rosa asks me. Do they think he's the murderer?

Of course not, I tell her. It's too grown up to explain.

In my arms Liv has fallen asleep. Her weight hurts my shoulders. I ask Rosa to get the buggy from where we left it at the back of the pews. Liv's cheeks are scarlet and a glittery rope of dribble runs from the corner of her mouth to the bib around her neck.

As I lay her in the buggy she startles and her fingers fly up and grab at a handful of air.

Alex is opening a can of beans. The kitchen smells of burnt toast. Washing-up is piled in the sink and about a week's worth of papers are on the table. He is trying hard to be a father on his own.

I don't allow myself to feel pity, not today. I ignore the mess and pull out a chair, move a bunch of dirty dish towels off it and sit down.

Hey, he says, that's Lacey's chair.

I look at him.

Joke, he says.

I keep my eyes on him.

I went to see Mawhinney, I tell him.

He looks at me coolly. Oh?

Yes, I tell him.

And?

And I don't understand –

212

Don't understand what? He turns down the gas under the pan.

All this stuff I find you've been telling him.

He frowns and pulls the toast out from under the grill. Turns it over just in time.

Really? What stuff?

Yes. Really, Al.

What do you mean, Tess? What stuff?

That we saw Darren Sims. Hanging around The Polecat. Is that what you told him?

Oh that, he says vaguely, yeah, well I probably did.

Probably?

OK. Definitely did.

He gives a little laugh.

Why?

He leans against the counter and looks at me.

Well, he says, slowly as if I'm a little stupid, because I did see him, believe it or not.

And me? You told him I did too?

I don't recall. Maybe. I might've said 'we'?

You did.

Ah –

According to him you did.

He says nothing, stirs the beans. The back door opens and shuts.

Now that really is Lacey, he says.

But I don't turn around. I don't do anything. Behind me, I feel him come in.

Tess is just interrogating me, Alex tells him.

Lacey doesn't say anything. I turn and look at him. He

is standing there holding his keys and a bunch of papers. Something inside me tightens, curves. I turn back to Alex.

So did you? I ask him.

Did I what?

Did you really see Darren that night?

Alex looks solemnly at Lacey.

Yes, Tess, I did.

And you never said anything to me?

I don't know, he says, I really don't remember everything about that night –

I'm telling you, you didn't.

Do you want me to go? Lacey asks, still standing there.

No, I say quickly, of course not.

Alex puts two plates on the table.

Jesus, he says, I mean maybe I'm the one who should go?

Don't be so fucking stupid, I tell him.

He blinks.

He butters toast. Scraping butter on, scraping it off.

Come on Tess, he says, what's the big deal? You don't have to protect young Darren from anything. The police are only interested in evidence. But if he was hanging around, then they need to know.

If, I say and look at Lacey. I fold my arms and watch as he sits down at the table. I am glad to find I don't blush.

Alex goes to the stairs and calls the boys.

When I left you, he says, when I left the hut to go home. He was waiting on the shingle in the dark. I thought you saw him too.

Well I didn't.

OK, so you didn't. Sorry.

When I came out, there was no one there.

Alex shrugs.

So he'd gone –

Anyway, I tell him then, I don't see what's wrong with him hanging around there. I mean, so were you.

13

School will be closed on the day of the funeral and so will just about every shop or small business in the town.

Alex is hoping that Lennie's body will be released on the Wednesday and will spend that night and the following one at Sharman's, the undertakers in Halesworth. From there it will be collected and brought into town, but it won't go straight to St Margaret's.

It will come in down Station Road, Alex says. But, instead of going straight down the High Street in the normal way, it'll take a right across Barnaby Green and down Spinner's Lane before taking the road out past the golf course and up to Blackshore. There, it will make its slow way along the rough shale track, past the black-tarred, paint-peeling fishermen's huts and the chandlery stores, past the ferry and the crumbling harbour walls and the edge of the caravan site and, finally, across the sand dunes and onto the beach.

Timetables have been checked. The tide will be out, so the hearse will, apart from where it has to skirt the groynes, be able to travel over firm, damp sand as opposed to the shingle which, the undertaker worries, might play havoc with the tyres.

After about a mile, when it reaches the Tea Hut and the Sailors' Reading Room it will have to stop because there's no way for a car to get up there. Then will come the even harder, even stranger bit. Six men – Alex, Mick, John Empson, Geoff Farr, Kenneth Peach and Jack Abrahams, with Jim Dawson and (possibly, though yet to be confirmed) Vic Munro standing by as reserves – will carry the coffin up the steps and onto East Cliff and back along the High Street, cutting across Bartholomew's Green to the church.

Most of the town will be waiting, either in the church or outside it in the graveyard. It's lucky that St Margaret's – the finest medieval seaside church in England, the guidebooks call it – is so vast. Everyone can squeeze in. And just about everyone, it's thought, will want to.

Alex says this strange journey was Con's idea. That he wanted to give his mum a last look around the town. A way of giving it back to her, he says.

Rosa approves of the idea.

I want to go too, she says.

Darling, I tell her, you can't.

Anyway, it's not straightforward. There are problems.

The weight of the coffin for one thing. Alex never gave a thought to this when he made it – unused as he was to making coffins – but oak weighs far more than pine. Will six men be able to get it all the way up the steps to East Cliff without a struggle? Those steps, cut into the side of the cliff, are famously steep, and hard to negotiate at the best of times. An accident – with Lennie and the coffin crashing all the way down onto the prom – would be unthinkable.

There's the handrail on the left, Mick says, but nothing on the other side. And if you can't hold on, you need at least to be able to look up.

And those guys are all so old, I point out. Well John and Ken anyway and Maggie says that Geoff sometimes gets the shakes.

It might frankly be easier, Mick says, to carry the bloody church to the coffin.

The only way round all of this, Alex decides, is to practise. At nine one night the six pall-bearers meet in The Anchor and then go on to his studio where, in a kind of weird parody of a wedding rehearsal, they shoulder the empty coffin and carry it all the way down to the beach and then up and down those same steps. In the moonlit dark. Several times.

Will we see her? Jordan meanwhile wants to know. Will you be able to look at her when she comes in the church?

No, darling, I tell him, she'll be in the coffin – you know, the one that Alex has made? No one will see her, but we'll all know that she's there.

She's not there any more, Rosa quickly points out. Her soul is gone, you know. When you're dead your soul floats up and leaves your body —

Jordan is silent, holding himself tense and thoughtful.

I miss her, he says softly. I wish we still went round there.

But we do, I say. We do still go round there.

No, he says. I mean when she was there and used to give us tea and things.

I hug him close to me and kiss the hot top of his head.

He means she made things normal, Rosa says. That's what he means, don't you, Jordan?

Alex says that at first Max and Con were upset when they heard that the funeral was happening. They cried because they were getting their mum back and also because they knew they were losing her all over again.

Early on, at Lacey's suggestion, he took them to a post-traumatic stress clinic in Norwich. They went once and then gave up.

It was useless, Max said. They made us play with dolls and look at books. They ought to at least have Nintendo if they want kids to go to those places.

Mick and I laughed.

The three of them ended up drinking hot chocolate in Starbucks and then going shopping to HMV and Virgin instead which, as even Lacey agreed, was probably more therapeutic in the end.

We work things out in our own way, Alex told the

counsellor. I've got people to talk to and so have the boys.

Now, to Alex's annoyance, the woman has sent him pamphlets entitled *How to Grieve* and *Letting Go and Saying Goodbye*. Alex puts them straight in the bin.

When asked what he and the boys are planning to do with themselves the night before the funeral, he says they're going to hire a video and get a takeaway.

Work drags along. I haven't a clue whether I'm really helping patients or not. I almost haven't the heart to charge Edna Richards for her treatment, so unsure am I that I really picked up anything or had any real effect on her body.

After I close, I go slowly up the High Street with Liv in the buggy and get the evening paper from Curdell's. The place is busy for a Monday afternoon. At the counter, near the racks of postcards and boxes of Bic lighters, Jan seems to have a crowd of people, all standing around and chatting. I realise they're talking about Darren Sims.

It was on him, someone says. He had it on him.

Down in a ditch towards Blackshore, says another voice.

They don't think it's connected, says Caroline Antrich.

But they haven't arrested him, have they? Jan asks.

No one seems to know the answer to that.

Darren's only seventeen, someone points out.

Eighteen. Eighteen in December.

Seventeen, then.

That's a juvenile – is that a juvenile? asks Jean Almond.

I don't care what anyone says – a pain in the arse and all that but – not capable of violence, no way –

Stupid place to hide it, though.

Or not –

Some kids found it – playing around the ditches.

How'd they know it was Darren's then?

No idea. Fingerprints or something I expect.

I push Livvy up Lorne Road and onto Gun Hill. From up here by the cannons, I can look down on the beach, the sky, the sea. It's very windy, it nearly always is up here – a real, ferocious, flattening kind of wind. A few kids are trying hard to play cricket, but they'd be much better off flying a kite. Jordan would so love to bring his Demon Racer up here right now. Last time we tried there was barely any wind and he was so disappointed.

I haven't been a good mother lately. I know this. That day, when there was no wind, Jordan cried bitterly. It took an hour to get him out of his sulk. I can't remember what it felt like, now, to live in a time when we still worried about the weather and when a sudden lack of wind could feel like a tragedy.

I sit down on a bench and watch the rough aliveness of the sea, brownish and edged with a ruff of foam. Liv's awake, smiling. A tooth has finally come through. I still can't get used to that small serrated stump poking up from where before there was only wet pink.

I wipe my tears on my coat sleeve. It's so old, this coat, that it's barely worth paying the money to get it cleaned.

★ ★ ★

Jordan swears that all he did was tell Nat that Darren had found something in the ditch.

He made me, he says and his face is sullen and pinched. He forced me to tell. He said he'd hold me down and spit in my face if I didn't.

And did he go to look? In the ditch? I ask him.

Jordan says nothing.

Did you tell him where? Did he go there?

How should I know? he says. He's always going off and doing things without me.

Of course Nat isn't in his room. The curtains are still half closed, trapped between the radiator and the bed which is not only unmade but has its covers falling off, onto the floor. I drag the duvet right off and leave it on the floor. Kick a pair of trainers across the room. Things he will barely notice.

There's a smell of varnish or paint. Plates covered in crumbs are stacked next to PlayStation games and glasses containing the dregs of orange juice gone sticky and dark. All his clothes, clean or dirty – school uniform, socks, pants, tracksuit bottoms, endless T-shirts with logos – are trailed across the rug which is rucked up and thick with fluff and dog hair. Fletcher isn't allowed upstairs, but somehow he has perfected the knack of getting himself up those stairs and into Nat's room and slinking on his belly under the computer table and lying there, half hoping to be invisible, half waiting, guiltily, to be found.

★ ★ ★

It ought to be simple, just to go down there to the kitchen and ask Mick whether he knows where his son is. He glances up from where he's sorting the dirty washing into whites and coloureds.

I saw him with his coat on earlier, he says.

So he's out?

I don't know.

You're his father.

I know that.

Well, don't you care enough to know?

I go over to the sink where the tap's dripping and turn it off. Push down the lid of the bin which is jammed full and starting to smell.

What's happening to this place? I ask him.

What do you mean?

Everything – stinks.

You could empty the bin for once, he says. Where've you been anyway?

I took Livvy for a walk after work, OK?

Mick shrugs.

Fine by me, he says. And I know what he means – that it would have been, it used to be.

I sit at the table and put my hand on Fletcher's soft head.

He's almost thirteen, Tess, Mick says. I don't ask where he's going all the time.

Thirteen is nothing, I say. Thirteen is still a child.

That's not what you would have said – before.

Before?

Before all this.

I sigh.

Look, Mick says more gently, he's perfectly safe.

You've no idea, I tell him, whether this place is safe any more.

Don't be so on edge.

I'm not on edge, I tell him but my hands are trembling.

He looks at me.

I'm not, I say again.

Nat says he was just in the playground.

What, playing football?

No, he says, not playing. Just hanging out. And I never touched the knife, I never even saw it. I just went and told Darren he should tell someone, that's all.

How did you know it was a knife?

Nat looks at me.

Well, duh-brain, I asked him of course.

You went and asked Darren what he'd found in the ditch?

Nat rolls his eyes.

Yes of course. Why not? What's wrong with that? Was I committing a crime or something? He was dying to tell someone, you know.

Nothing's wrong with it, I say, but – well, why didn't you come and tell us?

He gives me a look as if to say that should be obvious.

Because you'd just have prevented me, that's all, he says.

Prevented you from what?

Dunno. From everything.

Nat, we wouldn't.

Oh yeah, you would. You do it all the time.

I look at him and feel a kind of hunger – for what? For the days when if I tried to hug him he didn't spring away from me? For the days when he didn't use to lock the bathroom door? For the days when he still smelled of his own sweet baby self, instead of the different, contaminated smell of the outside world?

He meets my eyes and his own are fierce, challenging.

What? he says.

Nothing. I didn't say anything.

I didn't mean him to get into trouble, Nat says quietly. I didn't know they'd think it was his.

I touch his skinny, nerved-up shoulder.

It's OK, I say. I can tell them, you see, that I know he found it. He won't get into trouble, not if I talk to Mawhinney, he won't.

Four times, Rosa tells me when I ask if they've really seen Lennie. We've seen her roughly four times.

Roughly? Rosa, for heaven's sake, what does that mean?

She screws up her eyes so tight that her freckles blur together.

I mean I'm not exactly sure of how many times. Sometimes I see her in my sleep. I don't count those.

And who's we?

Jordan and me. Let me see – she counts on her fingers – once on the beach near The Polecat, once at the end of the road where school is, and twice here.

What? Here in the cemetery?

Yup. Jordan and me were swinging on the big tyre and we looked up and saw her sitting just over there. She was there for ages, just staring at us the whole time we were swinging. I'm not lying, I swear we did. Ask Jordan. He saw her too.

I look at Rosa and she widens her eyes.

Even if you don't believe me, she says, it doesn't matter. It makes no difference. She'll still keep coming and I'll still see her.

I don't mean a ghost, she's saying to me as the wind blows and the church clock dongs the hour, I'm not stupid, you know. I know that ghosts don't exist, they aren't real.

Well, I ask her, what, then?

It was just Lennie. It wasn't scary or anything. She looked really normal.

What was she wearing?

Rosa narrows her eyes.

Um – jeans. I can't remember what on top. And trainers, the ones with the silver bits on them I think.

I take her small hand in mine.

Darling, I say, Rosa, listen. This doesn't mean I think you're making it up, I promise, but, well, do you think what you saw was in your head?

As if expecting this, she smiles and shakes her head at me in a benign and patient way.

In your imagination, I mean.

If she was in my head, then she wouldn't have been real.

People see things, I say, but she smiles again. She's not falling for that one.

Well then, I ask her, trying something else, why do you think you saw her? It's not normal is it?

It's not normal, no.

So – why? What do you think she's doing?

Rosa thinks about this.

Just being sad. I think she's sad.

Do you?

Yes. She looked like she wanted to be with us. And like she was missing us and – seeing her made me want to cry.

Because you miss her?

I do miss her, yes, but that's not why I wanted to cry.

Why then?

I don't know, Rosa says slowly. Maybe it's that I don't want to think of her being all alone.

Our lives are all around us. That's what I know now. The beginnings and the ends of them, some wrapped tight, pulsing, unknowable – others floating free.

Time is a made-up thing. Everything happens at once. I know that now. It's all the same – life, death and life again. Children know this. That's why they complain if you make them wait for anything. Waiting is dead time, nothing time, they know that. Waiting is a punishment, finally over when the moment comes.

Even after Lennie, life goes on. You think it shouldn't, but it does. Smoke topples out of chimneys, babies startle, kids shriek, cars draw up and stop and go away again, men get tired of things, the sea crashes snarling onto the shingle and then retreats, sparrows jump up and down off branches and out of trees, dogs sleep.

So why won't she let go?

Maybe she wants her heart back, Rosa says. Maybe that's what it is. I know if I was her that's what I'd want.

We sit on the low flinty wall that separates the cemetery from the playground.

So, I ask Rosa, if you can see her, why can't I?

Don't know, she says, her eyes far away as she chases a ladybird up a stalk of grass with her thumb. Maybe you could. But I doubt it.

Why?

She's silent, concentrating on the insect. I can see every single light-blonde hair all the way up the nape of her neck, the faint beginning of colour where her cheeks curve, the swirl of baby hair that turns into a cowlick at her temple and is charming now but will probably annoy her when she's older and vainer.

You don't want to see her, Rosa says.

It's not a question. She has the insect on her thumb, watching as it crawls over her grubby thumbnail. Tilting her head, careful not to lose sight of it.

I do, I tell her, but I hear my voice – adult, tired, without conviction.

No, Mummy, she says. Let's face it. You don't.

I smile.

You've got your mind on other things, she says. All the time. You're always looking out for something else.

She takes her eyes off the ladybird for one single second to look at me with narrowed eyes.

Am I? I ask her, surprised.

Mmm, she says.

Something?

My heart bumps.

Or someone, she says and she turns and smiles at me with eyes I don't recognise.

The ladybird flies off – a black frizz and whirr of wings. Rosa tuts.

Oh look, she says. Look what you made me do.

Mawhinney says I needn't worry about Darren. He says the knife has been ruled out anyway by forensics. It's not connected with the murder, he says. It's just a knife. A coincidence. So that's that.

I try to make him understand that I'm not worrying, that I just want him to know that it wasn't even Darren's knife to start with. How I know he found it – how Jordan and I ran into him just after he'd found something, that day when we were walking Fletcher at Blackshore.

What I mean, I tell Mawhinney carefully, is Darren wouldn't even own a knife.

Mawhinney looks at me and laughs.

Rosa and I walk down Fieldstile Road, turn right onto North Parade and then head down onto the beach.

No one's there, not a single person, not even a dog. I sit hunched on the windy shingle while Rosa mooches up and down at the water's edge, head down, looking at pebbles.

Every now and then she squats – legs bending easily beneath her – and picks up a stone, turning it over, but mostly leaving it. Or else stands and hurls it so it skims the dark water, bouncing along the way Nat must have taught her. When that happens she glances back to see if I've seen. I raise my hand and wave to show her that I have.

The sun moves in and out of the clouds, drawing long black shadows across the beach, throwing light at everything, then snatching it all back up again.

Rosa comes crunching up the shingle, holding something up to the light.

Amber?

No.

I take the pale brown stone from her. The wet makes it pretty but as soon as I wipe it on my jeans it dulls.

Too heavy, I tell her, you know that. Amber's light.

Amber's a type of plastic, Rosa says.

Right.

My kids are obsessed with finding amber on this beach. Not that they've ever found any. The only person who has is Mick. Mick, who rarely looks, yet once casually picked up a honey-coloured, translucent lump the size of a 10p piece – only to lose it again through the hole in his coat pocket. The children have never forgiven him.

Rosa holds her brown stone up to the light. Weighs it in her hand.

It's quite light, she says hopefully.

The sea is dull. Then sun comes out, glitter rushes across its surface and everything turns yellow. Then back to dirty as the shadows fall.

The shadows on the beach get longer, colder. I pick up my bag.

Look, I warn her, you mustn't go telling people about this. Not Bob for instance. It might upset him. And the boys – you won't tell Max and Con, will you?

Oh, Con knows, Rosa says quickly. Con's seen her too.

Oh Rosa, I say, come on –

He has! Rosa wails. Oh, how can I get you to believe me?

As a baby, Rosa was the quiet one. She'd lie in her cot and fix on something motionless like the curtains or the sun coming through the blinds and just stare and stare. Then suddenly she'd chuckle, as if she'd just seen something extraordinarily funny that none of the rest of us could see.

Now she's crying, from frustration and anger.

She's not here, I tell her as gently as I can. She's gone, Rose. You know that. Lennie isn't coming back, not ever.

She doesn't look at me but she doesn't argue either.

It's not fair, she says, still feeling the weight of her stone.

That's right, I agree. It's not.

She chucks the stone away so it lands with a plick in the shingle, immediately indistinguishable from all the others.

14

Lacey pulls up beside me outside Parsons' Tea Rooms, in full view of most of the High Street. He winds down the window. He looks tired and cross and his hair is all sticking up.

Can you come for a drive? he says.

What, now?

Yes, he says, I really need to get out of this place.

It's a cold and blustery day. I know that Alison Curdell is watching us, standing on the steps of the post office and twiddling her hair. Next to her the sign saying Antiques & Curios blows over, caught by the wind.

I'll have to phone Mick, I tell him.

He passes me his mobile as I get in and clunk the door shut. The car has dark red leather seats and smells of sherbet or something acid and familiar like that. There's a white paper bag of sweets open on the dashboard.

I didn't know you had a car, I say. I mean here with you in town —

It's not my car, he says.

Oh.

Mawhinney arranged for me to borrow it.

What shall I tell Mick? I say.

I don't know, he says without looking at me. Don't ask me. Tell him whatever the fuck you like.

I bite my lips and look at all the numbers and symbols on the phone. What shall I tell Mick? Suddenly it seems like a question I've been asking myself all my life.

The answerphone is on. I tell him a lie — to do with Maggie Farr and Polly Dawson and some tins of something.

I ask Lacey how to turn the phone off and he takes a hand off the wheel and does it for me. A click. I watch his fingers, long and quick. I know how to turn a phone off. I just wanted to see him do it.

What? he says.

Nothing.

Why are you upset? I ask him.

I'm not.

You are. I can tell you are.

Oh, he says, I'm just a bit fed up that's all. It doesn't matter.

As we drive up to the A12, I watch the hedges speeding past the window, the skeletal cow parsley, the flattened leathery dead thing in the road. Brownish fur, bit of dark red blood. Once an animal, now a part of the surface you drive over.

So, Lacey says, the funeral's on Friday.

That's right, I agree. But you know, I'd rather talk about something else.

On a table by the road someone has made a sign saying Fresh Veg. There's a bunch of carrots and a marrow. Also some purplish-pink chrysanthemums in a black bucket.

Fair enough, he says.

I think he seems angry with me. Then I think if he was, he wouldn't be asking me to come out with him. Then I think, this is madness, what am I doing, coming out with him?

At the crossroads, Lacey waits to give way and then turns a sharp left. Lorries shoot past on the other side, heading for Lowestoft or Yarmouth. On my left the marshes stretch, black and wet, and from the right comes the sweet pong of Blythburgh pig. Put British pork on your fork, the signs say. Signs that reduced Jordan to tears of disgust the first time he saw them.

I hear they're bringing in new staff, Lacey says. On the investigation. An attachment from the task force.

What's that mean, then? I ask him and he shrugs.

It doesn't mean anything really – just some fresh blood. But anyway, I think Mawhinney is a bit pissed off.

Really?

Yeah. He takes things personally. I think he genuinely thought he had something on Darren Sims.

But he doesn't?

No, Lacey says, Darren's not involved in this.

You're sure? I ask him and he flicks me a look.

Are you? he says.

Yes, I say. Yes. Of course I am.

At the turning to Blythburgh, Lacey stops and puts his hand on the indicator.

Which way? Left or right?

I'm in charge?

Yes.

Left, then.

He turns so sharply that the wheels make a noise on the verge. A van behind hoots to complain.

Where are you taking me? he asks.

I laugh. You'll see.

Where?

Just a place I know. A funny place. You'll like it.

But then before I can say anything else, he pulls in at the side of the road by the sign for Toby's Walks and stops the car.

I know this place. Two centuries ago or something, a young girl was murdered here. It's in the guidebooks – long enough ago for people to find it exotic, exciting. Now though it's a nature reserve, with walks mapped out and little signs for where the marshes are, and benches for picnicking. A lot of birdwatchers come here. They say in spring you can hear the first nightingales if you're lucky.

I stare ahead at the vast black conifers and bracken. If you listen hard there's always a gentle tick-ticking. I don't know what it is – just the sound that the forest makes, the forest floor.

Why have we stopped? I ask Lacey.

He doesn't look at me.

I don't know, he says, I'm sorry.

I laugh, but only because I'm nervous and I don't know what else to do.

I'm lost, he says. He says it with a serious face but when I dare to glance over at him, he says, No, not like that. I mean, lost in other ways.

You know what I mean, he says after a pause.

Don't say things like that, I tell him.

What do you want me to say then? he asks me. I mean it. What do you want to talk about, Tess?

I don't know, I say.

The truth is I can think of nothing to say that would be right.

He says, Do you want to talk about how much I like you?

I take a breath.

About how I can't sleep or work or think or do anything that isn't about finding out how I can next see you?

No, I whisper, not that.

He doesn't smile.

Well, what then?

I don't know. But not that.

I look at him — at his face with its pale skin and dark eyes, the sharpish nose, the arrangement of features that aren't anything much at first glance, but for some reason get better the more you look at them.

He shrugs.

I'm only doing what you said, he tells me.

What?

What you said you had to do. Spending time and waiting for it to wear off.

Oh.

Except it won't, he says. You know that. My feeling for you isn't like that. It won't just go.

Oh God, I tell him, I shouldn't have come.

He puts both hands on the steering wheel.

I would have made you.

Would you?

Yes, I would.

I keep thinking he might touch me but he doesn't. He just keeps both of his hands on the wheel.

I don't know anything, I tell him. I mean, what to do, what to think –

You're in a difficult position, he says quietly, because you want to please everyone.

I think about this.

Is that what you think?

I don't know, he says. I'm finding it hard to know what I think either.

He winds down the window. There are pops, creaks and rustles in the bracken. Animal sounds. A magpie flashes black and white in the clearing ahead.

A girl was murdered here once, I tell him.

Is that what they say?

Centuries ago. It's supposed to be haunted or something.

Oh, he says. Haunted by what?

I don't know, I say. A ghostly girl in white?

Lacey laughs and after a moment so do I.

As we drive up into Westleton, he has to slow for a brown pheasant which picks its jerky way across the road and into the hedge. A sign by the side of the road says, Apples And Kindling For Sale, £1.20 a Bucket.

I decide to tell him about Rosa and Jordan and Connor and how they say they've been seeing Lennie.

Yes, he says slowly, Alex told me that.

Don't you think it's weird?

He rubs his eyes and then smiles.

I think it's that daughter of yours. She has a big imagination —

You think so?

Huge.

I think about this — about Rosa. The Rosa-ness of her.

It's funny, I say. When you first have kids, you think you know what their limits will be, how they'll turn out.

Do you? he says.

I mean, you know they aren't you, that they're their own people. But you don't really believe they'll have all this energy and thought that is nothing to do with you.

He smiles.

Your Rosa certainly has that.

What?

Energy.

I look at him.

Yes, I say, she does, doesn't she? And it's nothing to

239

do with Mick or me. Sometimes we can't control it at all. It's a force of its own.

An alien force, says Lacey, and smiles again.

Yes, I say quite seriously, an alien force.

After a moment or two he says, She had a big thing about Lennie, didn't she?

It's raining slightly and the road ahead of us turns dull.

Yes, I say. She did.

The bookshop is in an old chapel with a corrugated roof and dense thickets of nettles and brambles growing on either side. Opposite is a post office and general store combined, where you can buy shampoo or stamps, painkillers or home-made coffee & walnut cake.

In the shop window, among all the ads for Bed & Breakfast and babysitters and stuff for sale, is a Suffolk Constabulary poster with Lennie's face on. I don't have to look at it, I already know what it says. It gives details of what Lennie was wearing and carrying on that night. I know these details now by heart: jeans, a red satin shirt, a silver bracelet, a soft, dark red leather clutch bag with a yellow smiley face sticker (stuck on by Con and never removed) on it.

Unlike the post office, the bookshop is always open. Always open and always deadly quiet except for the twitter of the starlings that nest in the roof. Inside, old books are piled everywhere and in all directions – on the floor, up to the ceiling and up each and every wall, some of the piles so high you feel they might curl right up over the arched ceiling and come creeping down the opposite wall.

Other stuff is also piled almost to the ceiling, tin boxes, broken chairs, old bedspreads, spider plants spilling over.

Lacey looks around him.

You like books? he says.

Yes, I say, I do like books. Do you?

He says nothing, just laughs to himself.

Some are stacked in formal glass cabinets, others crammed into cardboard boxes that are in their turn balanced on old wooden step ladders or spilling out of metal filing cabinets.

There's quite a bit of handwritten labelling and a system of sorts. Health, cookery, DIY, crime, history, France, Egypt and nature studies. And religion and philosophy and fiction, as well as Rupert Bear and sci-fi and sixties TV programmes. On the dusty brick walls are strange canvases of twisting, fleeting figures and shapes, all done in oils, many of them for sale.

Up in the area that you might call the till − though certainly nothing like a till is in sight − is an upturned Carr's biscuit tin and a broken wooden spoon. And next to it, a felt-tipped sign done on corrugated cardboard: Bang With Stick On Tin For Attention.

Shall I bang? Lacey asks me.

No! I whisper. Don't you dare.

The owner doesn't seem to be around. He never is. There's no one else in the place at all and no sound except for rain coming down outside. Or maybe it's inside as well, for some kind of creeper grows through the upper windows which seem to be pretty much wide open to the elements. Above our heads, bare light bulbs hang, attached to strings at different levels.

I undo my coat.

Have a look around, I tell him.

OK.

I'm going to fiction, I say. I think he might follow me but he doesn't. I glance back and see he has picked up a book and is leafing through it already.

Hey! he calls softly after a moment or two. Tess! Come over here.

He's not where I left him. Following his voice, I make my way between birdlife of East Anglia and Norwegian cookery. He is in the furthest corner of the shop, a little book-lined room all of its own, with a metal step ladder on wheels and a stack of empty cardboard boxes in the corner.

Look, he says. Come here.

What? I say softly.

He's holding a book in his hands.

This, he says. Looking at me and waiting.

I stand there, too hot now in my coat.

What? I say. Look at what?

Here, he says. Come here.

And I move right over to him. The book is small and heavy and old, with a shiny tassel of a bookmark.

I hold out my hand.

Let me see –

But he doesn't give me the book or pass it so I can look. Instead he puts it gently down and reaches forward and opens my coat. Pulls it wide open and holds it by the stiff wool lapels – and pulls me closer.

No, I say, laughing and resisting.

Yes.

No, I say more seriously. You mustn't.

Oh, Tess —

I can't do this.

You're not doing anything. I'm doing it.

I look up at the shelves. A sign above me says, Miscellaneous Theories.

He doesn't let go.

Are we in Religion? I ask him.

I feel him looking at me — at my shoulders or my neck or my face.

I blush hard.

Why are we in Religion? I whisper as he pulls me closer still and I smell the unfamiliar smell of his breath, see the shadows on his skin, the way the hair brushes his ears.

It's the quietest, he says.

Oh.

I put my face near to his neck. A pulse is banging there. I've done it now, I think.

But the whole place is quiet, I tell him.

I know, he whispers and he puts a hand on my head, pulls me to him, but this bit's the quietest.

His skin is warm.

I've never done this, I say as I feel the worry and the confusion of it and the mixed-up swish of both our bloods banging against each other.

Why? What are we doing? he says.

I don't know.

★ ★ ★

Afterwards, we go around the corner and stand by the duck pond and watch the ducks. There's a bench and a weeping willow and a wire-mesh litter-bin. We stand right next to each other, but don't touch.

Ducks love the rain, I say.

Yeah, says Lacey.

I realise I've never been here without my kids. I've never stood on the edge of this pond and not had to grab the hood of some child or other to stop it falling into all that weedy water. I've never in all these years with Mick pressed my face into the neck of another man.

Mallards are paddling up with their bright legs and eyeing us beadily.

Oh, I say, I wish we had some bread. We should have brought some.

You don't really think that, Lacey says.

No, I agree.

The rain is pelting down very hard now. I shiver. I'm terrified but I don't know what of.

I'm going to kiss you, Lacey says quietly. Not now, but later. Don't say anything because I'm going to do it whatever you say.

My heart swerves.

Not here, I tell him quickly. Don't do it here.

But I don't say what I should: don't do it at all.

When I get home, Alex is there with Mick. Nat too, sitting at the table and refusing to eat.

Hi, Mick says.

He says it perfectly calmly. Maybe he hasn't noticed how long I've been gone. Alex just looks at me. He looks stoned.

Liv is wriggling on Mick's lap. Sockless, the front of her babygro damp with dribble. I can see from her frantic face that she's been fretting for ages. As I reach out for her, she cries loudly in a sorry-for-herself way.

Sorry, I tell Mick, undoing my shirt.

I don't know what you're apologising for, he says.

For being so long.

You got wet?

I can feel my hair wetting my shirt, my shoulders.

It's pouring.

And you've been out in it.

Yes.

Alex laughs. I shove a damp breast pad in my pocket, feel the dragging sensation deepen as Livvy sucks.

Smell this. Nat thrusts a spoonful of yoghurt in my face.

Why?

He says it's off, Mick says wearily.

Hold on. I try to adjust my arm around Livvy so I can take the spoon from Nat. I can't just smell it.

I taste it. It's slightly fizzy.

It's way past its sell-by, Nat says. Admit it. He wants to poison me or something.

Nat goes and the door bangs. The room is quiet again. Alex starts to roll a joint.

So. Al went to Halesworth, Mick says.

Oh, I say, realising I've forgotten all about Lennie, the funeral. Oh my God – and?

And they haven't released the body yet.

Alex says it in a blank voice, blank and triumphant.

No? I say. But surely – ?

Tomorrow morning. Or that's what they're saying now, he says.

Can you believe it? Mick says.

But I thought it was supposed to be today?

It was, Alex says, but there was a cock-up. So tomorrow it will have to be.

Soon after Alex has gone, Jordan appears in the doorway, one hand sliding up the doorframe, the other delving down inside his pyjama bottoms.

Go to bed, says Mick. Straightaway Jordan looks at me.

You heard, I tell him without looking at Mick.

But he doesn't move, just gazes at me, eyes shiny with exhaustion. He's at the age when kids look old enough during the daylight hours, but then go back to being little all over again at night.

I sigh.

You want me to take you up? I ask him.

Yes, Jordan says and carries on looking at me steadily.

Mick makes an exasperated noise.

Well, of course, he says. I mean if you offer him that –

You're a hard man, I say to Mick. I say it half joking but the voice I use is not very jokey.

He looks at me as I clear the plates off the table and put them by the sink.

What's that supposed to mean?

Nothing, I say. Come on, boy.

On the stairs, I prod at Jordan's small hard bottom till he giggles and collapses back against me. Relieved, I breathe in his warmth and his bed-smell.

At the doorway to his room, he yelps.

What?

Ouch-y. I stepped on Lego, he says.

Shouldn't leave it lying around, then.

I didn't. It was Rosa.

I put him in bed and he immediately tugs the duvet up to his chin. As I kiss the bridge of his small nose, he reaches out for a handful of my hair. Holds it.

Where were you today? he says.

Oh, nowhere much. I had to see Maggie and a couple of other people. Just jobs and things. Why, what did you do?

I got worried, he says, yawning.

But why? Didn't Daddy say where I was?

He did but I was still worried.

Why, darling?

He says nothing. Just looks at me and his mouth stretches down at the corners like it does when he's going to cry.

What, darling?

His mouth stays down. I stroke his face – slide the palm of my hand all over it, feeling all the curves and dips and softnesses. He shuts his eyes. A tear squeezes down the side.

You weren't here, he says.

I'm here now, I tell him.

He gives a little sob.

I was worried, he says again.

Worried about what?

That something might happen.

Oh Jordan –

He sobs again.

Nothing's going to happen, I say, kissing his face. And I'm not going anywhere.

He says nothing.

OK, sweetie?

He blinks.

OK?

I might have to tickle you, I tell him. If you're not going to answer me, I might just have to do it.

And I do and I feel the wriggle of him, crazy beneath my fingers. I drink in his toothpaste-and-saliva breath. But in the end I stop, because he's just not laughing. Or at least, he is, but not quite enough.

Downstairs, Mick is sitting with the last of the wine. Fletcher is asleep at his feet. Mick has his shoes off and his feet are stretched out in their thick woollen socks. One of the dog's front paws twitches ever so slightly.

OK? Mick says.

He's just overtired.

I knew you'd take him up.

You think I shouldn't?

It's getting into a habit with him, that's all.

I shrug.

I just felt bad, I say. At being out so long today.

What do you mean? he says, staring at me. You're allowed to go out.

Yes, I say, but for so long.

I don't look at him. I don't know what I'm trying to tell him – whether I'm trying to tell him anything. The more I try to tell the truth, the more it feels like a lie. He sighs and pulls out a chair, puts his feet up on it.

I told you. You're a free agent, Tess. Please don't make me into this person who always wants you home. It's not fair.

Yes, I say, but the baby –

She was OK. And as you say, we could start her on some formula.

He twizzles his wine glass round and round on the table.

Friday, he says at last, is going to be difficult.

Yes, I say, I know.

He stops turning the glass, finishes the last mouthful of wine.

And after Friday, he says, I'm not sure exactly how life is going to be either.

I sit down.

How do you mean?

He looks me in the eye.

I mean us, Tess. Our family. You and me.

He runs his hands through his hair. It's getting long again – even though he always has it cut extra short, in a style I hate, just to save money. He has good hair. I watch as the thick, gold band of his wedding ring runs through all that hair.

I shiver, listening to the wind. Pull my cardigan round my shoulders.

I'm sorry, I say, I'm tired. And I don't know what you mean and I don't know what to say.

He looks at me.

It's just – I've run out of energy for saying things, I tell him.

Anyone would look at this family, he says quietly, and think we were happy.

I shut my eyes.

That's a weird thing to say.

Is it? he says.

You know it is. We're happy, aren't we?

You tell me, he says and he sounds almost angry. You tell me, Tess – do you like this? How is it for you? Are we?

I sit there and I can't speak. Panic shifts things around in my chest.

We've all been having a terrible time, Mick, I say. It's no one's fault.

I hear myself and think I sound like Lacey.

This goes beyond that, he says.

Does it?

I think so.

He hesitates.

If you want me to be different, he says, if you want me to change, you have to say how.

Yes, I say.

Yes what?

Just yes, I'm listening.

He stops a moment.

But you have to give me a clue, he says. Otherwise it's just not fair. The odds are just too stacked against me. Do you see that?

I nod.

I'm going to think about going back to work, he says then. The paper would have me. We could come to an arrangement. I talked to Blake.

You did?

Mick nods.

Today. I called him.

You want to do that? I ask him.

Maybe, he says. Maybe I have no choice.

What do you mean, no choice?

He's silent.

We're managing, I tell him. We have enough money.

It's not just money, he says after a moment.

I don't want you to change, I tell him. I'm about to continue and tell him that he doesn't have to go back to work either, when he stops me.

Don't, he says. Don't say anything now. I mean it. I'm not asking you for that. But do me the favour of thinking about it. We have to get through Friday. We have a lot to get through, you and me.

OK, I say.

You're important to me, he says and gives me a bruising look. He pushes back his chair and the dog wakes up, stretches.

We should get to bed, he says.

Yes, I agree. Bed.

Sometimes, when I carry Liv around for too long, I'm left with a memory of her in my arms, a heaviness you can't quite shake off. Or perhaps a lightness, an emptiness. That's what I'm feeling now, except the memory is of Lacey. His touch, his breath, the feeling of what might happen next.

Mick looks at me and I flush. If he looked inside me, he could probably see it too. If he wanted to.

15

Next morning, Lennie's body is brought to Halesworth. It is brought in an ambulance and put in the coffin that has been waiting for days now at Sharman's. Alex is there alone when they bring her. He won't have Mick, he won't have Lacey. He doesn't invite Bob either. Instead Bob comes over to us early. He does this a lot – he likes to see our kids before they go off to school. Especially Rosa.

Passing through the hall, I hear this:

Why do dogs always look like they're about to cry? Rosa is asking Bob.

You're right, I hear him say, I guess they do look kind of tragic.

Tragic, yes, Rosa agrees, as if they're about to cry. Do your dogs at home look like that?

I've almost forgotten, he says, what they look like at all.

It hasn't been that long —

Well, it's been a while.

But you'll go home soon, right? After tomorrow you can go any time?

I guess so, he says.

There's a pause and then:

I don't really want you to go, Rosa says.

Silence.

I've got used to you being here.

So what's that you're drawing? Bob says then. Shouldn't you be getting ready for school?

Not yet, Rosa says. In a minute. Fletcher — it's Fletcher, can't you see — ?

I can almost hear Rosa bite her lip and hold her breath. The big dark slope of her silence as she concentrates.

It's great, I hear Bob say then, a great picture. The eyebrows especially — you've got them exactly right.

Sad eyebrows, Rosa says, sad everything.

That's right.

I could draw your dogs if you like, Rosa says. If I ever get to meet them, that is.

That would be nice, Bob says. A special portrait. Maybe I should invite you over.

Yes, Rosa says, please do. Well, just ask my mum and send me a ticket. Or if you want, just the money.

I hear Bob almost laugh.

He's got a big tongue, that dog, Bob says.

No, Rosa says a little impatiently, that's not a tongue, that's a heart – Lennie's big heart in his mouth. Can't you see? Don't worry, he's not going to eat it –

In the hallway, I hold my breath. Fortunately Bob is laughing.

You're a funny little girl, he says.

Well, and you're a funny man, Rosa says. Do you want to sit together? At the funeral?

Another chunk of silence.

If we're allowed, Rosa adds. We might not be allowed.

That afternoon – Thursday afternoon – turns suddenly beautiful. The sky, which was inky with threatening storm, clears and bright white sunshine soars across it. The sea sparkles. It isn't warm exactly, but you couldn't say it's cold either. No-coat weather, definitely.

I've done a morning at the clinic, but my last patient cancelled. I go home early to find Mick still barely dressed, padding around the house in slippers and cardigan, like an old man. He hasn't even shaved.

Are you OK? I ask him.

Fine, he says.

Really? You don't look at all fine.

He shrugs and doesn't answer but I catch him frowning once or twice. I don't know if it's me, or just his own thoughts unwinding in his head.

He says he'll walk Fletcher after lunch and go on to get the kids from school.

Are you sure? I say. Normally when I haven't got clinic in the afternoon, I do it.

Stop being guilty all the time, he says. Would I offer if I didn't mean it?

Liv is in her cradle seat in a corner of the sitting room. The seat has a row of blue, mauve and orange plastic beads strung in front of it, but Liv is much more taken up with watching Rosa's kitten who's batting a piece of scrunched-up paper across the floor.

She keeps her eyes on the kitten, both fists pushed in her mouth. Kicking her feet sharply every time the kitten jumps.

I pick up the kitten in one hand and in the other the piece of paper which, I see, is covered in Rosa's neat meticulous drawings, her handwriting. All her drawings are like this – sturdy, detailed and repetitive and packed with information. She's like a cave painter, her art teacher at school says.

I open up the scrunched paper and the kitten yowls. I drop her.

On the paper are a succession of pink crayoned hearts and the words, A Map Of Where To Find It – followed by Rosa's initials and her age. Underneath are piles of long wavy blue lines and a picture of a woman standing on top. A person standing on the waves. At the bottom, Rosa has written: Keep Out.

I put the paper back on the table and pick Liv up. She smiles and almost laughs when I bundle her into the buggy. It's like she knows where we're going. It's like she does, even if I don't.

★　★　★

We go down the High Street, in the direction of Gun Hill. It's still bright but very windy. Things falling over, bins and signs banging. Outside the grocer's a woman is yelling and yelling at her child to get into the car. In the road is a pile of manure left by the brewery drays. By the post box, an old man with a stick stands very still and bent over and further on an even older woman travels down the street in a little electric disabled car with a flag on it. She waves to a boy who comes out of Somerfield and picks up cardboard boxes and takes them back into the shop.

I want Liv to fall asleep but she doesn't. She sits up as straight as her almost five-month-old back will allow, straining and following everything that's going on.

We go past the Marie Curie shop, where Maggie is possibly sorting black bags of stuff in the back, and the butcher's. No one in there at all. At Suzanne Hair Fashions, Sue Peach can be glimpsed through the glass, foils in her hair, holding a cup of something.

At the foot of Gun Hill I hesitate, as if going up there is really an option. Then, after thinking about it for a second or two, I turn the buggy and head along North Parade towards the pier.

Though I don't know that's where I'm going till I get there. Or maybe that's wrong. Maybe I do know.

It's really not cold but still the wind along the front stings your cheeks and makes your eyes water.

I feel happy and excited for the first time in a very long time. Because it is a weird day, a mad, glittery day, uncanny and unseasonable. Because the sea has a million different colours slipping over its surface and my heart just nearly explodes when I see it – all that water and the pier, with its tangled mass of metal. And because Rosa may well be right. From where I stand it could just be a huge spidery animal crawling, belly slung low, into all that water.

He's perched on a filing cabinet over by the window, drinking something from a polystyrene cup. Tipping his head back, watching the sea.

I stare at him.

Why are you here? I ask him.

He turns and looks happy and pleased and careful.

Why are you? he says.

I really don't know, I say because it's the truth, and I go bright red and take a step back. He laughs. From the other side of the room Mawhinney's watching us. Mawhinney and a thousand others. The whole room buzzing – more police than I've ever seen in there.

Good news actually, he says. They think they might have something. The National Police Computer, a profile that fits. It's something, anyway.

My heart contracts.

They've found a man?

A suspect. A better one than Darren Sims, anyway. Mawhinney's over the moon.

My God, I say.

I know, he says. It's a shock isn't it.

Look, I say, do you need to stay here?

He looks at me.

What, now?

Yes, now.

No, he says, not really. They're finished with me.
Though I'll have to see Alex later.

Come for a swim then, I say.

He looks at me as if I'm mad.

A what?

Over by one of the computers, Mawhinney is talking
to a blonde woman in uniform.

A swim? I say. Or if you want, a paddle.

He chucks his cup in the bin and folds his arms and
laughs.

OK, he says.

OK?

He glances over at Mawhinney, who is bent over the
computer now as the woman scrolls along the screen.

Yes, crazy woman, Lacey says. Come on then, yes, let's
go.

Maybe I do really mean it about the swim. Or maybe
it's only a way of getting him inside The Polecat with
me. Whichever it is, as I dig the key out and put it in
the lock and turn and yank it open, my hand is trembling. He lifts the buggy up the two wooden steps and
we're in.

Sand underfoot. The grit sound of sand on wood.

The curtains in the hut have bold oranges and lemons
on them – leftovers from the sixties, from someone's

mother. I tug them now along the little stretchy curtain wires and light falls in. The windows are dirty but the light outside is bright. A spider has spun its web across one of the corners and in pulling at the curtain I break it. It falls and hangs for a moment on a thin string – a tiny, balled-up, bouncing dark red thing – before dropping to the wooden floor where sand, dust and, I suppose, old sandwich crumbs combine.

My little hut, I tell him.

Lacey looks around.

It's a mess, I know.

This is it? he says. Where you come?

I haven't been here in a while, I tell him and I can't tell what he's thinking. Not properly since –

We take a step back from each other. Suddenly I'm embarrassed.

It's tiny isn't it? I say almost in a whisper, because it is, the walls are coming closer every minute. I used to think it was big, I add, when I first got it.

Bigger than you think, he says, from the outside.

Some are much better than this, I tell him. Some have – oh, I don't know, some go back further.

He looks at me. I touch my hair, my face.

The ones towards Blackshore are bigger, I tell him.

He says nothing.

We've been meaning to do it up, I say.

Have you?

Yes.

I look at his eyes. My chest and knees have gone hot. Will he kiss me?

Livvy sneezes – once, twice – and the moment breaks.

It needs a paint and a clear-out, I continue, moving an old broken table football game of Nat's out of the way.

What do I wear, he asks me then, For this swim of yours?

Over there – I indicate the endless stiffened costumes hanging over on the wire coat hangers – take your pick.

He looks at them.

Unless you don't want to.

Are you going to? he asks me.

Of course I am, I tell him and I pull up my shirt to show I'm ready underneath, costume on.

He grabs the trunks nearest to him, old and baggy, Mick's from about five summers ago. His face is impossible to read.

Shut your eyes, he says.

The sun's still out, but there's no one around, only an elderly couple throwing a piece of wood for their dog and, further down towards Blackshore, a couple of guys dragging a dinghy with flapping orange and pink sails out of the water.

We crunch down over the shingle and I spread a blanket with a towel on top and put Livvy on it. I try to put two other towels on either side of her, but she immediately starts fussing, wanting to get onto her front.

My swimsuit is way too small – it's from back before Jordan was born – and I had forgotten how it's all shiny and baggy and wearing out at the sides. Also how the legs keep riding up so I have to pull them down all the time. Driving me insane. It seemed OK when I put it on, but I never go swimming with anyone but the kids. Now I realise I must look terrible in it with my bottom hanging out and my thighs all cheesy white and marked with tiny dark veins.

I hope he isn't looking at me. He's not. He's frowning at the sea. So I look at him. He's good without his clothes, just fine – pale but kind of streamlined and purposeful. A pencil sketch of a man. I like him. As I knew I would.

He turns to me and laughs.

Are we really going to do this? he says.

I don't know, I admit because part of me is losing heart. My arms are goose-pimply, though the air is actually surprisingly warm.

But he wades straight in.

You think I'm just a city boy, he calls over his shoulder without stopping, still going in.

I laugh.

I never said that.

You think it, though. You think I can't get wet.

I don't, I swear I don't.

Come on then, he says. He is in up to his knees. He grabs little palmfuls of water and rubs them on his thighs, his waist, his chest. Shudders and laughs.

I wade slowly towards where he stands. The first moment of putting my feet in is a shock but at least the waves are gentle, little washy, slappy ones, tipping their icy weight over my knees but never higher.

He holds out his hand.

This is mad, I say.

I glance back at Livvy who has rolled right onto her front but seems happy enough, lifting her head to wink at the sun. I take it. I take his hand.

He squeezes my fingers.

It was your idea, he says as I gasp at the cold, I'm just reminding you of that.

I don't know what got into me, I tell him. I've never in my life swum in November.

Suddenly he lets go of my hand and dives off under the water. Comes up gasping a little way away. Head all slicked blackly down and smiling.

I can't do that, I tell him, laughing. Don't expect me to do that.

He swims off away from me, a steady crawl with his head right down. Meanwhile I move myself along, feeling the shingle shift and roll under my feet. Occasionally a pebble drifts across the top of my foot, lifted and pulled by the motion of the water. I try not to think of what's down there – the pincers and tentacles creeping over the cold and eerie sea bed.

Now the water is up to my waist almost. I can feel it, the brown swollen weight of the water all around me. Back on the shore, Livvy is suddenly small. The sun slides under a cloud and in a second the whole sea looks dark and achingly cold. The loneliest place in the world.

I turn. I can't see Lacey.

Where are you? I call.

I can't see him anywhere.

Hey! I shout. Hey!

Then, under the water, a hand is on my waist and he comes up beside me. Water falling off him.

Oh, I say. Because the sea is still dark.

What is it? he says.

Shall we get out?

You haven't got in yet.

No, I say, but I think I might have had enough.

But it's a waste, to get out now.

And he puts both hands around my waist and pulls me down so quick that I gasp aloud at the shock of it.

But before I can even take a breath, he takes my whole face in his hands and kisses me so hard and deep on the mouth that all other sensations are swallowed in that single one. His mouth on mine, hot falling away from my body, limbs gone. Livvy gone, the shoreline gone, the brown water gone. For a few liquid seconds, there's us and me and him and only the pure smooth terror of that kiss.

And then the sun comes out again and turquoise shadows chase over the water and the whole world lights up.

I put my two wet hands on his two wet arms and glance towards the shore.

It's OK, he says. Don't worry – I can see her.

No, I say, I didn't mean that –

He touches my face. What, then?

I like it, I say and he smiles.

Again, I say. Please – do it again.

He still holds my face, but he stops, looks at me.

You're not afraid of someone seeing? he says.

Yes, I tell him because it's the truth. A little, I am.

He puts his arms around me and my teeth bang as he looks at me but it isn't from the cold and wet or only partly anyway. It's because I've done it now, the thing I never thought I'd ever do. It's happened, I've done it and I'm terrified because it changes everything.

In The Polecat, there are plenty of towels, but all of them smell stiff and musty. The blankets are better, cleaner. There's even an old goose-down duvet, thin and scrunchy and lacking a cover.

Livvy fell asleep on the beach, but I managed to get her back in the buggy without waking her. This is a rare thing. Normally she sleeps so lightly – the slightest touch startles her back.

We dry ourselves without talking and put back on most of our clothes. Then I lock the door and he helps me pull the two old mattresses, children's ones – lumpy and with a pattern of stars and planets on them – down onto the floor and cover them with the blankets.

We still don't speak. We just get under the duvet and lie there in each other's arms. And it's the best thing yet, just lying there so close and listening to his heart, his breath, and on top of that my own and then the soft, quick in and out of Liv asleep.

This is exactly what I was afraid of, I tell him when we've been lying there in silence for a while.

What? he says.

That it would feel this good.

★　★　★

Moments pass. We still have all these clothes on us, layers and layers of them, but I can feel him pressing against me, getting closer.

I can't, I say, suddenly panicky. I can't – do it.

He moves his head so he can see my face.

Can't do what?

I am trembling so much that my voice shakes.

Sex, I say. I can't have – sex – with you.

He laughs.

Hey. He kisses me near my mouth. Hey, shush, it's OK.

I kiss him back. I kiss his shirt and then his jumper. Wool that smells of him.

You don't have to do anything, he says.

No, I tell him, you don't understand. I don't mean because I shouldn't – though I shouldn't. I mean, I haven't done it for about a year, I don't know if I can any more.

He pulls back a little and looks at me.

Since the baby, I tell him as flatly as I can. Well, since before. I mean, Mick and I – we just haven't.

I wait for him to speak but he says nothing and I can't see his face. He feels for my fingers and covers them with his, interlacing them, squeezing, holding.

So there you are, I tell him in the calmest voice I can do, I'm – frigid.

He laughs.

No, I tell him. It's true. You don't understand – you couldn't, you're too young. I'm this old, frigid woman and you're young and –

I'm not so young, he says.

You wouldn't know, I tell him, how having kids changes you.

He says nothing.

I'm thirty-nine, I tell him, I mean it. I'm not like your –

I don't say it.

Not like my what?

Your – young girls.

He laughs again.

I thought plenty of old women had sex, he tells me. I thought they liked it.

Hmm, I say.

From behind me he grasps my hands by the wrists, holds them, circles them, strokes them. I feel a stirring of something and then it tapers off and I feel my eyes close. Maybe for a moment or two I sleep.

It begins to get dark and Livvy wakes and cries and I feed her. She's a good baby, a good girl. None of the others would ever have been quiet and easy for half so long.

When Nat was the same age he'd cry and cry, hardly drawing breath, and would only stop if Mick held him upright against his shoulder, triumphant and beady-eyed, for hours on end. Livvy has never demanded half as much.

I feed her there on the little lumpy bed with Lacey. And the noise of her sucking loudly and happily with him right next to me feels so strange and easy that I find I can barely speak to him or look at him while it's happening.

You love your kids, he says.

It's not a question, just a statement of pure fact, the way he says it.

Afterwards, I put Liv down on the mattress next to us and I get up and find some tea lights in a drawer. While I strike a match and light them, one by one, Lacey leans over Liv and pulls the cuffs of her babygro up over her wrists, does up the top popper. He does it carefully, like a person who has never touched a baby before. Then he puts his finger on her hair – just touches it with one finger as if a whole hand might be too much. Seeing him do it gives me a pain somewhere in my body, I don't know where.

All we need now is a drink, he says.

I remember the bottle of brandy.

Alex brought this, I tell him.

What? That night?

Yes that night.

He's madly in love with you isn't he? Lacey remarks so suddenly that I stare at him.

He's mad, I say. He's bonkers, raving mad.

Did Lennie know? Lacey asks me.

That he's mad?

No, about – you.

I don't know, I tell him. No, I hope not.

Why? Lacey asks. Why do you say he's mad?

I shrug.

He just is. Always has been. There's something about him. He's not reliable, you know. Not in any way. Lennie knew what he was like, I can promise you that.

Did she mind?

I shrug, try to think.

She was the practical one, is all I can think of to say.

He's lost without her?

Yes, I say, he is.

He can't function, Lacey says.

I think about this.

No, I say, you're right, he can't.

I hesitate, look at Lacey.

He was never – I mean, you and Mawhinney didn't think – ?

No, says Lacey quickly, we didn't.

He thought you did –

He was jumping to conclusions, then.

I smile.

That's it, I say. That's exactly what he always does.

Jumps to conclusions?

Yes. Always.

Why? says Lacey. Why do you think that is?

Why does he do it? I don't know.

Perhaps he likes the drama.

Yes, I agree. Perhaps he does.

I pour brandy into two chipped teacups and we lie back, not touching, watching each other. It's like every time we spring apart we're afraid to come back together.

After a moment he glances at his watch. I already know what the time is, I know it's half past four because I read it upside down a minute ago.

Don't you have to get back? he says.

Yes and no, I tell him. Not really. Not yet. Why? Do you?

I ought to drop in on Alex later, he says.

I watch the walls of the hut bend and change shape in the candle-light.

But not yet, he says.

Tell me, Lacey says, because I have to know. What's it like between you and Mick?

What's what like?

I don't know. Things. Everything.

I already told you –

Not just that – I mean the rest.

I huddle on the end of the mattress, my chin touching the furred cotton of my shirt. I miss Lacey now and I want to get close to him again but I don't know how to.

I feel suddenly miserable.

Oh, I tell him, please. Don't ask me stuff like that.

Do you love him?

Yes, I say, without looking at Lacey. Of course I do. He's a good, good man. How couldn't I?

Lacey lays his arms across his knees, same as I'm doing, and looks at the floor.

It doesn't always follow, he says quietly.

I ignore him.

And he's a good father, I tell him. A really good father.

I take a breath.

But? Lacey says.

I hesitate.

Saying it feels disloyal.

Saying what?

What I feel –

Have a go.

I shrug.

He doesn't make me feel like this, I say.

Lacey reaches for the brandy.

That's just because you know him, he says.

And I don't know you?

No, he says. You don't.

I look at him, so far away from me.

So don't make me talk about it. It feels wrong to complain about him. It feels – lazy.

We are silent for a moment.

That's why I can't – have an affair, I tell him.

He seems to think about this.

Is that what you think I want? he says after a moment.

I don't know, I say. I don't know what you want.

No, he says. You don't.

That's what Mick always says, I tell him. That I don't know what he wants –

That's hardly your fault –

No – but he says I claim to – to know, I mean.

Lacey keeps his eyes on me.

I can't keep myself away from you, he says. That's the truth. I told you. I think about you all the time and I can only really get on and do things that have to do with you.

I put my face in my hands.

This feeling I have for you, he says. It's huge.

I feel the same, I tell him. It's like I can't breathe. It feels like I love you.

But you don't, he says.

Don't I?

No.

It feels as if I do.

Love is just a word, he says. An overused one.

Now that we've got love out of the way, I think I might want him to touch me again. I ask him if he will.

He looks at me but he doesn't move.

Where? he says. Where do you want me to touch you?

The blood comes up in my cheeks all over again.

I don't know. Just – anywhere.

He still looks at me. So much distance between us.

What is it? I ask him. Don't you want to?

I want to, he says. His voice is different – low and cracked.

Well then?

You come to me, he says. Come on. You come over and ask me.

He pulls me onto him, on the mattress. All my skin has gone, dissolved. There's nothing between us, nothing left but us. I kiss him and he kisses me back. At first softly and wetly and slow – and then harder and deeper. We do that part for so long that my lips feel blurred, hot with blood.

When I've had too much, I pull back and try to sit up.

I don't know what I feel about Mick any more, I tell him. And that's the truth.

Though everything I say to him is beginning to feel like the truth.

Oh? he says.

No, I say. That's what I mean. It's true that I love him, but I don't know what sort of love it is or what our future is or what I feel.

No?

No.

And you want to find out?

I don't answer this. I sit back instead and take the brandy cup up from the floor and sip. Feel my lips burn after the kissing.

Do you?

Oh, don't ask me that, I tell him.

He takes the cup from me and puts it down on the floor next to the mattress and then he pushes me gently back and starts to unbutton my shirt.

I don't mind if you use me, he says. I don't mind if you use me to find out.

No, I tell him.

But don't expect me to be heroic, he says softly.

What? What does that mean?

He carries on unbuttoning.

I hold out my hands and touch his face.

I didn't know whether I should do anything about you, he tells me, when I met you. I couldn't decide, you know.

I listen. I listen to him undressing me. I notice that Liv is awake and listening too.

She's awake, I say.

Shh, he says. I tried to stay away. But you kept blushing every time I saw you. It was a dead giveaway.

He pulls my shirt right off and lays a cool hand on the hot skin of my stomach. I reach for it, for his hand, but he pulls it quickly away.

He puts a kiss on my neck. I feel it somewhere behind my eyes as well as up between my legs.

Can't we just hold each other, I ask him as he takes his clothes off.

No, he says, we can't. That wouldn't be enough.

But, I say, I can't — I can't do it.

It?

This — sex.

He smiles.

Tess, he says, it's not such a big thing, you know. What you're doing is, you're making it into a big thing.

But it is — a big thing —

No. Shh. It's not, it's easy —

He undoes my bra — my awful feeding bra — and touches my breasts.

I shut my eyes and lift my hips so he can get my knickers off. Then, just as he thinks he's going to enter me, I stop him and I push him over on his back and I kiss his goose-bumpy balls, the hard furred inside of his thighs. Still tasting of sea. He makes a little noise as I take him in my mouth and lick the salt and the mauveness of the slit that is him. It's good to hear his small gasp of surprise.

16

Liv and I head back up the High Street in the dark. It isn't that late, in fact the evening is just beginning. The street is deserted but in The Angel they are just moving through from drinks to the dining room, ready to sit down among all those pink linen tablecloths and silver cutlery. Through the low bay windows I can see the black and white clothes of the waiters, the glint of silver, the sparkle of chandeliers.

Empty cardboard boxes and crates are piled up outside Somerfield and Ann Slaughter is putting rubbish bags on top of the wheelie bin outside The Griddle. She nods to me. Some kids are shouting and hanging around outside Mei Yuen's.

I try to think what I am going to say to Mick. I know

I can't tell the truth, but I can't bear to lie either. I think I may just tell him I've been in The Polecat. I think I may just – But I don't get beyond this thought. Mick must have heard the gate, because he opens the door and rushes out before I can even get the buggy up the path. His face is white, his breath coming in terrible, jagged gasps. Nat hangs back in the doorway behind him, holding Fletcher by the collar.

He grabs at my arm. Have you got Rosa?

No.

My stomach does a flip.

Rosa? No. Why?

I stare at him.

Mick – what's happened? Where is she?

His face terrifies me.

Oh my God, I say, beginning to cry. Where is she, Mick, tell me! Where's she gone?

He stands absolutely still for a moment.

Right, he says, I'm calling the police –

Wasn't she with you? I say. When did you see her – ?

Inside, Jordan is sitting on a kitchen chair in his pyjama top and pants and bare feet, crying. His sleeves are wet with tears and snot. There are tears in his hair. Pasta sauce on his pyjama top. I pull him onto my lap and wrap my arms around him.

Rosa's gone, he says again and again, shuddering, sobbing, Rosa's gone.

Hey, I tell him. Darling, don't cry, I swear it'll be OK, we'll find her.

I say these words over and over while Mick explains. He speaks slowly and carefully but in between each word his voice tightens as if he can't quite breathe.

Rosa was here at teatime, he says. She was very helpful, unloading the dishwasher and grating the cheese for the pasta. Not in a mood or anything. Perfectly normal Rosa. She ate a big plate of spaghetti.

And fromage frais, Nat adds. Two of them.

He kicks at a chair leg as if his limbs are too large for the space, which maybe they are. The laces of his trainers are undone and fraying.

But − she kept getting up, Jordan says, still heaving with sobs. To look out of the window −

No, Mick says, that was before. That was long before tea, Jordan, please shut up and let me just tell Mummy.

Jordan gives a little sob and I wind my arm tighter around him, flesh on flesh, leaving no space between. As Lacey did to me barely an hour before.

Mick tells me that he went out the back to take the rubbish out, keeping the door on the latch so that Fletcher couldn't escape. Then when he came back in, Rosa wasn't there but he didn't worry because he thought she'd gone upstairs.

And anyway she did go upstairs, Nat says. I saw her. She was drawing in her room −

Pictures about Lennie, Jordan says.

I look at Mick and try to take this in and suddenly I feel sick − my insides sick and light, skin damp.

And?

And that's the last time any of us saw her. In her room,

like Nat said. She's been missing since at least six, maybe earlier.

Oh God.

I put Jordan down on a chair. I am trembling so hard I can barely speak.

Right, I say. Right –

Mick pushes his hands into his eyes.

Jesus Christ, he says.

But she wouldn't just go, I tell him then. Mick, she wouldn't. She's not allowed to just leave the house – you're sure she's not here somewhere, asleep?

Mick looks at me as if I'm mad.

We've searched everywhere, he says. What do you think? The garden, the road, we've looked bloody everywhere –

And you've checked she's not at Alex's? Or with Bob?

Bob's out looking for her now, he says. On the beach and along the front. He won't stop. He says he's staying out there until he finds her.

I stand up and my stomach tips.

We have to call the police. Or Mawhinney.

Mawhinney is the police, Nat says.

Livvy begins to cry and Mick picks her up out of the buggy. He pats her vaguely, holds her against him.

I was only waiting, he says, for you. I was just desperately hoping she was with you somewhere. I mean, where the fuck were you, Tess?

Mawhinney says he'll come straight over.

Mick starts phoning everyone we know, everyone who

knows Rosa. I meanwhile pull on a coat and go out with Nat. To the graveyard. It seems to me quite possible that Rosa might go there. Being Rosa. Especially now. Especially the night before Lennie's funeral.

St Margaret's is immense and silent in the half-light from the moon. The white metal gates are pulled across the porch and locked. I try the handle but it won't turn.

I thought they never locked it? Nat says.

Sometimes, I tell him. It's because of Lennie — tomorrow.

The cemetery's dark and windy — just two exterior lights shining their cold beams on the grass. We go over to the spot next to the dark spreading yew where Lennie's grave is already dug. Nat shines the torch in and we both look at the deep drop, the glossy, sharply spaded sides, the black, black earth.

He doesn't say anything. He just looks. I touch his shoulder.

Come on, boy, I tell him. Let's just walk around —

As I walk, I concentrate on keeping breathing, on taking big sensible breaths, keeping focused.

Rosa! I shout, struggling to keep the tears from my voice, Rosa! Rosa! Rosa!

In the darkness the sound of our voices is so huge and strange and loud, the edges of them so blurred, that we have to keep on stopping to wait for the echo to finish.

Rosa! a! a!

We strain into the silence, listening.

Nothing. Just the wind and a faint metallic clinking

279

sound, probably telegraph wires. And if you listen hard enough, if you strain, maybe a dull roar that is the sea. Nothing else. Nothing coming back.

Nat's quiet. I take his hot hand in mine.

What do you think? I suddenly ask him. Where do you think she's gone?

He says nothing for a moment, then, Well, you know how weird she is, the way she talks about Lennie as if she isn't even dead.

So –

Well, she might be looking for her – I mean, she's pretty stupid when it comes to Lennie.

She thinks she's seen her, right? I say. Nat makes a dismissive noise in the back of his throat, half laugh, half sob.

I try to remember where Rosa says she's seen Lennie. Try to think of what kind of crazy thing she might want to do.

The school? I say to Nat. Or maybe the pier?

He gives me a look. I know what he's thinking. He's thinking that even Rosa would never go there. That no one they know would dream of going anywhere near the pier car park at night – not now, not any more and especially not tonight.

Mawhinney sits in our kitchen. It's 11 p.m. Lacey too. Lacey has come not because he's with the police, but for me. I know this, but I'm not going to think about it right now.

I can't look at him. Tonight – now – I just can't let myself look. He knows what I'm thinking. Where the fuck was I? Where were you, Tess?

Mick has made coffee. He needs to do things, to boil kettles and move stuff around, to have reasons to get up and down from his seat. Now he has the phone on the table. He's been calling people. He is pale and jittery, unable to be still, even for one single moment. It's obvious, isn't it? Only action can bring Rosa back. Anything but sitting, in fact. Sitting and waiting is what makes you powerless. It's what makes disasters happen.

Meanwhile, we all keep looking at the door. Even Mawhinney does, even him, he can't seem to stop himself. Even though he must be used to these moments.

But maybe that's how it is when you've lost someone – that you can't help but believe that at any moment they will come walking through the door and it will all be over. Hugs and tears. Maybe that's how it was that night for Alex, before he called me, before the police came and he had to be told, he had to know.

If Rosa came walking in, right now, I try to think what I would do. She'd be hungry and tired and cross. Snapping at everyone. I'd get her crackers and milk – crackers with goat's cheese on and milk from the fridge without any lumps in. I try to fix on this – on the idea of what she'll ask for.

Mawhinney puts his radio down on the table.

He looks at me. Makes a face. Tries to smile.

The last thing you need, he says. Tonight of all nights.

Yes, I say. It is.

I feel almost calm now. The whole day has been unreal. And I swear to God that if it could just begin again I would be good – never complaining or making life difficult for Mick. I would never think of myself again, never, if I could just scratch this day clean and begin it again.

Are you OK? Lacey asks me. Can I get you anything?

No thanks, I say and I shake my head and my fake smile blots him right out.

Mick says he was going to call Alex again but then he thought why do it? If Rosa turns up there then of course he'll call us – and if not, then why put another thing on his plate, on this night of all nights?

Meanwhile Bob is still out looking. An old man stumbling along the shingle with a torch. Mick and I agree there's no point forcing him home. What else is he going to be doing tonight? He may as well be out there. Mawhinney has a whole bunch of officers out there, too. He says that in a place this small, it'll be easy. She can't have gone far. She'll be somewhere or other.

Somewhere silly, he says and I know he says it to reassure me. Little girls are strange creatures, aren't they? he says. Very hard indeed to say what's going on in those heads of theirs.

I get up and go to the toilet. My body empties – everything. I am perspiring. I splash cold water on my face, it drips down my wrists, into my clothes. I haven't washed since the sea. My arms and wrists still smell of it, of him.

I haven't been taking enough notice of her, I tell them

all as I come back into the room. Because the truth swoops in on me, sudden and terrifying.

Don't blame yourself, Mawhinney says.

But it's true, I say in a quiet dull voice. I haven't.

None of us have, Mick says.

Straightaway I resent how he has to lump himself in with me.

You've been a perfectly good father, I tell him. You've been great. You know it. You always are, you're fine.

Can she swim? Lacey asks after a moment or two.

Oh yes, I tell him. She's done three badges.

But, says Mick, she's not allowed in the sea alone, obviously.

She'd never try and go in alone, I tell him, horrified. Not now, not at night –

He agrees with me and he looks at Lacey.

She's quite sensible, I hear one of us say.

Mawhinney sighs and writes something down on his pad. It seems to be a phone number, but it could be just a scribble.

Lacey sits with his two bare hands on the table, perfectly still. His face is white and his eyes are pink with exhaustion.

He seems to think of something.

Is she upset? he asks us. Do you think she was perhaps feeling upset about tomorrow?

Mick looks at me.

Well, they all are, he says. All the kids, naturally. But not especially, no, no more than any of the others –

He seems to be about to go on, but then gives up and puts his head in his hands.

Then I remember.

No, I say. She is, Mick – she's been drawing these things –

In a stiff and unreal way, I feel myself get up from the table and move across the room. Fetching the scrunched-up piece of paper that I pulled from the paw of Rosa's kitten.

I open it out to show them. I wait for them to look. It now has a pale brown stain on it – tea or coffee – got from lying on the kitchen table all afternoon probably. But still – the careful words and pictures: A Map Of Where To Find It.

Look, I say. Look, she did this.

What? says Mick, What is it?

It's Lennie's heart, these pink things are hearts. And the sea. And there's Lennie –

Mick stares at me. I ignore him. Mawhinney leans over to see. So does Lacey. They all try to see. Why can't they see? I wait for them to understand.

A Map Of Where To Find It, I tell them.

It? says Mick.

Her heart. Look, I say, raising my voice now, surely you can see what it is – ? Can't you? It's a map –

Mick touches my hand.

It's just one of her little drawings, Tess. She's always doing these funny drawings, he tells Mawhinney.

A map of where to find it, I tell them again. Breathing hard, through my teeth.

But Lacey looks serious.

You think that's what it is, he says. That's she's off somewhere trying to find Lennie's heart?

I close my eyes with relief.

Yes, I tell him. Yes, I do. That's what I think.

Mick puts his arm around me.

Oh Tess, he says and I feel his body tremble against mine.

No, Mick, I mean it.

It's a game of hers, he says, the Lennie thing. A mad little game. Come on, you said so yourself.

I shake him off me.

It's not a game, I tell them. It's deadly serious. She thinks she's seen Lennie. She thinks Lennie talks to her. You know Rosa, Mick. I swear to you, she thinks it's absolutely real.

Mawhinney gets up and goes over and starts rinsing out his coffee mug at the sink.

Oh please, I say. You don't need to do that.

He looks odd and wrong standing there at our kitchen sink. His big wrists look suddenly futile as he lays the mug on the draining board and glances around for somewhere to wipe his hands.

I can't bear it. I hand him a tea towel.

Could I – can I have a cigarette off you? I ask him in a low voice. He's never smoked in my presence but I've seen him stop to light up the moment he gets out on those bald white steps of the pier.

He hands me the whole pack, slightly squashed and almost full.

Really, he says, when I try to give them back. You'd be doing me a favour. I'm trying to smoke less.

He hands the tea towel back to me as well. I put it to my face and use it to wipe away the tears that keep on coming.

When he and Lacey have gone, Mick and I go on sitting at the table and I smoke one of the cigarettes. Mick doesn't even mention it. I feel grateful for how it scoots up into my brain and steadies me. Smoke clings to every thought and I'm glad of something to hold. I am almost dizzy with fear.

Halfway through it though I stub it out on a plate.

I can't just sit here, I say.

No, Mick agrees.

We decide we'll take it in turns to go out looking. One staying with the boys who are at last sleeping, the other going out with a torch and maybe with Fletcher and just going anywhere they can think of to go.

Mawhinney has said to get a piece of Rosa's clothing ready. Something she's worn recently. Sniffer dogs are coming from Yarmouth. If she's not found during the night, they intend to cover the marshes at first light.

I slip off my shoes and go upstairs and flick on the light in her room, automatically picking up clothes from where they lie on the floor. School skirt, bobbly school jumper, stained with something. A sock with fluff on it. Her striped pyjama top is there among the felt pens and half-broken cassette boxes. Limp from being worn last night. I hold it to my face. The Rosa smell is unbearable.

And so is the sight of her messed-up but totally empty and unslept-in bed – unbearable. Maria lies hunched at the end of it, her paws folded under her and her two unblinking eyes fixed on me.

From the next room comes the loud up and down of Jordan's breath. I turn off the light and go back down to the kitchen.

Do you think this will do? I say to Mick, dropping the pyjama top on the table.

He doesn't look at it.

I'm going to be so fucking cross with her when all this is over, I tell him.

No you're not.

No, you're right, I'm not.

I go out there. I go all the way back to the pier, to the car park, to all the places that frighten me. The night is thick and empty of light and the sea sounds wild. Fletcher runs alongside, suddenly excited, trying to bite and snap at the lead, wanting to play. I didn't want him with me, but Mick wouldn't let me go alone without him.

I pull him in sharply. Maybe if Rosa could just hear him bark. Maybe –

Black wind rushes past my ears. It's a rough night. Out there, beyond the pier, you can hear the sea chopping and slapping its big wet jaws. A swell that would be dangerous if you were on it. Grey clouds skidding and racing across the moon, drowning out the yellow of its light.

Rosa!

I call for her – I call out for my daughter. I call out so many times I quickly lose count as one minute of calling and calling overlaps into the next. Every time I call, my voice is straightaway sucked in by the wind, and swallowed. My tears too, sucked away. My hair whips all over my face and I use my free hand, the one not holding the lead, to pull it back.

Rosa!

Fletcher barks once. His lonely, mystified bark, the one he does when he's either being left somewhere or doesn't know what's going on. It has a kind of scream at the end of it. He barks like that now, just once, and then once more.

We run down the concrete steps and go crashing over the shingle under the great concrete legs of the pier, the place where in summer kids chuck their used condoms and takeaway cartons. Water hits the graffitied sides of the pier, the breakwater, so hard you'd think it would come loose and float away. Fletcher barks again – he barks so hard and pointedly at the water, you really would think there was someone there.

Rosa!

We wait for a moment looking at the water, but we're looking at nothing.

I stumble back up into the car park. Two cars are parked there at the far end, but otherwise the tarmac expense is empty. No one uses the car park in November, especially not at night. Wind rattles the heavy chain on the boating-lake gate and an old fish and chip paper is lifted by the wind and hits the side of the phone box.

I shudder and tremble. Circles of cold close around me.

The moon is wrapped up in cloud at the moment that Lacey moves out of the shadows. As his arms come around me, I gasp.

Shh. It's OK, he says softly. Look. It's me.

In his arms, I can't move, can't go forward or back. I begin to cry.

What have I done? I say to him. Oh what? What did I do?

He puts his hand on my head, on my hair.

Shh, he says. It's not you, Tess, it isn't, it's not you.

But – my Rosa!

They'll find her, he says. They will, they'll find her.

I cry louder.

Fletcher whimpers and Lacey takes him from me and, keeping his arms around me or at least on me, he presses me against him and doesn't speak. I know he is trying to keep me all together, to stop parts of me flying off, and that he's a good person basically and that he knows less than I do and also that he can do nothing for me now.

Where is she? I say desperately. What can have happened?

I want him to tell me but he doesn't answer, he just says nothing. He doesn't say they've found her and he doesn't any more say it will be OK, he just says nothing and stands with me there.

17

Alex rings early the next morning. His voice is jagged and upset.

Where is she? he says. I don't believe it. I mean – where the fuck could she possibly go?

I try to speak but I can't. My head is hard and tight. I'm afraid of what I might say.

I don't know what to do, he says. How to help. Tell me, Tess –

We've lost her, I hear myself whisper. Al, I just know it – she's lost, gone.

Look, he says. Listen to me –

I try to listen. But I don't know what he says. All the time, other things creep in. Down the street is the clink of Doug the milkman delivering, just like any normal day. Birds doing things in the roof. Outside the window the sky is white, stripped bare by wind.

I'm half dressed, trying to drink a glass of water. If I don't drink, I won't be able to feed Liv, it's as simple as that.

We're just — waiting, I tell him, my voice shaky with tears. Oh God, Al, oh God.

I should have come round, last night.

There was no point.

Have you slept?

No, I say. Have you?

A little. I think so, yes.

He's silent for a moment.

Christ, he says. Jesus, Tess, I mean it. What's Mawhinney saying? Where could she have gone — ?

They're all out there looking, I tell him. So many of them. He says if she's out there they'll find her —

Alex takes a breath. Or maybe he's smoking. In the background I can hear Connor saying something to Max.

I'm sorry, I tell him.

What do you mean?

Today. That it had to be today — to have this — today.

Don't be so fucking stupid, he says.

A beat of silence. Tears are creeping down my cheeks again.

Look, he says, I've got Patsy here with the boys. Bob's shattered — I don't know what time he got in. Do you want me to come round?

There's nothing you can do, I tell him.

Be with you?

I don't need that.

Where's Mick?

Out there, with them.

When's he coming back?

I don't know.

The funeral will go ahead. It can't be postponed and no one wants it to be. Everyone's ready. The town needs it to happen now.

For Christ's sake, Alex says when I tell him Mick and I are still coming, neither of you need to be there. What does it matter? It will all happen with or without you —

We'll see what happens, is what Mick says.

I know what he means. He means that the afternoon is an unthinkably faraway place. So much could happen between now and then.

I start to think things. I think, if Rosa's just run away, if she's perfectly OK and just being naughty and hiding or something, then she will be there, she will somehow come to Lennie's funeral, I know she will. She has a watch. She knows when it is. She, more than anyone, would want to see Lennie buried, there beneath that spreading yew.

I want to be there, I tell Alex, panic mounting. I have to be there.

Tess, he says, why?

For Lennie.

You know what Lennie would want, he says.

★   ★   ★

292

The boys are watching a video, but only because I made them. Their faces are turned towards it, but they keep looking around them – Jordan at me, into the kitchen, Nat out of the window.

Jordan woke up this morning with a stomach ache and asked immediately about Rosa. Nat wants to go out looking for her again and he's angry with me because I won't let him.

Liv is asleep, but not for long. She's hungry and my milk is going. Fast. I can feel it. When I tried to feed this morning at about five thirty – weepy and tired – I was shocked at how little there was, just a thin blueish spurt and then a dribble, then nothing. Liv sucked so hard it hurt, then burst into furious cries. Then so did I. So, almost, did Mick.

Now my breasts feel small, useless.

It's the anxiety, says Maggie Farr who has kindly come over with a tin of formula. Tess, seriously – no one could keep on feeding through all of this.

If I can just keep drinking, I tell her.

You need to eat as well.

I'm trying to eat, I say but it's a lie. When Mick made me a sandwich last night I almost choked on it. My body is rejecting everything.

Mick has already put the bottles in the steriliser. Seeing that pink and blue tin of powdered milk and knowing what it means makes me cry all over again.

I don't want to get into all that, I tell Mick.

All what?

I don't want to start boiling kettles and sterilising.

He looks at me with a strained face.

But you said —

I know what I said.

You won't manage, he says, if she's hungry and crying.

I know, but I didn't want to stop yet. I wanted to keep going a bit longer.

She's quite old enough, Tess —

It's so final.

Tess.

I just don't want it to be — like this.

By lunchtime nothing has changed except that Liv has done it, she's taken a bottle. Mawhinney and his men are still out. Mick goes to take a shower and Maggie sits with me in the kitchen. I can't speak or think but Maggie doesn't seem to expect it. All I want to do is to sit by the phone and wait and Maggie lets me do it.

My two girls, I tell her and then I stop myself. Words, bursting up to the surface, but pointless. My two girls.

Maggie takes my hand.

She has on her black clothes already, even though Alex has expressly asked for people not to wear black. The brighter the better, he says, especially as Lennie hated black. A colour that sucked out the light, she said it was.

Maggie's black dress has red piping.

A compromise, she tells me. I know, I chickened out. I couldn't dress in bright colours. I just don't feel it, I just can't.

Tears slide down her face. I lean forward and tuck in her label which is sticking out at the back.

I feel I'm doing more harm than good being here, she says.

No, I tell her. No, it's not true.

She makes us some coffee. She makes it too weak because she's not used to making it in an espresso pot. She opens her handbag and gets out her sweeteners, clicks a couple into hers. We sit there and neither of us touch our cups.

There's washing-up piled in the sink. Maggie is so desperate to load the dishwasher and start washing pans that she keeps on touching the apron that Mick has flung down on a chair. Eventually I give in and let her. It's easier.

Rosa knows when the funeral is, I tell Maggie. And where.

Yes, Maggie agrees, but she carries on standing with her back to me. I long for her to turn so I can see if there is hope on her face.

When Maggie has gone, Mick comes back down. He has on his dark clothes, the suit we got dry-cleaned, the white pressed shirt that belonged to his father. I can feel him looking at me, trying to decide whether to say something or not. I feel him decide not.

The service is to begin at two. Lennie's body, already on its way from Halesworth, is to start the slow and winding journey towards Blackshore at one. The bells will start ringing then. An hour of bells. A sound not heard in the town since the last lifeboat tragedy, two decades ago.

Alex phones and I know what he's doing is telling Mick for fuck's sake to forget being a pall-bearer, to go and carry on looking for Rosa instead.

I hear Mick start to argue.

There's all those police out there, Al, I hear him say. It makes no difference whether I'm with them for that hour or not.

Mick pauses while Alex says something, I don't know what.

I'm already changed, he says uselessly.

He's silent a moment, listening to Alex. Then he says OK, then he puts down the phone.

I look at him.

Are you doing it?

No, he says. No, of course I'm not.

I hear him cross the hall and go into the downstairs toilet. I hear him shut the door. I hear him being sick.

After a misty, rainy start, the day has brightened and it's a lot like yesterday, with great sudden floods of sun swooping over the rooftops.

I make the boys eat a plate of sandwiches. Peanut butter and honey, anything they'll eat. I make too many – I am programmed always to make food for three. Jordan insists on putting two sandwiches on a plate for Rosa. He gets the clingfilm out to cover it and drops the box. The film unravels and gets in a mess. He begins to cry.

I wipe his tears and tell him it's OK. His hair is cool against my face. Together we smooth the clingfilm back over the plate and put the sandwich next to the bottles of formula in the fridge.

Nat sighs and looks down at his plate. His eyes are circled with tiredness.

What is it, Nat?

You know I don't like crunchy peanut butter, he says.

The bells have started. Mick comes down again, in jeans now, and finds me standing in the kitchen and holding a dishcloth and staring at the wall. He takes the cloth from my hands and gently pushes me into a chair.

No, I tell him, I don't want to. I don't want to sit.

Come on, he says.

I thought you'd gone, I say. Aren't you going? Out again?

In a minute, he says.

He stands there.

Tess, he says and his face is terrible, dark with grief.

What?

I need to know, are you going to leave me?

I stare at him.

What?

Am I losing you?

Why? I say. I am thinking of Rosa and unable to follow what he's saying.

Just tell me. Please. Is that what's happening?

I lay my head in my arms which are spread on the table.

I lost her, I say. It's my fault.

I did, he says. I had her. She was with me. I lost her.

No, I tell him. It was me. I didn't think – I wasn't paying attention. I was out, I was with –

He shuts his eyes.

You don't have to tell me, he says. I don't want to know what you've been doing.

So –

I just want to know about you and me, if we'll go on –

What do you mean, go on?

As a family, you and me.

I begin to cry, hard deep sobs.

Do we have to talk about this now? I say. Is this really the moment?

His face changes.

But Tess, he says, there are no other moments – we don't get any of these moments. Tell me, when are they? When do we get to talk?

He sits and he says, I'm sorry. But it's not just you, you know.

What do you mean, I ask him, confused, not just me?

He looks at me.

What I said – it's not just you.

What?

There have been times, he says, when I wanted to do something, too.

Something? I say. What do you mean? What sort of thing?

He shrugs in a horrible, hard way.

298

Something bad, he says. Something to cause – damage – to our relationship.

I look at him and taste fear in my mouth.

But – why? I ask him.

He shrugs. His eyes are cold.

Just to see.

See what?

His face is hard and tight.

See if our marriage survives it.

But, I say, you wouldn't do that –

Wouldn't I?

I mean, what about the children?

He looks at the table.

What about them?

I stare at his face and don't recognise him, the look on it, the look of a stranger.

If you want the truth, he says, there have been times when I didn't really think very much about the children.

Oh.

Does that shock you?

I don't know, I say.

Seconds pass. I'd have thought it would be impossible to think, but it's not. Just that each thought I have comes wrapped around a picture of Rosa.

When Lennie died, I tell him, feeling around carefully for words that seem true, I felt – well, I suppose – a little mad.

We all did, he says flatly.

I take a breath and look at him.

But –

No, he says, I mean it. You aren't the only one, Tess. All this time – it hasn't just been you –

I don't listen to this.

I had to find out, I tell him, I had to see whether I could be different without you. It's been so long and –

He waits.

We are so much a part of each other. Or we were – until Lennie had this – thing – done to her –

He seems to think about this for a moment. I hold my breath. He waits.

And were you? he says, a little coldly. Were you different without me?

I can't lie. I think of Lacey. His hands on my head, on my body.

A little, I say and I don't look at him. Yes, a little, yes I was.

And how did that feel?

It felt – oh –

I look at him and feel afraid – afraid of Mick, of my husband.

Good. It felt quite good.

A tear slips down. Outside the bells have changed and are making a different sound.

I thought it might be the answer, I tell him.

To what? he says. The answer to what?

I don't know. To – all this.

He doesn't ask what all this is. He sighs and pushes

his hands through his sleeked hair. Still he says nothing. He just looks at me.

I love you, I tell him. I haven't ever not loved you.

I hold out my hand for him but he doesn't take it, he doesn't move. I'm sorry, I tell him after a moment or two.

What for?

That I've been so bad to you.

Have you? he says. Have you been bad?

Yes, I say. Yes, Mick, I have.

The bells are still ringing. Above the sound, seagulls wheeling and screaming in the sky. Jordan comes in. He's changed and put on his corduroy trousers, the only ones he has that aren't jeans or tracksuit bottoms, that are half smart. And a T-shirt with Homer Simpson on. Toothpaste splashes on it.

I want to go to the church, he says, looking from Mick to me and back again. Why can't we?

Nat stands behind him with his hands in his pockets and looks at us as well. I sense a rare moment of co-operation between them. You can tell by their organised faces that they've been talking upstairs.

Aren't we going? he says.

Mick hesitates.

Let's go, I say to him suddenly.

What? he says.

To the church – please, Mick, let's just go there.

She might be there, says Jordan, unblinking. Nat says nothing, looks at the floor.

I look at him. I know Mick knows – that I am thinking the things that Jordan is saying. That they are useless things to think. That she won't be there, she couldn't, she can't possibly be.

But he doesn't say that. He looks at me and says, We'd better be quick, then.

St Margaret's is packed. There are even people standing at the back. Almost the whole of our town is in that church.

We sit at the front on the left-hand side with Alex and the boys. When Alex sees us, he shakes his head at us and then hugs us both. Tears on his face. Some people try to smile at us, others are careful not to look.

Bob, hair combed, face tight and rigid, is next to Patsy. After the service, he says, he's going straight out to look for Rosa again. Patsy has done as suggested and dressed in red – red shoes and bag, the lot. She stays very still, facing front. There aren't many other bright outfits, but one or two are scattered, like petals among the black.

There are some press in the church but no cameras apparently, as respectfully requested by Canon Cleve. And the burial is not to be filmed or photographed.

In front of us, on a plinth, is Lennie's coffin. Alex didn't want it draped in anything. He wanted the beauty of the wood to show. So there it is, naked, gleaming, huge. Jordan stares at it. He knows not to ask me if she's in there.

In fact, our children are perfectly still, perfectly quiet. I had thought they might be restless but they're not.

Even Liv stays quiet in Mick's arms, a string of saliva hanging from her soft, bunched-up mouth. Jordan sits with his small feet on the kneeler. He only glances around him when someone coughs or sneezes.

Alex holds both his sons' hands tight and stares straight ahead. I can tell that Connor has been crying, but he's OK now. He seems to be in a dream, or else he's tired, or both. I don't look at Mick. Instead I look up, at the tall, plain, light-filled windows through which you can always see sky, blueish cloud, tops of trees. Then I shut my eyes and for the first time ever in my life I pray.

Canon Cleve says that Lennie touched so many people. That was her gift. She will be remembered for her humour and generosity and her zest for life. When he makes a joke about her, a few people laugh. The laugh cracks the silence, lets everyone shift in their seats.

He says he hopes and prays that Alex and his family will be given strength to rebuild their lives, that they'll become a stronger family, bound together in love and grief by this tragedy.

Then he says, Let us pray.

A sudden memory comes to me, of Lennie making dough for all our kids in the kitchen and, when pieces of it got trampled all over the floor and the sofa and carpet, laughing and saying it didn't matter. Her face as she says it: It's only furniture. Her fingers and the wrists of her jumper covered in flour. When she pushes the hair out of her face, she has to do it with her arm, awkward, laughing.

I feel myself trembling all over. Mick turns to me and mouths, Are you OK?

I nod.

Jordan's kneeler is embroidered with beach huts – one red, one yellow, one blue. He traces their shapes with a finger, round and round, up and down, over and over.

I rest my head in my arms on the hard polished wood of the pew and now the sea comes into view – wobbling and sparkling on a far-off day – and Rosa is hurrying up the beach, bringing me endless brown pebbles and demanding to know if they're amber. And I wish that just one of those times, one pebble could be honey-gold and light as plastic and I could just say, Yes.

Let us stand, says Cleve.

Oh no, I hear myself mutter to Mick, I can't do this.

It's the hymn Alex and Lennie had at their wedding. Patsy is weeping silently.

Mick leans his mouth to my ear.

Do you want to go out?

I shake my head.

I'm fine, I tell him.

He does not sing – Mick never sings – but stares up at the carving on the choir stalls. The minutes pass and I won't allow myself to think or look behind me. And then eventually I do, I look down at the grey flag-stones and then I turn my head and see Lacey. He's right back against the far wall on the left, standing there with a couple of uniformed officers and he's looking straight at me. His face doesn't change, but he doesn't take his eyes away either. They are the last thing I see before Cleve asks everyone to kneel for the final prayers and Lennie's floury hands fly back at me again just as the cold grey floor comes up to smack me in the face.

The grave is almost three metres deep. That's what Nat tells me in the wide, cold porch as Sue Peach brings me a glass of water and someone else holds a wad of Kleenex to the cut on my head.

You got blood all over the floor, Jordan tells me as people shuffle past and try not to look.

You might need a stitch on that, says Sue but I grab hold of the Kleenex myself and I look at it and say no. I can tell I'll have a hell of a bruise tomorrow but the bleeding has already almost stopped.

I'm fine, I tell them and no one disagrees. Mick takes the children out to the graveside and tells me to stay sitting for a moment. I tell him I'm coming.

As the last mourners leave the church, Lacey is behind them. Up close his black suit is actually dark grey, his tie crumpled.

He squats down next to where I'm sitting on the cold stone bench and asks me if I'm OK and I just look at him. That's all. I just gaze and gaze at his kind face.

The burial is just family, but this of course includes us. We are all family. The rest of the town stands out there on Bartholomew's Green and watches as the coffin is lowered down on its ropes and put in the ground. Max can't stop himself leaning forward a little way to see it go in. Con begins to cry loudly. Patsy puts her arms around him, hugs him close.

In a pocket of deep silence, Alex takes some earth from the undertaker's trowel and lets it fall and then, more slowly, Bob does the same. In the church, he was weeping and weeping as if he'd never stop, but now he's calm, dry-eyed. Max takes some earth and lets it fall, but Con won't do it, he refuses.

When the trowel is held out to him, he turns and pushes his face into Alex's clothes and Alex staggers back a second, caught off balance, and then takes his hand and holds him close. Patsy shakes her head. Tears start to come down Max's face. Alex gathers him close as well.

It's over, I can see him saying. It's OK, it's over.

This, I think, this is the moment. I glance hurriedly around the graveyard, at the rows of stones leaning back like teeth. Nothing. No sign of anything. Just gravel and shadows and stone.

Then Patsy leads Alex and the boys away from the grave and out through the little gate that leads to the playground. It's a funny way to leave the cemetery but there's no other, not today, not if they want to avoid the crowd. We watch them take the long route through the playground, past the swings and the slide and the big tyre with the bark chippings strewn underneath, past the rough-mown lumpy meadow where on so many taken-for-granted summer evenings Lennie and I stood in the warm wind with mugs of tea in our hands and nothing on our feet, just shouting and shouting for our five suddenly deaf kids to come in for baths, or tea or bed.

A cold late lunch is served at Alex's, but we skip it. No one expects us to go. Even Alex has to be begged not to abandon it after half an hour and rush off to join in the search.

And then, just after five, Mawhinney comes round with a piece of news. He says that Darren Sims of all people has reported seeing someone looking very like Rosa standing right on the groynes down beyond Gun Hill. Yesterday evening, just before dusk.

What? I cry. Standing actually on the groynes?

Mawhinney folds his arms and looks me in the eye.

He says she was shouting at the sea.

Christ, says Mick and he looks at me.

Mawhinney says that Darren said it looked like she was perfectly happy and talking to someone.

Talking? To someone in the sea?

That's what it looked like.

But, for Christ's sake, Mick says, who?

Half an hour later, Darren is brought round to see us. He looks bothered, pink. His sweatshirt is muddy and on inside out.

I couldn't see anyone out there swimming or nothing, he says. I'm not being funny, but it looked like she was talking to the sea.

He tells us that he yelled at her to get down off the

groynes because everyone knows you don't go on them, that they're dangerous.

You were that close? Mick says and his face is pale and slicked with sweat. You could call to her?

Oh yes, Darren says. But she didn't hear a word of it. Or at least she turned round once but didn't do nothing, just looked at me and turned straight back again.

I sit. My head is bursting.

Ten minutes later, Darren's mum rings us. She sounds very upset. She explains to Mick that Darren did go home and tell her what he'd seen but she didn't believe him. She told him not to be daft and sent him off to pick up the two bags that needed collecting from the launderette.

Now, of course, she's kicking herself. All afternoon she's been in tears and can't concentrate on anything, not till she knows that little girl's safe.

The trouble with Darren, she says, is he's always coming home with these strange stories and I'm used to it. They never amount to anything, I swear they don't. I've learned over the years that the best thing really is just to ignore them all.

Livvy is crying and crying and won't settle. I take her upstairs and change her. In her nappy is the first poo made of formula milk – hard, brown, solid, of the real world. As I fold the nappy away and put it in a bag and clean her, she goes quiet and still and fascinated, following my movements with her clear, dark eyes.

Someone phones the squad to say a young girl has been seen getting into a blue van at Leiston, but from the description she is older than Rosa and Mawhinney says they're not going to follow it up, not at the moment anyway.

The six o'clock local TV news has Lennie's funeral on it and this is immediately followed by a report about Rosa. The picture they use is a school portrait, an awful one, in which Rosa – a smooth and alien child – smiles smugly at the camera against a sky-blue plastic background, her hair smooth, her collar down, her cardigan neatly buttoned.

You gave them that? I say to Mick.

It was the only one I could find.

From the tray in the hall?

Yes.

It was supposed to go back to school. You hated it, remember.

Oh, he says. Oh well.

I go and sit on the steps of The Polecat. I don't bother unlocking it and going in, I just sit there in my coat. It's all I've come for, just to sit.

It's dark. Seven o'clock. Seven or maybe half past. I don't know. I'm very calm now, unafraid. I sit there and I stare and stare at the rolling mass of the sea till the darkness comes up inside my head and I think maybe I can see right into it. As you can see into anything if you look at it for long enough.

I feel weightless, invisible, and in a strange way

everything is clear to me now. I even think that maybe if I stop breathing and remember where to look, I might be able to see my Rosa.

Eventually Lacey comes to find me, as I knew he would.

Oh, I say quietly. Hello. I thought you'd come.

He stands on the prom with his hands in his pockets. There is a strong wind blowing, a wind I must say I hadn't noticed till he arrived. But I do see it now, it's impossible not to, because of how his clothes flap, how he has to hold his coat closed. His big coat, the one he's wearing, makes him seem very far away, just a tiny speck really, though I wouldn't of course tell him that.

I do want to tell him that his face looks terrible, just daunted and upset and worse than I've ever seen it look, but my heart's fighting so hard with my mouth that I can't get the words out.

Tess, he says.

I shut my eyes. I can't look at him. I daren't.

I'm sorry, he says. Oh Tess, I'm so sorry.

He puts his hands on my shoulders, which makes me feel a little sick, but I don't stop him.

No, I start to say but already it's too late.

Come on, he says. Come on.

No, I tell him, pulling away now, suddenly frantic.

I'm sorry, he says. I'm sorry. I have to take you back now.

18

Rosa's body is found by a man out walking his dog on Covehithe Cliffs. He spots her down at the edge of the water as he walks along the gorse path above.

He says he isn't really looking down at the beach at all, but his eye is caught by the bright purple of her sweatshirt. She is floating, face down, nudged against the rocks by the tide. At first he wonders if it's perhaps an adult, in a wetsuit, swimming. But soon he realises the body is far too small to be out there bobbing around in the water alone.

He scrambles down the steep cliffside using his stick to help him, but the dog gets to the body before he does and starts barking furiously. He never goes in, the man says, but he always gets excited when he sees people in the water.

He is still hoping at that point that he has it all wrong and it's someone swimming. But as he gets closer, he sees it's a child, a girl. And that she has long fronds of seaweed grasped in her hands, he tells the police, her fingers wrapped tight around it, as if she's been trying to hold on.

A jutting rock is the only thing stopping her being washed back out to sea again, since the tide has finished coming in and is already on the turn. With some effort, the man pulls her out of the water and onto the beach. He turns her over. Her eyes are open and her mouth is blue. He feels for a pulse and thinks about trying to resuscitate her, but he's scared. He doesn't really know how to go about it. He can't quite catch his breath himself.

So he calls 999 on his mobile phone and then he goes a bit wobbly and has to sit down. He says it's very lucky he has the phone with him. He never normally brings it when walking the dog as he worries about losing it or leaving it somewhere. But as it happens he's expecting a delivery from Wrentham and grabbed it at the last moment, in case they arrived when he was out.

He lives up on Holly Lane, he says. Twenty-eight Holly Lane, Covehithe. That's the address. His name is Fitzgerald. The mobile phone is his daughter's but he sometimes borrows it. He wouldn't have one himself, he thinks they're a waste of money. How ridiculous, that he never learned to do mouth to mouth. He doesn't think he'll ever forgive himself. He feels terrible.

The paramedics assure him that Rosa has been dead some time – that no amount of resuscitation would have made a difference. But the man won't listen. He is terribly agitated and upset by the time they get to him and has to be given a hot sweet drink to calm him down. He keeps on repeating the detail about the phone to the police, even when they tell him they've got the point.

It's hard to tell how long Rosa has been in the water exactly but police believe it's close on twenty-four hours. It has to do with skin colour, how much water is in the stomach, how distended the lungs are. It's easier to tell with children apparently, because the changes happen more quickly and are more dramatic.

That night Lacey takes me all the way back from The Polecat to the kitchen at home.

It seems like the longest walk in all the world, that distance from the beach hut to our kitchen. Sometimes I don't think I'll make it. I walk and walk but my legs don't seem to touch the ground. But Lacey keeps his arm around me all the time, all the way up the street as we walk there in the dark, in the howling wind, the salt, the silence.

Even when we get in the kitchen, he keeps his arm around me. No one says anything. Everything's shifted and the rules have changed. There are no rules – there's only a phone call from Covehithe.

Mick is sitting there, crying. He is shaking all over and crying very hard, harder than I've ever seen him cry. Except for once – the time when Nat was born and for about half an hour we didn't think he was going to be

OK and I was too out of it to care, and then once it turned out he was fine, Mick wrapped his arms around me and just sobbed.

Just like this.

Mawhinney is there and two female police officers I've never seen before. One of them is gently holding Mick's arm, touching his shoulder. The other's got Livvy who's holding her floppy monkey and gazing around at all the people.

They're bringing her, Mick says. In the ambulance. After the police have finished with her. They were going to take her to the hospital, but I said not to, I said of course we'd want her brought here right now. I told them we'd want to have her with us at home. I knew you'd want the same.

I look at him and tell him that I do and then I open my eyes and my mouth and I scream.

I had Rosa at home. Second baby, easy birth. So easy that I remember laughing all the way through it. My memory is of a high, hot summer morning, a perfect cup of tea and an even more perfect, fuzz-headed seven-pound child. And Mick having to shampoo the carpet where I, forgetting the waterproof sheet, simply bent over, crouched and slipped my daughter out, easy and certain as a flower opening.

We carry her up and lay her on her bed, surrounded by all her soft toys and her Walkman, her private diary with the padlock. Maria the kitten comes and settles at the foot of the bed, ponching and ponching at the duvet with her claws just as if it was a normal bedtime.

In the end, Mick pushes her off and shuts her out. I don't blame him but I know Rosa would have been furious. What'd you do that for? She'd have sulked. What's Maria ever done to you?

With a pair of sharp scissors that I normally use for cutting the kids' hair, we snip off the wet clothes she's wearing. Then I get the bowl the children use when they feel sick at night and Mick fills it up with warm water and together we wash her with a flannel and soap.

I wish her small, brittle fingernails weren't all broken and torn, but at least they are clean for once. Bleached, almost, like tiny shells – I've never seen them so white. I take her coldish blue hand in mine and try to slot my own hot, trembling fingers in among hers but I can't. Already they're getting stiff and hard – and the soft pad of flesh beneath her thumb is starting to feel different and not like flesh at all but like something more solid.

Now and then, the room fades and I think I doze, but Mick nudges me awake.

Come on, he says. Clothes.

We can't decide what to dress her in. Eventually we agree that her blue jersey nightie and Gap hooded thing are best.

I don't want her to be cold, I tell Mick and I know how it sounds, but I still have to say it. All through this, he doesn't speak except when necessary and he doesn't look at me. I watch as he struggles to do up the bottom of the zip on her hooded thing.

I know Rosa likes the Gap thing, but I'm not so sure about the nightie. Being Rosa, wouldn't she have preferred jeans? Except that trousers would be almost impossible to get on her right now. Her legs are terribly swollen and no longer move so easily.

We leave the dolphin pendant round her neck. It's her favourite piece of jewellery, the only one she'll wear. Dolphins have magical powers, she says, it's like a talisman, a protection against, well, against all sorts of things.

There's a tiny graze on her forehead and another larger one on her chin — probably from the undertow of the shingle, the paramedics said. There's also a huge bruise on her shoulder but you can't see that now. Her eyes are shut, her eyelids dusted with mauve.

Before they closed her eyes, I looked. I insisted. What I saw was that they were already darkening, losing the spark and shine that is Rosa. I know she believes that your soul goes somewhere when you die. Obviously hers had already gone to that place. Knowing her, it would have rushed there, eager to be first. You could see this on her face — that her soul had spilled out of her far too quickly, leaving her somehow startled and bereft.

The police say we can keep her till morning but that then she will have to go to Ipswich so a proper post-mortem can be carried out. Though, based on the pathologist's initial examination, her death is not being treated as suspicious. She almost certainly just fell in the sea and drowned, they say.

But she was a good swimmer, I insist. I say it again and again to anyone who'll listen. But you can see they just daren't tell me what I already know: that it doesn't matter how far you can swim. Anyone can drown in a rough sea on a dark night.

We sit there all night with our Rosa. Sometimes we hold hands, Mick and me, and sometimes we hold onto each other, our whole bodies moving under waves of sobs, but mostly we just sit there in our separate silences. I see him gazing at his daughter, snatching his last hungry looks. I watch him doing this and I don't know what to say or how to feel.

As dawn comes and a greyish light moves over the chest of drawers, the bookshelves, the collection of ornamental cats and duck feathers, the pink dried-up glitter pens with their lids left off, Rosa's face seems to change again. It looks almost alive. A trick of the light, I tell myself – or else it's just that we've got used to it, to her, to this.

We both lean in and kiss her, first him then me, then both of us wanting to go again. Our girl. She doesn't smell bad – just of our family and of our soap and, slightly, of Rosa. Then we fetch the boys in to say goodbye. Mick says that's important, letting them see. Nat and Jordan look at her so carefully, as if the wrong sort of look could damage her. I feel almost proud of them, that they can look at their sister so gently.

Can I touch her? Jordan whispers.

Of course, I tell him and he reaches out and puts a hand on her cold, white forehead, on her smoothed hair.

Can she feel that? he says and my heart jumps as I tell him, No.

Yes, but if she was alive, could she? he says.

Yes, I whisper. If she was alive, yes.

He stands there and looks at her and thinks about this. I look at Mick. He is shuddering with sobs, his whole body moving. No noise, just shaking silently.

There is a time – I think so, it comes back to me later – when we all just stand and cry in the room together. That's the feeling I have anyway, though the moment has long slunk away, out of memory. I remember Jordan's small knuckles pressing on my face, the empty hungry smell of his breath. I remember Nat, the dark top of his head wrapped inside Mick's arms.

And when the ambulance comes, the men are so good. They creep up the stairs so quietly and carefully, as if a million babies were asleep in our house, instead of just Liv with her mouth wet and hands flung up in her cot. Fletcher barks as they come and then again as they go but I shush him and straightaway he shuts up.

As I stand there by the front door, I think I will never be able to let them take her, never be able to let her – that small blonde fast-asleep baby from that long ago summer morning – go. But in the end I surprise myself and it all happens quite easily, and I do, we let her, we do.

19

Lennie's heart is never found. Some months later though, something horrible is washed up in a plastic carrier bag at Dunwich. It turns out to be a heart – badly decomposed and a long time in the water. The carrier bag containing it has been sealed with duct tape – but not very well. I can't imagine what it was like for whoever had to open it.

Reporters rush to the town, only to be told it's nothing, the heart of a farm animal probably – maybe a cow, maybe a horse. Certainly not a human. No one has any idea why it was chucked in the sea in a carrier bag, but the truth is, people do strange things. Satanic ritual, one or two of the papers eagerly imply, but nothing the police say backs that up.

★   ★   ★

And no one is convicted of Lennie's murder either. The lead Mawhinney thought he had just petered out. Not enough evidence. It takes more than just a lead to get an arrest, he says, and even more to get a conviction. Mick always said that, after those crucial first days had elapsed, he didn't think the police ever really believed they'd get anyone.

The case stays open – Alex has been assured it will remain open for some time – but, though Mawhinney stays in touch, the murder squad leaves the town and the Dolphin Diner gets its storage rooms back and life returns pretty much to normal. One or two vindictive people continue to cut Darren Sims in the street and whisper about him in shops and pubs, and someone tells him he shouldn't ever bother showing his face at The Red Lion again.

But everyone knows who they are and no one supports them. Everyone agrees that Darren should be left alone. As Jan Curdell points out, since when did a low IQ make someone a murderer? Besides, Alex later admitted he could have been mistaken about seeing Darren. So the police have established for once and for all that there's nothing to link him to Lennie that night.

Actually, the knife Darren found in the ditch that time is indeed a lino-cutter. It is eventually traced back to a carpet fitter from Wangford who was laying a new floor in the Pool Room at The Anchor. How it got from there to the ditch at Blackshore is something no one has ever been able to explain. Even when the police interview the carpet man at some length – though there's still no forensic evidence to indicate this is the murder weapon – still no satisfactory explanation emerges.

Anyway, the man has a perfect alibi for the night of Lennie's murder. He was in custody in Lowestoft at the time, charged with drunken driving.

Anyone who knows Alex well knows he won't stay single for very long. After the funeral is over, after Rosa, it's only a matter of a month or so before he starts an affair with Gemma Dawson who has been helping out with the boys and who, at seventeen, is far too young for him. In the end, Gemma ditches him, but too late, Polly's furious. She never forgives him for distracting her daughter during her spring mocks.

So it's a relief when he falls for Ellie – single, thirty-ish, independent and with her own business making and selling wrought-iron garden furniture. Ellie's based in London but, after only a couple of months of knowing him, she puts her flat on the market and moves in with him and the boys.

Just to see how things pan out, she tells me. Nothing, after all, is set in stone.

I agree with her. Nothing is.

What makes me smile is that Ellie is far more like Lennie than anyone will admit. She's unimpressed by Alex for a start. She's tough, she's creative, she's funny – she's good with the boys. She rides a bicycle around town and the locals take an instant shine to her because of her red hair and the fact that she's not stuck up. She doesn't mind getting wet or dirty – crucial when you live with boys. Best of all, perhaps, she doesn't seem to expect miracles. Alex told me she's even written to Bob, asked him to come over and spend the summer, see his grandchildren.

I think they may marry. I really hope so. I've barely seen them this past year – all of us have been so busy with one thing and another – but I'm hoping they'll come up and stay soon. Besides, Jordan misses Connor desperately. Jordan misses everyone desperately.

Last time I spoke to Alex on the phone, he mentioned that he and Ellie are trying for a baby of their own, but that it's taking its time to happen.

Still, she's only thirty-three, he went on. She's still got all the time in the world, hasn't she?

Yes, I agreed, surprised to feel the tears spring to my eyes.

We didn't stay in the town, Mick and me. How could we? As well as taking a part of us, the place had lost all of its magic, all of its charm. It's not that I blame it for what happened to Rosa, but I couldn't go on being somewhere that reminded me – of what? Of how I took my eye off the ball for that split second – which is, after all, all it takes to lose just about everything you care about?

Most of all I found I couldn't any longer bear to look at the sea – at that grey and pitiless expanse, sucking and shifting its shadowy weight over the cold wet sand. Or I could of course, if I had to – but only for just long enough to call Fletcher back, or for Jordan to be able to run and grab his frisbee out of the foam. After that I'd have to look away, to turn. I'd have to run.

It took all of our strength to leave, but we knew, Mick and I, that leaving was our only chance of a future and we owed it to ourselves and the children to hang onto that.

We moved there to be safe but, in most ways, I feel safer where we live now. I'm amazed that Alex can stay there, that he loves it still. I think maybe Lacey was right. It makes you dizzy: too much water, too much sky.

Mick's new job pays him well. Silly money, he calls it. Everyone says he's fallen on his feet. He never really thought he'd go back into journalism – and he despises the paper for its bland complacency – but he sees it as a temporary measure.

The best thing is it's given him a push. Now he spends all his evenings and weekends writing his own stuff. I don't know if he'll be able to make a living at it, or even if he can write. All I know is, I love the look on his face when he's trying.

I know what will happen with Lacey. What will happen is that, sooner or later, one of these days, we'll find each other. There he'll be, standing in his dark coat on a crowded tube platform – or striding along the street among the bright lights and shop windows – and he'll touch my sleeve.

Come for a drink, he'll say.

What? I'll go, blushing. You mean now?

Yes of course now, he'll say, smiling. Why not now?

And we'll go and sit in a bar somewhere — a bar crowded with business people and their crushed-up suits and bags and phones — and in the space created by our new shyness, we'll talk and not talk and I'll remember him all over again, what I liked about him, how he confused me, threw me off course, how it felt, to have his body against mine.

I'll ask him how his life is going.

And he'll look down at the dirty, pine floor and then back at my face.

OK, he'll say.

And work?

A long story. Basically, something else came up, something I knew I could do better.

What? I'll ask him, unable to imagine what that something could be. What thing?

Not now, he'll say. I'll tell you all about it. Some other time.

And maybe I'll ask him how Natasha is. And he'll say he split up with her a long time ago, that winter actually. But that he's been seeing someone — a woman, an old friend he knew from long ago, from his student days.

It's all very weird, he'll add dismissively.

In what way weird?

I'm just — not sure it's going to lead to anything.

Well, I hope it does, I'll tell him truthfully, refusing the bait.

I suppose I hope so too, he'll say and then he'll glance at me in that way of his and I'll quickly look away and we'll both smile.

He'll be interested to hear about the move and will seem genuinely glad about Mick enjoying his work. He'll ask how the boys are getting on and I'll tell him fine, adding that Nat now towers above me, would you believe it? and he'll say that yes, he does believe it.

And Livvy? he'll say – and it will make me feel strange, to hear him speak her name, not just because I know he has a soft spot for my baby girl, but also because she was part of it. She was with us on that long ago terrible night.

A terror, I'll say – explaining how she's up and walking now, running around like a maniac, driving Mick and me crazy, getting into every cupboard and pulling things off shelves and so on.

Maybe he'll ask me who Liv looks like now and I'll laugh and say she's got Mick's black hair and black eyes but she doesn't look like anyone really.

She just looks like herself, I'll say.

Her own person.

Exactly.

And we won't talk about Rosa, but when we discuss the other kids, I'll see a question in his eyes and I'll answer it truthfully without speaking, because that's how it is with Lacey. Not everything comes down to words.

We'll both agree it would be great to meet up.

Well, I'll say, why not come over for supper some time?

I'd like that, he'll say and I'll tell him that he could see Mick and he could see the house – though it's still a mess with builders everywhere of course – and he might if he's lucky even get a glimpse of the kids.

And I'll pull a scrap of paper from my bag and we'll write down each other's e-mail addresses. He'll read mine aloud to check he's got it right and fold it away in his wallet, but we both know we'll never do it, we'll never e-mail. We know that, even as we write them down so carefully and as we fix on each other's faces for that one last time, we won't do it.

Maybe once or twice in my life, on a sad or shaky night, my fingers will hover over the keys. They may, occasionally, even go so far as to type in his address. But I'll always reach for the split-second safety of the delete. Mostly it will just be enough to see that scrap of blue paper with his handwriting on it stuck to my wall, to know it's there, to know it could be there, that it will continue to be there if I want it to be.

Rosa is buried right bang next to Lennie, as close under the yew as they could manage. Cleve was very good about it. Asked no questions, made no fuss, just made it happen. Leave it to me, he said and we did.

She is there and we are here and sometimes that is very hard, but that's why we still go down there, why we'll always go. Apart from Alex and his family, Rosa is what pulls us forever towards the town. She lies there and maybe one day we'll lie there too. I hope so. I used not to care at all about where I ended up, but I don't think I could leave my little girl there forever on her own.

Though she's not alone of course. When I'm there, I'm amazed at how I see the place through their eyes – Rosa's and Lennie's. Lennie used to say that the countryside around there scared her – that it had an energy that sucked you in, that snared you, whether you wanted it or not. I think Rosa understood that. And now I too am beginning to understand what she meant.

Because I know that, if you walk along past Blackshore and the ferry to the marshes, something strange happens. Sound and texture dissolve and all signs of human life recede and silence crashes into your ears. And that, once you're past a certain point, the cow parsley grows as high as your head and the sky clots to a palish green and the horizon dips and swerves and falls away.

And then, when you can no longer see a single soul or any sign of life save, to your right, maybe one small dark sail out at sea and, to your left, crowds of terns alighting in slow motion on the flats beyond Buss Creek, you can convince yourself that you're truly alone on the planet, that everyone's gone and there's no one out there but you.

Knowing this can cause a person's breathing to sharpen and their heart to tilt. Because, with or without the friendly souls of the dead, this place can seem like the loneliest and forlornest on earth.

And then, despite the crackle of insects in the gorse, the cry of the bittern, the brown gleam of the saltings, the eerie, mauve light that creeps in just before rain, you shiver. Because – smelling the coltsfoot coming off the dunes, feeling the sharp breeze that lifts your hair – you sense the truth. That there's no one at all out there to save you, should something happen.

Acknowledgements

Apart from the usual suspects – thank you Jono, Jake, Chloe and Raff! – a few special people made a difference during the writing of this novel. Jonathan Coe, Susanna Denniston, Esther Freud, John and Jackie O'Farrell, and Henry Sutton gave me unconditional fun and friendship through a dark winter. Philip Hensher generously told me things I needed to hear when I was down. Gill Coleridge and Lucy Luck believed unswervingly in the book right from the start, and Dan Franklin and Caroline Michel gave it the best home it could possibly have. And when I needed to remind myself all over again about babies, a small person called Izzy Thomas was somehow – magically! – there. One day you'll know how important a job that was. Thank you, Izzy.

JSM, London 2002